The mid-nineteenth century was one of the most inspirational times in the history of man. Discoveries in medicine, technology, science, philosophy and the adaptations to these by religious and political leaders influenced the world forever. Into this maelstrom of creativity, danced Lola Montez.

# THE DUCHESS

# OF LANDSFELD

## WHAT LOLA WANTS, LOLA GETS

*Dov Silverman*

Silverman, Dov
Duchess of Landsfeld, The: What Lola Wants Lola Gets

For more about Dov Silverman visit:
www.dovsilverman.wordpress.com
www.dovsilverman.com

Published by the Writers of the Apocalypse
www.apocalypsewriters.com

Cover art and assembly by K. J. Joyner, ebookcovers4u.wordpress.com
Edited by Leslie Fish, www.lesliefish.com

**ISBN-13: 978-1-944322-24-3**

*This book is dedicated to my wife.*
**Janet,**
*always wanted me to write
a story about women.*

*This is it.*


*I miss her.*

# *INTRODUCTION BY THE AUTHOR*

Lola Montez remodeled herself as a Spanish noble-woman, and changed 19th century history. In fact, she was born Irish and reinvented herself completely..

The world's most beautiful woman charmed, fascinated, captivated and lived off some of the most renowned men of her time. Lola bedded authors Alexandre Dumas, (*The Three Musketeers, Count of Monte Cristo*) Victor Hugo, (Les *Miserable, The Hunchback of Notre Dame*), Franz Liszt (composer, virtuoso pianist) Lord Palmerston (Great Britain's Foreign Secretary and Prime Minister), princes, kings, a maharaja, Czar Nicholas of Russia, musicians and students—while acting as a secret agent for England. Lola became courtesan to King Ludwig of Bavaria, who bestowed the title of Duchess of Landsfeld on her. She was the power behind the Bavarian throne. Lola brokered agreements between Russia and England, Obstructed an Austrian-French Alliance, thwarted Count von Metternich of Austria and defeated the Jesuits in a battle for political control of Europe. She caused the abdication of Ludwig, King of Bavaria. Second only to Queen Victoria in power, Lola Montez became the catalyst for the 1848 European revolutions and the confederation of Germanic States into the nation of Germany. Before her departure from France in April 1849, Lola had an intimate affair with Jung Bahadur, the King of Nepal. She participated in the Forty-Niner and Australian gold rushes. Her stage career ended when she became a religious penitent in Brooklyn, New York.

The newspaper reports were taken from Bruce Seymour's excellent, scholarly book *Lola Montez a Life* and *Lola Montez*, by Edmund B. D'Auvergne. Numerous other sources and files were used. I reworked some articles to correspond with the story. Lola was an inveterate liar, and her autobiography has little relationship to the facts.

Inspired by Barbara Tuchman's use of historical fiction to tell the truth, I sometimes extrapolate time and location about the most fascinating, intelligent and extraordinarily beautiful woman of her time. I believe Lola would have approved. Often, letters and newspaper articles have grammatical mistakes. Some have outdated phrases and words used in the 19th Century. I have not changed them.

—Dov Silverman

Dov Silverman is the author of the *Fall of the Shogun* five-book historical series that appeared on the *London Times* Best-Seller List and was published in German, Polish and Hebrew. Judah Magnus Museum published his *Legends of Safed*. He won a 1988 Suntory Mystery Fiction Award in Japan for *Revenge of the Good Shepherds*, published in Japanese; was Writer-in-Residence at Christian Brothers University, Memphis, Tennessee, USA, 1995; was a teacher at Writer's Digest Magazine Correspondence School, 1994-1997, published *The Kabbalist (Mysticism)* in English2007, Romanian 2009, Spanish 2012.

Dov (Robert) Silverman is the ninth generation of his family born in Brooklyn, New York. After 3 years as a US Marine Sgt. in the Korean War, he worked as a Long Island Railroad conductor, an auctioneer, and established Autar Microfilm Service. Working nights on the railroad and studying full-time days, he earned his high school diploma and went on to graduate Stony Brook University, New York, *cum laude*, at the age of 39.

Dov credits a spiritual meeting with God and a *Tzaddik* (righteous man), Jules Rubinstein, in the Brentwood (New York) Jewish Center, with setting him on the path of study, religious involvement and settlement in Israel.

The family include children Barbara, owner/founder of Docustar Technical Writing, the mother of Anav, former officer in the Israel Defense Forces, graduate of Bar Ilan University in psychology. Loriel, 21 is a Technical writer. Jeff Silverman, Dov and Janet's son, died of leukemia in 1979 at the age of 18. The family settled in Safed in 1972. There are now two great–grandchildren, Shira and Bar.

In Safed Dov taught English as a Second Language, was a high school principal, lecturer on teaching methods, a supervisor of English teachers, and taught Creative Writing at Universities in Israel and the United States. He served 4 years as a Safed City Councilman. His wife, Janet, was his editor and helpmate throughout their 50 years together. This book is dedicated to her.

## PUBLISHED WORKS BY DOV SILVERMAN

### <u>The John Mung Saga</u>
*The Fall of the Shogun*
*The Black Dragon*
*The Shishi*
*Tairo*
*To the Gates of Hell*

### <u>Other Works</u>
*Amphrithite*
*God's Dancer*
*Gold to India*
*Jewish Short Stories*
*Legends of Safed*
*Night Train to Ronkonkoma*
*Revenge of the Good Shepherds*
*Street Corner Society*
*The Dam Builder*
*The Eighth Day of Creation*
*The Fifth Marines*
*The Kabbalist*
*The Poor Farm*
*The Prophet and the Priest*
*Top Shelf*

# THE DUCHESS

# OF LANDSFELD

## *WHAT LOLA WANTS LOLA GETS*

*DOV SILVERMAN*

*BOOKS I &II*

# BOOK I
## PROLOGUE

***London, England, June, 1843:***

Outside the Foreign Affairs Office on Downing Street, worn cobblestones reflected the hot sun and the stench of horse manure filled the air. Great Britain's Foreign Office was a dingy affair; an iron picket fence flanked both sides of a large oak door where a small polished brass plaque read: Secretary of Foreign Affairs for Great Britain, Lord Palmerston.

Lord Palmerston quietly directed the most militarily and economically powerful nation in the world. At the moment he was listening to Lord Henry Brougham say, "...and a woman such as Lola Montez could be the one you seek. She is unquestionably the most beautiful female in the world."

"I understand she dances?"

"An acceptable Hornpipe. Her Spanish dances are intense cavorting, but amateurish."

"What about this Spider Dance people speak of?"

"It is her version of the Tarantella, a frenzied Italian peasant dance thought to cure the Tarantula's bite. She does her own interpretation, which consists of shaking the spiders off her skirts. She raises the hem so high, men in the first three rows swear she doesn't wear knickers."

"What about the ladies in the audience?"

"None. If the Tarantella is on the program, women are not allowed. Miss Montez sold out every one of her three nights at the Globe Theater."

"And you say she can't dance?"

"Men pay to ogle her."

"And you?" Palmerston asked.

"I ogle quite well, thank you. She is the most stunning woman I ever encountered. Her eyes are large, exquisite chalcedonic blue. They suggest the bedroom, or spit lightening, as she did the first night when some dance aficionados hissed her Flamenco. She stopped in the middle of her dance, strode to stage front center, and gave them what for. The men cheered and ran the hissers from the theater. She then carried on with her performance. The third night Watkins, who calls himself an art critic, had his cronies try to interrupt her dance."

"Why?"

"She rebuffed his advances on opening night."

"The cad. What happened?"

"He announced out loud that Miss Lola Montez was actually Dolores Gilbert from Limerick, Ireland. Lola completed her dance, but on her second curtain call— for more than half the audience was cheering—she waited for the applause to stop and then went at Watkins like a wildcat. Fisticuffs ensued. He fled the theatre with his cronies.

"You mean she struck him?"

"She hit him fore and aft. Watkins ran."

"I would like to meet this lady. But your previous report indicated she had raven black hair; isn't that unusual with blue eyes, for a Spaniard?"

"Watkins was correct. She's as Irish as Paddy's pig."

"Are we talking Irish Catholic?"

"Anglican."

"Reformed Catholicism."

"She also hates the Jesuits."

"Why?"

"No idea."

"Find out. She interests me."

"She interests every man. Women are insecure in her presence."

"Give me the full report."

Lord Brougham attempted to hand over a sheaf of papers but Lord Palmerston waved them off. "Read the pertinent features," he said as he lit a pre-packed, long, thin, opium pipe. "Will you join me?"

"I'd be asleep in a blink of the eye," Brougham demurred.

"It helps me relax," Lord Palmerston said, and a fragrant blue cloud floated across his desk. He slouched in the large straight-back chair, closed his eyes, inhaled and allowed the smoke to curl out from between his thin lips. His broad shoulders relaxed and he pushed off his slippers.

Lord Brougham cleared his throat and read, "Dolores, Rosanna Gilbert, now called Lola Montez was born to Ensign Edward and Eliza Gilbert in Limerick, Ireland. 1818. Eliza, the mother, was fourteen when she gave birth."

"The mother is now thirty-nine, and the daughter twenty-five.

"The small age difference is what caused the friction between them. The mother is a beauty in her own right. They were often taken for sisters. But any woman in the company of Lola Montez pales by comparison. The mother sent Lola away to boarding school, first in Scotland and then in France."

"Is she intelligent?"

"The Mother, not so: she is exceedingly self-centered. Lola is too, but extremely bright and intellectually aware. The Scotch taught her academic discipline, and the French school is considered the most progressive in Europe."

"How could an Ensign afford such an education?

"He didn't. Ensign Gilbert died of cholera in India, four years after Lola's birth. She grew up there and speaks Hindi, French, English and some Spanish. The woman is gifted with languages."

"Who paid?"

"The mother remarried a Major Craigie. He is a most honorable man, from a good family, and decorated in action. He is now a full Colonel, and took on the responsibility of a father to Lola. He has generously supported her."

"Is Lola's relationship with him better than with her mother?"

"Any relationship is better than with her mother. Lola hates the woman. She blames her mother for her growing up alone in boarding schools, with no family to go to on holidays or vacations. Lola never acknowledged her step-father as her benefactor. She took his generosity as her right and his duty."

"A bit ungrateful, what?"

"More so because it could hamper a good officer's career. He was recently made acting Adjutant General of the Army in India. Lola's dancing and her escapades aboard ship to England are certain to be talked about in the barracks here and abroad."

"Colonel Craigie's name is familiar. I believe it is on a list for promotion to General."

"He is respected by his superiors and juniors alike."

"If he performs well, I will see to his promotion. Tell me about Lola's escapades that might ruin Craigie's reputation."

"Lola's mother is a social climber. To please the Governor General's wife in Delhi, she attempted to make up with her daughter by inviting Lola from Europe to the Punjab mountain resort in order to seek a worthy husband. Lola was then eighteen. The mother selected a wealthy sixty-five year old retired judge. The wedding would have been in London, as the judge was recalled earlier than expected. On the four month boat trip to England, Lola upset many of the passengers by outright flirtations with almost every male aboard, including the deckhands. Amongst them was an ensign Thomas James, on leave from his regiment in India. They became especially friendly. James is one of those empty-headed swashbuckling officers. He like Lola, must be the center of attention. At first he attended to Mrs. Craigie, and he might have bedded the mother. Towards the end of the journey he spent all his time with Lola. In England he called upon Lola. The mother pushed Lola to marry the old Judge. The dashing Ensign and Lola eloped."

"What was the result?"

"Unsatisfactory. He was looking for a feminine showpiece to display at regimental balls, military outings, and social events, to further his career."

"According to you, he had the most beautiful woman in the world."

"But Lola sought romantic love. And what Lola wants, Lola gets."

"Is she so much of a fireball?"

"A living volcano. She carries a stiletto, and has brandished it on occasion."

"I can't use an uncontrollable wench no matter how beautiful."

"Controlled to do what?"

"Hmmmmm…" Lord Palmerston puffed a fragrant cloud of smoke toward the ceiling, then sat up and put the pipe aside. "I am contemplating promoting Miss Montez's stage career, which would give her entree into George Sand's social group."

"Send her to Paris?"

"It is the continent's intellectual whirlpool."

"A French cesspool."

"The future of Europe is planned there. Envoys from Hungary, Russia, Bavaria and the Germanic states attend. The greatest writers and newspaper editors of our time visit George's salon. Austria will send Count von Metternich to Paris. Our English newspapers copy most French news articles, word for word. Of late, George Sand is less active on our behalf. We require someone more energetic.

Lord Brougham made a face. "George Sand is a lesbian."

"Actually bi-sexual, and has served us well. If she could control and instruct Miss Montez, we might gain a valuable source of information."

"No one controls Lola Montez," Brougham said.

"She is disgustingly self-centered. Neither England nor anything else would come before her own interests. Her temper tantrums make her unreliable. I don't trust her." He stood, paced the floor, and added, "Having stated my dislike of Miss Montez, I would be remiss not to mention her intellect and her nanny."

"Strange bedfellows, intellect and nanny."

"This bogus Spanish dancer is quite bright," Brougham admitted. "She is well read, and knows how to use her knowledge with men of power. Her favorite ploy is to allow them to expound on a particular subject, believing that—like most women—she will be compliant and respectfully docile. She then attacks like a pirate wielding a cutlass, chopping their legs off at the knees."

"When she brings them to this humble position," Lord Palmerston chuckled, "Is she wise enough not to make enemies?"

"Smarter: she indicates that she can further embarrass them unless they consent or agree to her point of view. This is how she made it onto the stage of the Globe Theatre; she browbeat the theater manager."

"I see. Where does the nanny enter into this?"

"She exerts some control over Lola."

"Tell me more."

"Manuela is a Sikh slave."

"But fifteen years ago you wrote the law abolishing slavery throughout the British Empire."

"True, but in the furthest reaches of the realm, enforcement is unreliable."

"How does a Sikh earn a Latin name?"

"At age four she was sold as a slave, by her parents, to the Spanish Ambassador in Delhi. He wanted a companion for his daughter of the same age. Later, upon transfer, the Ambassador gifted Manuela to the French Ambassador in Calcutta, who in turn passed her to the English Ambassador for similar purposes. She was educated along with the Ambassador's children. Manuela is a most intelligent servant."

"How did she become nanny to the Gilberts?"

"She outgrew her usefulness as a child's companion, and was purchased by Mrs. Liza Gilbert as nanny to Lola because of her fluent English. The mother had little to do with raising Lola."

"You assume this Manuela has the influence I seek to control Miss Montez?" Palmerston asked.

"Sometimes."

"Explain."

"Lola usually gets into trouble by carrying to extremes her need to be right. If possible, Manuela manipulates the situation.

"Tell me more about this Sikh slave."

"My information comes from Army intelligence. They do not pay attention to slaves."

"They certainly paid attention to Miss Montez."

"She is hard to ignore. Do you wish me to have the slave interviewed?"

"Observed. First I want to meet this Smoked Irish Lass."

"Lola is not Black Irish."

"She must be descended from the Spanish Armada survivors."

"Possibly. Her thick jet-black hair yes, but her skin, although dark, has the Irish blush of roses in her cheeks—and sensual lips of natural vermillion."

"Brougham, you are a ladies" man. How do you come to be so taken with Miss Montez?"

"Meet her, and your question becomes superfluous. Personally, I do not like the woman. I admire her beauty."

"Is she beddable?"

"I've never before heard the noun conjugated as a verb. Yes, very. Shall I arrange a meeting?"

"Please. Give my secretary the information. Tell him the appointment should be my last of an evening. Before you leave, tell me why you are so positive she can be brought between the sheets."

"Lola's second voyage to England from India was even more sexually adventurous than the first. There were witnesses?"

"Wasn't she still married to this James fellow?"

"He agreed to a formal separation."

"Why not a divorce?"

"Anglicans are much like Catholics in this regard."

"We older Anglicans are," Palmerston said. "The newer ones steer a narrow path between Lutheranism and Calvinism. Does she go to confession?"

"In Spain, yes. On the ship certainly not, nor since her arrival in England."

"What the devil took place on that voyage?"

"Miss Montez spent almost four months locked up in Lt. George Lennox's stateroom. He is aide de-camp to the governor General of India."

"Hmmm, primarily because his uncle is the Duke of Richmond, the wealthiest man in England."

"All aboard the *Larkin* were aware of their shameless behavior. The ship's captain spoke with Lola. She sent him packing. Passengers said it was improper for Lola, who remains legally married, to spend time in a man's cabin throughout the night. The couple was shunned on deck, the dining room, and the ballroom, and appeared to care not a whit. The two were seen kissing, he with his tunic undone, she in her petticoat. Witnesses saw him putting on her stockings."

"And the plot thickens," Palmerston said, rubbing his hands together. "Brougham, will you join me in some port?"

"Yes, it will lubricate my vocal chords."

Lord Palmerston poured the tawny wine from a crystal decanter, and offered a long-necked goblet across the desk. "Is there more to this escapade?"

"Where Lola is concerned nothing is simple. Colonel Craigie, her stepfather, arranged ahead of time for his sister Catherine from Scotland to meet the *Larkin* in Portsmouth and take Lola to Edinburgh. Lola made short work of Catherine Craigie. Lola and Lt. Lennox took the stagecoach to London where they set up in the Imperial Hotel on Tavistock Row. "

"In the same room?"

"Yes."

"How did they register?"

"He signed as the Second Earl of Chichester. No questions were asked about the lady."

"Lady, indeed. I'm anxious to meet this Montez woman."

"Most men are, but I doubt she'll serve your information-gathering requirements."

"I'll make that decision."

"Enjoy yourself."

# CHAPTER 1

## NANNY MANUELA

I began my service as Lola's nanny at age seventeen, three years older than Lola's mother. She gave birth to Lola three months after my daughter's birth.

Since childhood I served as a companion to the children of various ambassadors. I also served as a sex slave to these important men. This is a common practice with female slaves. I usually took precautions to prevent pregnancy, but the Spanish ambassador raped me.

I hated the child inside me until I held her in my arms. My heart melted. I love my Princess. She is my life.

I placed her with a retired servant from the English embassy. I knew Dadi as a good woman; her name means grandmother in Hindi. She lived in the English compound and helped me give birth.

Dadi loved Princess as much as I, but she also needed money and a slave receives no salary. I was dependent on gifts from the Mistress, and the Gilberts were thrifty. Like most slaves, I bargained with shopkeepers for the family—and kept the money I saved them to pay for Princess' upkeep. I suckled both babies, for Mistress feared her breasts would increase in size. English women prefer small breasts. Their men like large ones.

The first time Master Gilbert saw his daughter he said, "This is the ugliest baby I've ever seen." The child looked like a little monkey. She had a wild crop of black hair, and dark hair on her arms and legs. Four years later Master Gilbert changed his mind. Lola's thick dark hair accentuated her wide blue eyes, which could open so large you thought you would fall into them. The body hair disappeared. She was the most beautiful child one could imagine.

Mistress Gilbert showed the baby off to the wives of superior officers, but all little Lola ever wanted was her mother's attention. She followed Mistress around the house repeating, "Yook at me, Mommy! Yook at me!"

As Lola grew older she became not only an exceptionally lovely, bright child, but a willful one. She formed her own opinions and clung fiercely to them. The less she understood a subject, the more adamantly she argued about being right.

As she grew, people stopped and stared at her. At first she became upset with this. I tried to explain, but it was the Battalion Sergeant Major who told her, "Darling, you're a stunner."

The older and more beautiful Lola became, the more distant grew her mother. The child developed a stubborn streak, quick temper, and was fearless—qualities she inherited from her father. He died of cholera in India. Lola kept her childish recollection of the dashing British officer, and cherished that memory. I learned in the Spanish school that unreturned love is the most powerful, for it can't be faulted by collision with reality. So it was with Lola's father. He never took real interest in Lola, so she embellished his memory.

After an appropriate mourning period, Mistress Gilbert sought a husband amongst the army officers and abandoned Lola to me. We were now living in Calcutta, and the most attractive matrimonial prospect for family, money, and future in the Army was Major Thomas Craigie. Eliza Gilbert was a beautiful woman, and at nineteen in the full bloom of youth. She set her sights on the Major, and achieved her objective.

She never allowed Lola to interfere with Major Craigie's duties or her own desires, so the child became my responsibility. The less mistress Gilbert saw of Lola, the more pleased she was. This became difficult for the little girl who desired her mother's attention. On the other hand, it allowed me to support Dadi and send my little Princess to the English School for I had free rein with the food and shopping expenses.

Major Craigie took his role as stepfather seriously. I don't know that he loved the child, but to him it was a military duty. He acted as a gentleman, and often slipped me a rupee or two.

In addition to sending my daughter Princess to the private English school, I hired a Sikh master to teach her our religion—which I had never learned. Sikhism is a religion of one God. I stopped praying to the Hindu and Christian gods. The ideal in Sikhism is to combine both Shakti (power that resides in the here and now), and Bhakti (spiritual qualities of the past and future).

I became confused about taking money from the Mistress by my bargaining. Christianity condemned it. I read about controlling the Five Evils: Anger, Lust, Infatuation, Greed and Ego. Saving money by bargaining and keeping it for myself wasn't greed, nor anger, infatuation or lust. I controlled Shakti from my position as a slave, and used what power was available to make life better for my daughter. It was a reorganizing of priorities.

My schooling was the finest in India. I studied with the children of the ambassadors, and I served as a companion for them. Lola grew up playing with the Hindu children. They were far more adventurous than the military children in the compound, and Lola was a natural leader.

On one occasion a group of older boys attacked her and stole a doll from her friend. Lola picked up a stick. The boys fled. She chased three of them into the nearby slums where adult White men feared to enter in broad daylight. She cornered them, she beat them, took the doll and returned it to the little girl.

This fearlessness remained in adulthood, and almost killed her on several occasions. People accused her of being self-centered and stubborn, which was true, but these traits were minor compared to her confidence. She believed that if she attacked hard enough and fast enough, she would be proven right.

Growing up in Calcutta for Lola was fun. She played with the Hindu children, became a favorite of the Battalion Sergeant Major, and mimicked perfectly the different English accents from the ranks. She had a phenomenal memory. Languages came easily and she had good study habits. She completed assignments ahead of time, and became a Gold Star pupil in the Calcutta School for Children of British Officers—but Lola was sent to Scotland for advanced schooling because of her courage.

Someone convinced her that if she showed no fear to a Cobra, it would not attack. Thousands of Hindus die each year from Cobra bites. Lola would find one of these venomous snakes and play with it. She often drew a crowd. She would dance with the snake. She had no music, but then, she would dance in the house and garden to silent tunes only she heard.

Lola loved attention, and she did not receive it from her parents. Her mother learned of the snake dance. Mistress used the incident to convince newly promoted Lieutenant Colonel Craigie to send Lola to be educated in Scotland, near his sister Catherine. I believe Mistress Gilbert didn't want her daughter around, as Lola stole the attention from her. She also made Mistress seem older in the minds of her social group.

The mistress ordered me to chaperone Lola on the four-month sea journey. I was sea-sick. The ship's Captain, Thomas Agnew and his wife Laura, took charge of Lola. They answered complaints from passengers who described Lola as a precocious child who, without invitation, would perform her own dances and use knitted stockings as puppets. She interrupted cribbage and shuffleboard games with her performances. A natural mimic, she poked fun at passengers and crew, including the Captain. She became more than an annoyance. Few said farewell when we docked in Portsmouth.

Lola found schoolwork easy; the discipline of the Scottish boarding school was not. The teachers and House Mother were strict. This control caused Lola to rebel. She once took off all her clothes and ran from the school grounds to the nearby market stark naked. She began to perform one of her dances until she was captured, wrapped in a horse blanket, and brought back to school.

Eventually, strictness served Lola well. She learned

self-discipline, at least regarding her learning. She never did apply this self-control to her temper. She suffered a lonely childhood because she tried to dominate every friendship. Rather than make friends she attempted to control them. Often she wore the Hindu sari to class, meals and into town. She wanted attention. She insisted I continue to wear my traditional clothes when accompanying her. It gave her an exotic aura.

Scotland can be cold and is quite damp. I wore woolen underclothes with long sleeves under the short-sleeved Choli vest. Lola argued with me about the under-clothes. She said it disturbed the ambiance as perceived by others. To argue with Lola, even when she was a child, caused her to battle until she won or worked herself into a state of hysteria. I simply ignored her complaints.

Winter accomplished what arguments could not. We both stopped wearing the Hindu dress until spring.

When Lola becomes aggressive, I stand back and let her stroppy behavior run its course. If she realizes she's wrong she will either not speak of it or, if you are of a lower social status, she might even apologize. On occasion she apologized to me, a slave. But I never once heard her express regret to her social equals or those of higher status. It is one of her quirks that I could never quite understand.

On more than one occasion I witnessed her helping the lowliest caste Hindu sweep the garden paths. No one asked her to do so. She often stole from the kitchen to feed her native friends outside the compound. She always saw the poor. They were visible to her; she never looked away. Lola often tried to lessen their trouble, but she opposed government by the people as in the American experiment begun sixty-five years ago. She preferred the English social system with a Regent, House of Lords, House of Commons and defined social standing.

Lord Palmerston once asked her how she could support the English stratified social system when she insisted on being elevated to royal status. She answered, "I am Lola Montez. There are those God intended to be privileged. Special people such as you, Napoleon and myself will find a way to break through the system and attain an appropriate level in society. Then we shall lead according to God's will."

"Are you saying God makes mistakes at birth?"

"No! God wants us chosen ones to see the needs of both lower and upper classes. Then we will lead to improve society. "

"What about the middle class?"

"England is the only country with a middle class. Great Britain rules one fourth of the earth and a fifth of its population. The sun never sets on the Empire."

"What about the possibility of Europe developing a middle class?" Palmerston asked.

"It will never happen," Lola said

"Why?"

"They don't want it. They adore their aristocracy."

"What about the French?"

"Influenced by the American sickness," she said. "You English with Russian help defeated the French. Who in his right mind would expect the dregs of Europe to form a viable society in America?"

"Those slaves, serfs, poorest and uneducated Europeans defeated England in 1776, and again the war of 1812," Palmerston said.

"Your first loss was because of England's King, German George, hired Hessians to fight an English war."

"And how to explain our second loss not twenty-five years ago?"

"That is even clearer," Lola said. "America declared war on England for impressing American seamen into the British navy to fight France. You were Foreign Minister and did not want war. England impressed unwilling American sailors into your battleship crews. That weakened your Navy, and the French knew it. The Americans took advantage of your war with France. But you didn't really lose that war; the treaty of Ghent resulted in all lands occupied from the outbreak of hostilities to be returned on both sides."

"Academically you are correct, but we lost over a thousand of our best soldiers at the battle of New Orleans alone. These British regiments had just defeated Napoleon's army, yet they fell in droves to farmers and backwoodsmen like Andrew Jackson. Americans don't adhere to the rules of combat. They actually aim for the officers first."

"That is what makes them Americans. They write their own rules."

Lord Palmerston poured two glasses of port, and offered one to Lola. "You are an amazing woman," he said. "Your grasp of history is exceptional." He asked Lola to take up the glass of port. She replied that she didn't drink.

"Why?" he asked.

"I do not like the taste, and it slows my thoughts."

"Excellent!" he said, and raised his glass. "To Miss Lola Montez. May you serve the Empire well!"

He drank. She straightened in her chair and said, "I am descended from Spanish royalty. I am served, not a servant."

"And so you shall be attended, by Lords and Ladies on the continent."

"What is it you want of me?"

"To offer you three choices." Lord Palmerston handed Lola a sheet of paper. "You are holding a voucher for one thousand shillings. You may leave it on my desk and walk out. You may take the voucher and say you will do what I ask, but not implement my plan. Everything said here will be forgotten. However, accept my proposal and do as requested, and I will arrange a trip to Spain for you and your servant. There you will study dancing to improve your professional technique."

"Who says I need improvement?" Lola demanded.

"My agents."

"You should hire better agents."

"And you should learn to accept constructive criticism."

"What if I do as you say?"

"When you leave for Spain you will receive a second voucher for five thousand shillings. On your return I will arrange for your appearance in Her Majesty's London Theater, where I guarantee you a warm and hospitable reception."

"That will depend on my performance?"

"Your beauty will assure applause. My agents will guarantee three curtain calls."

"My Lord, what is it you want of me?"

"Enter the salon of George Sand, to listen, learn, and report to me."

"George Sand the editor and writer?"

"Yes."

"She is a woman I truly admire, but George Sand is in Paris."

"She runs her own newspaper there, and will introduce you to other members of the press. I will organize theater engagements in La Ville Lumière. This exposure, and introductions by Lord Brougham, will give you entrée to the elite of Europe. You will meet the most influential men of our time. Then report to me, and attempt to influence these men according to my instructions."

"How can I influence them?"

"Powerful men have powerful desires. "

"They call you the Mongoose for a reason. You nip around the subject, then jump in for the kill. "

"Can you make a decision now?" Lord Palmerston asked.

"Yes."

"Yes, to which question?"

"All. I will accept your money, go to Spain, take dancing lessons, then go to France and meet George Sand. What is it you expect me to learn from her?"

"The value of information. You have the rare ability to understand history and evaluate its effects on current events. I will give you the opportunity to make history and serve your own purpose in search of a prince."

Lola motioned for me to come forward. "Should my nanny deposit this voucher in the Bank of England?"

"No. Take it to Yeshaia Caspi at the building site of the West London Synagogue."

"A Jew?" Lola asked.

"A Rabbi," Palmerston said. "Do you object doing business with Jews?"

"I never met one."

"Caspi is prudent and honest. Most important, he can transfer money to all of Europe and the middle east by just writing a note to his fellow Jews. He is also a prime source of information. Other countries despise their Jews. I use them."

"I would like to meet Mr. Caspi."

"Have your servant do it. He will not speak with you."

"And why not?"

"You are a woman."

"So is Manuela."

"He will speak to her through his wife. Don't be insulted; his is a primitive religion."

"We have spoken of money, spying, traveling, dancing, religion and sex. Except for the latter we agree."

"We may now discuss sex," Palmerston said. "Would you prefer your nanny leave?"

"I prefer to engage in sex rather than discuss it."

For the first time that evening, I saw the most powerful man in England hesitate. He blushed, raised his glass of port in a toast to Lola.

Lola asked, "Are you familiar with the *Kama Sutra*?"

Palmerston choked on his Port, dabbed his lips with a serviette, and said, "A Hindu sex manual, isn't it?"

I knew Lola's answer; I had taught her that five

thousand year old manual of love, and she was a good student. She described in detail the first ten positions. I watched Lord Palmerstone's face as Lola spoke, and he was dumbstruck.

"Foreplay," Lola concluded, "can be marking with nails or teeth, and slapping if requested. For a grander sexual climax, manual manipulation or oral sex, or both, bring both partners to a pleasing pinnacle of enjoyment."

A heavy silence hung between the two. Palmerston then asked, "Did you really study all this?"

"Of course," Lola replied. "How else can one be a grand courtesan? That is my goal. Boat and bridge builders study their trade. You studied history at Edinburgh and Cambridge before entering politics. I am preparing to capture a duke or a prince."

"And where did Nanny Manuela learn this *Kama Sutra*?"

"She is a Sikh from India, was bought as a child companion to the Spanish ambassador's daughter. He also paid for her *Kama Sutra* lessons. That is why she was passed on to other ambassadors. She served your English ambassador in Delhi. He tried all 60 positions depicted in the manual."

"I never realized the manual contained illustrations."

"Shall we go to bed? I will teach you."

"You and me?" Lord Palmerston asked.

"I assume you made arrangements," Lola's smile lit up the room. "You scheduled this interview as the last appointment of your official day for the purpose of sleeping with me, did you not?"

Lord Palmerston bowed, saying, "Miss Montez, I am

confidant you will do well in the service of Great Britain." He came out from behind his desk, offered her his arm and led Lola into an adjoining room. I heard her say, "Then you should increase the amount of that voucher."

He did.

# CHAPTER 2

## JEW TOWN

Inquiries about London's West End convinced Lola that I should go to Rabbi Caspi with the voucher and two of the biggest and toughest looking footmen she could find. They knew that area of London: the largest city slum in England. The closer we came, the more gaunt and ragged were the children, adults and animals. Garbage was everywhere. Open sewerage waited for the next rain to move along the channels in the middle of the streets. One of my guards explained these streets were passable by carriage only because of the construction of the new synagogue. When I left the carriage I looked deeper into the West End. Truly, we could not have gone further. Refuse, garbage, and even people lay in the streets blocking passage. I don't know if they were dead, sleeping or drunk. The coachman said, "It's a little of each."

A young bearded man met me at the gate and directed me to the women's entrance at the side of the building. I entered a room with a balustrade overlooking the center of the Temple below. A middle-aged lady appeared to be teaching a group of young women. I explained my mission and she led me outside to a small apartment in the rear. Her husband was in another room full of books, arguing with a group of men. He left them and entered the room where we waited. He didn't look at me, but sat sideways to me at a small table. His wife directed me to sit. I began,"My Mistress, Madame Lola Montez..."

He interrupted. "Ain devar!"

His wife interpreted, "It's nothing. The Rabbi will not speak to you. Do you understand Yiddish?"

"I never heard of that language."

"I will translate. What is it you wish?"

I used Lord Palmerston's name, and saw the Rabbi's eyes snap toward me and then away, which meant he understood English. This was proven when I finished and he waved off his wife's translation, speaking to her in English. She in turn asked me if I understood. I hand-ed two vouchers to his wife. One was for two thousand shillings now, and the other for ten thousand shillings in Spain. Lord Palmerston had certainly loosened his purse strings after his first lesson in *Kama Sutra*.

"No problem," the Rabbi said. He stood and went back into the room of men, who were still arguing, and shortly returned with a purse which he gave to his wife. She insisted I count the money. She asked, "When are you leaving for Spain, and which city will you visit?"

"We leave England in two weeks for Cartagena."

The Rabbi didn't wait for a translation, but took a quill and wrote a note. He asked his wife, "What is this lady's name?"

I answered. He wrote, then handed the paper to his wife, who offered it to me.

Still facing away from me he said, "Please tell the lady that she will be visited by a Jewish merchant from Lisbon, to whom she will show this letter. He will ex-tend credit up to and including ten thousand shillings.

Ask her, is that satisfactory?"

"Most agreeable," I answered, "But you need not call me Lady, as I am Miss Montez's slave."

The bearded man abruptly turned toward me, an intense scowl on his bearded face. "Slavery was abolished years ago. We Jews were once slaves. Demand your freedom!" He slammed his fist on the table and turned away.

"I must remain a slave," I explained, "If I wish to return to Calcutta and see my daughter."

"Hmmmmm!" He grunted and pulled on his beard.

I asked, "Could I send money through you to Calcutta?"

"Much easier than Spain," the wife answered. "It is against the law for Jews to live in Spain. We can only travel through it, to and from Portugal."

"Could my transactions remain private? I mean, separate from Lord Palmerston or Mistress Montez?"

"My husband is tight-lipped. I would like it if he speaks more to me than to his friends in there." She indicated the other room where voices were being raised.

"What are they arguing about?" I asked.

"Our religion is all about arguments," the Rabbi said. "Someone says yes, another says no, and a third says maybe. We argue to get at the truth." He realized he was talking to me and clapped his hand over his mouth.

His wife smiled and asked, "What sums of money will you be transferring to Calcutta?"

"Today I have eighteen shillings," I said and took out my purse to pour the coins on the table.

The Rabbi's wife jumped back in fright shouting, "Oy Ve!!!"

I almost fell over backward in my chair and the Rabbi spun around to see what was happening. He raised his hands and motioned for me to back away. I did.

"She doesn't know," The rabbi said to his wife.

"What is it I don't know?"

"The pig," he said, "Is an unclean animal. Isn't your purse made from a sow's ear?"

"Yes, most are."

"Had your purse touched this table we would have to throw it out. Your money is in the pig-leather purse, and it would make unclean the table we eat from."

"I didn't know. Will I be able to clean the money and bring it again?"

"Give my wife your daughter's address. I will send a voucher to her for eighteen shillings. Bring non-tainted money next time."

I felt vulnerable clutching the large sum of money on the return trip through the slums. It was getting dark. London at night can be dangerous, but the sight of two burly guards standing on the coach's rear platform and the coachman up front with whip in hand kept the villains at bay.

I was worn out from the adventure, but Lola now had money. She insisted on shopping, the very next day. A born spendthrift, she frequented the most fashionable dress and hat makers. She never discussed price, but only handed me an amount of money and left me to pay the shopkeeper. This was good for me; I haggled and received lower prices, and kept the difference. In this case it was more difficult, for Lola insisted I charge everything to Lord Brougham's account.

When I questioned the wisdom of this, she laughed and said Palmerston would endorse the expense. She said he had never made love before in any but the missionary position.

Lola was in such good spirits that she insisted I order a dress, jacket and expensive cloak. "It gets cold in Spain," she said. We visited shoe and hat makers. Lola purchased bonnets and hats decorated with exotic bird feathers. She charged them, and the crinoline cages for skirts, and under that the steel hoops to hold the petticoats. Boned corsets were worn over linen chemises.

She purchased several shawls to match the dresses. Lola insisted the skirts be fitted tightly to reveal her tiny waist, and the bosom cut low and pressed up by a busk to accentuate her breasts. I believe she started a new fashion which spread to France and became known as the Princess style.

Three days later, on my way to market, a horse-drawn carriage stopped in front of me. The carriage door swung open and a gentleman inside tipped his top hat saying, "Lord Palmerston would speak with you." It was Lord Brougham.

We rode in a carriage of his design. He built the one-horse carriage to save on the expense of extra horses, footmen necessary to handle them, and to reduce the animals' excrement in the streets.

I find the British quite strange. Aristocrats looks down on businessmen, yet they invest in factories, shipping, and grain. They make jokes about the Scotch being excessively thrifty, yet I find Englishmen even more so. They speak of Victorian morals, but it applies only to the lower classes. They say Englishmen are overly formal, with no sense of humor; I found this to be true in India and England, but only when other English people are about. Alone, Englishmen are quite relaxed and amusing.

In the carriage Lord Brougham was amiable, even jovial. Two jokes I recall; "How can you identify a Dogwood tree? By its bark" and, "See here, waiter, I've found a button in my salad. That's all right, sir: it's part of the dressing."

Our carriage stopped behind a livery stable on Market Street. He motioned me to remain seated, and his face became serious. "If your Mistress ever again takes advantage of Lord Palmerston's generosity by charging things in his or my name, I promise to make her life most difficult." His eyes and the set of his jaw spoke in the understatement of Englishmen when addressing important matters.

A second carriage pulled alongside ours, and I transferred over. I curtsied to Lord Palmerston. He tipped his top hat and motioned me to be seated opposite him. He raised his cane, tapped twice on the ceiling and the carriage moved on.

"This may seem a strange way to meet," he said. "But spies are everywhere."

"If they are watching you..."

"They are."

"They saw me enter your carriage."

"Perfectly acceptable behavior for a Lord of the realm. They will think I am cheating on my wife. Your recognition of the possible danger strengthens my belief that you are the correct person for the task I have in mind."

"Sir?"

"Similar to the three-point option I made your mistress. Your point of view is different from Mistress Lola's. You will see and hear things that most aristocrats never dreamed of."

"You wish me to spy on the servants?"

"Of the powerful. In your daily forays to the market, pay attention to what and how things are being sold. Pay attention to new buildings, houses and businesses. Listen to soldiers. Are they happy, paid well? Where would they like or not like to be billeted? Always ask yourself the question, why? Listen when your mistress mingles with other aristocrats. Valuable information is often revealed in casual conversation."

"That would require much writing."

"Rabbi Yeshaia Caspi's Jews will forward your letters to me. Do not send important information by ships' mail. We monitor them, and they us."

"Who are 'they'?"

"Foreigners."

"But I am a foreigner, am I not?"

"Hopefully working for Great Britain. Do you remember what I said to Mistress Lola about the three things she could do?"

"I have no problem doing any of the things you described."

"We find your Mistress' correspondence written in your handwriting."

"Mistress Lola dictates to me."

"Will she do so with her reports?"

"I expect her to either dictate or have me put the report in a more grammatically correct form. She has little patience with sentence structure."

"Good. However, in a separate letter I wish you to comment on Mistress Lola's observations. Agree, disagree, but tell the truth."

"You wish me to spy on my mistress?"

"Observe."

"Will I be paid?"

"Fifty shillings a month will be sent to your daughter through the Rabbi."

It was obvious and logical that the Rabbi was Lord Palmerston's man. He had told him of my daughter. Fifty shillings a month was a fortune for a native family in Calcutta. I thought of Lord Palmerston's three alternatives. "Yes," I said. "I am grateful for your generous offer."

"Do your job well and there could be added gratuities."

Upon my return I drew a bath for Mistress Lola. As I washed her back I said, "Lord Palmerston made the same three offers to me."

"What does he want you to do?"

"Spy for him."

"On me?"

"That too."

"How did you answer?"

"I volunteered."

"What!" Lola shouted and spun around in the tub. The sponge flew from my hand and water sloshed onto the floor. I started to dry the floor but Lola screamed, "Why do you betray me?"

"I did not betray you. And I didn't lie to Lord Palmerston."

"How can that be? You will report to him?"

"I must."

"Then you betray me."

"No, my little Lolita. I will take his money, and I told you of his offer. That means you will be on guard when you dictate to me."

"But you will still be spying on me."

"There is an old Hindi saying, 'The spy you know is better than the one you don't.' If I refused, Lord Palmerston would hire someone else."

"Hmmm!" Lola murmured, turned and slipped down into the water. "Another hot bucket," she ordered. When I returned with the water she asked, "Is he paying you well?"

"Yes."

"Take the old Mongoose's money, and I'll dictate the reports."

This was my first real step towards freedom. The yearning in my heart to join my daughter became more than a dream. Her marriage into a good family was now a distinct probability. I treasured these thoughts. Like a hoard of jewels I hid them in the secret recesses of my heart. I peeked and played with them. I spent hours revising them as the money I sent to Princess grew. I dreamt day and night of a dowry and matchmaking: the trousseau, and musicians, entertainers, menu for the parties before and after the wedding. There was so much I did not know; I had never attended a Sikh wedding.

# CHAPTER 3

## THE SPANISH EXPERIENCE

Lakshmi, the Hindu Goddess of prosperity and good fortune, smiled on me during our trip to Spain. We left Portsmouth on a sailing ship and transferred in Marseilles. There we boarded the *Janet Del Carmen,* a new steam-driven paddle-wheeler. I did not suffer seasickness aboard the steamship. In France a delegation of Sikh businessmen boarded, returning to the Punjab by way of Algeria. Among them was Guru Rama Singh, their spiritual advisor.

Mistress Lola remained socially engaged from late afternoon into the night. This allowed me time for three full evenings of private lessons with the Guru about Sikh weddings. He was easy to speak with. His smile was relaxing and his speech was measured and deep. His mahogany skin contrasted with his long white-white hair and beard. His dark eyes sparkled and his laughter lightened my heart.

He described the wedding ceremony and expressed surprise that my daughter was unmarried at the age of twenty-four. I explained that she waited for my return. He smiled and said, "The English are most correct when they say; 'Time and Tide wait for no man'." Years later I came to understand the full meaning of this phrase, and wondered if in some mysterious way he knew.

"The Sikh wedding," he said, "Is the most religious

act husband and wife will ever share. It is more than a legal contract or physical union. It is the merging of two souls into one, called 'a blissful union'. The couple circles the person performing the ritual four times while hymns are sung. It is proper for a Guru to perform the wedding, but any knowledgeable Sikh man may preside. In doing so he symbolizes the greatest Guru of the past, Granth Sahib Ji. The perambulations represent the couple's commitment to Sikhism, the Guru acting as witness.

"It also reminds the bride and groom that from their union will spring life. Their obligation is to teach the new soul in preparation for its journey through this world. The Guru in the center represents the fundamental basis of Sikhism: there is only one God. The congregation supports this principle. Guru Rama explained that parents may arrange a marriage, but only with the consent of both the boy and girl. The two must be above the age of fourteen. It is proper to consider wealth, family status, and educational factors in the search for a partner. There should be similarities in the couple's approach to God which determines the betrothal. Marriage to a Sikh is preferred but not mandated, keeping in mind that a compatible religious marriage has a greater chance of success. A Sikh may marry someone of another religion, but the person should believe in one God, be humble, and earn his bread by honest means. There is no ritual for divorce. The husband and wife become 'Ek Jot Doe Murti', one spirit. This soul cannot be halved.

"While the marriage ceremony is taking place, the Milnee is performed where wedding gifts are exchanged between families."

Guru Rama said I could hire people to act as my family. He questioned me about my real name and parents, but I do not remember them or my name. He gave me the Sikh name Inderjeet: "One who wins the love of God".

What a beautiful name. I repeated it aloud. I asked him to say it. When I gazed into a mirror or saw my reflection in a cabin window I said aloud, "Inderjeet." It felt wonderful to own a real name. I practiced writing it in Hindi and Latin letters.

The ceremony continues when the groom sits to the right of the Guru and the bride on his left. The parents and couple stand, while all guests remain seated. The Guru requests God's blessing on the marriage and the wedding hymn is sung. Guru Rama sang it in a deep mellow voice:

> "Cry out to God for guidance in that which you wish to achieve.
>
> The Guru Granth Sahib Ji stands as a holy witness for you.
>
> Live a sanctified life and in the presence of the sanctified thou shall experience only the sweetness of life.
>
> You are the destroyer of fear. You are the Lord our God, merciful, kind, and beyond the knowledge of man."

Then the bride and groom stand before the Guru. One end of a saffron shawl is draped over the groom's shoulder and held in his left hand; the other end is draped over the bride's shoulder and held in her right hand. In this position the vows are taken. A hymn is sung while the groom leads his bride around the Guru, both holding the scarf.

There are speeches, music and communal songs. These are followed by parties which can be for one evening or several days. I wished to follow the Guru Rama, to sit at his feet and learn, but obligations to my daughter precluded such action.

In the Port of Algiers, Guru Rama blessed me before leaving the ship. The last word spoken from his holy lips was my name, "Inderjeet."

It took three days from Algeria to anchorage in Cartagena, in Spain. We contacted Lord Palmerston's agent at once; his office was on the same wharf where we docked. He was a big bellied Scotchman who rolled his R's and ate his sentences, but most efficient and energetic. He bounced from one side of his desk to the other, shuffling papers for us to sign. Having done so he set us in an open carriage, gave orders to the driver in Spanish, which I understood, and off we went. Our luggage followed.

Lola ordered me to speak Spanish with her, and she told me to ask the driver to tell us about Cartagena. I thought the driver's smile would break his face. A ninth generation Cartaginian and a lover of his birthplace he said, "My city has the taste of Rome. They conquered Hannibal's army and occupied Carthage two hundred years before Christ. To the right you see the walls of the ancient coliseum. Those Roman arches beyond the coliseum supply our water from the five hills surrounding the city. Through the centuries different civilizations built here, but Rome's influence is strongest.

"Spain's treasure fleets used this as their port of call in the Spanish Main. French and English pirates hovered outside Cartagena like vultures, hoping to pick off our ships laden with gold and silver. From time to time these buccaneers tried to capture the city itself. We have beautiful beaches on the Mediterranean. Beyond the mountains are The Fields of Cartagena, the most fruitful plantations on earth. You think I exaggerate? Instead of precious metal we now export vegetables, melons, lemons, and oranges. Figs olives and honey. This is the finest and richest place on the Spanish Main. See the steeples of the beautiful churches."

"Is it true," Lola asked, "That the Inquisition continues in Spain?"

The driver's features hardened. "Napoleon Bonaparte abolished it," he said. "It exists only in a weaker form. This subject we don't speak of." He turned his back and pointed out an old Roman customs house.

We arrived at a small but attractive villa overlooking the port. Flowers formed a carpet of colors on both sides of the white marble steps. A woman in a long black dress, buttoned at the collar, appeared at the entrance. Her body and stance were those of a twenty year old; her aristocratic face and silver hair indicated an age of sixty. She studied Lola with intelligent dark eyes, nodded and said, "Welcome to my home, Signora Montez. If you are not too tired, your first lesson begins after refreshments."

"Fine," Lola said, "But refreshments are unnecessary. I am ready now."

"My name is Madame La Rosa, and suggest you use

a more sophisticated word than 'ready'. The words 'prepared' or 'eager' are more appropriate. The moment one opens one's mouth he or she falls into the listener's mental social classification."

I stepped towards Lola, thinking she would explode. She dug her fists into her hips and said, "I am here to learn dance. I know how to speak. I am Maria Dolores de Porris y Montez. My parents were nobles at the court of King Ferdinand until the Carlists exiled my family."

I knew she lied about her birth. The older woman's expression did not change yet, I believe she also knew. Lola often stated this lineage, with such absolute certainty that she was rarely questioned or challenged even by those who knew the truth. She intimidated people, but not Madame La Rosa. The elegant woman standing before us stood unimpressed. She lifted her chin and repeated, "My name is Madame La Rosa," and beckoned us into the house saying, "'Lola' is too personal a greeting for someone of my station. Except for family, lovers, or those of the highest aristocratic station, no one should use your first name."

I sighed in relief as Lola relaxed and entered the tiled ante-room. "My lady," Madame La Rosa cautioned Lola, "There is a Spanish axiom; 'You must not show your feelings. Anger is a form of mental suicide'."

I thought, if this were true, Lola would have killed herself long ago.

"You must control your temper," Madame said. "Put your anger to use; never let it rule you."

After this conversation I witnessed a change in Lola's tantrums. They were more calculated, and she sometimes feigned anger to get her way. Still, she would never learn to curb her violent temper.

Madame La Rosa was a hard taskmaster, but Lola never complained. I tired just watching them exercise, dance and repeat everything over and over. Madame insisted that Lola wear high heels at all times and balance a book on her head. She balanced the book while eating, going to town, and even when she attended her toilet. Lola's stance became even more elegant. She learned to walk so it appeared she floated across the floor. The high heels of her dancing shoes and her stance made her taller than most men. Madame explained, "Height is a tool to dominate men." Lola wore high heels from then on.

The Cachucha is a solo Spanish folk-dance with castanets. Madame chose this as the first of four dances in Lola's repertoire. Lola added the Hornpipe as a fifth. The lessons were long, exacting, and exhausting to both teacher and student. Twice Lola made me join them. My attempts caused both women to laugh. They made me try again. In frustration Madame La Rosa burst out "Klutz!" and motioned me to take a seat. I had heard Rabbi Caspi use this word to a son who had spilled milk in the kitchen. I questioned Madame La Rosa, who admitted she was a Converso. Her father's family had fled the Ukrainian Jewish pogroms a hundred years ago. "I am a safe Catholic now," she said, and attended church every day, refusing to teach on Sundays.

# CHAPTER 4

## TO WORK

Madame La Rosa polished Lola's versions of the Fandango and Flamenco, but felt the Bolero too slow for the excitement Lola brought to the stage. "As a dancer," Madame told Lola, "You possess earned grace. It is artificial. With practice and time, you will develop natural elegance. You burst with energy and enthusiasm. That you must offer the audience, that and your beauty. Success will be yours."

Lola and I walked to the market. She, balancing a book on her head, always drew children who tried to imitate her. A crowd had gathered around a man who jumped about, flailing his arms and legs frantically in the air. His body gyrated, elbows, hands, and feet twisting and turning. "What's wrong with him?" I asked a bystander.

"He's a stevedore. Carried a bunch of bananas on his shoulder, and a tarantula bit him in the neck."

"And that makes him crazy?"

"No. He's Italian. They believe the dance will burn out the poison and prevent him from dying."

"Does it work?"

"Más o menos," he answered in Spanish. Lola heard the conversation. Her grasp of the new language was amazing. She told the story to Madame La Rosa in broken Spanish.

The older woman's face glowed in one of her rare smiles. "The Tarantella you perform is a dance based on that man's actions, but I just had a vision of how to improve your version to suit your energetic style."

"After seeing that man," Lola said, "I came to a similar conclusion. But how to perform this dance to make it more exciting without looking wild and crazy?"

"Dance your version for me," Madame said, and called, "Jose!" Her guitarist entered the foyer. "The Tarantella," she commanded.

Jose played, Lola danced, Madame Rosa watched but said nothing. Lola finished. "Well?" she asked.

The older woman stroked her chin. "Your concept is good. The Tarantella is rarely seen on stage. Most women do not possess the energy or stamina to perform it. Men appear as idiots when they try. The woman must dance just athletically and sensuously enough to excite the audience. It is a delicate balance and a difficult combination to achieve."

Madame La Rosa stood, and snapped her heels on the tiled floor making two loud claps. The guitarist struck several vibrant chords.

Madam La Rosa strode to the center of the tiled floor and took her stance, hands held high over her head, long-nailed fingertips touching. Her body moved in time to the music. She kicked her dress, showing a shapely leg. She whirled back and forth with several short leaps, cracked her heels on the tiled floor, then stood out of breath, hands on her hips. It took a moment to regain normal breathing. She pointed at Lola. "The Tarantella was written for you. This will be your signature dance. Every muscle from your little toe to the tip of your hair must be strengthened. I promise no one else will attempt to copy this from you. It will be too difficult."

"When do we begin?" Lola asked.

"We must sit and develop the story, in dance, about the deadly spiders. They attack you, the beautiful young maid. Then you defeat them by dancing, shaking them off, and smashing your heels down on them."

"I will show some leg while doing it."

"And petticoats."

"And bosom?"

"You've got enough bosom for two women," Madam said. "I'll design your dress so either your breasts or their eyes will pop out. This will be your dance." The two women laughed, embraced, and pulled me in the circle with them.

"It must be unique," Lola said, "Explosive, and tell a story in movement."

"Yes, because singing is not your forte." Madame said.

"What do you mean?" Lola demanded. "My voice has been praised by professionals and singing coaches. You are neither of those!"

"You are correct," Madame La Rosa said, "And I am not wrong. Where did you sing for those professionals who praised your voice?"

"In their ateliers and salons."

"And their evaluations were correct. You project a professionally acceptable voice for a studio. However, you lack the power to fill a crowded theater with this charming voice. And I am a professional singing coach."

Lola responded by changing the subject rather than admit defeat. "My version of the Tarantella has been well accepted."

"I seek the highest accolades for you, not mere acceptance." Madame had learned not to argue directly, but said, "Theater audiences applauded your beauty and vitality. Now we must work on receiving praise for your originality and presentation."

I doubted the two women would work well together. They were both strong-willed people. Changing something Lola considered perfect wouldn't be easy, but once again she surprised me. Lola herself made the most unique changes to the dance and her own costume. First she built on the story in dance about a young girl who is attacked by the deadly spiders. She added more spiders. This required her to dance more wildly, shaking her skirt and seven petticoats to be rid of the vermin. Guided by Madame La Rosa, she used her high-heeled dancing shoes to stomp the spiders into the floor. This she did while keeping time with the music.

Each shake and frenzied stamp of her foot exposed more and more leg. This led to a prolonged argument between teacher and student. The costume designed by Lola and sewn by me was praised by Madame La Rosa. The music selected by Madame was praised by Lola. Lola's underwear caused the problem.

Women's pantalets were a new concept. Madame La Rosa had no problem with the skirt or low-cut bodice and off-the-shoulder blouse. She admired the whalebone corset which pushed up Lola's ample breasts. The hooped cage I fastened at the waist supported seven delicate petticoats. The chemise and stockings were no problem. The new pantalets made trouble.

Neither Lola nor I ever wore them or knew women who did. The new fad had detractors. Doctors and men of science wrote that the private parts of women need fresh air. Lola was convinced by Madame La Rosa to wear pantalets because when she bent over or mounted a carriage the hoop would lift the dress, petticoats and chemise exposing everything to everyone. But Lola insisted on having pantalets with a split to allow fresh air. Madame La Rosa insisted I put buttons on the pantalets to close it. Lola stood her ground arguing in Spanish that she must have fresh air circulating between her legs. She maintained that she would allow no one to touch her there by unbuttoning the pantalets during formal occasions. It was the custom of young boys summoned onto a ballroom floor to crawl under the hooped skirt with a chamber pot, and place it so the lady could make pee pee without having to leave the room.

Lola shouted, threatened, and screamed, and by virtue of her anger won the argument. No buttons were used. Madame La Rosa had met her match.

Prior to our leaving Spain, a Portuguese cloth merchant insisted on showing his merchandise. Unimpressed, Lola left us. Madame was taking her siesta. When alone, the man whispered, "Rabbi Yeshaia Caspi asked me to visit you. How may I be of service?"

I had forgotten the arrangements made in London's West End, but I had 100 shillings to send my Princess. This enormous amount of money was earned by me arguing down the prices after Lola accepted them. This involved moving our luggage, shipping, purchase of materials for costumes and numerous other items. I was proud of myself, and bought several yards of the Jew's material to thank him for transferring my money. He in turn gave me a package containing the equivalent of ten thousand sterling for Lola's account.

The night before our departure, Madame La Rosa arranged a private dinner for the three of us. She directed the conversation into subjects which made it clear that Lord Palmerston was involved. "Most people," Madame La Rosa said, "Misunderstand a courtesan's position in society. The term is feminine, and means one who attends court of a royal or powerful person. The masculine term is courtier. The Royal Courts of Europe remain the center of state governments. A country's social, economic, political, religious and military life is decided there. After the fall of Napoleon, Prince von Metternich of Austria established national Congresses throughout Europe, but the aristocracies—formerly the feudal Lords—controlled the kingdoms. A less formal venue for these aristocratic courts is called the Salon. It is an informal meeting place. There, lords and ladies, artists, business people, military and newspapermen gather to share ideas and plan the future of the world. Countess Lievian and George Sand, both in Paris, are the most successful courtesans in Europe. They attract influential people from England, the continent, and America. Prince von Metternich will soon be posted to Paris. He will attend both salons. George Sand is most important because she owns a newspaper, is Europe's most famous authoress, and is politically engaged with other newspaper owners. Newspapers shape the thoughts of the educated, and the educated lead the people."

Lola unobtrusively signaled that she wanted me to

question Madame La Rosa. We had prepared for this meeting. "How would you describe the role of a courtesan?" I asked Madame La Rosa.

"She serves as an informal method of conveying information to visiting notables, and relays their replies," Madame answered. "The courtesan is a third party used to reduce friction between potential adversaries. It is also customary for the courtesan to sleep with such people."

"Prostitute myself!?" Lola exploded. "Never!"

"In this, the highest class of society, it is not considered prostitution," Madame said.

"Aren't most of these noblemen married?" Lola asked.

"Yes," Madame answered, "But aristocrats rarely marry for love."

"You mean they don't go to bed together?" Lola asked.

"Of course they do. That is the reason for their marriage. They wed to continue their noble bloodlines, increase the family fortune, and bind political or economic alliances. Sexual gratification and companionship is sought from amongst the courtiers and courtesans. By having intercourse with men, courtesans obtain sexual pleasure, as well as wealth. The more natural the sex, the easier it is to obtain information and money. You, my dear Miss Montez, are in an ideal situation. Lord Brougham will provide you money and introductions to the wealthy, powerful and influential. You also will be gifted for your favors from those men you entertain."

"Should Mistress Lola pretend orgasm?" I asked.

"Of course!" Madame said. "Preferably it will happen naturally, bur skill at pretence is necessary. Most married women pretend in bed. They receive clothing, jewelry, a home, food, and recognition for their service. Why shouldn't you?"

"But in India," I said, "Women usually enjoy sex. Men study the *Kama Sutra* to learn how best to pleasure a woman."

"I do not know about Hindus. Frenchmen are good lovers," Madame said, "The Italians better. The worst are the Germans and the English. They climb on, enter, give a few furious pumps, then slide off satisfied they have proved their manhood. The situation of unsuccessful orgasms for women has reached epidemic proportion with the English."

"I lived in India and England," Lola said, "But never heard the lack of a sexual climax described as a medical problem."

Madame La Rosa radiated one of her rare smiles and asked, "Are you familiar with the medical condition called Hysteria?"

"Of course..." Lola said. "You mean... The hysteria is because of lack of sex?"

"Of successful sex."

"How can you know and the doctors don't?"

"They know, and make a very good living from this sad malady."

"I can't believe it," Lola said.

"What is the treatment for female hysteria?" Madame La Rosa asked.

"Pelvic massage." Lola answered. "I don't know what or where a pelvic is."

"Between your legs, my dear," Madame said. "That

part you don't want to cover with buttons on your panta-lets."

Lola blurted out, "You mean to say women go to doctors so they can masturbate themselves?"

"No," Madame said. "The doctor masturbates them."

"How often?"

"As often as necessary. I met a woman who went three times a week."

"How does the doctor do it?"

"With his finger."

"Why didn't she do it herself?" Lola asked.

"Because she's a proper English lady," Madame answered. With a twinkle in her eye she continued, "As aristocratic Spaniards, you and I are not troubled by that problem."

Lola started laughing. She emitted those deep-throated, lusty guffaws. From such an elegantly beautiful person it was odd, yet genuine and infectious.

We three laughed until our sides hurt.


The steamship journey to England was pleasant. Lola usually wandered off after dinner to flirt or seduce the young men aboard ship. Sometimes she returned to our cabin in the early hours of the morning. There were occasions when she walked in evening clothes to our cabin, passing those going to breakfast or on deckchairs taking the sun. She rose late, but never missed our afternoon lessons in Spanish. We held our own high-tea as the passengers shunned us. We discussed *Kama Sutra* at the evening meal, and then she was off again on her own.

She had a terrible row with the Captain. He came to

our cabin to criticize Lola's evening escapades because the passengers were complaining. Lola actually attacked him with her fists. He was a big man and smiled at her ineffectual efforts—until she pulled a stiletto from her waistband. Then he fled the cabin. For the remainder of the voyage the Captain ignored us and we took our meals in the cabin.

My teaching the Hindu sex manual to Lola had begun after the separation from her husband. When Lola came to me about her sexuality, Madame La Rosa would have said she was suffering from hysteria. I understood Lola's problem and explained how she could relieve herself by effective masturbating. She questioned me closely about sex, and I mentioned the sixty different positions of the *Kama Sutra*. She ordered me to purchase the book and teach her. I taught her the various positions for intercourse and how to entice men. She compared the flirting instructions to hunting.

Lola was good with rifle or pistol. On several occasions she embarrassed the young officers who took her to the shooting range or on a hunt. She was, as I've said, fearless. My most important contribution to Lola's sex education was knowledge that the act should be fun and prolonged for maximum enjoyment. At first Lola told me every detail of every sexual encounter. It wasn't long before she wearied of talking and I of listening.

My concern was to protect her reputation. Alas, I failed. Lola didn't care what others thought. Her name suffered, but she never failed to attract the eyes of men—and the jealousy of women. When she appeared, the young, old, married, and single swiveled their heads to watch her elegant bearing, sensual body and lovely face, with those large blue eyes gazing from under curved dark black lashes and long ebony tresses.

We two also studied the Hindu approach to the eastern courtesan in the *Kama Sutra*. I consider it superior, more practical and straightforward than the Anglo-European attitude.

"A courtesan should form friendships with people of power. She focuses on those of wealth in positions of authority and influence."

Lord Palmerston impressed on me the concept that influence is preferable to power. He was keen about Lola developing relationships with newspaper people. He diagramed with quill and ink a fictitious Lord or politician with authority who gives twenty percent of his control to an underling. He proved mathematically that this man had reduced his own authority to eighty percent, but if he influenced another to act on his behalf, he increased his authority by twenty percent. Thus, Madame La Rosa and I had stressed focusing on newspaper and literary men. These people influence literate society. Literate people determine the future. Lola and I discussed these subjects as professionals planning a business venture.

We agreed that Lola's goal should be to capture and marry a prince. She would use the theatre to gain attention. We based our plans on the careers of Fannie Ilssler and her sister, Theresa. These Austrian ballerina/courtesans captured many hearts, and usurped several fortunes, on their theatrical way to Theresa marrying Prince Albert of Prussia and becoming a Baroness.

First Rule: the courtesan, through her intimacy with the powerful, influences others and acquires wealth. She seeks men of high birth for money and influence. Newspaper editors and owners are able to manipulate both the nobility and the masses. Newspapers shape the thoughts of people who can read. Those who read control what is being called the New Industrial Society.

The order of priorities for the association of a courtesan with a man is the acquisition of money, power, and enjoyment—all three, if possible. The courtesan must speak intelligently, think before acting, and never lose her temper in public. The latter was a primary concern. The methods of extracting money are numerous. We discussed them.

One can contract debts for the sake of her lover, then cancel the purchase and keep the refund.

Pretend to be ill, and charge the cost for treatment and vacations to recuperate.

Pretend to sell jewelry, furniture, or cooking utensils because of lack of funds.

When I told Lola this, she opened her fan, brushed the air onto her face and said, "I'll handle the explanations; you manipulate the sales."

In India, when a lover arrives the courtesan greets him with a smile and revealing dress. She uses betel nut and betel leaves to encourage his vitality.

"But Lord Palmerston said he will supply me with the Pope's wine!" Lola said.

I produced a bottle of Vin Mariani along with a poster picture of Pope Leo XIII recommending the French tonic wine for rejuvenation and relieving pain. Madame La Rosa gave the wine to me before we departed. It contained coca leaves whose elements, when extracted by the alcohol, become ten percent cocaine.

According to Madame La Rosa, Queen Victoria, Lord Palmerston, and those who could afford to import Vin Mariani did so for its aphrodisiac qualities. Lord Palmerston vowed to keep Lola supplied with the cocaine-infused wine in order to seduce men. Early in our voyage Lola decided to try this bottle on a young aristocratic rake. It had worked so well that she had to fend him off the remainder of the voyage.

In addition to my teaching the *Kama Sutra*'s advice to a courtesan, we studied how to avoid pregnancy. The rhythm and withdrawal methods were obviously not for a courtesan. Lola was religiously against abortion. Fanny Ilssler had a daughter out of wedlock with Prince Leopold of Sicily, which almost ended her career. I taught Lola how to insert a small vinegar-soaked sponge with a string. It always protected me.

We discussed how to select, evaluate and entice a potential lover and how to extract the most money, using trickery, even blackmail. When a courtesan finds her lover's ardor waning, she should get possession of all his best property and allow supposed creditors to confiscate art, furniture, jewelry and other valuables in satisfaction of some pretended debt. Later the bogus creditor will sell the repossessed items and make payment. If the lover is rich, and behaved well towards her, the courtesan should treat him with respect; but if he is poor and destitute, she should get rid of him as if she didn't know him.

How to get rid of a lover: The duty of a courtesan consists in forming connections with suitable men, obtaining wealth and information from the person who is attracted to her, then dismissing him after she has taken away all his possessions or usefulness.

To recognize the behavior of a waning lover: He gives the woman either less than is wanted, or something else than that which is asked for. He keeps her in hopes by promises. He pretends to do one thing, and does something else. He does not fulfill her desires. If he forgets his promises, or does something else than that which he promised, the courtesan should end the relationship.

Lord Brougham sent a dossier with instructions; Lola and I were to learn from the experiences of Princess Dorothea Lieven. Her salon in Paris was second only to that of George Sand. The Princess, not an aristocrat, was born in Riga, Russia. A beautiful young girl invited to the court of Catherine the Great, Czarina of Russia, she married Prince Andre Lieven at the behest of Czar Alexander—who appointed him Minister to Berlin, and then Ambassador to Great Britain. In London the Princess used her cleverness, personality, and beauty to become an important conduit for information to and from various embassies. She became a recognized force in international politics. Czar Alexander said, "If Princess Lieven wore pants she'd lead Russia's diplomatic corps."

She is reported to have slept with all the leading politicians, English and foreign. The Princess developed liaisons with Prince von Metternich and Lord Palmerston. However, Palmerston rejected her overtures to Austria, on behalf of the French, to stop the Russian invasion. She defied Palmerston. He retaliated. Palmerston used his secret relations with Czar Alexander to have the Princess and her husband recalled to Moscow after two decades in London. She soon abandoned her family and moved from Moscow to Paris. There she re-established her salon and political intrigues.

Lord Brougham cautioned us to be clear, concise and truthful in our reports. He warned, "The sun never sets on the British Empire, and Lord Palmerston regulates its rising and waning. He is not a forgiving man."

Prior to our arrival in London, Lola and I discussed the three A's of a courtesan: to aim, attract and arouse men she marked for conquest. Lola insisted she would not become involved with older men. I pointed out that they were the richest, most powerful, and supremely gullible. Lola insisted that she would not spend her time in bed trying to arouse an erection that would not satisfy her needs. I countered with the Pope's Wine saying, "It worked for Lord Palmerston, who is in his seventies. If necessary, keep a young lover to satisfy you. The younger the better: you can teach him."

Lola didn't concede the point but changed the subject. At least she didn't explode as she used to before our sojourn with Madame La Rosa.

# CHAPTER 5

## HER MAJESTY'S THEATER

Never again did we meet Lord Palmerston. Lord Brougham guided us.

I was wary of Lord Brougham. He did not like Lola or Lord Palmerston's plans for her, yet when we arrived in England everything was arranged and tidy. We were housed in a fashionable London apartment.

Lord Brougham's agent explained that Lola would appear at Her Majesty's Theater. We later learned that pressure was put on the playhouse manager to accept Lola's performance between acts of the existing program. This was occasionally done for reputable performers. Lord Palmerston's agents invaded the streets, taverns, and private clubs, chatting up the coming appearance of Lola Montez and her Spider Dance. In addition, those newspaper people in the service of Lord Palmerston wrote of the trials and tribulations of this Spanish noblewoman forced to flee her country. Lola was portrayed as an innocent aristocratic victim of historical events, compelled to earn a living on the stage.

We two laughed when reading the articles aloud to each other. But then, two days before the performance the atmosphere became serious. Tickets sold out. They were re-sold at three to five times the original cost.

Journalists found us. They blocked the front and rear of our building. The police arrived before we left for the theatre, and I allowed the Sergeant to enter the apartment. He was a large, powerfully built man. Newspapermen tried to force their way in with him, but with one shove he sent three sprawling and shut the door. "Decorum. That's what is required," he said. "These scandalmongers don't know the meaning of the word."

Her debut only two hours away, Lola was on edge "What is it you want?" she demanded.

The Sergeant's face smiled but his eyes were not happy. "Madame," the Sergeant began but was cut off by Lola shouting. "I am Donna Maria Dolores de Porris y Montez! My parents were nobles at the court of King Ferdinand. Address me properly."

"Madame... I mean, Miss Donna Maria Dolores: is there anything you can do to satisfy that bunch outside so they will leave? Their carriages block the street. The citizens are complaining."

"That's your problem!" Lola shouted. "If you English cannot afford patience for an artist, then to hell with you!"

"But Miss Donna Montez," the Sergeant persisted, "The people on this street also have a right to quiet and decorum."

"You big oaf, is decorum all you worry about? Shortly, I will make my premier appearance at Her Majesty's Theater. My show has been sold out for days. The neighbors can wait."

"Not outside this apartment, they can't," the Sergeant said. He put his thumbs in his belt, threw back his shoulders and said, "I have my orders, and brought enough men to enforce them."

Now the Sergeant's face was as angry as his eyes.

Lola's eyes flashed blue lightening. He said, "If my lads start cracking heads, the newspapers will blame you. I'll see to that."

Lola screamed, "You don't know who you are dealing with!"

I quickly stepped in between the two as Lola reached for the stiletto in her waistband. I covered her knife hand with both of mine and asked, "Is it possible for the Sergeant to say that Miss Montez will address the newspaper people at the stage entrance of Her Majesty's Theater in thirty minutes?"

"That might do," he said. "I'll make that announcement. I'm going to remove them and clear the street one way or another."

"Could you and your men escort Miss Montez to her carriage so our departure will not be delayed?"

"Your departure is my fondest desire," The Sergeant said. He mocked us with an exaggerated bow and closed the door behind him.

He certainly heard Lola shout and curse like an army drill sergeant; her early education included the parade grounds of Calcutta. I stared at the door expecting the policeman to barge back in. It remained closed, but Lola's mouth did not. The shouting in the hallway and the street made it doubtful anyone heard Lola's detailed description of the Sergeant's ancestors.

True to his word he cleared the hallway, porch, and eventually the entire street. He met us at the front door with that same exaggerated bow and said, "Madame your carriage awaits."

Lola slapped his broad smiling face. It reminded me of the old Hindu joke about the flea having sex with an elephant and the flea asking, "Did I hurt you, dear?" I must have smiled for Lola looked at me and said, "If I could get him in the Spread Eagle position, I'd kick his balls so far up his arse he'd think he had eggs for breakfast."

I laughed. She laughed and it broke the tension. Lola was in good spirits when she stepped from the carriage at the stage door. Newspapermen surrounded us. The theater manager brought a semblance of order to the rambunctious crowd of reporters shouting questions. Lola appeared unaffected and forthright with her answers. She ignored those relating to her Irish lineage, marriage, and Spanish ancestry. She actually answered questions that were not even asked.

"Yes, it is true I performed the Tarantella before, but I modified the dance to be so much more exciting. Those who have the pleasure of seeing me perform will be pleasantly surprised by my interpretation."

I was proud of my little girl. She had the newsmen eating from her hand. They hung on her every word. Her beauty impressed all.

"I take leave now," Lola said. "I must arrange my costumes and makeup, and exercise before my appearance." Stage hands stopped the crowd from following us inside. Several well-wishers threw bouquets.

The manager showed us to a dressing room where two actresses were dressing. "Out!" Lola shouted. "Out right now!"

"And who the hell are you, Ducky?" one actress demanded.

"I am Maria Dolores de Porris y Montez. My parents were nobles at the court of King Ferdinand of Spain."

"Well, kiss my royal ass," the actress said, "I took you for the bloody queen of Sheba." She came forward, prepared to fight. Lola balled her fists and raised them. The theater manager inserted himself between them, pleading, "Ladies! Ladies! We can settle this amicably."

"They go!" Lola shouted

"Or what?" the actress demanded, reaching over the manager's shoulder, trying to get at Lola.

"Or I go, and this little twerp," Lola tapped the manager's bald head with her fan, "Can dance the Tarantella himself."

The manager turned white, and while struggling with the angry actress he stammered, "They're standing in the aisles and out the doors! Miss Montez, be considerate. They'll rip this place apart."

"I am reasonable." She pointed at the two actresses. "They leave, or I do."

Lola had her way. After the door closed behind the arguing trio, she began stretching, pirouettes and leaps. I helped her dress, and we waited.

I found waiting difficult. Lola always appeared detached and calm at times like this. Before her stage appearances she remained quiet. I do not know if or where her thoughts wandered, but should anything disturb this contemplative mood she would explode like Vesuvius, covering all with curses and threats.

That's exactly what happened with a knock at the door. It was a young curly-red-headed man holding a bowler hat in one hand, a pad and pencil in the other, and saying, "I'm a newspaperman sent by Lord Brougham to interview Miss Lola Montez."

"NO!" Lola screamed. "You speak to him! Protect

me from these callous bastards!"

I slipped outside, closed the door behind me and grabbed a passing stage hand to guard Lola from being disturbed.

"My name is Donald Ewart, Esquire," the young man said. "We can talk, without being bothered, in the basement."

I followed him down the wooden steps leading under the stage. We passed a maze of ropes, pulleys and moveable platforms called elevators that reached to trap-doors in the floor above. "Does Miss Montez use any of these modern contraptions in her performance?" he asked.

"No, but we were warned about the new gas lights ."

"Because in another theater ballerina Clara Webster's costume caught fire, and she died."

"In front of the audience?"

"Yes. There's a movement to ban gas lighting."

"What newspaper do you represent?"

"The *London Dispatch* and *London Standard*. If you follow Lord Brougham's instructions to give me an exclusive interview, other newspapers will copy my articles of Miss Montez's debut. Lord Brougham has much influence."

"What do you mean?"

"His agents have been touting Lola Montez in the pubs, bars, clubs, and on the streets. They occupy a good part of the front benches."

"Please be brief," I said.

"When in the act will Miss Montez perform the Spider Dance?"

"The third presentation. The Cachucha first, the

Hornpipe second, and then the Tarantella."

"Do you consider this Spider Dance to be lewd?"

"Not at all. This piece is an expression of carefully researched authenticity, as interpreted by Miss Montez in ballet for the edification of her audience. Miss Montez's beauty is not in question. That she performs Pointe-Work on her toes, while most ballerinas still walk flat footed, is an indication of her dedication to the art." Mr. Ewart scribbled away and he justified the agony I went through memorizing this answer. "Miss Montez darns her own special slippers to be able to perform on her toes." Actually I did the darning, but we thought it would give Lola a down-to-earth image for all the factory workers who would be in the benches. The boxes right and left of the stage would be filled with aristocrats and nouveau riche. The balcony was for whoever else attended.

"Did you know that poets, playwrights and authors Robert Browning, Lord Byron, and Charles Dickens are in the audience?" Mr. Ewart asked.

"They are in for a stellar performance."

"Is it true that Miss Montez is the illegitimate daughter of Lord Byron?"

"Rubbish!" I said. "Her proper name is Maria Dolores de Porris y Montez. Her parents were nobles at the court of King Ferdinand of Spain, until the Carlist's revolution."

"Rumors abound of Miss Montez's errant activities aboard the ship to England. Can you comment on this?"

"I certainly can. Have you ever seen Miss Montez?"

"No."

"You then have the pleasure of expectation. Miss

Montez has been proclaimed the most beautiful woman alive. She gives her heart to her audience, a dedicated professional performer. Her leisure activities are often exaggerated and cruelly distorted by those jealous of her beauty. Men whose advances are rebuffed by her forthright manner deride her."

"Certain people claim Miss Montez is actually Eliza Gilbert born in Limerick, Ireland?"

"Does Lord Brougham pay you?"

"I hope so."

"Ask him that question," I said, and left to prepare Lola for her entrance.


Lola stood in the right wing of the stage and I behind her, hidden from the audience by the curtains. She knew this was her opportunity for a giant step on the road to success. She felt the theatre manager pat her bare shoulder as he passed and went front stage center. The gaslights at floor level glowed brightly.

His stentorian voice boomed throughout the theater. "Ladies and gentlemen: for your pleasure and edification, tonight Her Majesty's Theater presents Miss Lola Montez." He continued while Lola mentally prepared herself to burst onto the stage. She knew this was her time. She was prepared.

"Without further ado," the Stage manager boomed, as he signaled to the musicians in the pit, "I present, Miss Lola Montez, the Spanish aristocrat, performing the Cachucha." Then he hurried back behind the curtain to clear the stage.

The First Violinist raised his bow. The orchestra took his signal, and music filled the theater. The audience roared their approval as Lola exploded onto the stage.

Her first dramatic leap took the audience's breath away. She skipped lightly across the stage, returned to the center and took a stance. Suddenly the gas-lights lowered and the theatre was plunged into darkness. Then slowly flames on the extreme right and left gave forth all their light. The stage manager directed several stage hands with highly polished copper reflectors used to transfer the light onto at Lola stage center.

She posed, exposing her right leg above the knee from under her voluminous skirts. Her breasts were pushed up to form beautiful golden mounds under her exquisite face. The audience in the boxes, the rows and balcony collectively drew in their breath, and it sounded as a sigh of the Thames when the river ran out with wind and tide.

Lola held the pose. Then, in time with a single drum–beat, she clicked her castanets. Other instruments joined. The music quickened, and Lola made a second leap followed by a magnificent two–step, clicking her heels in perfect time to the music across the wooden floor. She whirled back and forth from one side of the stage to the other.

The audience was momentarily silenced by her athletic performance, and then began to clap in time to the music. The sound of the audience's approval energized Lola, and she put forth all her strength to make the dance even more dramatic. Lola skipped off stage to me.

I quickly tied a cord around her left wrist, attached to a male dummy. This Madame La Rosa had thought up. Lola returned to the stage with one of her finest leaps, and the crowd responded in surprise at her dance partner attired in traditional Spanish costume.

Lola danced with the life-sized doll. She whirled it around. She threw him to the floor at her feet. With a flick of the wrist he leapt back into her arms. Lola's unique manipulation of the doll drew thunderous applause. She bowed and bounded off stage, followed by a roar of approval from spectators, stage hands, and actors standing behind the scenes.

I worried Lola might not have enough energy for her next performance and tried to get the manager's attention, but he was already announcing the Hornpipe. I helped change her costume. Lola was smiling. She had the audience's approval; that is what she lived for. When she smiled like that everything around her looked beautiful.

The only clothes Lola wore from the first dance were the corset revealing her cleavage, and the sparkling tiara glistening in her ebony-black hair. For this dance she dressed in a sailor's white button up pants, white-and-black striped tight-fitted shirt showing her full bosom, with a red sash around her slim waist.

The First Violinist blew a boson's whistle. Lola took her mark. A concertina struck up the old seamen's tune, and a bagpipe joined. I handed Lola two cutlasses. She pranced onto the stage, her knees raised high and toes pointed. She hopped from one foot to the other, arms folded in front of her breasts, but low enough for them to be seen. She bowed with the left leg forward and then with the right leg. She sliced the air with the cutlasses, laid them on the floor, and in time with the music imitated hauling the lines to raise the sails and climbing hand over hand into the rigging.

The musical accompaniment stimulated the audience to stamp their feet and clap in time with Lola as she danced around and in between the swords. The musical instruments increased the tempo. Faster and faster the music drove Lola's steps. I expected her to collapse.

Then she stopped. The music stopped. Lola took a deep breath, and her eyes spat fire as she reached down and picked up the cutlasses.

She was angry at the First Violinist, and stalked toward him, front stage center. The man looked up in wide-eyed horror at Lola brandishing the swords. He and I both thought she would attack. Instead Lola crossed the weapons in front of her breasts, bowed to the audience and received a standing ovation. She saluted with the swords and danced off stage.

She wilted into my outstretched arms. "Can you continue?" I asked.

"She must go on," the manager said. "They'll destroy the theater, else. I am going to announce the Spider Dance!" He pointed to a large stage-hand. "You," he said, "Down on your hands and knees. Let Miss Montez sit on your back."

He had another stagehand support Lola from behind, and he instructed me, "Get her dressed. I'll tell a few jokes to give her time. The show must go on!"

The manager walked onto the stage and signaled for quiet. He announced, "Miss Montez needs a few minutes to change costumes. I thought to tell you a couple of funny stories, but on the way to the theatre a sad thing happened. I passed the wool factory, where they have a massive coal pile to fuel the new steam engines. An old lame dog, thin as you've ever seen, staggered to the coal pile. He sniffed it, licked it, and ate a few chunks of coal, cracking them with his few remaining teeth. Suddenly he threw back his head and howled. Then he ran around in circles before he collapsed in front of me, rolled over on his back, four feet stiff in the air."

"Dead!" Some of the crowd murmured.

"No," the manager shook his head, "That dog just ran out of fuel."

Lola's eyes were closed but she must have been listening, for she laughed with the audience. I hurried to get her elaborate costume on, and gave her sweets made from honey for energy.

We heard the stage manager ask the people, "How can you tell a dogwood tree in the dark?" The crowd responded, "By its bark!"

He asked, "How can you tell when a tree and a dog are dead?" The crowd echoed, "When they lose their bark!"

I signaled the manager that Lola was ready.

He made the introduction. The theater lights lowered. The orchestra struck up the first chords of the Tarantella.

Lola put every bit of her talent and strength into this dance, and received thundering applause.

It was after her last curtain call that the trouble began. The following was written be newspaperman Donald Ewart.

*Those center stage, in the first three rows of*

*the aisles, swore they saw Miss Montez's knickers. Some Toffs in the boxes complained they should have been treated to that sight as they paid more for their place. Others were offended by shouts from the benches that she had a slit in her pantalets to air out her Pusey. A Toff in a lower box took umbrage. He called those in the front rows 'swine!" He used other unprintable words. A large man from the aisles jumped up and grabbed the aristocrat by the lapels of his velvet jacket. He dragged him over the rail and would have landed the man down into the aisles when his comrades caught hold his legs. A tug of war ensued. Workers held the head and shoulders while friends had the man's legs. In the tug of war the gentleman's trousers came off. The rail and side of the box collapsed under his weight. The fight was on. The Toff's against the workers. The Irish in the balcony, always prepared for a good punch-up, came pouring down into the melee. The Gaelic mob did not take sides. They walloped everyone. Some brandished shillelaghs. The Toffs broke chairs and used the legs as clubs. Those in the aisles used the benches as battering rams. I saw a few knuckledusters. The manager turned off the gas and the theater went dark. The fight spilled into the street where everyone could see who he was thumping. Lola Montez exited by the rear door of the theater where a carriage awaited.*

As reporter Donald Ewart predicted, most morning newspapers were reworked versions of his article. Ewart also wrote for the afternoon papers, "I look forward to Lola Montez's next appearance, but it will not be in Her Majesty's Theater as the play-house will be closed for repairs. Miss Maria Dolores de Porris y Montez is a celestial body that appears once in a lifetime. Lola is a lithe tigress. She contains a bright nucleus which enters a highly eccentric orbit as she leaps and flits across the stage. Until last night, ballet belonged to the French and Italians. Lola put Spain and England in their category by dancing the Hornpipe on her tip-toes. From the boxes to the balcony she received accolades. From this reporter, rave reviews.

Miss Montez is not only a successful performer but a student of the art of dance. One of her most interesting observations indicating her dedication and professionalism is, that although the sun never sets on the English Empire neither does it shine on a national school of dance. Spain, France, Holland, Belgium and the Germanic States all boast state supported schools of the arts. England does not. Miss Montez believes something should be done about it."

From the *Daily News* I read, "Lola's physique is as beautiful as her face, which is dominated by flashing blue eyes that can challenge or promise. Her supple body assumes physical attitudes undreamt of, yet retaining the artistic stature of a premier ballerina."

From the *Tribune*, "Lola Montez is a superior mime. By use of her body, limbs, and expressions of her lovely face, she graciously translates her movements into a monodrama for the audience. At one moment her actions are provokingly seductive. Then, she slams her heels down on the wooden stage. Plants her fists on those lovely hips, thrusts her ample bosom forward taunting every man, any man, to approach her if he has the courage. What a gift Spain has given to English theater!"

From the *Mirror*, "I was grateful at last to see a Spanish dance by a Spaniard. Miss Lola Montez does not have the buoyancy or remarkable grace required of a prima ballerina, but her passion and beauty draws the audience into her performance."

"Of course I am a Spaniard!" Lola shouted. "And I am equal to any prima ballerina living or dead." She pointed to the newspapers. "Read! But from the bottom of the pile. I know you try to protect me. I smell that Mongoose, Palmerston, behind all this flattery."

"He certainly wasn't behind the ovations you received last night, and the multiple curtain calls."

"His flunkies occupied the first three rows in the aisles, and led the crowd. They even applauded when I just stood there."

"They applauded your beauty."

"Manuela, don't you become one of those sycophants. I need you to tell me the unvarnished truth. "

"I have not, nor will I ever lie to you," I answered. This, of course, was the biggest lie I ever told. Lola was incapable of hearing some truths, and unforgiving to those who spoke them. I removed the bottom three newspapers from the pile. They were *The Chronicle, The Age* and *The Era*. I read, "There are truly pro and anti-Lola cliques. The former being more vocal and strategically placed in the theater's central aisles. They cheered and complained Miss Montez's act was too short. Some Toffs in the boxes thought it was too long. The Irish in the balcony only wished to see Miss Montez's new knickers with the split in the middle. There is no doubt that Miss Montez is a tigress, at the epitome of her sex. A Spaniard she is not. Her real name is Eliza (Betty) Gilbert born in Limerick, Ireland. Although separated from her husband, Lieutenant Thomas James, she is still legally his wife under British Law. This presents a problem to those Keepers of the Commandments. Mistress Lola is not one of them. She is an adulteress, an imposturous and an agile gymnast. Certainly not a dancer."

"Next!" Lola shouted. I dropped that paper and opened another. "Miss Montez, who disappeared from Britain after she was hissed off the London stage, returns once again to foster her false Spanish credentials on a gullible public. The Manager of Her Majesty's theater and impresario Charles E. Carasso should have stopped this adulteress from appearing. She is an amateur dancer, separated from her husband but not divorced. She flaunts her beauty in a funambulist demonstration of athleticism. Some of my colleagues in the morning journals praised Miss Montez's performance even before she appeared on stage. The only truly Spanish dance was the Cachucha, the Hornpipe, obviously British and the Tarantula from Calabria, Italy." Lola pointed to the next paper and I read from the *Herald,* "Miss Montez is a superior pantomimic and by using her body and limbs she projects her message. Her feet require years of training to execute the intricacies of a danseuse such as Fannie Issler."

I put the article down and picked one I had put aside. "From the afternoon edition of the *Times*," I said, "A Spanish dance by a Spanish dancer. Miss Montez's dance is not characterized by remarkable grace or buoyancy, but it has much intensity. To compare her to other ballerinas is a mistake. She will be underrated by many in ballet who set the standards by French and Italian criterions. Lola Montez does not display pirouettes, entrechats and her agility is more athletic than artistic. But every gesture and attitude she expresses, she does so with great passion. That passion is transmitted from the stage to the audience. Dona Lola Montez is exquisitely beautiful in form and feature. She possesses the ability to represent various emotions in rapid succession with coherence and consistency."

"Was he also paid by the Mongoose?" Lola asked.

"Lord Palmerston only paid the morning papers," I lied. "Why can't you enjoy praise when it is truly given?"

"Because I danced well," Lola said. "Those literary clods couldn't make a pimple on my artistic arse. I will visit these idiot editors who hire hacks. I will give them hell."

I feared Lola's reaction would come to this, and changed the subject by saying, "While you were performing, one of the actors approached me to ask you to appear at a benefit show for himself."

"Did you inquire to his needs and his background?"

"He has been out of work for six months. And only picked up a small part for last night's show. He used to be a star performer and much sought after as a leading man, until rheumatism struck him down."

I was shocked when Lola said, "For a fellow artist I must do it." I knew her as a self-centered baby who, through childhood, followed her mother around saying, "Yook at me Mommy! Yook at me!" She was a selfish adolescent and an egotistical adult. However, when it came to those less fortunate, she was generous to a flaw.

In the coming years Lola never refused a legitimate request by artists, firemen, or hospices for help. She was often in confrontation with the law and did no benefits for the police. She once raised a goodly sum for a synagogue, and never accepted a fee for charity. I have seen her place money in the hands of the poor and donate to those less fortunate. She sought out the needy. I never understood why. It seemed contrary to her character, her background, and personal relationships which were mostly stormy. In any discussion with her peers or betters she always had to be right, and never backed down no matter how the truth or proofs contradicted her.

Lola's appearance at this benefit was a stunning success. She gained the admiration of London's theatrical world. The actor for whom the charity was held said twice the number of people attended than he hoped, all because of Miss Lola Montez.

We arrived in a phaeton serviced by four matched black horses, a footman and driver in full livery. London's artistic community paid her homage. Lola's performance was hailed by some newspapers and derided by others.

True to her word, Thursday afternoon we entered the offices of *The Clarion* unannounced. Lola's large hooped dress had to be forced through the door. She headed straight for the inner office with the capital letters EDITOR and threw it open. A tall thin man was bent over a desk, pencil in hand, making marks on a printed page. He had another pencil behind his left ear and a chewed-up cigar in the corner of his mouth. Stunned by the sudden interruption and then by the beauty standing before him, he asked, "May I help you, Madame?"

"Help me!?" Lola shouted. "You uncouth lout, get rid of that saliva-covered cheroot and address me as Dona Lola de Porris y Montez."

"Yes. Miss Montez." He threw the soggy cigar into a brass spittoon. "How may I be of service?"

"Fire that idiot Blake who wrote such wicked lies. He called me an adulteress in your newspaper."

The office door was still open, and I stepped aside as the editor shouted to all those gaping faces outside looking in, "Get Roger Blake in here!"

A big man with bald head came hurrying from amongst the desks in the outer room. He asked the Editor, "What is it?"

"This is Dona Lola Montez. You wrote an article calling her an adulteress."

"Yes sir, because she is."

Lola whipped out her dagger and leapt at the man. Surprisingly quick for his size, he took refuge behind the editor. There were several moments of noisy ducking and weaving before the Editor relieved Lola of the weapon.

He sent the frightened reporter from the room, closed the door and listened patiently to Lola for an hour. We three dined together, and then Lola ordered me home. She spent the night with the editor.

The following day there was a flattering article about Lola and her Spanish heritage and heroic escape from the revolutionaries in Spain. There was also a visit from Lord Brougham which changed our plans.

# CHAPTER 6

## TO PARIS

**Downing Street, England:**

"Only big men can make big mistakes," Lord Brougham said.

"And you constantly remind me of them," Palmerston answered. "This Montez woman leaves a trail of destruction. She could bring down all of London, possibly even our government."

"You gave her the idea that newspapers control public opinion. She wants to be famous."

"Let her be famous someplace else. She spent three hours with one editor, bedded another, and was wined and dined by the Lord Mayor of London. Get her to hell out of England."

"To George's Salon in Paris?"

"Yes. Montez has the potential to be a successful agent. We need information about Prince von Metternich's move toward France. It should be simple to arrange a performance for her on the Paris stage. She received enough publicity here."

"Do you have specific instructions for her?" Brougham asked.

"Von Metternich is the Austrian key to blocking Russia's move west. He is trying to form an alliance with France. He will be transferred to Paris to help the

Russians and the French facilitate an agreement. The thirty-nine Germanic States are strategic to blocking this move. Bavaria is the largest, richest and most powerful of these small Kraut countries. The key to Bavaria are the Jesuits. They run King Ludwig and control most of Europe."

I will attend to it."

"I want you in Paris."

"To monitor Lola?"

"That too. Don't become involved with her. She is as dangerous as a keg of black powder in a smoke-house, and clever too. You will be appointed Ambassador to France. Lola can be an important window on the act being played out between Russia, Austria, Hungary and France. I require information. The prize England seeks is the wealth and military power of the Germanic States; our Royal family is of Germanic stock."

"And King Ludwig controls most of the Germanic states."

"No! The Jesuits do. Infiltrate and investigate them."

I had barely enough time to reach the synagogue in London and pass two hundred pounds to the Rabbi for my daughter in Calcutta. This was more money than I ever sent. I made it by giving tidbits of information to various newspaper men at the theater and to those who waited for me when I went shopping.

The Rabbi named two Jews in Paris that I could trust, and he cashed Lord Palmerston's voucher for Lola.

We traveled by coach to the London docks, where I supervised the loading of our baggage. Lola spent time on the bridge with the captain, and the night in his cabin.

We docked in Le Havre, where the luggage was sent by coach to Paris. We took a river steamer up La Seine to the capital of France. Our luggage arrived before us at the luxurious King George V Hotel.

My first duty was to contact Marcus Goldberg in his shoe-repair shop, where he changed our English currency to francs. French money was accepted or easily converted throughout Europe.

On my return, I told Lola of the beautiful new dress shops. Instead of visiting a seamstress in her home or inviting her to yours, one could purchase from places where clothes were stored. Here everything was now done in the store.

Paris was wonderfully exciting: wide boulevards with so many people, all fashionably dressed. The cafés, bistros were crowded with street musicians and artists ready to sketch ones portrait.

Lola spent more money on clothing in three hours than our vouchers were worth. She refused to pay cash, but signed Lord Brougham's account to be billed at the British Embassy. She even selected a dress for me.

We took dinner on the Boulevard and hired an open carriage back to the hotel. I was exhausted. Lola wasn't. She had me stack selected London newspapers on the floor next to a writing desk. She spread out negative articles about her from the London newspapers. She prepared to send rebuttals to these editors, and thank-you notes to the positive ones.

She had me purchase a multiple writing device which held five quills and would duplicate each letter five times. I helped her arrange the paper and ink, and Lola wrote letters to the editors.

"Sir:

"I had the honor of dancing at Her Majesty's Theater on Saturday. The English public received me in so kind and flattering a manner, I am cruelly annoyed by reports that I am not the person I pretend to be. But that I have been long known in London as a disreputable character. I entreat you, sir, to allow me through the medium of your respected journal, to assure you and the public in the most positive and unqualified manner, that there is not one word of truth in such a statement. I am a native of Seville and in the year 1833, when I was ten years old, was sent to a Catholic lady in Bath, where I remained seven months and was then taken back to my parents in Spain. From that period until 14th of April last, when I landed in England. I never set foot in this country and never saw London before in my life. The imperfect English I speak I learned at Bath, England, from an Irish nurse who has been many years in my family. The misfortunes caused by the political events of my country, obliged me to seek a livelihood elsewhere, and I hoped that my native dances might be appreciated here, especially those Spanish ballets that are new to the English...[1]

---

[1] Taken with slight revision from *Lola Montez* by Bruce Seymour, page 39

"Believe me to be your obedient and humble servant,

"Lola Montez"

I inserted the letters, addressed the envelopes and posted them to London with the concierge. He introduced me to a reporter from *Le Figaro*, who gave me a gold Napoleon for one letter.

The French, If you speak their language as Lola and I do, are warm and quite generous. Lord Brougham was not. He appeared at our apartment door without invitation, and pushed past me shaking a fistfull of bills in Lola's face. "Where do you get the right to sign my name on these accounts?" he bellowed. "You obligated Her Majesty's government to pay an exorbitant amount for your frills."

I expected a violent reaction from Lola. Instead she fluttered her long dark eyelashes, gave a coy smile, and said, "We both receive orders from the same man. Ask Lord Palmerston if he objects."

Brougham stepped back, measuring the beauty before him, and said, "Palmerston thought he bedded you. I think it was the other way around."

Lola tilted her head, smiled, and blinked her blue eyes at Brougham. His neck bulged and his face turned red until he looked like a bright apple ready to explode. "I wouldn't touch you with..." He sputtered to a frustrated silence, turned and stormed out.

The bills were paid. Lola could write her own addendum to the *Kama Sutra* for courtesans.

The new clothes forced us to cull older clothing. Lola ordered the clothes given away. I kept them, and I sent a cart load across the Seine to the Jewish tailor. It meant extra money for Princess.

In fact, the money remained with the Jew in Paris. A letter informed a Jew in India to pay the specified sum to my daughter. Princess confirmed the payments by mail. She told of her studies and how she yearned for me to return.

I sensed a change in her writing, and it worried me. I thought it might be due to the death of Dadi, the old English Nanny. Some of my questions went unanswered.

I began to plan how to leave Lola and return to India. This would require money. Should I disappear or attempt an equitable parting?

Suddenly another opportunity for financial gain arrived in an embossed envelope delivered by a footman: An invitation for Lola to attend George Sand's Salon.

Lola was ecstatic. She danced around the apartment singing, practicing her bows, nods and snubs. She pulled out all the new gowns and we spent the rest of the day deciding which would be most appropriate. We chose a fine red velvet evening dress, with a low-cut bodice framed by white Belgian lace to reveal and emphasize her sculptured cleavage. A thin, crafted, silver belt accented her tapering waist and smooth rounded hips.

For two hours we debated the hairstyle. Her thick, ebony curls shone like black fire. That, more than anything else, gave her the appearance of a Spanish grandee. She wished to show her tresses with a small tea rose behind her right ear and a see-through veil. I argued for no veil, a simple part in the middle, the dark hair framing her blue eyes, tied in a bun at the back with a decorative silver sword skewering the bun and matching the belt clasp. Lola relented

She ordered me to obtain a list of guests who attend George Sand's Salon. I slipped the concierge several francs in accordance with the acronym TIPS: To Insure Personal Service.

He guided me to a bistro where servants of the wealthy gather. It was across the Seine not far from my Jewish tailor. First I called on Lord Brougham. He simply directed me to George Sand saying, "She is also in our employ." With a letter of introduction, I hired a carriage and arrived at a villa in the center of Paris.

White crushed marble formed a semicircular path to the front entrance. Inside the large gravel border, flowers, shrubs, and a host of miniature trees flourished, each selected for its shape, color and form. I told the driver to pull around to the servants' entrance when the front door opened. A handsome man called, "Whom do you seek?" Taken aback by the abrupt greeting I blurted out, "Mademoiselle Sand."

"I am she."

And so it was. Attired in fashionable men's clothes, with shoulder-length hair, she was smoking a cigar. She struck a pose. Her fists dug into her sides, she eyed me as one would a horse on the auction block.

"I am the servant of Donna Lola Montez," I said, "Here at the suggestion of Lord Brougham. This is my letter of introduction."

"Come down from there." She waved me inside. "I thought you would be wearing a sari."

"When Donna Lola appears in public, I wear the sari. French weather sometimes makes it impracticable."

"Good! If you want people to pay attention you must command it by voice, action, and clothing". George Sand threw back her head and stood to her full height, taller than most women. She waved both hands inward, indicating her clothes. "I wear men's attire. It is more comfortable and practical, and before people realize I'm a woman I enter places proper ladies do not go. I understand your lady is a pistoleer?"

"She shoots targets and hunts."

"Is she good?"

"Very."

"Excellent. We shall have sport with these effete aristocrats, and take a few ducats from them. Now tell me what I can do for your lady."


On my return, Lola stopped me from explaining my first impressions of George Sand.

"Tell every detail of her house, gardens, furniture and art," she demanded. "They will define her more accurately than the way she prepared to meet you."

Lola often had wise insights. George Sand loomed large in her mind as a scion one of France's wealthiest families and celebrated European authoress, newspaper editor/owner, literary publisher/ and mistress of the most prestigious salon on the continent. "Unification and control," I said, "Is the prominent theme in her home, clothing and actions. The gardens, villa and interior are all part of one plan: to create the perception of a refuge from the world. It is built to isolate those she wishes to manipulate."

"Did she manipulate you?"

"Easily. She put these words in my mouth. The villa has twenty-seven rooms for guests to sleep or entertain in. There are two well stocked libraries, a smoking room, and playrooms for adults and children."

"What can a playroom for adults contain?"

"Two billiard tables, a special room called an 'alley' for playing ten-pins, several dart-boards, chess, check-ers and professional gambling tables with roulette. Mademoiselle Sand takes part of every bet and donates it to charity. There is also an indoor pistol range."

Lola patted a stack of Sand novels. "Quite a lady."

"She is not a delicate type of lady."

"I've heard about her escapades. But tell more about the house."

"The servant's quarters are behind, close to the most elaborate and organized kitchen I ever saw. It stretches the entire width of the villa. Carts deliver into prepared stalls behind the house. Refuse is burned or composted for the well-kept gardens. Butchers for meat, fowl, and fish are in separate stalls and have their own ovens. Soups and vegetables have their own places, and there is a small building for pastries and sweets. There are seven chefs and a Master Chef, and a separate building for servants' uniforms. Women wear black blouses with a white over-dress. Men wear blue, green, or yellow vel-vet waistcoats, knee-length white silk trousers, and buckled shoes with white silk stockings. Their shirts are white linen, ruffled to the chin. Everything is meant to blend with this theme of isolation from the outside."

"She wants her guest's attention," Lola said. "Now tell me about her. Is she beautiful?"

"Not in the sense of feminine attraction. She is a

handsome woman with a good figure. Her personality is her most attractive quality. You can feel the power exude from her. She steps close to you when speaking. It frightens and excites. She is aware of this, and does it purposely."

"Why?"

"To put one off balance. She asks a direct question and demands an immediate answer with her eyes. It is her way of getting at the truth and controlling the conversation."

"Does she employ other means of interrogating people?"

"I did not recognize any."

"Your education in the foreign embassies serves you well." Lola said. She pointed to a tureen on the credenza with money for tipping. "Take two sterling. You did well. Tell me more about George Sand."

"Very opinionated."

"She's earned the right."

"She suggests you trade the dagger in your belt for a riding crop or small horsewhip. She says the words Dago and dagger are synonymous in France, and throughout Europe, for Spaniards."

"My reputation precedes me."

"I agree with Madame Sand. A woman pulling a dagger and swinging a riding crop are two very different things. The former can be prosecuted, and the latter makes the man look foolish."

"Are those your words?"

"No, hers. I told you she can manipulate people."

"What do you think?" Lola asked.

"I'll buy a riding crop."

"Anything else?"

"She's interested in your ability on the pistol range. She wants to shock some of her elegant guests with your prowess."

"Pleased to oblige."

"Baroness Sand left me alone in the library with a newspaper folded open to this article. She meant for me to read it, and I did. When she returned I was holding the paper, and she said, "Take it with you.""

I handed the paper to Lola, and she read: "George Sand's reputation came into question when she began sporting men's clothing in public. She warranted the clothes are sturdier and less expensive and more comfortable than the dress of noblewomen. Sand's male attire allows her to circulate more freely in Paris than most females. It gives access to settings from which women are excluded. She smokes tobacco in public. She rides to hounds fully a-straddle and not side saddle as a lady of breeding.

"Her behaviors are remarkable for a woman of her station and lineage. As a baroness she and other upper-class wives live physically separated from their husbands, without embarrassment, provided no blatant irregularities become public knowledge. She cares not what others think.

"Poet and critic Charles Baudelaire describes George Sand: 'As stupid, heavy and garrulous. Her ideas on morals have the same depth of judgment and delicacy of feeling as those of janitresses and kept women... The fact that there are men who could become enamored of this slut is indeed a proof of the abasement of the men of this generation.' Flaubert is an unabashed admirer. Honoré de Balzac, who knew Sand personally, once said, 'If someone thought George Sand wrote badly, it was because their own standards of criticism were inadequate.' He also noted that her treatment of imagery showed her writing had an exceptional subtlety. She has the ability to 'virtually put the image in the mind of the reader.'

"George Sand was born Aurore Dupin in 1804. She is France's most famous woman writer. She is even better known as lover of the celebrated composer Frederic Chopin, and often described as a frigid, bisexual, nymphomaniac."

"Ho! Ho! Ho!" Lola's deep throated belly-laugh filled the room. "I am going to enjoy meeting this woman."

# CHAPTER 7

## GEORGE SAND

One cannot fault Lola in her preparation for meeting George Sand. I enjoy the task of researching people. It is their history that interests me: who they are, who they pretend to be, and how they achieved their position. These facts all relate to our future. It also makes the high and mighty more common.

George Sand was my first subject. Her writings inspired Fyodor Dostoevsky and Ivan Turgenev. Her personality inspired the character Prince Orlofsky in Strauss' "Die Fliedermaus". England's Elizabeth Barrett Browning penned several sonnets to "the large-brained woman and large-hearted man, self-named George Sand." Thackeray wrote: "Her wording recollected the sound of village bells sounding softly on the ear." John Stuart Mill compared her literature to a symphony by Haydn or Mozart.

I felt it important to read to Lola an excerpt from George Sand's autobiography about her religious experience. In reference to God she was a maverick, yet she believes in the Almighty.

She wrote, "I found myself before the church altar:

I had forgotten all: I knew not what was passing in me; with my soul rather than my senses, I breathed an air of ineffable sweetness. All at once a sudden shock passed through my whole being, my eyes swam, and I seemed wrapped in a dazzling white mist. I heard a voice murmur in my ear, *Tolle, lege* (Take up and read.). I turned round, thinking that it was one of the sisters talking to me—I was alone. I indulged in no vain illusion; I believed in no miracle; I was quite sensible of the sort of hallucination into which I had fallen; I neither sought to intensify it nor to escape from it. Only I felt that faith was laying hold of me—by the heart, as I had wished it. I was so filled with gratitude and joy that the tears rolled down my cheeks. I felt as before that I loved God, that my mind embraced and accepted that ideal of justice, tenderness and holiness which I had never doubted, but with which I had never held direct communion, and now at last I felt that this communion was consummated, as though an invincible barrier had been broken down between the source of infinite light and the smoldering fire of my heart. An endless vista stretched before me, and I panted to start upon my way. There was no more doubt or luke-warmness. That I should repent on the morrow and rally myself on my over-wrought ecstasy never once entered my thoughts. I was like one who never casts a look behind, who hesitates before some Rubicon to be crossed, but having touched the farther bank sees no more the shore he has just left."

George Sand and Franz Chopin spent the winter of 1839 together on the island of Majorca. I read newspaper summaries of her novels, *Indiana* (1832), *Lélia* (1833), *Mauprat* (1837), *Le Compagnon du Tour de France* (1840), *Consuelo* (1842-43).

Lola read them all. She never took notes, but internalized what she considered important. She would bring the conversation around to her knowledge of the subject where she could sparkle. I never met a more clever woman than Lola. She had intelligence, was witty, physically strong and fearless. Her temper was her Achilles heel. She tried to overcome this flaw by always being right, and this often led to confrontations.

We were interrupted by a footman with a message from George Sand. I read,

> "My dearest Donna Maria Dolores de Porris y Montez. It is with great anticipation I await your arrival this evening. The following are suggestions to make your accommodation into my Salon efficacious. Do not be affronted if my initial greeting upon your entrance is not overly enthusiastic. Later we shall talk privately. I suggest you draw as little attention to yourself as possible. Your beauty will be recognized. Become a wallflower if you can, and observe. I will appoint one of my confidants as your guide.

> "Your servant is quite educated, quick–witted, and hopefully will wear her sari this evening. It will draw attention to you rather than you toward yourself.

> "Sincerely, George Sand"

Our entrance and introduction to George Sand may have been discreet, but Lola made certain our arrival was noted. We rented four matched blacks drawing a large ornate polished black coach with gold trim, a driver and two uniformed footmen.

No fuss was made at our entrance to the ballroom, but heads turned. Lola wore a shimmering red, form-fitting gown. A silver tiara sparkled in her ebony black hair, and a diamond pendent shone from its resting place in the cavernous cleavage between her breasts.

The brief greetings offered by George Sand were discreet. My sari drew attention. We slipped off to the side, and remained standing against the far wall while music flowed from a string quartet. Lola asked, "When you met George Sand this afternoon, was she smoking a cigar, wearing a cravat, waistcoat, and man's stovepipe trousers?"

"Yes, with riding boots."

"If her hair was pulled tight and clubbed at the back she would look even manlier."

"My assessment of Madame Sand is that she achieves the impression she wishes to exhibit."

"Your initial description was accurate," Lola said. "George Sand oozes confidence and power. The only good thing my mother ever did for me was to hire you as my nanny."

I bit my tongue to keep from saying, "I am your slave. Nannies receive a salary, not presents."

A tall beautiful woman with a low-cut white sequined gown and high silver beehive hairdo moved next to me, saying, "Your hostess assigned me to explain the names, rank and importance of those you see."

"You wish to speak with my mistress."

"No, it must appear I am speaking to you. The words are for Donna Lola Montez."

Lola nodded and I replied, "Please continue."

"Do you really understand what takes place in the

Salons of Paris?"

"This is our first visit to a salon." I answered.

"Your spoken French is excellent." She covered her lips with a fan and said, "Reply as if I am speaking to you. There may be professional lip-readers observing."

That revelation changed the lighthearted atmosphere into a highly charged environment. I scrutinized the smiling faces. They now appeared as deceitful masks.

"The fate of countries and their people are decided in this ballroom," the woman said. "The details are sorted out in the embassies and capitals of the world. England may be the economic center of the world and the German states the fragmented scientific power, but France is the cultural capital of the universe. It is here the mighty meet. In the salons of Paris wars are begun, peace initiated, and plans for the future made.

"The man speaking to Lord Brougham is the Russian ambassador, and is looking to form an alliance with Prussia and France to take over the German States. Lord Brougham may appear friendly toward the Russian, but he and Prince von Metternich are opposed to his plan. The Prince wants the Germanic states for Austria. England wants Russia to remain where it is and keep France isolated."

Without turning her head or moving her lips Lola whispered, "Is von Metternich here?"

"No, He was recalled to Prussia."

The wealth of information that poured from this lady's ruby red lips was amazing. It seemed none of the royalty slept with their spouses. Theirs were arranged marriages, and both went their own way as long as there was no scandal. Invitation to the Salon was an unwritten guarantee by George Sand of aristocratic prudence. Diplomats sought out the lonely wives of royalty as a source of information and pleasure. Courtiers hunted male and female patrons for financial support and sources of information to be peddled. Same-sex relationships were common and communal sex selective.

Lola's eyes brightened. She wanted to dive into this maelstrom of genteel-looking aristocrats and tear them apart. She was aroused, and that could be dangerous. She had the ability to evaluate and catalogue information, but her memory was selective. If she saw no value in facts and figures, she forgot them.

By some unseen signal conveyed to the woman, she stopped her monologue and said, "Madame Sand wishes to meet with you privately. Please follow me."

The moment we moved, people apparently interested in other things turned to watch us follow George Sand from the ballroom. Our guide whispered, "This is Madame Sand's manner of announcing her approval of you in her Salon."

We entered a private room behind the bandstand. Our guide took her leave and closed the doors behind us. George Sand struck a pose in the middle of the ornately decorated room, right foot forward, fist on hip. She puffed a cloud of blue cigar smoke to the ceiling and stripped Lola from head to toe with her bright brown eyes. Lola appeared to enjoy the examination.

"You and your servant made a wonderful impression," George Sand said. She pointed at the riding crop tucked into the silver belt at Lola's waist. "So you took my advice about the dagger. Whatever made you carry such a weapon?"

"I had rather not say,"

"My dear little Lola," George said, "You and I will be sharing our most intimate thoughts and ideas. You are about to enter the information business. It is essential I know you. You, my dear, must trust me implicitly."

The two women locked eyes. They held each other's gaze without flinching. Lola reached up and rubbed a tiny scar over her right eyebrow and said, "I was twelve years old. It was the central church in Granada. I made confession and was doing penance."

"What did you confess to?" George asked.

"That is personal."

"Much of what you do in the service of Lord Palmerston will be even more so."

Lola thought and finally said, "I masturbated."

"What was your punishment?"

"To walk on my bare knees down the center aisle from the church entrance all the way to the altar. The aisle was strewn with pebbles.

"How could you possibly stand the pain?"

"I couldn't. They beat me. Three Jesuits tore off my clothes. I was naked and bloody at the altar. The three took turns trying to rape me. They were too large and I too tight. One with a ring punched me unconscious."

She touched the scar over her eyebrow, and I wondered if there was a better liar in all the world. Lola never saw Granada. I cannot remember where the scar came from, but am certain it didn't happen at age twelve. I cared for her as a baby until today, and cannot recall her ever meeting a Jesuit.

The story turned George Sand's sharp brown eyes into limpid pools of consolation. She stepped close to Lola, gently brushed her fingertips over the scar, then brought both index fingers down to the bulge of Lola's breasts and ever so lightly touched them. She continued tracing her fingers down to the silver belt and below, leaving a faint trail in the red velvet gown. Lola's hips were drawn forward, magnetized by the two fingers. George Sand leaned forward and kissed Lola on the lips. The two stood mesmerized, staring into each other's eyes. I dared not move for fear of breaking the spell.

In a husky voice George asked, "Would you like to spend the night?"

Lola shook her head from side to side.

"Another time perhaps." George stepped back, tugged the sleeves of her jacket and re-lit her cigar saying, "Your servant Manuela made quite an impression in her sari. She's been invited to sleep over with the Swedish cultural attaché, He considers her Hindu manners erotic."

"Erotic!" Lola quipped. "If he had any idea of her experience with *Kama Sutra...*"

George interrupted, asking me, "Are you a practitioner of that ancient art of sex?"

"I have been instructed."

"And she instructed me." Lola said.

The foreplay between these two powerful women excited me, and I was damp between the thighs.

"Would you like to see this Swede?" George asked me.

I looked to Lola, who nodded. "I would."

I thought George was leading us to the door to re-enter the ballroom, but she stopped at a large painting left of the doorway and swung it back on its hinges. In the wall a two foot long slot looked through a silk wall-hanging. It allowed a hazy view of the ballroom. George peered through and said, "The tall blond gentleman with monocle, speaking with the bearded Pole: that's Sven Avid Svenson."

"He is a big man," Lola said.

"And well-endowed below the waist," George said. She asked me. "Do you think you could handle him?"

"I have been celibate for some time." My nipples were swollen and pleasurably sensitive. I squeezed my thighs together. I knew what I wanted, but Lola was required to answer. She must have seen the desire in my eyes. I almost climaxed looking through the peep-hole. Lola said, "If you want, go."

I asked, "What do I do now?"

"A servant will direct you to an adjoining room. The Swede will come to you." George pulled on a silk rope, and a servant entered. George instructed him to take me out by the rear door and inform the Swedish Cultural Attaché.

"Should I leave by myself," Lola asked, "Or should I wait?"

"Your servant seems like a full blown healthy woman. If she knows the Hindu sex manual, we might be in for a long wait. How old is she?"

"Thirty seven. A year older than my mother."

"And how old are you?"

"Twenty-two."

"And I am three years older than your mother. Would you like to watch?"

"We can observe them?"

"It's fascinating."

"I never watched before."

"It can be as exciting as participating. We'll share a glass of wine before they meet. My servant will let us know."

"I don't usually drink"

"Lord Palmerston mentioned that, but this is a special wine I would like you to try." George Sand poured two glasses and sat facing Lola. "I have a list of names given to me by Lord Brougham. Almost all are newspaper owners, authors, and other architects of public opinion. He wishes you to appear on the Paris stage as a way of introducing you to the public. I will arrange meetings with theater managers, playwrights, and those other wealthy supporters of the arts. Some of these names you will recognize, such as Liszt, Chopin, Flaubert, Alexandre Dumas, and Dujarieir. You may not wish to sleep with me, but they will want to sleep with you. They are powerful men with potent sex desires. That is how you will earn your way into our society and glean the information hoped for by your mentor in London."

"Could I try smoking one of your cigars?"

"Have you smoked before?"

"Cigarettes. I can roll my own with one hand. You are impressive sitting there puffing away on the cheroot."

"What impression do I impart?"

"To hell with the world."

"Good! People's thoughts are usually so mundane that their voices aren't worth hearing. Even out there in my ballroom, with the cream of western society, most of what they say is merde. Spying may seem exciting, but it can be extremely boring. You must remain alert for that one snippet of information, inadvertently mentioned in casual conversation, which might lead Palmerston to a correct prediction that will change history."

A bell tinkled. George stood, clinked her wineglass with Lola's, and they drank. George walked to another picture in the rear of the room. It too swung away from the wall and revealed another aperture through which they both gazed.

The Swedish attaché and Manuela were standing in the middle of a bedroom. She was helping him off with his jacket, speaking in French. Attaché Svenson said, "You are a fascinating woman."

"You don't even know me."

"I am looking forward to correcting that."

"May I take your vest?"

He shrugged out of his vest. Manuela reached up to undo his cravat.

Lola whispered to George, "She taught me from the book of *Kama Sutra*, but I never thought of her using it or my being able to observe."

"Listen," George hissed.

Manuela was undoing his shirt buttons and saying, "We are not children, so let us make the most of this opportunity." She pulled the shirt open, exposing a massive hairy chest.

"What do you suggest," the Swede asked.

"We each have our own sexual fantasies. Rarely do we share them. Tell me yours and I will attempt to accommodate you."

She placed the palms of her hands over his nipples and massaged. He threw back his head and groaned. "I have such fantasies," he said. "But tonight you are my guide." He covered her tiny hands with his large hairy ones, moved them up and down his body and said, "I want to see what is under your sari."

"Then remove it."

A bit clumsy at first, the Swede pulled off the flimsy head-scarf. He became more adept undressing Manuela until she stood naked before him. "You are beautiful."

"He's correct," George whispered. "Your servant is a mature attractive woman."

"I never thought of her like that. She's my nanny."

"Even nannies have sex. Manuela is no blushing virgin."

"She has a daughter my age."

"You would never know it."

"She's removing his trousers," Lola said. "My God! Look at that erection! She has both her hands wrapped around it and the head is sticking out. Oh dear."

"It is eleven inches long," George said. "In one of our communal orgies I measured it."

"I never saw anything so large. She is pushing him back against the door."

"We have an Italian who measures a full thirteen inches, but his is not as thick as the Swede's."

Lola became aware of George's hand slipping between her thighs. She thought to protest, but didn't. Her fascination was with Manuela's instructions to the Swede. The big man stood in the doorway. He spread his legs the width of the door-jamb and his hands over his head, spread-eagled. Manuela kissed his nipples and massaged his erection. His pale hairy body visibly changed color from white to pink to red. Manuela warned him that if he moved his legs or arms from the door-jamb she would stop.

The big man trembled. He threw back his head and stuttered in Swedish. Manuela grabbed his scrotum and while closely watching his face applied pressure. His back arched, and his head struck the door. At just the moment he was about to break his grip on the door-jamb she released her grip and took his manhood in her mouth. George's fingers found the opening in Lola's underwear. She probed and Lola shivered. George said, "Your servant's playing with fire. Most of us make the Swede lie down, and we determine the depth of his penetration."

The Swede's shout alarmed the two watchers. He reached down, pulled Manuela's head from his penis, lifted her off her knees and high in the air. He thrust his hips forward, worked his body between her outstretched legs and lowered her onto his throbbing shaft. Manuela's head lolled back in ecstasy, but it kept going deeper and deeper until she was full and overwhelmed by the size of it. She was gasping, raking his chest and arms, and she bit him on the neck. He rushed across the floor, carrying her on his penis, to the canopied bed. In his haste he knocked the wine bottle off the credenza.

Lola was being massaged by George. Sweat stood out on her face. "I've seen that wine label before," Lola whispered to George. "I drank it with Lord Palmerston. It's the Pope's wine."

George smiled, placed her hand solidly behind Lola's neck and drew her close. Their lips met. Their tongues sought each other. They touched, and both bodies magnetized. They tore off their clothing until they stood naked, gasping with desire. George whispered, "You are the most beautiful woman I have ever seen. I am going the ravish you. If you can walk after our love-making it will not be my fault."

Lola swung her right fist catching George on the jaw. George staggered, then moved forward smiling. "If it is rough you want, I am the one to administer your punishment."

She moved closer. Lola slapped with her left hand, then her right. George did not attempt to protect herself. She brushed her breasts against Lola's breasts, and Lola fell into her arms whimpering, "Mommy, don't beat me." George reached down into the pile of clothes and removed the riding crop. She slapped it across the palm of her left hand.

"Ohhh! Ohhh!" Lola wailed. "I'll be good to you."

# CHAPTER 8

## THE ELITE

We remained overnight in the chateau. Lola never spoke of that evening, bur she ordered me never to leave her alone with George Sand.

The maid woke me early. She said our carriage was sent back last night, and Madame Sand's personal carriage would return us to the hotel. The Swedish cultural attaché wished to speak with me. I met him.

He took off one of his rings and placed it in my hand. It was an ornately engraved gold ring with a large blood-red ruby. I bowed. He kissed the back of my hand, saying, "I will call on you." From slave to courtesan in one evening. I hefted the ring in the palm of my hand. It posed a problem. I couldn't sell it while the Swede and I were in a relationship, and I couldn't wear it. My ring and little finger fit into it at the same time.

Lola had an appropriate gold chain in her jewelry box. She agreed; the ring rested in the cleavage of my bosom.

The remainder of the week was quiet and Lola subdued. I worried about her and said so. "Do not concern yourself," she said. "Tell me of your experience with the cultural attaché."

"Exciting." I held up the ring. "We began with the standing position. I excited him until he lifted me upon his erection and rushed me to the bed, where he plunged to the full depth. It hurt. He is large, and exploded inside me. I finally made him understand that it was painful for me, and he should lie back. I worked his erection again to its full length and mounted him. We both enjoyed that."

Lola pointed to the ring hanging from the chain she gifted me. "He certainly showed his pleasure. Will you see him again?"

"He said so."

"Then you too can be a spy."

"I may already have useful information."

"Did you write it down?"

"No.

"You must. Palmerston insists."

"I didn't know I would spy on anyone but you."

"Palmerston thought you could glean information from servants of the aristocrats, but on your first night you bedded an embassy official. Did you learn anything from him?

"Sweden intends to remain neutral."

"They are afraid. They lost one third of their land to Russia."

"How did that happen?"

"Sweden sided with Napoleon. He lost. Russia grabbed Finland from the Swedes."

"Sweden will sign a non-aggression treaty with England and France, but refuses to become involved in hostilities."

"Palmerston must be informed. He will try and stop the agreement with France. You've done well. Is there anything more?"

"The Swedes will unofficially support Denmark

against a Prussian invasion."

"How can they remain neutral?"

"I asked that. He said, Sweden is now sending weapons, cannon and ammunition over the border. If war breaks out between the Danes and Russians, Sweden will allow volunteers from the Swedish army to enter Denmark."

"Volunteers indeed." Lola laughed. "How did you get him to talk so much?"

"I asked about his beloved Sweden, and he never stopped. Some men talk when they get excited."

"Write it. I'll add my views and you send it to that English twit, Brougham."

Within an hour of receiving the report, Lord Brougham appeared at our apartment.

"You did well," he told Lola. "Sweden's diplomatic approach to France is unexpected. We had an understanding with the Swedes to isolate the Frogs." He questioned Lola, and because she turned to me for answers I thought Brougham suspected I was involved. He would learn of my assignation with the Swedish Ambassador. Everyone in the Salon watched everyone else.

Brougham told Lola, "This information is exactly what we want. We also need you to listen to discussions regarding advances in science and agriculture. For example, an American invented a steel-tipped plow. It will open up millions of hectares of rocky land for cultivation. There will be an increase in food. Populations and wealth will grow. In this age of industrial evolution, information is power."

To Lola's request for financial reimbursement for expenses, he replied, "I paid the bills for your dresses, the coach and four, with driver and two footmen. That is enough."

Lola pointed to our report in his hand. "That is worth much more."

"Will you attend the Salon tomorrow?" he asked.

"Of course," Lola replied.

Brougham withdrew a drawstring purse weighted with francs. He placed it on the table between them, saying. "You will soon be introduced to Alexandre Dumas. He and George Sand will pair you with the manager of the Paris Opera House. Convince him to support you for an intermission performance. I will see that the newspapers print positive articles about you." He pointed to the purse. "Lord Palmerston expects you to justify the expense."

"We've done that!" Lola snapped and motioned me to take the purse. Brougham left without a by-your-leave.

Although we received two notes from George Sand requesting our presence, it was three weeks before Lola had the confidence to accept. Lord Brougham wanted an explanation. I replied in writing that Lola was ill. We did go to meet with Hippolyta Barren, famous choreographer for the Paris Opera, who agreed to choreograph four of Lola's dances. Lola practiced the new moves for hours on end. I kept busy sewing, fashioning new costumes, and feeding information for cash to my newspaper friends.

True to his word, Lord Brougham stoked the flames of publicity. On the 24th of March the newspaper *Le Corsaire* complained that, "Although Lola Montez dances the most voluptuous boleros, and is perhaps the only woman who can perform the dance of the gypsies (the Tarantella) in all its romantic energy, she was being denied a chance to appear in French theaters." *The Journal des Theatres* stated, "There is no hope we will see Lola Montez dance at the Opera; is this then the only stage in Paris where Europe's most enlightened public may applaud a talent worthy of praise?"[2]

We returned to the Salon. I had strict instructions never to leave Lola alone in a room with George Sand, which Lola did not explain. Our second entrance to the Salon was quite different. Lola didn't walk in; she practically danced into the hall. Her breasts appeared ready to pop out of the low-cut gown. Her blue eyes sparkled; ruby lips, seductively moist, were framed by ebony curls that drew the eyes as fireworks do on Bastille Day.

George took charge of Lola and introduced her to Alexandre Dumas. His book *The Three Musketeers* was being serialized in the newspaper *Le Siècle*, and Lola had read every installment. She asked, "Why do you call your book *The Three Musketeers*? They haven't shot anyone, but there is much swordplay."

Dumas laughed and said, "Ma Cherie, for such a beautiful woman I will have them fire their weapons in next week's publication." He also led Lola to a private room where they spent the night.

I and the Swedish Attaché retired to the same room as before, and I began by instructing him in the Rocking Horse position. He sat cross-legged on the bed with his back against the head-board. I knelt over his erection and lowered myself onto him. In this way I determined

---

[2] (Page 72, Lola Montez, Bruce Seymour)

the depth of penetration, and I also controlled the rhythm. By looking into his eyes I determined when he might explode. By watching his eyes dilate I prolonged the ecstasy and we climaxed together.

I chose the upside down position for our second coupling. He lay face up on the bed, I turned my back to him and straddled his body. I lowered myself to control the depth of penetration and choose the moment of my climax.

By the time of my third position, "Hips Up", I was lubricated and relaxed enough to place two pillows under my thighs and allow him to mount facing me. He was gentle at first, but then took his penis in his hand and moved it within me from side to side, up and down, then round and round.

It hit a particularly magic spot, and I screamed and squirted. He plunged in and out again and again. My legs lost their strength and fell from his body. I lay completely spent with his full weight on me. He panted in my ear, "I love you! I love you!"

I panicked, thinking he wanted to marry me. Then I realized he was married; his wife was here. She was probably being serviced in another room by a young courtier. Life was becoming more interesting, and I wondered if he would gift me again.

He did: a gold brooch depicting Noah and the ark, with tiny gem-encrusted animals entering the craft. This one piece was two years' earnings for a Hindu shopkeeper. My little Princess would have an impressive dowry.

Lola dictated information gleaned from Alexandre Dumas. She said, "Richard Hoe of New York perfected a rotary printing press. By fastening lead type around the circumference of a large cylinder and cranking it, he created a rotating press. The paper was fed from one continuous roll. The speed of the drum determined the number of sheets printed. The machine was powered by steam. He coupled this with an automatic ink-well and cutter. Thousands of sheets could be printed by two men in an hour. It would revolutionize the newspaper and book-printing industry."

Dumas was a weapons collector. Lola revealed her knowledge of guns, and he told her of an invention by a Frenchman; the barrels of muzzle-loading muskets were scoured to make the Minie ball spin when fired. This gave a more predictable trajectory and greater accuracy. The Frenchman was also working on a breech-loading rifle. I never found out what that meant. Lola said Lord Brougham would know; "He wears breeches every day."

My Swede liked to talk about cooking, especially of preparing fish. To me, all fish tastes like paper. If you put sauce on, it is just paper with sauce.

He also said von Metternich would return in a month by way of Poland. Lola considered this important. She surmised Palmerston had an agreement with the Poles to hold the Russians from linking up with the French. The British wanted to consolidate the Germanic states into one government, for the British royal family was German. What von Metternich wanted was a mystery. He appeared to contradict himself by making alliances and overtures to Russia, Prussia, France, England, the Germans and Poles at the same time. Lord Brougham explained: "Von Metternich is the most astute politician alive. He is called King of the continent. Palmerston is second to him."

"I thought you would be more loyal," Lola said.

"Loyalty is not in question. Palmerston leads the greatest economy and military power in the world. Von Metternich commands a second-rate army and a non-existent navy. Austria's internal economy is healthy, but exerts little financial influence abroad.

"What game is Metternich playing?" Lola asked. "He is making treaties with everyone."

"Very astute," Brougham said. (It was the only compliment to her that he ever made.) "Lord Palmerston calls von Metternich's ploy the Balance of Power. If Russia moves too far west, the Austrian supports France, or Poland. He gives them weapons, mercenaries etc. until a war between the two becomes a standoff. Then he steps in, negotiates a settlement and takes whatever helps Austria, while promoting the Catholic Church's grip on Europe."

"That would be the Jesuits," Lola said.

"Yes," Brougham answered, "but Metternich is always directing Austria to become the supreme military power in the world."

"He requires a navy," Lola said.

"Where can he find a readymade navy?"

"France," Lola said. "It poses a threat of invading Great Britain. From France the Austrians can access the North Sea and Atlantic Ocean. Von Metternich needn't occupy Holland, Belgium or the Nordic countries. He would control the English Channel. He'd bottle up all their ports."

"Von Metternich," Brougham said, "Is thinking beyond that. He plans to take Italy and its merchant fleet. It gives him entre' to the Mediterranean, Adriatic, Ligurian, Tyrrhenian and Ionian Seas. He wants to control the Levant, middle-east and Africa, with access to the Far East."

"That's half the world!" Lola said.

"England is presently the world's greatest power," Brougham said. "We intend to continue in that role. Let the Europeans compose music, produce art, and write novels. We will take their money, build our cities, and guard our island with the British Navy."

"Why Isn't Britain interested in occupying other countries?"

"We don't have enough people. We control them instead. India's population is ten times ours. We use the Worthy Oriental Gentlemen to keep order. Hindus police the Muslims. Muslims police the Sikhs. The Sikhs keep everyone else in place. When we have real trouble, we call on the Gurkhas."

"What about China?" Lola asked.

Lord Brougham's head snapped around. "Never mention that country again. I want you to learn more about this scouring of the inside of musket barrels from Dumas."

"I see him tomorrow."

Later, I asked Lola why Brougham became ruffled about China.

"It is the best known secret in Europe," she said. "The Chinese emptied the European coffers by addicting the west to spices and tea, but trading only for our gold and silver. Britain, being the greatest sea power in the world, suffered most."

"You mean the English are low on money?

"Not only the English, but most of Europe."

"How will they cope?"

"That is why Brougham told me to keep quiet. He is a moral man, but his orders come from Palmerston: 'Get the gold and silver back from China'."

"That means war."

"Not quite. Wars are expensive, but opium is not. It is addictive, and eventually physically harmful. It is also dirt cheap in India. England sells its manufactured goods and broadcloth in India, and takes payment in opium. It sells that to the Chinese, who readily become addicted and want more. The Europeans only take silver and gold in payment. Tit for tat."

Doesn't the Chinese government object?"

"There was one Opium War in 1840, and the Chinese lost. There will be another. China will lose again."

"Why?"

"England wants to open up the interior population of China to the drug. The Chinese do not have a navy to stop them from bombarding their port cities."

"Why do not the Chinese simply give up trying to beggar Europe, and accept other goods in trade?"

"Pride," said Brougham. "The Chinese like to believe that they are as superior to all other men as the gods are above them. That's why they call their land 'The Middle Kingdom'. To maintain that pride, they cannot leave off playing Beggar My Neighbor, even when it does them harm."

I shook my head. The Implications were confusing. I put out Lola's clothes for tomorrow's meeting with Alexander Dumas.

He and Lola met for lunch with Leon Pillet, manager of the Paris Opera. Hesitant at first, Pillet succumbed to Dumas' words and Lola's beauty. He agreed to arrange Lola's Parisian debut between acts of Gromental Halevy's *Le Lazzarone* in the renowned Paris Opera House.

# CHAPTER 9

## PARIS

Once the capital of Bourbon Kings and Napoleon Bonaparte, Paris radiated out from the Cathedral of Notre Dame. One million people dwelt in the cultural center of the western world. The majestic Paris Opera House was its jewel.

The talented and adventurous from all countries poured into this capital city. New moral, economic, and political dynamics developed. Dreams of a world driven by industry, powered by steam, worked by commoners and led by the aristocratic intelligentsia prevailed. The nouveau riche mingled with artists and royalty in theaters, salons, cabarets, and clubs.

Rarely were they invited to the homes of royalty. If so, admission was through the servants' gate. Although the French Republic was established with the blood of the high born, power returned to the noble survivors. Spencer's economic concept of "Rule of the fittest" justified Government by aristocracy.

George Sand had no aristocratic encumbrance. Her father owned an inn. She was the world's most accomplished female novelist, was independently wealthy, received a government pension and title of Duchess. She invited outstanding personalities from all classes to her Salon. A more diverse mix of the charismatic people from the western world would be difficult to find.

Lola met Gustave Flaubert, Eugene Delacroix, Honoré' de Balzac, Frédéric Chopin and other personages. Standing off to the side, I listed the names for Lola. She required me to describe the clothing worn by those with whom she spoke. We later sat, and Lola added snippets of her conversations. I had to file these under countries. When I questioned, she replied, "I am thinking of touring Europe." I realized she would use these names to be hosted by the affluent and recommended to theater managers. We compiled a list of the wealthy and influential. We were invited to every country between the Atlantic Ocean and Asia. Lola copied George Sand and took to smoking cigars. She enjoyed smoking. I choked and never tried again.

With abounding energy, Lola continued her dance lessons. She and Madame Hippolyta Barren concentrated on specific routines. Lola exercised her body and her voice. Her voice was cultured, but not strong enough to carry in a theater. She continued to exercise her vocal chords, but agreed not to sing in the Paris Theater. Often she helped me sew her costumes. She was an excellent seamstress.

Several cases of the Pope's wine arrived. I stored them with our luggage. Lola's debut was to take place on the morrow.

Friends and agents of Lord Brougham, George Sand, and Editors Lola had befriended, campaigned on her behalf in the journals, clubs, the race track, and the Salons. The Paris Opera House sold out. The resale price of tickets reached three times those published in the afternoon newspapers. By show time tickets resold for astronomical sums. The theater had standing room only. A pin could not be inserted amongst the standees.

My little Lola stood in the wings, allowing the tension to build. She, who had not made a dozen professional appearances, readied herself to step onto the world's most prestigious stage. She appeared calm and composed. She did stretching exercises as the audience began to chant, "Lola! Lola! We want Lola!"

I whispered, "Good luck." She smiled, came up on her toes, and leapt out before the audience. She appeared on her toes in the new style, and Paris was the cradle of ballet orthodoxy. At first people cheered. Then, realizing she was balancing on tip-toes, they went silent.

Lola signaled the conductor to stop the music. In dainty strides Lola went front stage center and while balanced on one toe removed the garter from her other leg and threw it out to the audience. A roaring cheer broke the silence. Men in the front boxes fought for the garter that graced the leg of the most beautiful woman in the world.

Lola performed El Olano and Les Boleros de Cadiz. Towards the end of the first piece, this knowledgeable audience became restless with the unorthodox innovation to their theater. Papers later wrote, "Dona Lola Montez seemed determined to violate the rules of French/Italian ballet. Her beauty and stage presence is what carried her through. But beauty cannot excuse bad taste."

Two major newspapers praised Lola's performance, claiming, "She astonished and charmed the audience with her new style, agility and beauty." A friend wrote in his column, "Lola Montez surprised and enchanted the audience."

The majority of papers praised Lola's beauty but decried her artistic proficiency. They declared; "She will never again appear at the Paris Opera."

They did not count on Lord Brougham. He bundled George Sand and Alexander Dumas into his carriage and took them to a meeting with Pillet. The theater manager resisted. The pressure brought on him by this powerful trio was enormous. "Lola," he said, "Is not professional enough." In the end they overwhelmed him. Lola would appear between acts one and two of *Le Bal de Don Juan*.

Once informed, we wrote to the editors of all major newspapers requesting they publicize her appearance. She went daily to Madame Hippolyta Barren for lessons. Lord Brougham convinced her not to repeat the garter episode; Aficionados considered it more suited to the cabaret.

An overflow crowd packed the theater. Tickets brought premium prices. The audience, accustomed to more sophisticated entertainment, booed and hissed Lola. One wag in the boxes shouted, "It looks more like the Can Can than ballet."

The *Journal des Theatres* which fought for Lola to appear wrote: "It's perfectly excusable for the young Spanish dancer to dare to mount the boards of the foremost French theater; but it is far less so that the management should convince itself she belonged there."[3]

Other newspapers extolled Lola's figure, her eyes

---

[3] P.74 *Lola Montez* by Bruce Seymour.

and the beauty she projected. Regrettably, they decried her ability to perform. Lola was finished in Paris. Despite some newspapers questioning her Spanish lineage and ability to speak Spanish properly, neither mattered to those attending George Sand's salon. They accepted Lola by virtue of her beauty, intelligence, charisma, and George Sand's approval. Lola continued her dance lessons.

Lord Brougham developed a new plan for Lola, involving the Dutch King, William II, in Amsterdam. He and his Russian wife were incompatible, and their disputes spilled over into the public arena. A recent incident took place at a public house. The couple threw dishes and silverware at each other.

Lola would be introduced by the English ambassador with the objective of becoming the King's courtesan. He was fifty-two years old. She met his son, the Duke of Orange, in the Salon and thought of bedding him.

No one foresaw Franz Liszt.

I doubt Lord Brougham could have prevented what happened, but Lord Palmerston recalled him to London, "to grease palms and twist arms in Parliament".

In the salon, Alexander Dumas introduced Lola to the world's most renowned musician. From the age of nine, when his genius became public knowledge, Franz Liszt grew in fame, prestige, and wealth. Kings vied for his attendance, showering him with lavish gifts. The Czar of Russia sent a handful of diamonds. Liszt threw them to the audience.

He disdained snobs, falseness, and mediocrity. He loved music. Through it he transformed himself and his audiences, presenting emotional images of life and views of nature by integrating melody, harmony, rhythm, and tempo. At age thirty-three he was tall, lithe, handsome, with shoulder-length hair almost as dark and vibrant as Lola's.

Their meeting appeared like watching storm clouds, when lightning illuminates the billowing haze from within: fear and beauty, male and female, two glorious human beings. The passionate, creative nature of the man cried out with joy at the magnificent beauty of the woman. Lola's exuberance, her tigerish boldness, her frank and scintillating conversation, contrasted with her erotic physical attraction. The combination of beauty, intelligence, and intellect mesmerized Liszt. He and Lola walked off, leaving Alexander Dumas and George Sand agape.

I overheard Lola commenting on Liszt's creation of the symphonic poem. He challenged her comprehension. She blew a cloud of cigar smoke in his face, smiled and replied, "A tone poem is a piece of orchestral music that conjures up a story, painting, or scenery. It is a blending of musical composition and spectacle."

Franz Liszt threw back his head and laughed. Heads turned, and he said for all to hear, "My dear Dona Lola Montez accurately phrased my achievement better than I." He turned to Lola and asked, "Do you understand my use of Thematic Transformation?"

Lola inhaled and let the cigar smoke curl out from her ruby red lips, saying, "The transformation of a theme takes place similar to any musical variation. However, in your hands, the transformed theme takes on a life of its own."

"Madame Montez," Liszt said, "You are the most

pleasant breath of fresh air I have experienced in a long time. Will you join me in a carriage ride by moonlight?"

Of course she agreed.

I doubt either one saw the moon.

Lola made me proud. I recalled helping her study for her music examination in France; the two questions Liszt asked were part of the reading program.

I didn't see Lola for three days. She arrived wearing new clothes and appeared radiant. "Pack my things," she announced, "I leave for Dresden in two hours."

"What's in Dresden?"

"Franz is giving a concert,"

"But what of your obligations to Lords Palmerston and Brougham?"

"To hell with them!"

"What about the money?"

"Money be damned. This is love! I always wondered if I would know true love."

"Lola," I said, took both her hands, and gazed into her electric blue eyes. "You are a courtesan. Love is dangerous."

"Why can't I change?" she demanded.

"I don't know. But you are burning the candle at both ends. When it reaches the middle, there will be darkness."

"No more talking. Let's pack."

"Will we need warm or light clothing?"

"A little of both, but you are not going."

Taken aback, I blurted, "What will your mother say?"

"She hasn't bothered to write in years."

"I am obligated to watch over you."

Now Lola stood, took me by the shoulders and kissed my forehead. "My dear Manuela, this is your vacation from me. The apartment is paid for. The Swede will keep you warm. You can go across the river and listen for information from the servants."

"What if Lord Brougham returns?"

"Tell him you are a servant and do not make decisions for me. Now start packing."

"How many cases of the Pope's wine do you want?"

"Not necessary. We cannot keep our hands off one another."

"Careful," I warned. "He fathered three children by Countess Marie d" Agoult, and several more around Europe."

"Where did you learn this?"

"Across the bridge, from the servants."

"What else do they say about my genius?"

"He is generous and treats people for what they are, not who they are or where they come from. He supports the poor and sets up schools. He earns fantastic sums to play, compose, or teach. He gives his earnings to charity in whatever city he appears."

"How does he survive?"

"He accumulated a fortune before he reached twenty-one. Do not get pregnant."

""I don't intend to. Unless, of course we marry."

"He may be a true genius, but he abandoned the countess after twenty years."

"Twenty years of life with him would be worth everything. Enough said!"

The coach arrived for the luggage. Franz Liszt followed in his traveling coach. They departed, and for the first time in twenty-five years I was alone. My thoughts were of Lola and what I must anticipate to serve her.

I found myself dusting and cleaning, which the hotel staff ordinarily did. I delivered money to the Jewish tailor. While there I ordered two dresses appropriate for either side of the Seine. I put aside my sari and drew less attention. Across the Seine in the cafés, cabarets, and restaurants, I made friends and eavesdropped. I recorded the contacts and news according to their order of importance, and posted the information to Lord Brougham in London.

He wrote back, furious at Lola's flight with Liszt. He insisted I remind her she remained in the employ of England. He returned to Paris and expressed satisfaction with a piece of information I sent. It came from a maid whose husband worked as a blacksmith, mainly in wagon construction. His employer received an order to recondition one hundred and fifty freight wagons, and build fifty new ones, for the government. The blacksmith, along with wheelwrights, carpenters and harness makers, would keep the wagons in repair on the journey.

Lord Brougham asked me to learn the destination. I later told him they would be traveling 250 miles with four horses to a wagon, but I did not know where. He calculated the distance on a map and said, "It's a troop supply convoy to the Alsace Lorraine region, probably Strasbourg."

"Austria," I said.

"The French must anticipate a Russian incursion. Two hundred and fifty supply wagons will feed three French divisions for a month. The French are keeping their word to England. Palmerston must be informed." He started to shake some coins from his purse, grinned, and then handed the coins and purse to me. "You've earned this," he said. I curtseyed, thanked him, and went to the tailor.

I experienced a sense of freedom never known before. I made friends and acquaintances in the public houses and markets. My Swedish lover was attentive, talkative, and generous. I no longer visited the Salon but met him at fashionable hotels, inns, and guest houses. He revealed news that presented a moral problem.

Two months earlier the British Army, under the incompetent leadership of General Elphinstone, was wiped out by the Afghan Akbar Kahn's tribesmen. They surrounded the British Fort in Kabul. As terms of surrender, Akbar Kahn promised safe passage and attention to the wounded left behind. The British would be provided with food, fuel, and safe escort to Jalalabad 90 miles away.

January is the height of winter in the Hindu Kush. Temperatures dropped to twenty below zero. The mountain passes were blocked by snow.

Against the advice of more experienced officers, Elphinstone accepted the terms of surrender. He led a column of 16,000 English,and Hindu troops and their families out of Kabul. Akbar Kahn kept his word, and gave his attention to the wounded left in the fort. He slaughtered them all.

He sent his tribesmen to attack the weak and lame at the rear of the retreating British column, and his trained fighters moved ahead to block the mountain passes. Of the 16,000 evacuees, only one British doctor with ten

Indian soldiers reached Jalalabad.

Great Britain's weakness was exposed; the English did not have enough troops to retaliate. India, Afghanistan, and the Middle-east was in ferment. The Swede said, "Ranjit Singh, leader of the Sikhs in the Punjab, intends to take advantage of the chaos among the British. He will found a Sikh Commonwealth." Knowing my Sikh heritage, he explained. "Ranjit Singh is quite clever. Educated at Oxford and Cambridge, he hired European and American mercenaries to train his army, especially the artillery corps. One of those mercenaries is a Swedish agent. Ahmed Kahn delivered the greatest defeat ever to the British Army, and is conspiring with the Russians to take over the Khyber Pass. Russia wants to access year-round warm-water ports in the Bay of Bengal and the Arabian Sea. Both lead to the Indian Ocean, Africa, Asia, and Antarctica."

My Swede enjoyed talking about these things. He explained that the British spread themselves too thin. They ended the Opium War with China and signed the Treaty of Nanking. When I questioned why the Europeans who profess Christian morals would want to force this addictive drug onto a peaceful nation, he laughed, "Money, my little Sikh sweetheart. The Chinese controlled the spices, silk, and tea we Europeans craved. For a hundred years they would not accept any of our products in trade. We were addicted. They took only silver and gold in payment. So much of Europe's currency went into China, there is hardly enough left to support our economies. We bought cheap opium in India, and crammed it down the Chinese throats until they became addicted. We then forced them to pay us in precious metals. Tit for tat."

"It doesn't seem very Christian," I said.

"It is consistently Christian. Whether you are Greek Orthodox, Roman Catholic, or Protestant, money conquers values."

"But I do not see the connection between these things, the Sikh army and the British in India."

"Power perceived is power achieved," the Swede said. "Sixteen thousand British slaughtered in eight days. England appears weak. Afghans smell fear as a shark does blood. They will continue to attack the British. The Sikhs under Ranjit Singh know the British must regain respect or lose India, their Jewel in the Crown. The English must punish the Afghans to regain respect. To accomplish this they will withdraw troops from the Khyber Pass. When they do, Ranjit Singh will proclaim an independent Sikh state in the Punjab. He will invite the Russians to help him against the British. The Sikh army grew from thirty to eighty thousand. They are equipped by Russia with modern muskets."

My misgivings of betraying the Sikh military was overcome by a sense of duty, or maybe it was my greed. I sent this information to Lord Brougham, also warnings about Russian advances into Western Europe. The Czar will try and make allies of the French. Russian agents are infiltrating the near and middle-east. A German Prince believes, because of the slaughter of Elphinstone's English Army, that Russia will take advantage of British weakness and secure a warm-water port with year round access to the Indian Ocean.

I spent several hours questioning myself on how, and what, or even if I should pass on this information about a Sikh uprising. Would I betray my people? I decided it wouldn't be betrayal. If I learned of it, in only a short time these facts would be common knowledge in the Salons of Europe. The press would print it.

I contacted Lord Brougham. He rewarded me. My Princess was a wealthy woman. She would have a dowry to match a Rajah's. Oh, but to see my child again and hold her close!

Other than my yearning for Princess, I enjoyed life without Lola. She wrote me from Dresden with a list of things for shipment to her in Basel, Switzerland. "Franz," she wrote, "Is the most exciting man I ever knew. His mental attributes equal his physical qualities. My own strong nature is matched by his. In making love we both yield and conquer, conscious of each other's needs. He is interested in *Kama Sutra*. What a beautiful personality! I never met anyone like him. The royals, wealthy, and powerful, flock to him, but he remains unchanged by their adoration of his musical genius. His generosity is boundless. He gives without the desire to receive. He holds in contempt those in high places who are not suited to perform their duties and help the common people. He and I agree people should be free. We also believe governments should be led by an educated aristocracy. If the dregs of society are given an equal vote, the nobility will be forced to fund, house, and feed them. Even the Americans, proclaiming equality, require land ownership to vote or stand for political office.

"You wouldn't believe how many invitations we received to visit homes, palaces, and spas. I could travel from England to St. Petersburg without the need to pay for a hotel. I keep a detailed list of these offers. Franz does not; he just travels, shows up where he wants, when he wants, and says, 'I'm here!' People are overjoyed to have him. I love him. He is smart, fresh, noble and attentive to me.

"A vagabond accosted me on the Boulevard. I beat him with my riding crop. Franz reached out with those magical fingers, that produce the world's finest music, and he threw the man several feet through the air!

"Life is wonderful. We travel from city to city. Everything is anticipated by our hosts, who beg for the opportunity to please us.

"Give your full attention to this list of my things. Act quickly so I may find them waiting for me in Switzerland. "

I worked through the night. Next morning, the concierge shipped the crates to Basel. I included the following letter.

> "My Dear Dona Lola, the items you requested are on their way. You have no idea how close you were to becoming Mrs. Alexander Dumas! Monsieur Dumas is a reputed rake and bon vivant. With the publication of his *Les Trois Mousquetaires*, he is at the height of his career. The Duke of Orleans is Dumas' royal patron. The Duke gave a ball In Porte-St.-Martin. Dumas took his latest female escort, Mademoiselle Ida, Ferrier to the ball. When he introduced her to the royal couple, the Duke smiled and said, 'Surely it is only your wife to be that you would think of presenting to me and my wife.' The message

from the Duke, who is not only Dumas' patron but also his publisher, was a royal decree. Dumas had to marry Mademoiselle Ferrier. The wedding took place last week. It might have been you. Your humble servant Manuela"

Lola wrote from Florence, Athens, Berlin, and Amsterdam, where she met the Dutch King William—the same she had planned to seduce. Franz Liszt owned her heart.

She also gathered information and sent it to Lord Brougham. Most of the information I gathered came from reading foreign newspapers given to me by my Swedish lover.

In Dresden, Lola fought with a theater manager. A policeman confronted Lola with a summons sworn out by the manager. She ripped it up, threw the scraps in the policeman's face, and beat him with the riding crop.

She arranged a party to a shooting gallery, where she put six holes in the Ace of Spades playing card and sent it to the theater manager. He filed another complaint. She and Franz left for Basel and made it across the border ahead of the police.

Liszt accepted an invitation to stay at Prince Heinrich LXXII palace in Lowenstein. There he spent much of his time alone, working in the music conservatory on the palace grounds. Bored, Lola took to walking Prince Heinrich's St. Bernard dog. She taught him several commands. The Prince became angered when Lola and the dog trampled his favorite flower bed. She cut off the blossoms to make garlands for the St Bernard and the

Prince's horse. This angered the Prince, but he said nothing. Lola tried to make conversation with the servants, but they didn't understand French and she knew little German. Franz had his work. Lola found boredom. I think of the phrase, "Idle hands are the devil's playground."

The Prince hosted a garden party for his guests. Liszt excused himself to work. The setting was outside on the lawn, where a screen of trees hid the orchestra. Local farmers and tradesmen were the musicians. Their rendition of the folk music was unrecognizable. When a particular sour note sounded Lola made a face. She saw this annoyed the Prince, and she made more improper gestures until the Prince called for the musicians to leave. A child's choir replaced them. Children climbed into the trees and sang traditional folk songs. Several minutes passed before Lola jumped up with her hands over her ears shouting, "I cannot stand a minute more of this bawling!"

The Prince came to his feet, and dismissed the children. One little boy straggled behind. Lola ordered the St. Bernard to stop him. The dog easily caught the boy and pinned him to the grass with a large paw. The Prince ran to the animal, pulled him off and brushed the boy clean. Then the Prince turned to Lola. "Madame," he said. "I am master of this house, and you will leave." He stalked away.

Other incidents followed. The one receiving the most attention was Lola's ability to roll her own cigarettes with one hand, while conversing with reporters about another row with a policeman. What did not appear in the newspapers was the unexpected break-up between Liszt and Lola.

She suddenly appeared at our hotel in Paris, and never said a word. I believe she truly loved Franz Liszt, but never mentioned him again.

My Swedish consort revealed the story. After Liszt's piano recitals in Stockholm senior composers, musicians, and critics gave a dinner party for Liszt. No women were invited. Lola appeared on Liszt's arm and disregarded those who gawped. She remained quiet as speeches honored Liszt. Then he spoke. His reply was unrehearsed and finished to polite applause.

The French Ambassador jumped to his feet, pointed at Liszt and shouted, "You! You, who owe so much to France for your musical education and success, failed to mention our great Republic and all it did for you!" Liszt started to apologize when an Austrian composer shouted, "Vienna had more to do with his foundation in music than all of Europe combined!"

"He was born and educated in Hungary!" another shouted. Someone took a bowl of soup and poured it over the Frenchman's head. A fight ensued. Plates, food, and chairs were thrown. Liszt protected his creative mind; he sat down and closed his eyes.

Lola exploded. She jumped up on the head table and began beating the bald heads with her riding crop. Those who fought back received a kick or bowl of soup in their laps. She cowed the entire group. When Liszt opened his eyes, Lola stood on the table and all the men stared up at her in awed silence. He offered his hand to her. She stepped from the table to a chair to the floor, and Liszt dragged her off. She screamed back, "Not one of you would make a pimple on Franz's ass."

According to my Swedish lover, Liszt took Lola back to the hotel. He excused himself, went to the hotel concierge, and requested am estimate of all the furniture in their suite. He emptied his pockets, wrote a voucher for the remainder, and ordered Lola be locked in for two days while he made his escape.

My Swede told me Liszt admitted to confidants that Lola was the most beautiful thing in the world. She disturbed his muse and distracted him from his music. He could not abide the interference.

Lola returned to Paris and the unofficial headquarters of the creative class on the Champs-Elysee: the Café de Paris, at the corner of the Rue Taitbout. Down the wide boulevard at the central Place de l'Étoile stood the monumental Arc de Triomphe. Alexander Dumas, Balzac, and Alfred de Musset took lunch there. The eccentric Lord Seymour, founder of the French Jockey Club, owned a table. Cezanne, Manet, and Degas displayed their works on the sidewalk. Editors and newspaper owners frequented the Café.

Lola penetrated this exclusive gathering of painters such as Camille, Delacroix, and Roseau, and writers Victor Hugo and George Sand. Louis Daguerre photographed Lola. Her beauty attracted men. Her intelligence, wit, and ability to express herself fascinated these molders of European society. She argued as an equal, never seeking refuge behind her femininity.

Lola gained the respect of those who made a difference in Europe. Her shell-like ears, although concealed under beautiful ebony tresses, heard much amongst Europe's elite. She dictated to me, and I reported to Lord Brougham.

She once confirmed what Brougham already knew; Queen Victoria despised Lord Palmerston on personal and moral grounds. The Queen referred to him as a whoremonger. On political grounds, although head of a constitutional monarchy, her power was restricted by law. Influenced by virtue of her personality, the Queen and Palmerston clashed. Victoria came from Germanic royalty, Saxe-Coberg. She married her first cousin Albert from the same family, and they both believed in rule by inherited nobility. Palmerston regarded the monarchy as a self-serving institution. He desired to maintain England as the greatest power in the world, and he held uneducated royalty in contempt. He was a genius at undermining the House of Lords.

Lord Palmerston's reaction to Lola's report on American correspondent Margret Fuller's talk to the members of George Sand's Salon must have sent him for his opium pipe. Miss Fuller was an advocate of women's rights and an abolitionist in America, and she became the first woman war correspondent in the history of journalism. Ralph Waldo Emerson recommended her to George Sand. Miss Fuller spoke fluent French, and she talked of her coverage of the Franco-Moroccan War. The lecture became a prediction of the demise of the British Empire.

She began with the debacle of Lord Elphinstone's Army in Afghanistan, and she confirmed information I had passed on to Lord Brougham. The Brits were militarily involved in the east, with China, Afghanistan, and India. She brought everyone to the edge of their seats by saying, "England is militarily spread too thin. The sun may never set on the British Empire, but it is swiftly descending on Great Britain. England is now being outperformed industrially by countries whose economies and populations are expanding. America is foremost among them. If our American experiment can survive the national disgrace of slavery and give women the same rights as men, there is no doubt America will lead the world into the twentieth century."

There were polite guffaws and tittering from the aristocratic audience. She continued, undisturbed, and set her listeners back into their overstuffed chairs. "The industrial age originated in England, but today, in 1844, British technologies are outdated, inefficient, and obsolete. The Germanic states, your beloved France, Russia, Sweden, Italy, even Japan in the Far East, are surging forward developing new technical innovations and improving those in use to compete for international markets. The condenser for recirculating steam back to water revolutionized American railroads. With open immigration, America receives an endless supply of cheap labor. America encompasses an endless supply of natural resources. How many of you know the phrase 'Fifty-four, forty or fight'? "

Only a few hands were raised. Miss Fuller asked, "Can anyone tell me what it means?"

The Russian political attaché said, "It refers to latitude and longitude defining the Americans' demands for a northern border with England's Canada. It is called the Oregon Territory."

"Will you tell the good people why it is so important?"

"Miss Fuller, if I do, then it is officially from the Russian government."

"Hasn't your government already negotiated away

your rights to the Americans on the Russian River in Oregon?"

"Yes," he replied. "The Spanish and French have also left North America."

"What is meant by the Yankee phrase 'Manifest Destiny'?" she asked him.

"This policy is encouraged by your American President James Polk. It means Americans are ordained by God to expand westward throughout the continent, from the Atlantic to the Pacific Oceans. "

"Thank you, sir. To put into perspective how the Americans are taking advantage of British weakness we must go back to the Louisiana Purchase in 1803. Thomas Jefferson purchased a million square miles from France for only four pennies an acre. That swath of land west of the Mississippi stretches from Louisiana on the Gulf of Mexico to the new Canadian/English border. This isolated the Oregon territory and the Mexican state of Texas. We took over Oregon and will soon annex Texas into the Union." Margaret Fuller looked at her audience and said, "I see blank stares. Many of your maps do not show Oregon, Texas, and other vast areas. They are marked as wilderness. But that wilderness contains lumber, coal, endless buffalo herds, precious metals, broad rivers, and grazing land. To give you an idea of how large America is, France could be placed in the newly acquired Oregon Territory and still have eight thousand square miles left over. You can fit England, Wales, Ireland, and Scotland into the state of Idaho.

"America exposed England's weakness in the War of 1812 when we Americans thrashed the British at New Orleans. It left Mexico vulnerable. America won the

1812 war because Emperor Napoleon Bonaparte forced the Brits to fight him in Europe and the mid-east. Now history is repeating itself. Britain is once again spread too thin. Her forces are fighting in the far, near, and middle-east. They try to patrol the Caribbean against pirates while being challenged economically by Europe and America. The only way the Russians can be stopped from controlling all of Europe is by a consolidation of the thirty-nine German states and an alliance between Germany, England, and France to oppose the Russians."

Frenchmen in the audience came to their feet shouting, "Never! Never will France allow one English soldier on our soil."

The Britons in the audience didn't know whether to be proud of their predicted role as savior of the French or be upset at the prophesied decline of the Empire.

I found it difficult to follow the international alliances; they appeared to be conflicting. My Swedish friend revealed that Russia and England opposed an Austrian-French alliance to keep the Russians out of France. Austrian Chancellor von Metternich led the negotiations and struggled to control the German States. I thought Austria, Hungary, and Germany to be cultural allies. I questioned Lord Brougham.

He claimed von Metternich did not care who won in any dispute. He used the term "Balance of Power." Von Metternich would supply enough weapons to the weaker side so the struggle continued. In the end both sides would be damaged, and Austria could walk in and dictate terms.

Lola's information, gleaned from her acquaintances, changed according to whom she slept with. She reported on a multiple barrel machine-gun being tested in Sweden, the French experimenting to make dynamite more stable, and uprisings in Poland against the aristocracy.

The money she received from Lord B should have been enough to support us, but Lola insisted on the best in coaches, clothes, and entertainment. She accepted gifts from her lovers as her due, and I pawned and sold them. Lola entered places where women were forbidden, puffing her cigar and challenging men in the gambling halls, at ten-pins, and shooting galleries. They quickly learned she was a great pistoleer and ten-pin bowler, but a poor gambler and good loser. She lost a fortune at games of chance.

Then one evening George Sand introduced Lola to the wealthy and famous newspaper owner, editor of *La Presse*. My little girl might have been a courtesan, but she was a romantic at heart. I warned her, infatuation could be dangerous for a courtesan.

# *CHAPTER 10*

## TRUE LOVE

Alexandre Dujarieir and Franz Liszt were opposite personalities, Liszt a calm person contrasted with Dujarieir, an impulsive one—though nothing compared to Lola. He expressed irritation, not outward anger. An intellectual, he engaged in lengthy arguments using short pithy sentences. This singled him out from the obtuse aristocratic society he lived in.

He was tall, slim, with an easy smile. His dress was in the latest style. For Lola, his mind and manner of expressing himself attracted her. "We know not how to converse," he said. "Intellectuals are as scarce as kings' jokers. There is no sophistication in our legislature. If our elders spoke less and thought more, our social, political, and religious ideas would generate a dynamic, compatible society. Our youth think and talk brilliantly; they are full of vim and vigor, fired with enthusiasm for the love of living and creating, but the Old Guard restrains them."

In 1844 Lola learned the true meaning of *joie de vivre*. Dujarieir and Lola publicly matched wits. The couple became the main attraction of every gathering. Their conversations were topical, rational, and edifying. Her beauty, his reputation for innovative thought, raised these two keen minds to the top of Parisian invitation lists.

The standard annual subscription rate for most newspapers was eighty francs. Lola gave Dujarieir the idea to halve the price and seek advertisers to make up the shortfall. He did, and doubled his readership—then doubled it again when he convinced his friend Alexander Dumas to serialize his books exclusively in *La Presse*.

Lola also took credit for the third doubling, but I gave her the idea: a special supplement that involved news oriented to those on the other side of the Seine. The most popular column was gossip about royalty. The lower price increased lower class readership and drew more advertisers.

Dujarieir became wealthy. but success earned him enemies. Several papers closed, leaving publishers, journalists, printers, and vendors unemployed. Lola and Dujarieir contributed to charitable organizations, but there was anger in the streets.

In the fall of 1844 Lola told me to plan her wedding to Dujarier for the spring. The wedding party would tour Spain with Dumas and his wife. I reminded Lola that she remained legally married to Captain James. She ignored me.

Uncertain if English law would be enforced in France, I knew better than to renew the discussion. Life was good to both Lola and me. She had found true love, and I, additional sources of income. The information given to Lord Brougham I re-sold to newspapermen. I bargained hard with money changers and shopkeepers for Lola, never keeping more than half of what I saved.

My money went to Princess. I planned to join her, arrange her marriage, and live in relative luxury. I once

told my plans to the Jewish tailor, and his look reminded me of the Sikh holy man when he said, "Man plans
and God laughs."

The success of Dujarier and his newspaper earned
him bitter enemies in the industry. He became the object
of venomous attacks, and responded with a series of
articles. In one he chastised the owner of *The Globe*, his
main competitor. He also came across a debt owed by
one of the *Globe's* editors to *La Presse*, and published it.

The vituperative response angered Dujarier. He replied in a vindictive front-page article. The brother in-
law of the offended editor, 25-year old Monsieur Jean
Baptiste Rosemond de Beauvallon, worked as a dramatic critic for the *Globe*, but he had once worked for
*La Presse* until Dujarier fired him. Baptiste held a
grudge and used his brother in-law's dispute to implement revenge. Jean Baptiste planned the tragic rendezvous.

A Madame Albert, once Dujarier's lover, also considered herself wronged by him. She knew of the argument between the two newspapers and Jean Baptiste's
hatred of Dujarier, and decided to take advantage of
both. She fueled Baptiste's loathing with made-up stories Dujarier had supposedly told of him. Then she invited both men to a grand risqué party where the women
were young courtesans, actresses, dancers, and circus
performers. Lola wanted to attend, but Dujarier convinced Lola that her reputation as a legitimate actress
would be damaged. Her appearance at the Porte St Mar-
tin Theater in *La Biche au Bois* would draw fewer aristocrats and reduce the box-office income. He went
alone.

The gayest blades in Paris attended. The most beautiful single women in France were invited. Mademoiselle Lievienne, acting hostess for Madame Albert, was the most beautiful. Her full figure with luxuriant breasts and derriere, displayed in a form-fitting sequined gown, riveted the eyes of every man and the envy of the women.

The oldest person attending was Roger De Beauvoir, aged thirty-six, known as the Beau Brummell of Paris and a friend of Dujarier. The two became immersed in the gaiety. Corks popped, sounding like a battalion of musketeers shooting. Champagne flowed, and bottles were cleared to make way for more.

Dujarier started a drinking duel with De Beauvoir by proposing a toast to his stovepipe trousers. De Beauvoir responded with a toast to a cartoon character in *La Presse*. After each toast, glasses were refilled, and it went on until the hostess asked for the floor to be cleared. The guests moved to the sides, and men took to fondling the women. Mademoiselle Lievienne's derriere came sashaying by, and without thought Dujarier reached out and caressed it. She spun around, and scowled.

"M-mademoiselle," Dujarier stammered, "Please pardon me. I fear I drink too much."

The elegant woman looked down her aquiline nose at Dujarier's outstretched hand. Several silver sequins sparkled in his palm.

"Yes," she said, and stalked off.

Roger De Beauvoir straightened Dujarier's tie, patted his chest and said, "You have good taste, my friend. Mademoiselle Lievienne's buttocks are the best in the house." He reached out and snatched two glasses of champagne from a passing tray. "Let us drink to Mademoiselle Lievienne's derriere."

The dinner service and food were cleared, and a place made for a musical quartet and dance floor. Green felt cloths for gambling covered the tables. Dujarier, like Lola, was a poor gambler but a good loser. He started to take a seat when Jean Baptiste approached him saying, "You personally accepted a piece written by me for publication in your newspaper. It is over a month. Why the delay?"

The subject of business at such a gay occasion violated accepted rules of etiquette. Those within hearing expected a rigid reply. "Dumas' serialization will be appearing for some time," Dujarier explained. "You cannot expect to compete with him for newspaper space."

Jean Baptiste's face smiled, but his eyes flashed fury. He bowed in apology and took a seat at the card table with Dujarier.

The game Lansquenet entails two decks of cards. One of the players is the banker, who declares how much he will open his bank for betting. The other players may take part in the betting, up to and including the amount set by the banker. The cards are shuffled. The first card up is the dealer's. The second card goes to the player on his right. Thereafter, cards are turned up until one of the dealt cards is matched by its numerical value, not including the suit (hearts, diamonds, clubs or spades).

The atmosphere at the table was festive and the conversation light and lively. Dujarier continued to drink.

He had the bank and overestimated the amount of his money, and Jean Baptiste realized the mistake. First to act, he bet the entire amount Dujarier had stated: 2,500 francs.

"You feel lucky?" Dujarier asked. He turned over the Ace of spades for himself and the King of clubs for Jean Baptiste. The third card was an eight, the fourth card a six, and the fifth card a King. Baptiste won; he broke the bank. Dujarier pushed all his chips toward Jean Baptiste, who smirked, "Monsieur Dujarier, you are short seven hundred Francs. Everyone at the table heard your limit: 2,500 francs."

"I too heard your wager," Dujarier said. "I believed I covered it."

"Are you going to default on your debt, as you did about publishing my article?"

"Sir, is it my honor you question?"

"Your mathematics is in doubt."

"Again you impugn my integrity in public!"

"Do you seek an affair of honor with me?" Baptiste demanded.

Dujarier came out of his champagne stupor to realize the situation had become serious. In all his years as a newspaper editor and journalist he had made many enemies, but none ever challenged him in public.

The manager of the games establishment moved in to maintain order. Dujarier addressed him, "Ronald, will you please give this itinerant seven hundred francs? My servant will settle with you in the morning."

The owner hurried off to get the money. Dujarier turned his back on Baptiste and left the party. In the cold, sobering night air Dujarier realized he might have really insulted Baptiste.

He tried to dismiss it as being too trivial to worry about, and returned to his apartment on *Rue Lafitte*. Lola immediately sensed something wrong, and attempted to learn the cause. Dujarier put her off. He left for his office to contemplate the situation. He slept at his desk and worked until noon—when two military officers appeared before him, Comte De Flers and Comte D' Ecueville. They informed Dujarier they represented Monsieur Jean Baptiste who had been publicly insulted the night before by the tone, words and manner of Monsieur Dujarier. Monsieur Baptiste required an apology or satisfaction.

"I will not apologize to that word-slinging pettifogger," Dujarier said, and handed them two of his personal cards. "Make arrangements with Monsieurs Dupree and Dubois."

The men left, and Dujarier collapsed into his chair. He had fired a pistol only three times in his life, twice with Lola at the shooting club. There he had witnessed Jean Baptiste's expertise with the weapon.

As the challenged party he could select the weapons. He rushed to meet with Alexander Dumas. The author, an experienced duelist, hurried out from behind his desk. "I heard!" He embraced Dujarier, held him at arm's length, and looked into his eyes. "Alexander Henri Dujarier, you are my closest friend. Cannot you find it within yourself to reconcile this dispute peacefully?"

"If you mean a public apology, never!"

"French honor kills more of us than wine."

Dujarier pulled away and took a saber from the wall. He made a couple of slashes in the air.

"The way you handle that, he'd hack you down in a minute. I exercise at the same gymnasium as Baptiste. We have fenced. He is well trained."

In disgust Dujarier replaced the weapon. "I never fought anyone. As a boy I found words more effective than fists."

"Jean Baptiste may not be as good as you with words, but he has killed with pistols."

"What should I do?"

"Get the hell out of Paris."

"I cannot. My family honor is publicly questioned. I would be shunned on the Boulevard, in the Clubs, and in my profession. Pistols should do."

"No! No! No!" Dumas said. "Foils."

"But you said he's an expert swordsman?"

"And he is. But with foils, when he and his seconds see how inexperienced you are, they will surely accept any conciliatory gesture as satisfactory."

"And if I don't make a gesture, or they won't accept?"

"By keeping your right side toward him, your foil facing him, with right elbow against your body and your chin behind your right shoulder, the chances are you will suffer only a superficial wound. According to the rules of chivalry, that is sufficient."

"But I lose the duel."

"Better than losing your life."

"But I watched Lola. She points and fires."

"Your woman is a natural. She's been shooting since childhood."

"It looks easy enough."

"It is not. Most deaths from firearms are not because

of the Minie' ball hitting a vital organ. The pistol ball carries pieces of clothing deep into the wound. It becomes infected. Most die from blood poisoning. It takes a while."

Dujarier went pale, stroked his chin and thanked his friend. They embraced and parted.

That evening Monsieur's Dupree and Dubois arrived at Lola's for dinner. They did not mention the duel, but Lola became alarmed. Their attitude and lack of conversation heightened her concern. Dujarier convinced her to attend rehearsals for her stage appearance. He had business with his guests.

The two visitors explained to Dujarier that they had failed to convince Jean Baptiste's seconds that no insult was given or intended. "Baptiste will not accept our explanation," Dupree said. "He demands a public apology."

"I don't remember what I did or said to warrant such a challenge."

"Wine often leads the heart to danger," Dubois commented.

"I take it reconciliation is out of the question?" Dujarier asked.

Both men nodded and Dubois said, "We spoke with Baptist's seconds. Our conclusion is that Jean Baptiste manipulated you into this situation."

"Does it make a difference?"

"A man of your stature and wealth must be more careful."

"If I survive this," Dujarier quipped, "I will drink less and listen more."

"Baptist's seconds signed the following document,"

Dubois went on. "Our signatures are also affixed."

Dujarier read, "We, the undersigned, declare that in consequence of disagreement, Monsieur Dujarier has been challenged by Monsieur Baptiste in terms which render it impossible for him to decline the encounter. We have done everything possible to conciliate these gentlemen, and it is only upon Monsieur Baptiste insisting he is the wronged party, that we have consented to assist them."[4]

Dujarier pulled himself together and asked, "What now?"

"As the challenged party," Dupree said, "You may choose the weapons."

"What about writing quills at ten paces?"

Both men remained silent.

"Must I decide now?"

"It is customary," Dupree said. "The duel will take place tomorrow morning at ten."

Dujarier recalled the unwieldy weight of the saber in Dumas' study and said, "Pistols!" His voice cracked and he looked away. The men shrugged, and left.

When Lola returned from rehearsals she harassed, besieged, and beleaguered Dujarier until he told her of the duel. However he changed his opponent's name to Roger De Beauvoir. "You can't shoot!" Lola said. "Why did you choose pistols? And what did you do to upset that fop?"

"It was the wine talking."

"Jesus Christ!" Lola shouted.

His jaw set when he said, "It is a matter of honor."

---

4 (Page 91, *Lola Montez* by Edmund D" Auvergne)

Lola rubbed her forehead to stimulate her thoughts. She understood honor, and realized he must go through with this. "Your saving grace is that Roger De Beauvoir will be more concerned about his choice of clothes than weapons."

"Can you show me how I can wound him slightly? I really don't want to kill him."

"I watched both of you shoot, and doubt either will harm the other. After you both fire and miss, you will bow and walk away, honor intact."

"I hope so. Will you teach me what to do?"

"Who is supplying the pistols?"

"Dumas. He sent them to Baptiste's— I mean, De Beauvoir's seconds."

"You will be offered both. Select one. Your seconds will supervise the loading. Do you have a pistol in the house?"

"No."

"This will have to do." She pulled a small pistol from her waistband saying, "An American from Philadelphia thought I need to be protected. Dueling pistols are much longer. Do you know how many paces you will have?"

"Thirty paces."

"Good. Neither one of you will hit the other. Understand, you and Roger will stand back to back, then each take fifteen paces, turn and fire."

"That's it?" Dujarier asked with a sigh of relief.

"No!" Lola said. "That is not it."

"What else is there?" Dujarier demanded. "I point the gun, pull the trigger. Voila!"

"Voila on your father's mustache! You don't pull the

damned trigger; you squeeze it, gently, like when you touch my nipples. There is a fraction of a second between the hammer sparking and the black powder exploding. That fraction of a second is the difference between a hit and a miss. The pistol must remain on target."

"Can I aim for his leg?"

"Aim for his belt buckle. The seconds will be lucky you don't shoot them."

"You must think me a fool for not knowing these things."

"I love you all the more for it. You know I am an audacious woman. Some think me foolhardy. When my honor is questioned, I fight. I will not prevent this duel. I understand honor. And if that bastard even scratches you, I'll put a bullet through his eye."

For the first time. Dujarier smiled. "I believe you would."

"And when you turn to fire," Lola said, "Point at his paunch and squeeze the trigger. Remember, only present your right side. It gives him half the target. Having discharged your weapon, bring your arm back to your side, protecting your vital organs. Bend your elbow so the pistol is in front of your face. Now come with me."

"Where to, at this time of night?"

"The Shooting Gallery."

"Gaspar won't open up now."

"He will for me," Lola said, and handed Dujarier his jacket.

Snow fell lightly on Gaspar's capped head as he looked down from the upstairs window and moaned, "Why do you wake me up?"

"To give you fifty francs," Lola shouted. "You can take the money and go back to sleep. In that case I will shoot your balls off. Or you can open the gallery for an hour, in which case I'll give you fifty more francs when we are done. Then we all go to sleep."

Gaspar opened the gallery.

Lola set up a silhouette target of a man at thirty paces. She loaded and reloaded for Dujarier. He hit the target twice in twenty shots.

The snow cushioned the carriage wheels and horses' hooves as they rode home. Neither spoke. They spent a sleepless night together.

# CHAPTER 10

## THE DUEL

***March 11, 1845,***

"Manuela!" Lola called from upstairs, "Prepare a hot breakfast and put out Alexandre's warm long coat, scarf, and the fur hat I bought for him."

"No fur hat!" Dujarier called.

"Put it out," Lola countered. "The pond is frozen, and the wind is whipping the snow flurries over the ice."

They ate very little. At nine our carriage arrived. Lola tucked in Dujarier's scarf, tried to close his coat collar button, and gave him a kiss. His smile was forced. He handed me an envelope, saying, "I am indebted to the restaurant owner for seven hundred francs. The check is inside."

"Why worry about that now?" Lola asked.

"I gave my word to send it first thing this morning."

Lola eyed him with suspicion. He avoided her gaze, kissed her passionately and entered the carriage.

Lola tried to appear unconcerned. She ordered a bath drawn. As there was a dress rehearsal today, I made ready her costume. While I was drying Lola's hair she asked, "How much did Alexandre say he owed the restaurant owner?"

"Seven hundred francs."

"But he wrote a check?"

"I didn't look."

"Even if it was cash, the envelope he handed you was quite large."

"Do you want me to get it?"

"Yes. Something is not right."

I watched Lola remove several letters and documents from the large envelope. The check floated to the floor. I tried to hand it to Lola, but she was preoccupied with the other papers. One was to Dumas. "My dearest friend, find a check for one thousand francs which I owe to you. Thank you for your attempt to teach me how to shoot. And if I should leave Paris, please look after my darling Lola."

"Dujarier doesn't believe me," Lola said. "He thinks he's going to die. De Beauvoir is a worse shot than he."

"Your man is taking every precaution," I replied.

"Does he really think I would allow him to risk his life?"

"You can't take away his honor and have the same man."

"Manuela, you are wise beyond your years." Lola held up another letter. "Ha, this is to me."

"'My Dear Lola,'" she read alout, "'I am going out to fight a duel with pistols. This will explain why I wished to leave early. I need all the composure at my command, and you would have excited in me too much emotion. I will be with you at two o'clock, unless... Good-bye, my dear little Lola, the dear little girl I love. Good-bye, my dear, dear little girl I love so very much.'" Lola broke down sobbing. "I will save this letter. In time to come, when we are older, we will laugh at this whole affair."

The following document sobered her. It was his last will and testament. She said, "He really is taking this too seriously."

The last letter set Lola in motion. She came off the bed shouting, "Get my warm long skirt and jacket, gloves and walking boots. You dress warm, too."

"Where are we going?"

"To see Dumas. He'll know where they are."

While Lola dressed I read the last letter.

*"My Good Mother—*

*"If this letter reaches you, it will be because I am dead or dangerously wounded. I shall exchange shots tomorrow with pistols. It is a necessity of my position, and I accept it as a man of courage. If anything could have induced me to decline the challenge, it would have been the grief which the blow would cause you, were I struck. But the law of honor is imperative, and if you must weep, dear mother, I would rather it be for a son worthy of you than for a coward. Let this thought assuage your grief: My last thought will have been of you. I shall go to the encounter tomorrow calm and sure of myself. Right is on my side. I embrace you, dear mother, with all the warmth of my heart. Dujarier."[5]*

We hurried to Dumas" house. Lola charged into the study, tracking snow over the carpet and shouting,

---

[5] *Lola Montez* by Edmund D"Auvergne p.93

"Who the hell is he fighting?"

"I am not at liberty to say," Dumas replied.

She recalled Dujarier making a mistake when he told her who he was dueling. Her beautiful bronze skin went ghostly white and she gasped, "Jean Baptiste."

Dumas's chin fell to his chest and tears came to his eyes. Lola had her answer. "You fool!" She grabbed Dumas by the lapels of his smoking jacket and shook him with rage. He did not resist. Lola shouted, "My love is a dead man!"

"I tried to stop it," Dumas said.

"Where?" Lola shook him. "Where is the duel?"

Dumas shook his head. "He may lose his life, but I will be damned to eternal hell if I will allow you to steal his honor."

Despite shouts, threats and tears from Lola, Dumas refused to reveal the location. We were hurrying back to the house when we saw our carriage come into the circular driveway.

Lola pulled open the carriage door, and Dujarier's bloody dead body fell into her arms.


It was the largest funeral cortege of the century in Paris. Pall-bearers were Honre' de Balzac, Joseph Mery, Emile Di Girardin and Alexander Dumas.

Second-hand accounts of the duel appeared in all the papers. We received a first-hand account from our carriage driver Alain, and I made certain that the newspapermen questioned him. The newspaper exposition of the unfairness of the duel led to a court case. Jean Baptiste fled Paris for Rome just ahead of a warrant for his arrest.

Alain, our coach driver, was a big, older man with a fierce handlebar mustache. He came from a military family; his father was in Napoleon's Iron Guard. Alain had retired as Sergeant Major.

He explained how he drove to where the doctor and seconds waited. The three men entered the carriage with Dujarier, and they rode through the cold deserted streets to the Bois de Boulogne behind the Cafe Madrid. After a half hour of waiting the doctor approached Dujarier, who used the carriage to block the winter wind, and said, "You have fulfilled the requirements of honor and may leave with your integrity intact."

"We shall give Baptiste a while longer," Dujarier answered.

At eleven o'clock, an hour after the appointed time, the doctor again approached Dujarier and requested him to go home. Dujarier shouted, "My honor has been impugned."

"You are in no condition physically or mentally to continue under these conditions."

"My good doctor," Dujarier said, "You may leave. I will not."

At eleven-thirty the doctor and the seconds convinced Dujarier to leave the field with his honor intact. Just as they were entering the coach, a carriage burst into the Bois de Boulogne. Jean Baptiste alighted with his seconds and doctor. An argument ensued between the seconds as to the time of arrival. Baptiste called over to Dujarier who was shivering with cold, "Shall we postpone this affair of honor? You decide. If so I will challenge you again."

Dujarier undid his scarf, threw it into the snow, and

said, "Let us get on with it."

Jean Baptiste's seconds had been in possession of the weapons overnight. On inspection Dubois, Dujarier's second, put his little finger into the bore of one of the pistols. It came out black. He held the blackened finger up for all to see and said, "According to the rules, these pistols were not to be fired before this duel."

"On my honor," Jean Baptiste said, "I did not fire a ball from this weapon. I tested it with black powder only to see that it would ignite. I did so with the other weapon also. Its barrel is also blackened."

Dujarier's seconds looked at him for a reply. He snapped, "Get on with it."

Dujarier's doctor stepped forward and said, "No! You are in not in condition to participate in this duel. You're shivering and couldn't hold a pistol straight if you knew how."

"I am capable and I will have done with this!" Dujarier replied.

The pistols were primed and loaded. Dujarier had to be reminded how to hold the weapon pointing to the ground. He and Baptiste each stepped off fifteen paces, and faced each other. Dubois held a white handkerchief at arm's length. As soon as he let go of it, Dujarier fired. The pistol ball kicked up dirt and snow ten feet from where he stood. Baptiste raised his pistol slowly and, against all rules of the duel, he took excessive time to aim carefully. So much time did he take that his own second shouted, "Shoot! Damn you, shoot!" Dujarier forgot all he had been told. He didn't turn sideways to present less of a target. He didn't raise his pistol before his face to protect his side and face with his arm.

Baptiste fired.

Dujarier stood rigid. The snow swirled about his feet. Then he collapsed, a bullet through his throat. Blood gushed out. The doctor was first to reach him. Spitting blood, Dujarier's last words were, "Did I behave honorably?"

"Yes, my friend," the doctor whispered.

Alain our coachman, who had seconded many duels between army officers, questioned Baptiste's coachman. The driver admitted to driving Jean Baptiste to the shooting range where he practiced with both pistols, using Minie' balls on targets at thirty paces—all against the rules. The coachman also told Alain that they arrived at the dueling field shortly after ten, but stayed out of sight while he was sent to spy on Dujarier. The moment he reported Dujarier preparing to leave, Baptiste ordered him to hurry to the dueling ground.

I saw to it that the information from both coachmen was published in the newspapers. The disclosure led to a summons being issued by the Paris police against Jean Baptiste, for murder. Lola also dispatched a summons – and she challenged Baptiste to a duel. He never received it. He fled to Italy.

Lola was honestly committed to Dujarier. He was more to her than her husband or Franz Liszt, who flashed through her life like comets. Dujarier really loved her. He also left her eighteen shares in the Palais Royal Theatre, worth twenty-five thousand francs.

When those who consoled Lola had left, and she could listen and hear my words, I spoke to her in Hindi. "Na jaayate' mriyate' vaa kadaachin naayam bhuthva bhavithaa na bhooyah:ajo nithyah saasvato'yam puraano na hanyate' hanyamaane' sareere."

("The holy *Bhagvad Gita* tells us that you can kill people, but you can never kill a soul. No weapon can cleave it, no fire can burn it, because the soul is immortal. The *Gita* also says: 'For death is certain to one who is born...thou shalt not grieve for what is unavoidable.'")

The luxury of grief is allowed little time in the entertainment field. Tears must be dried and the show must continue. Three weeks after Dujarier's death, Lola appeared at the Porte-St.-Martin Theatre, in *La Biche au Bois*. She was hissed, and she antagonized the public by voicing her scorn at them from the stage. Lola's theater career in Paris was finished.

The Royal Court absolved Jean Baptiste's seconds. Hearing this, he thought it safe to return to Paris.

He was mistaken. He did not consider the newspapers, the railroad, and Lola Montez. She wanted revenge. She kept the fires of Baptiste's dishonor burning. on the Boulevard and in the clubs and parlors of Paris' elite. The newspapers had lost one of their own in a blatant act of cheating on the field of honor. Public pressure forced the Court of Cassation to send Baptiste for trial, on the charge of murder, to the High Court in Rouen. The railroad had just opened a line to Rouen, and the ninety-mile trip from Paris could be made in comfort in less than two hours. Dujarier's friends, admirers, and fellow journalists were so numerous that two cars were added to the regular train. That was insufficient to accommodate the Paris crowd. A special express train of ten cars was arranged just for the trial.

### March 25—March 30th 1846

The case against Baptiste was based on his violation of the Code of Honor. Particularly, that no weapon used in the duel should have been handled or practiced with prior to the duel. Prominent duelists such as Dumas, professors from the universities in Rouen and Paris, testified that this was an ironclad rule and was understood by Baptiste who was a known duelist.

The people of Rouen poured in to see the rich, famous and powerful attending the trial. The courtroom could not accommodate the crowd, and it flowed out into the street. The courtroom windows were opened to let in fresh air and allow those outside to hear. The witnesses had to push their way through the crowd to stand before the judge.

Except Lola. The crowd parted for her. She wore a black Cashmere shawl and form-fitting black satin gown, and she was the cynosure of all eyes. Though a year had passed since the duel, her voice was choked with sobs, and the reading of Dujarier's last note caused her to shed floods of tears. She declared that had she known it was Jean Baptiste with whom her lover intended to fight, she would have communicated with the police and prevented the duel.

"I would have gone to the rendezvous myself," she cried with characteristic spirit. In her Memoirs Lola added that she would have fought Baptiste herself, and her life-story testifies that this was no empty gasconade.[6]

Jean Baptiste was convicted of premeditated murder and sentenced to seven years in prison. It was the testimony of the two carriage drivers, Lola's heartbreaking testimony and her artful reading Dujarier's letter to his mother that sealed Baptiste's fate.

---

[6] *Lola Montez* by Edmund D"Auvergne description P. 104,105

# CHAPTER 11

## EXPULSION

Not long after the funeral, friends of Dujarier faded away. Few invitations were received to Salons, theater, or public events. Requests to attend social gatherings were even less. The newspapers no longer mentioned Lola.

A message from Lord Brougham directed us to meet him at George Sand's home. He received us in the study. George closed the doors and Lord Brougham said. "I am being posted to Bavaria. Prior to departing, I will arrange a tour of Europe for Madame Lola."

"Why should I leave Paris?" Lola demanded.

"The Austrian Foreign Minister, von Metternich, is returning to Paris. He will not attend any function to which Lola Montez is invited, has been invited, or will be invited. He declared you persona non grata in Paris."

"Who the hell does that Vienna Schnitzel think he is?"

"He is the chancellor of Austria, senior representative of the Hungarian monarchy, a brilliant tactician and politician who manipulates most of Europe," Brougham said.

"You have been identified as a spy for England," George Sand added. "Your information about the French rushing troops and wagons to the Austrian border stopped a Russian invasion of France. You ruined

Metternich's plan to unify the German States."

"Consider yourself fortunate," Brougham said. "Von Metternich controls a larger, more efficient spy network than England. He usually kills our agents."

"You never mentioned that before," Lola said.

"Your agreement is with Lord Palmerston. I implement his wishes."

"What have you arranged for us?" Lola capitulated.

"A tour of the Lowlands, Poland, Russia, and the German States. Our consulates in these countries are working on your behalf. Belgium and the Netherlands will be first."

"Where do we go after entertaining the Dutch?"

"Westphalia. While you're in Holland, we want you to meet King William. He is still arguing with his Russian wife."

"I'll think about it."

"Think about this: you are being paid to keep us informed."

"I have done so."

"You took an unauthorized vacation with Liszt."

Lola's cheeks turned crimson. A hard glare appeared her eyes. Before she exploded I said, "We need to know our departure time. Preparations must be made to send our luggage."

"Of course," Lord Brougham said. "The cities and dates will be delivered shortly. Von Metternich will arrive soon, and you must be gone."

"We will try," Lola said.

"I am pleased you said we," Lord Brougham smiled at me. "Your maid is helpful."

"Manuela is not your average servant," Lola said.

"Her education is superior to that of most courtiers in Europe."

"We appreciate her efforts," Lord Brougham said.

"Most men try to please me," Lola noted. "You don't like me."

Lord Brougham massaged his clean-shaven chin and mused, "You are blessed by God with beauty beyond compare. How you use God's gift I find repulsive."

"I use my beauty to survive in style."

"Your style of living is far above the survival level. England spent a small fortune on you."

"And received a large fortune worth of information in return."

"You could have married princes, dukes, men of wealth and power, and do so much good for society."

"The society be damned!" Lola snapped.

"No!" Brougham burst out, "You be damned! If you had as many penises sticking out of you as have been stuck into you," Brougham's face was livid, "You would appear like a bloody porcupine!"

Lola opened her mouth to reply but nothing came out. Brougham turned and stalked from the room. A flood of laughter erupted from Lola's belly and she guffawed, even slapped her knees with both hands. She laughed so hard her make-up ran with the tears.

"He didn't mean that," I said.

"Oh yes he did. I didn't think the pompous ass had it in him. He's probably right; I would look like a porcupine. He is also correct about helping society; it was one of Liszt's virtues which endeared him to me. He never took payment for concerts, but donated his fees to the poor."

"He also had great personal wealth," I said.

"I must think on this. You see, I love society; it's people I don't like."

Much of my time involved selecting clothes for traveling and storage. I made a quick trip to the tailor, who gave me names of Jews in Antwerp and Amsterdam.

The British Embassy could not arrange a meeting with King William in Amsterdam, for he and his wife were attempting reconciliation, so we moved on.

From Amsterdam we journeyed overland to Dortmund, in Westphalia. Newspapers, posters, and discussions in the clubs and cafés by the English Embassy staff promoted Lola's appearances. Her performances sold out.

Theatre critics praised Lola as an artist. Unsophisticated audiences were easily pleased. An incident in Westphalia received unjustifiable attention in Frankfurt.

We left the theater in a hired carriage. A Westphalia policeman attempting to control the crowd held us in the alley for some time. Lola sent our chauffeur to bring the policeman to her. When he opened the carriage door, Lola struck him with the riding crop on top of his helmet. Then she slammed the carriage door shut on his arm, tapped on the carriage roof and off we went, dragging the officer for ten meters.

We weren't long at the hotel when the policeman reappeared, with a citation. Lola tore it up and threw it in his face. He began writing two new citations. We left the city.

Our arrivals in Frankfurt and Berlin, the Prussian

capital, were heralded by newspaper reports of the incident. The demand for tickets increased. The shows sold out.

Lola made acquaintances with men of wealth, title, and power, and she dispensed the Pope's wine liberally. She received many expensive gifts, two offers of marriage, and three as courtesan to titled aristocrats. One showed us a palace he would give her if she agreed to be maintained there. Lola spent time with these men, dispensing her favors and the wine, but she declined all offers, saying, "I wish to see Poland and meet the Czar in St. Petersburg. Besides, it's a small castle."

I sold many of the gifts for her through the silversmith in Antwerp and the cheese-maker in Amsterdam. My daughter confirmed that the money arrived, and the amount far surpassed my original goal. I remained longer for Lola's sake – and, I must admit, for my own greed. The accumulation of money became so simple, I now thought in terms of a royal marriage for my Princess.

# CHAPTER 12

## POLAND

Frankfurt and Berlin were accurately described by philosopher Arthur Schopenhauer as having a "healthy climate, beautiful surroundings, the amenities of large cities, the Natural History Museum, superior theater, opera, and concerts, fine coffee, well-kept houses, good water... and better dentists."

Warsaw was different; it belongs to Russia. There was only one concert hall in the Polish capital. Homes, businesses, and government buildings were all built from unfinished lumber. Only the main boulevards were paved.

Czar Nicholas II had appointed General Ivan Paskievich Viceroy of the Kingdom. The iron-fisted ruler used the Russian secret police to destroy the morale and will of the people. He forbade the Polish language, placed Russians in positions of power, and imposed cultural imperialism by edict, action, and the bayonet. Entire village populations were transferred to Siberia and replaced with Russian peasants.

The Poles hated Ivan. They referred to him as the Black Dwarf. Five feet tall, he brought darkness to their country and despair to the life of every Pole.

Lola's appearance became a most welcome surprise to the people of Warsaw. The glowing Andalusian star who had graced the Paris stage would appear in their opera house! The people were elated. The theater sold out for the first, second, and third performances.

The closest box to the stage belonged to Ivan Paskievich. When the Black Dwarf laughed everyone laughed. When the little man clapped with his small delicate hands, those around him pounded their hands together. When he stood to his full height of five feet, those close by remained seated.

A section of his Russian supporters, who applauded when he did, led the cheering for Ivan Paskievich after Lola's final bow. He stood and took his bows, then whispered to an aide to invite Lola to his box. He had read everything he could about Lola. He collected photos of her, and read one article repeatedly:

> *"It is indisputable that in this, her twenty-sixth year, Lola is extremely beautiful. Her bitterest detractors never denied her magical loveliness. This was reinforced by sparkling vivacity, and personality, without which we should never have heard the name of Lola Montez. A human masterpiece of this sort is as much a source of trouble in a community as a priceless diamond. Everyone's cupidity is excited, probity and honor melt away in the fierce heat of temptation. The upright think that here at last is a prize worth the sacrifice of all the standards that have hitherto guided them. St. Anthony, after forty years of sainthood, succumbs—and is glad that he does. Even Poland forgets her woes when Lola appears."*

The Black Dwarf met Lola, and New energy coursed through his sixty-year-old frame. He, the master of legions, at whose frown a nation paled—why should he not grasp this treasure? Who should say him, nay?"[7]

Informed of the invitation, and aware of the Paskievich's importance, Lola saw him close up in the nearest box to the stage. She rejected the invitation because of a previous appointment.

She left to make a benefit appearance for a group of actors. Lola accepted no money for her performance and donated to a public kitchen organized by the Sisters of Charity. Her rejection of the love-struck Viceroy Paskievich inspired him. Lola wrote in her diary: "While on a visit for breakfast to Madame Steinkiller, the wife of the principal banker of Poland, the old Viceroy again sent to ask my presence at the palace at eleven o'clock. I was assured by several ladies that it would be neither politic nor safe to refuse to go, and I traveled in Madame Steinkiller's carriage. I heard from the viceroy a most extraordinary proposition; he offered me the gift of a splendid country estate, and would load me with diamonds besides. The poor old man was a comic sight to look upon – unusually short in stature, and every time he spoke, he threw back his head and opened his mouth so wide as to expose the artificial gold roof of his palate. A death's-head making love to a lady could not have been a more disgusting or horrible thought. These generous gifts I most respectfully and very decidedly declined. My refusal to make a bigger fool of one who was

---

[7] *Lola Montez* by Edmund D"Auvergne P. 52

already fool enough was not well received. [8]

"The next day the Viceroy's colonel of gendarmes and the director of the State Theater called at my hotel. They urged the suit of their master. They tried persuasion then argument. It availed them nothing. They insinuated threats, a grand row ensued. I showed both men out."

The following night Paskievich did not appear at the theater. His personal box remained empty. The house was crowded.

Three rows of Paskievich's Russians took seats nearest the stage, and they hissed and booed during Lola's performance. She exploded, rushed to the footlights, and shouted at the Viceroy's hirelings. She screamed the truth, telling them of the Prince's offers of estate, privileges, and wealth in return for her affection.

The audience found the story more entertaining than her dance. She said she refused Paskievich's gifts because she found him disgusting. She called him an ugly dwarf – and received thunderous applause from the Polish audience. The people saw their aged former Princess stand in her box, applaud, and then bow to Lola. The Poles grabbed the nearest Russians and pummeled them. The fight poured out into the street, and the outnumbered Russians fled. Lola found herself carried shoulder high by the Polish crowd out into the street and to her hotel. She became their heroine.

Unintentionally, Lola ignited the passion of the Polish people for sovereignty. Their intense hatred for the Russians turned into violence. Warsaw became a

---

8 Lola's Diary.

cauldron of boiling emotions. The odor of revolution permeated the capital city. Riots and looting of Russian businesses took place. The Black Dwarf called out his Cossacks. Mounted, with saber and musket, they put a swift and bloody end to the spontaneous uprising.

While we were preparing for a late dinner, a message arrived that a warrant had been issued for Lola's arrest—the charge: inciting revolution. The police were on their way.

I informed Lola. She ordered the servants to barricade the front and rear doors with furniture, and produced a pistol. A policeman appeared at the front door, and she threatened to shoot him. He stood dumbfounded, warrant in hand, looking over the pile of furniture into the muzzle of the pistol.

Lola's hand remained steady, the pistol cocked and her eyes flashing lightning. The policeman stammered, "A lady does not act in such a manner."

Lola aimed at his forehead and asked, "Do you wish to bet your life I'm a lady or not?"

He turned away from the gun muzzle and consulted his colleagues. They could not agree, so they left to ask at headquarters how to proceed.

I sent word to the French Consul. He arrived, saying that as a French Citizen Lola was under his protection. (She was not in fact a citizen of France). The English Consul later acted likewise.

Paskievich wearied of the entire incident. He sent a verbal message to both consuls that the arrest warrant remained in effect, but would not be implemented for twenty-four hours. He suggested we leave Warsaw. We did.

While in the coach, traveling through the barren snow-swept Lithuanian landscape, Lola made one of her astute observations that gained her acclaim amongst men of importance. Speaking about Poland, she said, "Where political, religious, or military authority has free rein, oppression is absolute."

I replied that our destination was St. Petersburg with an invitation arranged by Lord Brougham to Czar Nicholas. The Russian Czar is Poland's real ruler, and a despot of the highest order. She turned away and asked, "What would you have me do? I must convince the Czar to provide me an invitation to the Dutch Prince Wilhelm, who is again having trouble with his Russian wife. While in the Russian capital, we can earn a small fortune spying and making some intimate friends."

"But neither of us speak Russian," I said.

"Liszt once told me that French is the language of their upper class. He performed in Moscow and Petersburg."

We had no problem with the language. Her performance of the Spider Dance was enthusiastically received, and the Czar asked her to dance for his Cossack guard.

These wild bearded men were a change from the genteel smooth-faced courtiers of the Russian elite. The Cossacks were bearded, mustachioed killers. They wore knives and a cavalry sword at their waists. Their Kuban (a large black fleece hat) covered a shaven skull with one long lock of hair always hung over the left ear. They believed an angel sat on their right shoulder and the devil on their left, and they used the lock of hair to brush the devil off their shoulder. They also believed that upon dying they went directly to hell for having killed their enemies, but the angel, realizing they killed in defense of their country, would pull them out of hell by that same lock of hair.

They wore a long overcoat called a Burka, and a sheepskin cape. The Burka was held together by a belt from which a leather money pouch hung. They were a loud, rowdy bunch, who drank hard and ate prodigious amounts of food. They used fighting knives to cut meat and bread, and their hands to stuff it in their mouths. They cleaned their greasy hands on their beards.

When Lola danced they didn't stop eating or drinking, but slammed their fists on the board tables in time to the music. Lola performed her Spider Dance, and the noise stopped. They gaped at her beautiful figure flitting across the floor, showing more and more leg as she stomped the detestable spiders.

When she finished, the Cossacks erupted. They toasted Lola with mugs, glasses and bottles. They pulled off their boots, filled them with liquor and drank. They began chewing their boots to show how their fathers had outlasted Napoleon. They drank from their hats, and every man in the room tore his money-pouch from his belt and threw it at Lola's feet. A Russian officer emptied a large bread basket to collect the pouches. He then led us to safety as the drunken Cossacks danced on the tables, fighting under them, and it became a wild uncontrollable melee.

The following afternoon we had a private audience with Czar Alexander. He was a tall man with a full head of hair, standing militarily erect, the epitome of what a ruler should look and act like. In a letter from Lord B, prior to our meeting, the Englishman warned that he thought Czar Nicholas mentally unstable. I can say that neither Lola nor I saw any indication of intellectual or emotional insecurity. His opening words to Lola were, "Lord Brougham tells me you are considering going to Amsterdam. I will give you letters to my cousin Anna Pavlovna, wife of Prince Wilhelm II." He smiled knowingly. "She would appreciate it if Wilhelm found a temporary distraction. The two need a period of separation to restore marital bliss."

"I shall endeavor to entertain the Prince," Lola promised. "That is, until your cousin regains her energy."

"Yes," The Czar said, "Energy is the correct description. The Dutch must remain calm. Holland is the key to Belgium, and Belgium is the back door to France."

Both Lola and I included that information in our letters to Lord Brougham. There was more to come. How we learned that information will never appear in history books.

Count Benkendorf, the Minister of Foreign Affairs, led Lola and me into the Czar's presence and made the initial introduction. He then escorted me out so that Lola and the Czar might be alone.

I was sitting in the anteroom when four large, disheveled looking men of high rank burst into the room. Their soiled uniforms indicated a long journey. They brushed by the outer guards, pushed aside the palace guardsmen and stormed toward the closed doors to the Czar's receiving room.

Count Benkendorf leapt between the men and the door, and they stopped. With his fist clenched behind his back, Count Benkendorf knocked three times on the door. The four men demanded to see the Czar. Benkendorf pointed to their dust-covered greatcoats saying, "You've ridden hard. What's the problem? Why approach the Czar in such a manner?"

"We have fifty thousand men who will die in the Caucasus Mountains," one General said, "If food, ammunition and warm clothing are not soon delivered. "

"How can that be?"

"Since spring we fought minor battles pushing the Persians and Turks into a cul-de-sac. We are in position to finish their armies, but cannot."

"Why not?" Benkendorf demanded.

"The Muslims are well supplied by the French. They have the new rifled muskets that shoot better and further than ours. Mountain fighters from Turkestan are pouring in. Soon they will be hunting us."

"If it's more men you need," Benkendorf said, "I will authorize a division of Cossack cavalry."

"Keep your goddamned Cossacks," another general said. "They know how to pillage and rape, and can only fight from horses. In the mountains we cannot use horses. We left your Cossacks to guard the supply wagons, and they stole more than we had. That is why we are here. We need supplies and mountain fighters. Without them we face total defeat!"

The doors behind Benkendorf swung open. "Defeat?" The Czar thundered, "I refuse to accept any defeat!"

"We will lose everything we fought for in the Caucuses," one general replied, and all four bowed.

I was shocked when the Czar indicated that the generals should follow him into the room. The Czar's tunic was not buttoned correctly, and he had forgotten to put on his royal sash. I pictured Lola half naked in there, but the conversation carried on until the doors closed.

I had no idea where she could be.

It was some time before the Czar, Benkendorf, and the officers re-entered the anteroom. The men drank a toast to success. As the Czar led the four generals from the room, he looked at me. His eyebrows raised so far they got lost in his hair. He placed a key in my hand and said, "The closet behind my desk."

Dumbstruck, I remained seated until they left the room. Then I entered the receiving room. No one was there. I whispered, "Lola!" Then again, louder. I heard a knocking. Using the key, I opened the walk-in closet behind the Czar's desk. Lola emerged and threw her arms around me. "I'm saved," she said. "I thought he forgot. He locked me in here so they wouldn't see. Who were those men he was arguing with?"

"Generals from the Army of the Caucasus," I said. "They need to be resupplied."

"Yes." Lola pointed to the Czar's desk. "Take paper and quill. I also heard their conversation," she said. "I'll dictate what I heard, and then you add to it."

So two British spies, using the Czar's personal stationary, wrote crucial military information that resulted in a major change in policy by Prussia, England, Austria, and France.

I never told Lola that the Czar had forgotten her. He asked to see Lola before we left, and he apologized for locking her in the closet. He said, "Whenever I imprison one of my subjects unjustly, I compensate them for time lost." Then he placed a thousand rubles in Lola's hand.

She curtsied and said, "I fear your highness will be a poor man."

"Fear not," he laughed. "I am also the judge."

# *CHAPTER 13*

## ST. PETERSBURG, WESTPAHLIA, MUNICH:

Lola challenged the Russians at ten-pins, gambling, and in the shooting galleries. They gave up their money, harboring hopes of an evening alone with the most beautiful woman in Europe. She smoked cigars and showed her legs while dancing.

The Russians loved Lola's unconventional behavior; not so in Westphalia. Lola's reputation for garnering police warrants and causing riots in England, France, and Poland preceded her. The same occurred in the Prussian capital of Berlin. Her previous appearances in these cities sold out because of her notoriety. Today people demonstrated against her.

The authorities canceled her Berlin performance on moral grounds. She raged through the hotel cursing, breaking vases, and tearing paintings from the walls. She insulted anyone who looked German. The theater manager came to deliver her performance fee. She hit him in the head with the purse. I picked up the money and shoved him out the door. The manager's toupee hung from the money bag. Our laughter broke the tension.

Early next morning Lola prepared to visit Berlin's newspaper editors, where she wanted to make her case to the public. The concierge appeared with a bill for damaged articles in the hotel. A tersely worded invitation from the British Consul followed. He wanted to meet us at eleven. I used the money from the theater manager to pay the hotel damages.

A male secretary ushered us into the Consul's office. On his way out he removed the guards and locked the doors. Leon Favish, the British consul, stood six foot two inches. He held himself upright with an easy smile showing even white teeth. Greying chops grew down his firm jaw. His voice approached a deep baritone when he quoted from a letter. "Lord Brougham writes: 'Your information from the Russian capital of St Petersburg is much appreciated. It confirmed our assessment of Prussian, Austrian, and Hungarian intentions. Your evaluation of the Czar's Army in the Caucuses is equally important. The strategies Russia and France hold for Belgium and the Netherlands are most significant. The unwelcome reception you received in Westphalia and Berlin reflects nothing on your theatrical abilities. We suspect an Austrian spy in our service. Von Metternich learned you procured this valuable information, and he is a vengeful man. Beware'."

Consul Favish put the letter aside. "We can no longer trust the mail, not even the new telegraph. They are infiltrated. The following is a verbal communication from Lord Brougham's courier. He says, 'Von Metternich knows you are planning to visit Amsterdam in pursuit of Prince Phillip.'"

"Yes," said, Lola, "I hold a letter of introduction from Czar Nicholas to his sister Princess Pavlovna in Holland."

"Lord Brougham suggests you stay away from Holland. Von Metternich is preparing similar demonstrations to those you received in Westphalia and here in Berlin."

"Where would he have me go?"

"To Munich."

"That's in Bavaria?"

"Yes. Your goal, to seduce King Ludwig."

"Who is Ludwig?" I interrupted, "What makes him more important than King of the Netherlands?"

"Ludwig is King of Bavaria. He commands the most organized army among the Germanic states. Munich is the cultural center of the independent German kingdoms. For Von Metternich to succeed in confederating the Germanic states, he must control Bavaria. Prussia and Russia will then invade France and Belgium. All of Europe will be theirs."

"Ludwig has a wife and seven sons," Lola said. "What makes him accessible?"

"He loves beauty," Favish replied, "And you are the most beautiful woman I ever saw." Lola nodded and he continued. "As a young man the king frequented Italy and Spain, and he made an extensive study of their art. His life is dedicated to the splendor of women. For fifty years he imported historic and artistic works of the Italian and Spanish masters. He reconstructed Munich. It boasts the most ornate public buildings, museums, theaters, stadiums, roads, and bridges along the Isar River. His stellar achievement is the founding of Munich University, one of Europe's finest. The sons of Germanies' elite study there. Through education Ludwig hopes to control the other German states.

"The university has the finest school of architecture in the world. Its influence can be seen in Munich's public buildings. They rival those of Rome, Florence, and Milan."

The consul came from behind his desk and stood in front of Lola. He looked down at her breasts and nodded approvingly. She smiled. Consul Favish said, "King Ludwig's weakness is beautiful women. He has built a Hall of Beauty. When he sees an exceptionally stunning woman, whether commoner or aristocrat, he invites her to the castle. A court artist paints her portrait. He beds her, then displays the portrait in the hall. Once Ludwig sets eyes on you, there will be an invitation to sit for a portrait. Lord Brougham will arrange an introduction through your appearance in the Royal Theater."

"Is the King a lecher?" Lola asked.

"No. He is germanicly discreet. He beds his beauties and arranges liaisons with courtesans; that is his right as King. His wife, Queen Theresa, accepts this. The people love them both.

"He is a wonderful administrator. At his desk before cock crow, he watches every coin spent by his council, demands explanations and justifications for all projects. Two areas of interest for King Ludwig are beauty in the city and his Hall of Beauty. Although he was a fine battlefield commander, he leaves the military and politics in the hands of the Jesuits."

"I hate the Jesuits."

"Good. We hope you can give us an insight into their methods of spying, especially vis-à-vis a union of the German states. They too wish to govern the continent. Bavaria and Berlin are the leaders of the 39 Germanic countries. Half are Catholic and half Protestant."

"You said nothing of Ludwig's religion or appearance. That Pole, Paskievich, offered me a castle, land, and title. I refused. He is repulsive. "

"The King is a staunch Catholic, in his late fifties, a bit taller than you. He is considered a handsome eccentric. His people hold deep affection for him. When dressed for official occasions Ludwig appears impressively kingly, but he is an unconventional man—at times slightly bizarre. He often wanders the streets in the same clothes he works in at his desk, his pajamas. In colder weather he forgets to change shoes, and wears slippers and a sleeping robe in the streets. He walks without guards, and is always looking for ways to improve his beloved city. He checks the sewers or chastises the owner of a house in disrepair. He speaks with vendors in the markets to see their prices are fair and their food fresh and clean. He checks the purity of the water and visits the alms-house. Most of all he inspects the breweries. Germans love their beer, and Munich brews the best. Its sale supports half the population."

"He sounds like a man I want to meet," Lola said.

"He is hard of hearing,"

"Fear not," Lola said, "I will speak up. What languages does he speak?"

"German, French, of course, Italian, and he enjoys trying to improve his Spanish—which is another reason Lord Brougham thinks you will impress the King."

"How do I contact Lord Brougham?"

"You will not. Use your servant Manuela to reach Lord Brougham. You should not be observed communicating with him." Consul Favish handed Lola a purse heavy with Bavarian guldens. "For services rendered."

Upon our departure from the consulate, Lola insisted

we visit the Hamburg Bank. There we exchanged the gulden for Berlin marks. We then made for the premier dress shops.

Lola spent most of the money that evening. She knew exactly what she wanted, and price never influenced her decisions. We returned to our hotel suite exhausted, and lazed around the next day receiving the purchases and preparing to ship everything to Munich. By this time I had expected to be on a ship to India. My greed and Lola's need required that I remain.

Greed trumped my need to return to my daughter. Money came so easily, I couldn't stop. The Jewish money changers greeted me with their warmest smiles. I kept recalling a story from the Old Nanny who cared for my daughter. They were watching a band of monkeys hopping from roof top to roof top, stealing food. Nanny asked my daughter, Princess, "How do you catch a monkey?" My Princess answered, "Run, and grab him."

Nanny pointed to the pack of monkeys scampering over the rooftops, swinging from rafters, leaping into trees. "Could you do that?"

My child looked at the chattering band of rogues and shook her head in the negative. Nanny presented an empty urn used for carrying water. "Around the neck of the pitcher you tie a rope. Make it fast to something solid." A banana appeared in Nanny's other hand. She placed the banana in the bottom of the pitcher and told Princess to take the banana out of the pitcher. My daughter put her hand in, but once she grasped the banana she couldn't remove it without lifting the vessel into the air and stretching the rope. "Your filled fist is larger than your hand. The monkey will never let go.

You can walk over and lead the animal to wherever you want."

"Why doesn't the monkey let go and escape?"

"Because he is a monkey."

I am now that monkey. It is my deep fear of the poverty, misery, hunger, and death I witnessed in the streets of India that make me unable to give up the money. The average Indian is dead before the age of thirty.

On October 5th, 1846, we arrived in Munich.

Our accommodations at the Munich Hotel were luxurious. Everything in the city appeared sparkling clean. People soaped and scrubbed their stoops and walks every morning. Before the sun came up, street cleaners finished sweeping. Women who picked up horse droppings stood at every cross–section; they sold the manure to the city to fertilize the municipal gardens.

Munich retained the quaintness of a village but with the atmosphere of a beautiful, dynamic city. King Ludwig's palace monopolized one end of the main thoroughfare, Munich University, hospital and dormitories the other end. In between stood banks, theaters, artists, cabinet makers, silver and goldsmiths, doctors, dentists, livery stables, clothing stores and three farmers' markets. Policemen in uniform marched in pairs. They could have stepped from Hans Christian Andersen's fairy tale, 'The Steadfast Tin Soldier'. The national colors red, black, and gold predominated. The buildings of symmetrically cut stone promoted the sense of stability. Colorful women's clothing breathed life into the city. I loved Munich.

Lord B. summoned me to the Embassy; Munich's Minister of Culture had rejected his request to feature Lola in the Royal Theater. The Minister cited her temper tantrums, her violent behavior toward policemen, and two outstanding (but unenforceable) warrants for her arrest. Neither Lola nor I were aware of the negative articles appearing in German. They highlighted her disruptive activities in England, France, Poland, and Westphalia.

According to Lord Brougham, the people of Munich wished to see her Spider Dance and were blasé about Lola's episodes. Munich hosted the most talented, controversial, and contentious performers in the world. However, the Bavarian people cherished order. Order was dictated by authority. No one protested the Minister of Culture's decision to exclude Lola.

She exploded like fireworks. It took time for us to converse rationally. We agreed that, beauty being her strong point and the King's weakness, she must meet Ludwig. She insisted it be today. She handed her jewelry box to me and said, "We must succeed here in Munich. Cash it with the Jews. Hire a coach, a driver, and two footmen."

"Wait until tomorrow," said Lord B. "The King receives the public starting at eleven in the morning." Lola agreed—but would not walk, be escorted, or carried in a palanquin, the three hundred yards from the hotel to the Palace. She was adamant. "To arrive for a meeting with the King, one must be appropriately attired and escorted."

I walked the Bayerischer Hof to Rubinstein's Jewelry

Emporium. It was Oktoberfest in Munich. The buildings and bridges were decorated, people dressed in their most colorful clothes. A carnival atmosphere prevailed. Strolling musicians played, string quartets, Oompa bands consisting of tuba, trumpet and trombone. The University provided drum and bugle marching units. The Fire Brigade staged a mock alarm. Not to be outdone, the Police marched in various formations back and forth across the *Promenadenplatz.* I loved Munich. What a joyous city: a multitude of red cheeks and smiling faces.

Rubinstein's Jewelry Emporium was a wonder in itself. Gems glittered, gold and silver gleamed from dark felt trays, yet there was an understatement in wealth which blended with Munich's cultured environment. I presented the letter from the money changer in Berlin, and a man escorted me to a private room.

Jules Rubinstein was ninety years old, and had suffered from a right-side stroke. His cheek and eye were disfigured, but his mind was not one bit inhibited. I placed the jewelry box on his desk. Before I opened it, "'Sha," he said. "Tell me about yourself."

I began telling him about Lola. He stopped me again, saying, "I wish to know about you."

I began by claiming, "I am a servant."

He pointed heavenward and said, "We are all God's servants. Now tell me about you. Do you have a family?"

I told him about Princess. His one good eye was so compassionate, I began to sob. I spoke a long time and he listened. I slumped forward, completely drained. Mr. Rubinstein called for tea. We sat in silence waiting for it to brew. "Your story of the monkey and the banana makes a good point," he broke the silence, "But in your case it is a mistaken comparison."

"My greed keeps me with Lola."

"True, but the banana is no longer there. You managed to slip the banana out of the trap and send it to your daughter. How old is she?"

"Twenty-six, the same age as Lola."

That one eye looked at me with the question that forced my heart into my throat. Princess was a mature woman. I had difficulty accepting that. He pushed the teacup toward me. I regained control. "Isn't it time for you to return to India?"

Suddenly I realized Lola was also my daughter. "I cannot leave until Lola is secure."

"Your mistress will always be vulnerable. Danger is the best part of her life. She must be the center of attention, challenge authority and spend more money than she earns. It is her nature. You may call a leopard a tiger, but you cannot change its spots."

In my heart I knew he was right. In this same heart is a conflict between love for my Princess in India and love for my Lola.

Mr. Rubinstein gave me enough money on account to prepare for the meeting with the King. He would evaluate the jewelry and settle later.

My return to the hotel was remarkable. For a few moments I forgot all problems. Street lights were decorated with silk banners and ribbons, and the slightest breeze set them afloat. Gaily colored lanterns stretched from rooftop to rooftop. The night intensified an already festive atmosphere, filled with music, singing, free beer, and dancing in the streets. The aroma of roasting sausages, whole lambs and pigs cooked on outdoor fire-pits permeated the air.

I returned to reality. Mr. Rubinstein's revelation of my greed and Lola's need hurt my ego. I argued with myself about my feelings for Lola as my child. I knew her better than my own daughter. I felt very close to her, and felt guilty for it. Mr. Rubinstein explained the greater love I have for my Princess. "Since Princess is not with you, she cannot return your love. Unreturned love is the strongest element of affection."

"How can that be?"

"You love Lola?"

"Yes."

"She at times shows affection for you?"

"Yes."

"There are times she is petulant, peevish even abusive?"

"Quite often."

"Therefore you fault her. You cannot fault your daughter, and so she remains perfect in your mind and heart. Isn't it time you got to know your Princess?"

My first thought of leaving Lola was that she would be alone. In four years her mother did not write. For Lola to be alone could be dangerous. She had the ability to fool people; rarely did they fool her, but she often fooled herself. She did not like to be alone with herself, an attribute that made her a good courtesan, but vulnerable.

I found myself in front of Schmearsahl's Livery Stable, and there negotiated for a carriage, a matched team of four horses, and two coachmen for the morrow at

10:30 a.m.

It took five minutes for us to enter the carriage, drive
from the Promenadenplatz onto Max-Josephplatz to the
Palace, and be escorted through the large doors to a seat
in the audience chamber. Several petitioners awaited
their turn. Lola looked at them, and turned on the Major-domo saying, "I am Maria Dolores de Porris y Montez. My parents were nobles at the court of Spain's King
Ferdinand. King Ludwig will want to see me without
delay."

Stunned by the haughty voice, beauty, and arro-
gance, the Major-domo retreated. He returned followed
by Count Silvanus Springer who said, "Madame Montez, every Bavarian citizen has the constitutional right to
meet and discuss with his King that which is most important to him. You are a foreigner, therefore last in the
order of priorities."

Lola noticed that the Count left open the door to the
King's reception room. She raised her voice and shouted
in Spanish. He did not understand a word. Lola knew
the King loved to speak Spanish, and few in Munich
were capable of holding a conversation in that language.

The count recovered, "Madame Montez, are you a titled personage?"

"Titled?!" she screamed in Spanish, "Of course I am
titled! Under the King of Spain I was Countess Maria
Dolores de Porris y Montez. My parents were nobles in
King Ferdinand's court. Alas, the rebels exiled my family and stripped all land and wealth from us." She handed
an envelope to the Count. "This is a Letter from Czar
Nicholas II to his sister the Princess, in Spain. He com-

mands her to receive me at Court."

"Madame Montez," the Count bowed as he opened the envelope, "I do not speak a word of Spanish. Use German or French, please."

"I know a bit of Spanish," King Ludwig said, as he approached behind the Count. He took the letter from the count's hand, scanned it and looked up. His eyes settled on Lola's untamed breasts. Lola too followed the King's gaze and inhaled deeply. It was a fatefully erotic moment. "Come," Ludwig said, and escorted us to his reception room.

The King stopped before his desk and turned to face Lola. She stepped closer to him. Her dazzling beauty and hint of a smile on those ruby-red lips caused him to blush. Ludwig, the ardent admirer of beauty, was held by her brazen eyes. Blood rushed through his veins and youthfulness long forgotten welled up between his thighs. Without thought he nodded to Lola's breasts and asked, "Are these of nature's making?"

I gasped. Lola reached past the King to the desk behind. She took up a pair of scissors, placed the point under the lace string restraining her bosom, and cut. Her breasts exploded out of their confinement, the nipples hard, erect, and pink as newly formed rose buds.

The Count coughed, choked, and then hurried from the room.

"Magnificent!" exclaimed the King, his eyes on the untamed quivering breasts. I produced a kerchief to cover Lola. The King hesitated, and for a moment I thought he would remove the kerchief. He strode to the door and ordered the guards, "Send for a seamstress!"

There was shouting outside the reception room. It

echoed through the palace. Four women hurried in to repair Lola's bodice.

Lola gazed over their heads at the King. Her electric blue eyes challenged him. "Will your majesty see," she asked, "That I appear on stage at your Royal Court Theater?"

"Of course. How could it be otherwise? Let us continue our conversations in Spanish; it is such a vibrant language." The moment her lacing was repaired, he led Lola onto the veranda. I followed.

The two chatted in broken Spanish. "I will be in the theater for your premiere. My countrymen rarely hear Spanish music or see the dance from Hispania."

"I promise to make their introduction memorable."

"I cherish the anticipation. How much time do you require to prepare?"

"A week."

"Silvanus!" The King shouted, and the Count hurried onto the veranda. "Have the manager of the Court Theater schedule Madame Montez to appear between the first and second acts, and the second and third, a week from today."

# CHAPTER 14

## THE MUNICH THEATER

"What made you cut open your bodice?"

"I required his attention."

"The King's eyes almost came out of his head. The Count nearly choked to death. I taught you to become a courtesan; now I'm your student."

Lola wanted her money from the jeweler. I dispatched a messenger to Leon Favish, about Lola's appearance at the Court Theater. The walk to the Jewelry Emporium was pleasant, the information about the largest pendant in the jewelry box unsettling. "An imitation," Mr. Rubinstein said and offered his jewelers loop.

I peered at the magnified gem. "What I am looking for?"

"Examine the setting in which the stone sits; you will notice slight discoloration of the metal. View the chain."

"There is a hint of green".

"Correct. Gold never rusts or discolors. Also, there are no markings to indicate the amount of gold."

He passed a piece of metal to me. "Place it against the chain."

"What is this?"

"A magnet. Neither gold nor brass attract a magnet. Put it on the back of the brooch."

"It clings to it."

"It is of base metal, not gold. The next is called the bite test. Do not hurt your teeth, but bite down on the frame of the brooch. Now see if you can find your bite mark."

"I cannot."

"Now bite down on this." He produced a small tablet of gold with the markings 24 Karat stamped on its face. I bit, and my tooth-marks were clearly imprinted. He pushed an unglazed ceramic plate toward me. "Rub the gold across the plate."

It left a gold trail.

"Do it now with the pendant and chain."

There were two black marks on the unglazed dish.

"Shams," he said.

"How do I know this stone is not a diamond? "

"A real diamond that size, would never be placed in so cheap a setting. This is a clear gemstone worth perhaps a hundred marks. I could scratch its surface or smash it with a hammer. Diamonds are the hardest things on earth."

"I must inform my mistress."

"The other items appear authentic and of good value. I will advance you seventeen thousand marks."

I returned to the hotel thinking how to tell Lola. A man came up behind me and slipped an envelope under my elbow. I dropped it. When I looked up he was crossing the street, dodging carriages.

I found Lola dancing on the bed in front of a tilt mirror on the floor. She posed in one of her stage costumes. "How much did you get?" she asked.

"Seventeen thousand marks in advance."

She removed the dress and plopped down on the

bed. "We expected more than that for the large brooch."

"You were given it by Baron von Malthausen."

"Yes. I saw him at lunch. He is in this hotel for the October Fest."

"He gave you a fake diamond in a cheap setting. It's worth one hundred marks."

Lola jumped off the bed and stormed for the door shouting, "That son-of-a-bitch screwed my ass off!"

"Where do you think you are going?" I blocked the door.

"I'm going to knock that horny weasel on his ass."

"Dressed like that? The hotel will be in an uproar. They'll call the police."

"The police be damned. My Irish is up and there's no stopping me. Where's my pistol? Where the hell is it?" She rummaged through the dresser drawers throwing clothing about.

I grabbed her by the shoulders and spun her around. "You've hooked a King. He arranged your stage appearance. Now, you must be the wise old fisherman. Reel his Majesty in. If you cause another rumpus, the Germans will cancel your debut. Munich will shun you. Germans like order."

"How could Malthausen lie like that?" Lola asked. "He actually lied to my face. Can you imagine if people knew my jewelry was fake?"

I stopped from laughing. Every time Lola's lips parted she lied. The falsehoods rolled off her tongue as the Gospel flowed from John, Mathew and Mark. "We must think of a way to make him suffer."

"Suffering isn't enough," Lola growled. She found the pistol. "I'll shoot his balls off."

I held out the envelope hoping to distract her. "Open and read it," she said.

"This was sent by the British Consul, Favish."

"What does he want?"

"He is pleased the King received you so well. The information contained in this dossier is meant to help you understand Ludwig and the Bavarian people."

"Give me a supply of the Pope's wine," Lola said. "I'll have Ludwig drinking it from my boot."

"Lola, this is serious."

"Right now I would like to make that liar Malthausen suffer. I cannot tolerate liars. I'll arrange a wooden shack with a long table that cannot fit through the door."

"And what would you do with that?"

"Nail his tallywhacker to the table, set the place on fire, and just when he is beginning to fry I'll throw a knife onto the table."

"Where on earth did you learn something like that?"

"From your peace-loving Hindus."

"I am Sikh."

"Same difference. They did it to a Muslim who raped one of their women."

"He emasculated himself?"

"Yes."

"Did he live?"

"No. When he stumbled out the burning shack holding the bloody stump of his tallywhacker, they shot him."

"You saw this?"

"I was nine."

"You never told me!"

Lola smiled. "There are many things I haven't told you. The next one I won't tell you is how I will punish Count Malthausen. Now read Lord Brougham's message aloud."

"Please don't cut off his tallywhacker."

"He'll wish I had. Do you have the brooch?

"Yes,"

"Give it here and read that letter."

"King Ludwig is a 'Living Contradiction'. That is the heading of this intelligence dossier."

"Go on!"

"On formal occasions the King is the epitome of procedure, pomp and formality. On parade, his eye catches every fault. He is thus with accounts. He knows more about the country's finances than his ministers. He is generous to those he respects and harsh with slackers. He is punctilious, fastidious and bound by the European code of chivalry. He rises before dawn, goes to prayers (a devout Catholic), then attends affairs of state. This he does in his pajamas. Finishing before breakfast, he will wander the streets of his beloved Munich in the same attire. He is a frugal man, saving scrap paper for notes and rejecting frivolous requests for government funds. The Bavarian people love him, and Queen Theresa, though she is Protestant. Munichens are predominately Catholic. Although governed in religious affairs by the Jesuits, the people are independent thinkers.

"At sixty years old the King is six feet tall, weighs two hundred pounds, and fills a uniform. He is battle tested, and knows how to use saber, sword, and foil. He has led regiments, and divisions, in combat. He is an inspiring commander. In the Napoleonic War he was awarded the highest honors of merit, and was wounded twice. He maintains the best trained army among the German States. It is a small force in comparison to Prussia and Austria, but his soldiers are well equipped for defense. The Bavarian police force is an adjunct of the Bavarian Army. Von Metternich's casualties would be unacceptable if he marched on Bavaria. Ludwig in turn holds to the aphorism: 'Power perceived is power achieved.' During the October Fest you will see his military units on parade.

"The King's weakness is beauty. He loves beautiful women, and has a special gallery of beauties. When he sees a stunning-looking woman, no matter her station in life, he will arrange for her portrait and place it in his gallery. Then he beds her. The Queen birthed eight children. And accepts her husband's sexual exploits. He is discreet.

"The King's second priority in the realm of beauty is the city of Munich. Italian visitors feel they are back in Florence. Ludwig is enchanted with Latin culture, the countries, their language and art—especially Spain. Above all he cherishes his people, and they love him.

"He established a Constitutional Monarchy. Bavaria's Congress is called the Landtag. Ministers are elected by the people, and the King appoints those he deems fit. Ludwig is the ideal ruler in temperament, education, and morals. The people take pride in their King.

"He saved Bavaria from going bankrupt to Prussia. His father squandered most of the country's wealth, and the Bavarian Burghers rose up and forced the father to abdicate. Ludwig put the economy right. This embittered von Metternich. Acting for the Prussian Empire, he expected to push Bavaria into bankruptcy and take control, then dictate to the independent German States. Ludwig outwitted the Austrian; he returned his country to economic independence. The new Bavarian government ended von Metternich's plans. He never forgives or forgets."

"Ludwig and I harbor a mutual dislike for that Austrian bastard."

I ignored the comment and read, "Ludwig is proud to support the teaching of academic realism in the University. His goal is to train future leaders of the German Confederation of States. He hopes to unify them through these students. He also funds and oversees the Royal Academy of Fine Arts. His poems are published through the school. You will be dealing with an intelligent, sensitive man, trained since childhood to rule. He is a primary source of information.

"I wish you every success."

"This is unsigned," I said.

"You don't expect British Intelligence to sign something like that."

There was a knock at the apartment door, and I answered. There the concierge held a silver tray with an envelope which he offered to me. I reached for the letter, but he pulled it away. "The King's Seal," he said, and nodded to the elaborate wax stamp on the envelope. "Please present the tray to your mistress."

I did.

Lola tore opened the envelope and read. "His highness would like the pleasure of my company tomorrow morning for a tour of Munich. Yes! Yes! Yes! Reply immediately."

"Not necessary. Having worked at three different embassies, I know that a King's request is a summons."

"I need a new dress."

"No time. There are gowns you never wore; let's try them."

Lola jumped up on the bed and danced around. She tossed the letter to me saying, "I almost settled for a baron or a count. Tomorrow, as James Fennimore Cooper would say, 'I'm going to scalp me a King.' Put that letter in my diary."

"Remember *Kama Sutra*. It is the mystery of what rests between your thighs that will make the difference. All women have the same opening. How you stimulate your lover's imagination determines his gratitude."

"And that's what we are here for. Oh, how I wish I could be rich and famous! Not to need anyone to buy things for me. I want to buy without thought."

"Price never influenced you."

"True, but how little money I have."

"If you received sufficient funds, what would you do?"

"I'd be humble."

I laughed.

"What are you laughing for?"

"Let's prepare for tomorrow."

# CHAPTER 15

## GETTING TO KNOW YOU

Anticipating the King's arrival, the hotel's owner, concierge, and uniformed attendants waited at the hotel entrance. The sidewalk was wet from scrubbing. The October sun shone bright, the air was clear and crisp. Lola stationed me on our balcony to watch the palace. "The royal carriage is leaving," I reported. "He will be here in a minute."

The elegant lines of the open Landau Coach were painted red, gold and black, the colors of the Bavarian flag. The driver and two footmen stood behind the king. All wore the same colored livery.

"You can never again use a four-horse carriage," I told Lola.

"Why not?" she demanded.

"It would be bad form. The King uses only two horses. Now hurry."

Lola wore a large broad-brimmed sombrero-like black hat covered by pure white ostrich feathers. A high black Elizabethan collar pointed down into her formidable cleavage. Her dress was of pure white silk, with patterns of black hummingbirds in flight.

Ludwig wore a similar wide-brimmed hat topped by ostrich feathers. Without planning, the two had coordinated their dress. His white linen uniform had three golden medallions over his heart and a black leather belt crossing his chest for his sword, a black silk cummer-bund and polished black boots.

They made a stunning couple. People in carriages or on foot bowed to the King. He acknowledged everyone, affluent or pauper. He greeted Lola in Spanish and she replied, pointing at the two beautiful horses, "How did you know I love the Friesian breed? Their long hair is perfectly cropped. I can sense their power before they move."

"I thought you would appreciate the Spanish blood-line of these magnificent Andalusians," said Ludwig. "Their high-stepping gait is well synchronized."

"Where are you taking me?"

"To show you my beloved Munich." The King patted the seat next to him for Lola, and motioned me to a seat opposite. He took a royal blue blanket and covered Lola and himself.

"The horses' gait is so well coordinated," Lola said, "The carriage moves as if on glass. Did you know Spanish monks bred the Arabian bloodline with the native Andalusian to produce the Friesian horse?"

"I doubt there is another woman in the realm who can converse intelligently about horses in Spanish. Benedictine monks established Munich. The city takes its name from the word Munichen, which means Monk. They settled the fertile farmland in 1158, the same year Munich became a city".

"How did your family come to rule?"

"By virtue of bloodline, and deaths caused by the plague. In 1240 the city passed to the House of Wittelsbach, and remains in my family since."

"How did the Black Plague affect your people?" Lola asked.

I was proud of her. By asking questions she allowed him to lead the conversation, while she controlled the subject.

"The plague devastated Munich," Ludwig said. "From a prosperous trading center it became a graveyard. In two years the city lost half the population. Ten thousand died. It was 150 years before the plague subsided. The barrel makers initiated a ritualistic dance to cheer the survivors. You will see it this evening. The first Hofbräu brewery was founded in 1589 here. If you don't mind a rowdy bunch of fun-loving Bavarians for companions, we shall go to the Hofbräuhaus for lunch."

"It sounds grand."

The gaited clop of the paired Frisians on the cobblestones brought us to Marienplatz 1, Munich's city hall, a magnificent large circular building. Marble colonnades marched around the exterior, upholding a red-tiled peaked roof. The building radiated an aura of stability, order, and beauty.

"Munich's main streets originate here," Ludwig said. "They radiate out into the city, which is growing ever more rapidly."

"And will continue to grow," Lola said.

"I agree, but what makes you think so?"

"The English call it the industrial revolution: advances in science, engineering, and medicine. The steam engine is not only moving trains but ships, and machines. At speeds unheard of in the history of the world."

The King's smile broadened. "I look forward to discussing this with you," he said. "Now you must see St.

Peter's Church. There are two hundred and ninety-nine steps to the steeple. You can see the snow-covered Alps."

"Why not three hundred steps?" Lola asked.

"My father said the architect miscounted. To cover his mistake, he made up a superstitious tale about number three hundred being bad luck. Would you like to make confession?"

Lola and I had prepared for questions about religious observance. She answered, "The cathedral would probably collapse. I haven't been to church for a while. I pray alone. I talk to God, and will eventually answer to Him."

"I too am private in my devotions," Ludwig said. "I have official religious obligations as monarch, and these I fulfill. When the Jesuits refused to appear at my father's funeral, I became less public about religion."

"We share a mutual dislike of the Jesuits," Lola replied. "How is it that much of your military, politics, and all religious affairs are controlled by them?"

"Manicheans are Catholic. Jesuits call themselves the soldiers of God. I allow them to play at soldier. I control the Army."

"And politics?"

"People may elect whom they wish. I appoint all ministers to the Landtag. The laws are made there. Religion I leave to the Jesuits, but even there, I control the purse-strings. Not a mark is spent in the public domain that I do not sanction. They step to my command, like these wonderful Friesian horses."

We drove to the plaza Residenz Munichen. I became accustomed to the loud speech between the two. Only when people turned, thinking the King might be calling to them, was I conscious of his hearing problem. They conversed in broken Spanish, Often substituting Latin and French words to complete sentences. Oblivious to each other's language faults, they chattered on.

Lola signaled, and I withdrew a bottle of the Pope's wine with two long-stemmed glasses from my bag. I poured, and handed them to Lola. She passed one to Ludwig, who said, "I usually prefer beer."

"This wine will tickle your palate and embrace your innards," Lola said. "Beautiful Munich will appear even more desirable." She fluttered her eyelids and peeked from under the wide-brimmed hat with her bedroom eyes.

"How can I refuse such exquisite loveliness?" He sniffed and nodded approvingly.

The Residenz Munichen was a castle, fortress, and the ancient city capital. It once housed the Kings, Princes, and Bavarian royalty. The furnishings were a combination of styles and periods; King Ludwig integrated Classical, Baroque, and Rococo sophistications to create a fascinating impression.

He had enhanced the architecture. The tour of the fortress with exquisite tapestries, sculptures, and splendid paintings was both enjoyable and informative. He gave a personal insight into Bavarian history.

We drove to the English Park. The largest public gardens in the world stretched from the city center to the outskirts of Munich. The far-sighted project was planned and implemented by Ludwig's father. He had employed veterans from the Napoleonic and American Revolutionary wars to enhance the beauty of Munich.

The veterans learned agriculture, husbandry, and land-scaping to become employable, and filtered back into Bavarian society.

Fashioned by the hand of man, the English Park stood as a portrait of humanity's adaptation of natural beauty for practical living. A five-tiered Chinese pagoda graced the park entrance. Food stalls and straw-roofed booths abounded, and the stands sold food, handicrafts, antiques, and art. Beyond the commercial area, trees and lawns graced both sides of the wide paths. People picnicked on the lush green grass. Not one piece of trash in sight: a contrast to India. Here, clean streams leapt smooth river rocks. Colored carp swam in the lake with ducks and swans who followed children throwing crumbs. Couples punted the placid freshwater lake in slim shallow-draft craft. A small flock of sheep gave city children an opportunity to play with the animals. Sturdy stone bridges spanned the streams. Music of an Oompa band wafted across the pastoral scene.

"Are you prepared for lunch?" the King asked.

"My stomach is growling," Lola said.

"I like a woman with a good appetite. You will be rewarded at the Hofbräuhaus. I hope they have enough beer."

"How could the most famous brewery in the world not have beer?" Lola asked.

With an exaggerated wave of his arm, Ludwig bowed. "Alas, dear lady, I am the culprit."

Lola clapped her hands and joined in the farce. "Please, kind sir, do explain the plight of the beer-less Hofbräuhaus."

"I lowered the price of beer at the Hofbräuhaus.

People flocked there. They drink more than the owner can brew."

"Why did you lower the price?"

"So my soldiers, policemen, and the average workingman could afford a good drink. It is forcing local breweries to lower their price.

"How many people can this establishment serve?" Lola asked.

"On the ground floor are accommodations for eleven hundred. On the second floor nine hundred."

"I would enjoy sitting with the crowd," Lola said.

"My choice exactly." Ludwig beamed.

Our carriage pulled into the cobblestoned plaza. Five arched entrance ways led to the large basement room. Waiters and waitresses in folk costumes stood at attention waiting for us. The women held five large glass steins of beer in each hand. Ludwig dismissed them.

"How can those little women hold those liter-size glasses full of beer?" Lola asked.

"They would not be employed if they couldn't. The women must not be over five feet tall."

"Why?"

"That was the height of the brewery founder."

A waitress approached the carriage holding five steins of beer in each hand. The King declined, saying to Lola, "I normally drink a stein on arrival. Your wine piqued my palate. The world seems brighter. May we have another glass?"

I poured. They clinked glasses. Lola pointed to the large bronze statue atop the peaked roof and asked, "Who is that?"

"Wilhelm V, Duke of Bavaria from the 16th century.

He couldn't find a quality beer in Munich, so he built this brewery."

"The statue is much taller than five feet."

"It is six feet. Wilhelm commissioned it. He didn't like being short. Munichens say he sued the city for building the sidewalks too close to his backside."

We entered the Hofbräuhaus laughing. The basement was enormous and crowded. People sat on long wooden benches, at plank board communal tables, a raucous, rowdy bunch with red cheeks and blond hair predominating. Laughter and song filled the room. Waiters and waitresses whisked down the aisles, with foam flying off the heads of large beer steins. They plunked the glass mugs on the wooden tables. Now and then a waitress yelped and jumped as she was pinched from behind.

The laughter, like an outgoing ocean wave, subsided until silence filled the great room. The proprietor stepped up onto a tabletop, and raised a stein in salute to Ludwig. "Ladies and gentlemen, rise and give honor to our most illustrious King." The man giving the toast blew the head off his beer and shouted, "To King Ludwig! Long may he live and rule Bavaria!"

The crowd of a thousand echoed the toast and drank. Waiters and waitresses rushed to scoop up the empty mugs and refill them. Although out of sight, from the upstairs room came a roaring toast, "To the King, long may he reign!."

The King raised his stein, bowed to the people and drained his mug.

The crowd cheered, sat, and soon the boisterous laughter and music filled the vaulted ceilings of double

Roman arches, forming alcoves large and small where people ate and drank. The ceilings and arches were painted with floral designs. We sat on an upraised stage. On the other side of the room an Oompa band and dancers in folk costume performed. They wore short leather trousers, or aprons with suspenders, and knee-length white socks with polished black leather shoes.

A young man set a three-foot oblong silver tray before us, announcing, *"Hofbräuhaus Wurstplatte."* It was a large mound of mashed potatoes and another of sauerkraut on each end of the tray. In the center were steaming piles of wieners and links of pork, chicken, and beef sausages.

"I caution you," Ludwig said, "Try a little of each. More will come."

We served ourselves. No sooner were the dishes taken than a waiter returned, with another tray piled high with two-foot large, hot, soft, salted pretzels. Links of white sausage made of veal and pork surrounded the bread. Bowls of sweet mustard for dipping appeared with fresh steins of beer.

The waiter placed another tray and Ludwig said, "This is one of Bavaria's absolute favorites! Grilled sausage loaf with potato salad."

It was encompassed by lightly battered, golden, fried balls of sauerkraut mixed with ham. I wanted to loosen my corset.

"What happens to all the food we don't eat?" Lola asked.

"It's passed out the kitchen door to our coachmen and the poor."

Lola reached over and patted his hand under the table saying, "You are a good man." He smiled and Lola groaned as the waiter returned, with a roasted suckling pig stretched out on the silver tray lying in a bed of leafy fresh vegetables, holding a bright red apple in its mouth. "Oh no!" Lola moaned. "I cannot eat another bite."

Ludwig waved the waiter off, but made a circular motion with his hand for him to bring something else. He returned with another tray.

"You are looking at the epitome of Munich's gastronomic art," Ludwig said. "Traditional homemade Bavarian *Apfel Strudel*, with vanilla cream and raspberry sauce. You must try it! And this," Ludwig pointed to a three layer, moist, chocolate cake with cherries, covered with chocolate sweet cream and sprinkled with chocolate shavings.

"I so much wish to taste it," Lola said, "But my stomach rejects the idea."

Ludwig bowed his head, turned to the waiter and said, "Send the dessert to Miss Montez's Hotel."

The waiter bowed, stepped back and signaled the owner. Ludwig reached over, took Lola's stein and poured most into his stein. "Thank you," she said. "I could not finish it."

The Hofbräuhaus owner mounted a table and sang out in a lusty voice: "In Amsterdam there lived a maid, and she was mistress of her trade. *Oans, zwoa, g'suffa.*" One thousand people came to their feet, raised their beer steins in salute to the King, and sang:

> "There's the Highland Dutch and the Low-
> land Dutch,

The Rotterdam Dutch and the Gotterdamned Dutch,

Singing, glorious! Glorious! There's one keg of beer for all of us.

Glory be to God that there are no more of us,

For one of us could drink it all alone. *Oans, zwoa, g'suffa.*"

"What does that mean?" Lola asked.

"It's Bavarian for: "One, two, drink up."

"Must I?"

"It is good manners."

Lola raised her stein with the remaining beer, chanting, "Up to the lips and over the gums. Watch out, stomach, here it comes."

The crowd cheered her and the King to the door, out into the courtyard and carriage. We arrived at the hotel just in time to use the toilets. Lola had me cancel her practice at the theater.

On my return from the theater I stopped at the apothecary to purchase the sweet oil Lola ordered. I thought it was for her and the King. We had once studied a chapter of *Kama Sutra* detailing the oil's application.

# CHAPTER 16

## PERFORMANCES

"I wish to remain an eternal mystery to you, myself, and others", Ludwig wrote. "This is the only guarantor of a vibrant, fascinating future."

He requested Lola's company every day. Having missed one rehearsal, she couldn't afford to miss another. Time for her debut was short. She responded in a letter to his messages. "It will be my lifelong task to reveal and understand the mysteries of Europe's most beloved King. My heart quivers at the thought. My breasts swell in anticipation."

I advised Lola to delete the last sentence.

The evening before Lola's debut a strange thing happened. On our return from rehearsal she and the infamous Baron Heinrich Von Malthausen, he who had passed off a replica pendant for Lola's favors, came face to face in the hotel lobby. I expected fireworks. Lola brought her parasol forward, popped it open, spun it and smiled into his face.

I breathed a sigh of relief. By creating a public scene she could ruin her relationship with Ludwig. The King was even more enamored of her since she sent a decanter of the Pope's wine every night to him. He replied in poetry. One he translated into English:

"Happy movements, clear and near,

Are in thy living grace.

Supple and tender, as a deer

Art thou, of Andalusian race!"

Lola stepped closer to the Baron and fluttered her bedroom eyes at him. The bulge in the crotch of his tight-fitting trousers grew larger. She covered the view with the parasol in her right hand, reached out with her left hand and massaged his crotch. His jaw dropped. Gurgling sounds came from his throat. I was aghast, but no one at the desk or in the lobby noticed.

She withdrew her hand and passed the parasol to me. "Heinrich my dear," she said, "Why don't we rendez-vous?"

"Yes! Yes!" he stammered.

An older woman turned from the concierge and approached the Baron. They walked off arm in arm. Lola whispered, "The son of a bitch is going to kill that poor woman."

"What are you talking about?"

"Handsome Heinrich may be a Baron, but his purse is empty. He's married three wealthy widows. They all died under mysterious circumstances in the land of the Turks."

"What have the Turks to do with it?"

"Baksheesh. European police would investigate. The Turks take the money to look the other way."

"All three women died in Turkey?"

"Aleppo, Lebanon. It's under the Ottoman rule. He must have a connection to the city police."

"Will you meet him?"

"Oh, yes. First I want to have sex with him. It's a part of my plan. The cheap bastard is well endowed and knows how to use it."

"My God! Are you mad? You would jeopardize everything with Ludwig for a romp with a creature like him?"

"Maybe I am drinking too much of the Pontiff's wine."

"Cocaine is an aphrodisiac. It can also affect people's thinking."

"If you believe I'm crazy, say so."

"Your plan is crazy. And you are getting disruptive at rehearsals."

"You don't know my plan. And why criticize me for rehearsals?"

"You argue with the cast. Tonight you slapped the conductor, drove the stage manager from the set, and kicked one of the chorus girls."

"She upstaged me."

"Your imagination."

Lola took both my hands in hers, and pleaded. "Manuela, be patient. This is so stressful. I am not myself."

I reversed the grip, held her hands in mine and said, "On the contrary. You are yourself; and you must change. King Ludwig appears to be a genuinely good man. He is taken with you. Generations of courtesans dreamt to be where you are now. Why jeopardize everything?"

"Then help me," she pleaded.

We embraced.

### The Court Theater:

The King and Bavarian nobility occupied two large

boxes on the second tier, close to the center of the stage. The curtain came down on the first act of The Enchanted Prince, and the set was quickly dismantled. The stagehands assembled Lola's scenery. She puffed a cigar and waited as the orchestra tuned their instruments. Men swept the stage and raised the foot lanterns. She handed the cigar to me and slipped on her castanets.

The music for Bolero wafted through the theater. The audience heard the clicking castanets before Lola stepped onto the stage. She strutted out with arched back and chin held high. A noblewoman of Spain stood center stage. She looked directly at the King and bowed. He responded.

She challenged him with her body. Lola threw her shoulders back, breasts pressed forward, hands on her hips. Slowly at first, her body sensually moved in time to the soft music of the flute. The harsh clicks of her castanets signaled other instruments to join the haunting tune. The theater filled with music. The exotic suggestion of her defiant body dared every man in the room. I had witnessed this reaction before, but Lola's eyes locked on the King, and his eyes on her.

From my position backstage I saw the court ladies in the Royal box casting glances at Queen Theresa. She sat at Ludwig's side, her smile genuine. It never changed. Her fan did not flutter one jot. Yet it was obvious, Lola danced exclusively for the King. Driven by the music, she bounded on her toes to the right and left of the stage. Her castanets kept time to the seductive movement of her body. The King's eyes never left her. She whipped her skirts higher, revealing more leg than ever before seen on a Munich stage. The King applauded.

The Queen applauded, and the people applauded. The few dance aficionados remained silent.

Lola bowed and the curtains closed. Stage hands rushed to change scenery for the second act of the play. I helped Lola with her costume change. She performed the Cachucha and Spider Dance between the second and third acts. Critics were divided as to her artistic interpretation. Others, skeptical of her imaginative creativity, questioned the performance's Spanish authenticity. Lola received two curtain calls and warm applause, led by the King. An abundance of bouquets filled both her arms. The stagehands gathered more, I suspect most sent by the King.

Critiques in the morning newspapers were similarly divided between supporters and the naysayers. All praised Lola's beauty and the King for bringing the Andalusian, and a refreshing breeze of Spanish culture, to Munich.

Ludwig remained unconcerned with the technical intricacy of Lola's performance, or the ethnic legitimacy, or her cultural presentation. A man bewitched, he experienced a second period of youth and would not let it pass unattended.

Without rehearsals, the King dominated Lola's time. We took another carriage tour of Munich. Many of the outstanding neo-classical buildings such as the *Ruhmeshalle*, *Ludwigstraße*, *Königsplatz*, *and Maximilianstraße* had been commissioned by the King. Captivated by Lola, and inspired by the Pope's wine, he doted on Lola. I began carrying two bottles, then three, to satisfy their daily needs. Five days after Lola's stage appearance, Ludwig presented her to his court in the palace reception hall.

The Queen did not attend.

"*Mein Herten,*" he announced, "I present to you my best friend."

He spent evenings in our hotel suite. Lola soon complained, "This apartment is so small, I must ask Manuela to leave when we wish to make love."

The next morning the King's messenger informed us of our move to a more exclusive hotel next to the palace. Lola quipped, "If I get any closer I'll be living in the Palace."

"No! No! No!" I said. "Queen Theresa may be a Protestant in this land of Jesuit Catholics, but the people love her. Never antagonize her."

Lola jibed, "I should introduce her to Baron von Malthausen. He'd finish her off."

"Don't even think that."

The rooms in our new hotel were larger and more numerous. When we spoke, an echo resounded off the bare walls. "This should be spacious enough," I noted.

Lola did not answer, but pointed at the drapes. "Replace those with mauve-colored ones, and select furniture to match."

"We haven't funds for the move, the rent and furnishings."

"Send all bills to the Royal Treasurer." Lola handed me her ermine muff. "This is full of Bavarian marks. Use them."

"Where are you going?"

"To complete unfinished business at our old hotel."

Lola left. I began the selection of furniture supplied by the hotel. The concierge awaited me in the basement, and I lunched with him and his wife. While we were eating, the King entered. The three of us almost fell from our chairs trying to stand and bow at the same time.

"Where is Lola?" Ludwig asked.

"At the dressmaker," I replied.

I saw his brow wrinkle. "I shouldn't disturb her. He turned to leave, stopped and said, "Manuela, have you the Pope's wine with you?"

"Yes, Sire." I reached for my bag, poured a glass and handed it to him.

He held it up to the lantern light and said, "I never thought wine would take the place of Munich's good brown beer." He drank. "I am getting lazy in my old age. I cannot get up as early, and have fallen behind in my administrative duties. The only thing I do better..." He stopped, turned to leave, and we bowed. In my mind I finished his sentence: "...is fornicate like a rabbit."

Lola returned. Her face was relaxed, her attitude buoyant, and I knew she'd had sex. But with whom? She would eventually tell me; she always did. She skipped from room to room, complimenting me on my choice and placement of the furnishings. I told her about the King's visit, asking for a bottle of the Pope's wine. "His footman should carry the bottle," I said.

"Ludwig is oblivious to what others think. Because of his diminished hearing and loud voice, people underestimate him. He takes advantage of their stupidity. The King is a gentle, yet a daring and creative, soul. I intend to bring out the best in him."

I breathed a sigh of relief. "You don't know how happy that makes me, for it is the true mission of a successful courtesan. Now tell me, in whose bed did you sleep?"

"My favorite Baron."

"Von Malthausen?"

"Yes."

"You bedded him?"

"He thought he bedded me. Revenge is sweet."

Lola! Lola! Lola!" I moaned. "You could ruin everything. Was there a public display?"

"Yes."

"Oh dear! Tell me."

"Not until we eat. I worked up an appetite. Order a rare steak and five raw oysters. I'm going to frolic with the King."

"Isn't it enough frolicking for one day?"

"If the King is drinking the Pontiff's wine, so am I. We will both be ready. Leave a bottle with me, draw my bath, and order dinner."

Lola slurped down the oysters one after the other and replaced the shells on their bed of crushed ice. She pushed aside the vegetables, and carved pieces of fat and blood-red meat from the steak. She chewed with gusto, ate fried potatoes and German sour pickles for which she had acquired a taste. The wine complemented the meal. Dessert included Black Forest chocolate cream cake.

I do not eat oysters; a small piece of steak and half slice of cake satisfied me. If I consumed half of what Lola did I would be fat as a horse. She never dieted, gained, or lost weight. I had raised the child, but stood in awe of her. , Sometimes blasphemous, often brilliant, with thoughtful then thoughtless actions. Lola also possessed the energy and determination to implement her concepts.

She told me about the Baron., They spent most of the afternoon in bed., Lola explained, "I told Heinrich I saved the best for last., We each drank a bottle of our special wine. ,I stood him spread eagled, stark naked, in the doorway. I used the sweet oil to anoint every part of his body. His phallus responded to my attention, and I guided him to the bed but not onto it. I put him on his knees at the foot of the bed, placed a pillow for him to rest his head, then liberally anointed his anus with the sweet oil."

"Did that excite him?"

"It did. He became very vocal when I shoved the fake pendant up his arse."

"You what!?"

"He deserved it. The rotten bastard took advantage of me."

"How did you get it out?"

"I didn't."

"That must have been painful."

"Not for me," Lola laughed, "But he doubled up in agony. I led him to the door and pushed him into the hallway."

"Without clothes?"

"Naked!"

"Were there people?"

"Not until I screamed into the hallway, slammed my door shut and locked it. I heard doors opening, people yelling and shrieking. I got dressed and came here."

"How will he get that thing out?"

"I left the chain on."

"Who would...? I mean, where can he go?"

"To a doctor."

"Stark naked?"

Lola shrugged.

"Malthausen might tell Ludwig. He's a third cousin."

Lola looked at me with pity. "Do you really think the Baron is going to admit passing off a phony pendant, then having it shoved up his backside?" She laughed. It became infectious. "Have you ever heard the English idiom, 'a pain in the arse'?"

I began laughing and said, "He's certainly not a smart arse."

Lola replied in French, "*Ca va chier des bulles*!"

"What does it mean?"

"He will shit bubbles!"

I laughed harder. "You mean baubles." My sides hurt, and I wheezed, "He'll poop a pile of brown pearls."

"They'll have to bust his arse to get it out!" Lola was crying, she laughed so hard.

"His arse was already cracked before you shoved it in," I said, and we laughed so hard we had to hold each other to stop from rolling on the floor. I gasped, "I'm laughing my arse off. Did you tell him why you did it?"

"I did. He said he didn't understand. I told him I'd rip his ears off and shove them up his arse with the phony brooch. That way he would hear better."

A notice in the morning papers announced, "Baron von Malthausen will return to Prussia." Lola smiled.

My Irish imp, known by a false Spanish name, supported by a powerful King, would soon achieve her goal; wealth, fame, and power were within her grasp.

What more could she achieve? What more could I do? Lola no longer needed me.

I yearned for Princess, and began plans for my return to India.

# CHAPTER 17

## THE DUCHESS OF LANDSFELD

Ludwig visited every afternoon. We went to lunch, then toured according to the weather—the museums, the university, the city, its parks and sports centers. He never tired of relating the city's history and his future plans for Munich. We returned in the evening. He often read his poems or discussed political, economic, and even military problems with Lola. She was a good listener and problem solver. I attended them, and took notes. Mostly they sipped the Pope's wine and munched soft pretzels from the Hofbräuhaus. They ate, whispered, even giggled, then retired.

The King ordered a portrait of Lola for his Gallery of Beauties. She sat for court artist, Karl Stieler, posing in the late mornings. Ludwig often visited to talk with her as the artist worked. I assumed Lola was content with the King's generosity.

Not two weeks after we moved into the apartment I overheard her complain, "Ludi, my love, I wish to be your helpmate. The most valuable thing I can do for you is create a salon."

"For what purpose?"

"To gather intelligence on foreign countries."

"Bavaria has spies, infiltrators, and a network of agents."

"France, England, and Prussia possess these capabilities. Yet, all finance salons. Knowing what the decision-makers are thinking can be crucial for the future. Spies observe and listen, but rarely do they acquire the opportunity to influence decisions. A salon can help implement your strategies."

"Is the effort worth the expense?"

"Von Metternich, Palmerston, and the French support salons in every major country, including Bavaria."

"How would you approach this venture?"

"Copy George Sand in Paris. My salon in Munich will circulate, accumulate information, and hope to influence those in power. Ludwig, my dear, you are oblivious to your position as the natural leader of the 39 Germanic States. This puts you in conflict with von Metternich. He is trying to bring Bavaria, and all of Germany, under Austro-Prussian rule."

"I am aware of his goal and my status. So are the Germanic states. They want me as a figurehead to forestall von Metternich. They are a fiercely independent lot; not one is prepared to relinquish his sovereignty to form a united Germany.

"There is also the problem of religion. Half of Germany is Catholic and the other half Protestant. There are Calvinists, Lutherans, Roman and Orthodox Catholics. Only war will bring them together. Prince von Metternich is Prussia's puppet. He and they want war; I do not. He desires to establish a hegemony of Germanic countries."

"The French, Russians, and English would oppose him."

"My dear Lola, for this reason I give your idea of a salon consideration. Bavaria is the key to control of the

Germanic states. My army combined with von Metternich's could easily dictate to the German States."

"What would he do with your army and the organized Germanic states?"

"Push the Russians back into Siberia. Isolate Belgium, then Holland, and France. Britain will not cross the channel to oppose him."

"You and Bavaria are the key to von Metternich's success.

"Correct. The Austrians are prepared to accept fifteen percent casualties invading Bavaria."

"How many do they estimate?"

"Twenty-five percent."

"From my salon I could rumor forty percent, and hint that the Bavarian mountain fighters are trained to cut his supply lines in winter. The Prussia-Austrian troops would suffer the same fate as Napoleon: freeze and starve to death. You, on the other hand, will retain interior lines of transportation, communication, and supply."

"What an amazing woman! Whatever the topic, you clarify the subject and focus my view. If you wore trousers you would be in my Cabinet."

"All I ask is to whisper in your ear."

"What is needed to implement this salon?"

I dropped a crochet stitch when Lola waved her arms saying, "This apartment is far too small to entertain ambassadors, royalty, the wealthy, and host them on holidays."

Ludwig sauntered across the room fingering his chin. "My cabinet complained about money spent for this apartment."

"Who appoints your Ministers?"

"I do."

"Discharge those who oppose you."

"I rule by influence, not decree. There are times I'd rather not be King."

Lola went to him and rested her head on his chest. "This is your burden. It is also your calling. God placed you here at this time in history for a reason. Build a palace for me to serve you, and I swear by all that is holy, the cost will be justified. I will gather information, spread tales true and false to mislead your foes and encourage your allies. I'll hamstring the Austrians—my goal, to obstruct and confuse your enemies, identify your supporters, and ascertain traitorous friends."

"The latter is important," Ludwig said and kissed her forehead. "My enemies I know; it is my so-called friends I fear. You are the only one with whom I speak freely. You say the truth, not just what I want to hear."

"I will support your every endeavor." Lola kissed him passionately. She stepped back, her blue eyes flashed lightening, and she growled, "No one will ever harm you while I stand guard." She poured two glasses of their wine, and they retired.

Two weeks later, Ludwig discharged one minister and bought a large home near his castle. He summoned the court architects, and ordered the building razed to the ground. He adapted the foundation to a small but eloquently designed palace for Lola.

Two weeks after that, he formally received Lola at court. The King granted Lola Montez from Limerick, Ireland, the title Duchess of Landsfeld, Bavarian citizenship, and an annual pension of twenty thousand florins. The yearly income of actors, teachers, and bakers is 400 florins.

Money once again flowed into my account. Her new status drew politicians, manufacturers, foreign delegates, even the military.

Ludwig arranged for a second appearance at the Royal Court Theater. She performed between the acts of *Mueller und Mueller*. The critics remained divided in their reviews.

The audience was less appreciative. Some hissed her performance. Ludwig's agents detained the most vociferous. Those employed by the government were transferred to the hinterland. Two business establishments lost their validation plaques of service to the Royal Household. It became obvious; do not insult the King's favorite.

The corps of university students was also divided, the larger, local Catholic group against Lola. Influenced by the Jesuits, they claimed her an imposter: born in Ireland, raised in India, and educated in Great Britain. They said she was rude to Bavarians and disrespectful of Queen Theresa. The smaller but more dedicated group, predominately Protestants from the north, petitioned the King to establish a sixth student corps dedicated to Lola. He consented.

Some Munich newspapers described Lola as a Latin hellcat; she had publicly pummeled the first violinist, routed the theater's stage manager, and punched the Hotel concierge after an altercation about unpaid bills. Lola attacked the policeman attempting to settle this dispute.

Munichens disliked her conduct. They accepted the King's right to courtesans, but the lady should be unobtrusive. People recognized the King's prerogative to confer the title Duchess of Landsfeld, but they rejected his right to grant Lola citizenship; that would require the Landtag's confirmation.

People publicly disdained her. Twice she was attacked while walking the street, once forced to seek refuge in a local Hofbräu House. She antagonized some people and beat a man with her riding crop. Citizens cursed her and threw horse droppings.

The police arrived. Outnumbered, they called for the Army. Ludwig heard. He set out alone in his carriage.

At the scene he strode through the angry mob. The people bowed in respect, and a path opened through the crowd. He entered the Hofbräu House, offered his arm to Lola, escorted her through the crowd to his carriage, and safely to her apartment.

Forty university cadets, all having pledged themselves to Lola, arrived at our apartment soon after the King departed. These young aristocrats from various German States vowed to protect Lola with their lives. They posted guards. She in turn chose her colors: gold, red and black. I purchased enough colored scarfs for all. These young men, between the ages of seventeen and twenty, went out and purchased their own uniforms: white silk culottes, black velvet vests, jaunty rubicund caps with gold trim, and a golden sash.

They took the name Alemannians, and organized themselves as guards for Lola. They watched the house by day and night, and ran alongside her carriage when she left the house. Ludwig approved the young men's dedication, but he did not appreciate their presence when he visited. He avoided people unfamiliar with his hearing disability and loud manner of speech. He requested the students not attend Lola while he visited. I tied one of the scarves to the balcony rail as permission for the Cadets to visit.

A similar scarf caused a major problem.

A university professor noticed a student in his lecture hall wearing Lola's colors. He found it repugnant. and requested the young man remove the scarf or himself from the hall. The young aristocrat stood, recited his family titles and said, "Herr Professor, you may leave."

The cadre of students in the hall were anti-Lola. They swarmed the young man, and threw him out of the building. His head bandaged and arm in a sling, he returned with a number of the Alemannians.

A fight ensued, and the police arrived. Word of the incident reached Lola. She ordered me to arrange a meeting of her students at the Hofbräuhaus.

We took a private room on the second floor. Forty young men sat at plank board tables with large steins of beer, munching two-foot-long salted pretzels. Lola sat flanked by Fritz Piesner and two other student leaders. The young men read speeches and poems, to Lola, and sang songs praising her beauty and the courage of the Alemammians, and they vowed their allegiance to Lola.

She readily perceived the benefits of their support for her and Ludwig. All were titled aristocrats from the Germanic States, and they had their fathers' ears. In the future they would inherit their parent's titles and power. My little Lola could write valuable addendums to the

*Kama Sutra's* advice to courtesans.

But what happened next astounded me. Lola put everything in jeopardy.

I sat behind and to her right. The young men at the table all wore tightfitting knee-length trousers—culottes—that buttoned in a flap in front. It wasn't unusual for the bulge of the penis and scrotum to be seen through the cloth, especially if the man had an erection. This was the case of the seventeen-year-old sitting at Lola's right.

Her hand moved stealthily under the table until it reached his knee. I saw her squeeze, and him quiver. She began to massage his leg, moving higher with each stroke. What amazed me was her ability to follow and participate in the discussion at the table while doing so. Even more shocked was Piesner, the student leader, seated on her left. He stared wide-eyed at Lola's manipulations of his companion's penis, and Lola knew he was watching.

She reached out with her left hand and squeezed Piesner's scrotum. He gulped, choked, and blew the beer froth out of his mug. She whispered to him, "We will meet after." Her right hand never ceased to massage the young man on her right. Suddenly he stiffened and began screaming, "EEEEaaaahhhhh! EEEEaaaahhhhh! EEEEaaaahhhhh!"

A wet stain appeared on his trousers. He remained stiff as a board from head to toe. One of the young men down the table explained to Lola, "its epilepsy: the curse of kings, caused by inbreeding." Three young men carried the student away. Lola raised her glass of the Pope's wine. She did not care for beer, and said to Piesner on her left, "Do you know what the *Kama Sutra* is?"

He wagged his head. "No."

"Tonight I will teach you."


It was Lola's first experience with a virgin male. Piesner was twenty years old, well-muscled and mentally malleable. When alone with Lola I berated her in the strongest language. She had placed everything she worked and sacrificed for in danger. I made her tell me everything. I think she enjoyed reliving it. Lola climaxed once during her description.

"I undressed him, then allowed him to undress me. I stood him in the doorway and massaged him all over with my hands, my body and my lips."

"The Spread Eagle," I said. "Did he last long?"

"Not very. Then I took the same position and he worked on me."

"Was he attentive?"

"I instructed him. He lost control and took me standing up, ramming me against the wall and onto the small table near the door. I thought he'd go into an epileptic fit. His eyes rolled up into his head. Then he buried his face in my breasts and began to cry."

"Was that it?"

"Just the beginning. The boy is a sexual predator. If he marries, his wife will be bowed-legged and pregnant all the days of her life. I had to change the sponge three times."

"What did he do?"

"We fornicated. Six times."

"Six?"

"I never experienced anything like it. If there were a

seventh, I would have passed out. Instead, he collapsed. I dressed him and sent him out the servant's entrance."

Two nights later the distressed Piesner contacted Lola. His penis leaked, and he thought it might be a sign of the pox. I explained to him it was a strain; the muscles of the penis, overused, allows leakage. Six times in one night can be considered cruel and unusual punishment."

"I did not intend to hurt the countess."

"I meant punishment to your penis."

"Can I do it again?"

"Only you can answer that question,"

"I would like to do it every day for the rest of my life," Piesner blurted, "If the Duchess of Landsfeld agrees."

Lola and I smiled and I led him to the door.

The tenuous sexual situation was aggravated further. Unbeknown to me, Lola entered into a relationship with one of the Palace guards. Lieutenant Nusbammer stood six feet tall, with square, strong German features, light blue eyes, and blond hair, and he filled the uniform from boots to epaulets. How she maintained sexual relationships with him, the three student leaders—Piesner, Hertheim, and Laibinger—and the King, I do not know. She showed no ill effects.

These three young students who ran at the side of her carriage could no longer keep up. Her favorite person was Ludwig, her cherished lover, Nusbammer, for fun and exploration, the three students.

One evening she drank too much of the Pope's wine in preparation for Ludwig. They called him to convene an emergency session of the Landtag. Alone, and fired by the cocaine-laden wine, Lola summoned the Lieutenant. Nusbammer did not respond.

She flew into a rage. I followed her out into the night, and she directed our carriage to number 9 *Fruhlingstrafe*. We stopped there, Lola strode to the front doorway, gazed for a second at the line of bell handles, and proceeded to ring them all. A formidable middle-aged woman in night clothes appeared, demanding Lola explain her actions. "Step back!" Lola ordered. "I wish to see Lieutenant Nusbammer."

"He is not at home. He left earlier with friends."

"I will see for myself!"

"You will not!" The large woman jammed her meaty fists onto her ample hips blocking Lola. Lola raised her riding crop. The Concierge punched Lola so hard she flew backward into me, and we both ended up on the sidewalk. Lola was unconscious. I required a neighbor's help to put her in the carriage.

This episode made the front pages of Munich's morning newspapers. Articles attacked her for causing a public disturbance and being discourteous to the King and Queen. They accused her (rightly so) of influencing Ludwig to replace the Minister of Education with one of her friends. Detractors named our Salon the Lolaministerium.

Instead of hurting Lola, it strengthened her position. She became the King's confidant. She influenced Ludwig to approve yearly endowments for three families, all favored guests in our Salon.

The smell of wealth and influence drew more people to Lola. Many supported the new Alemaine student's corps. The young men added a gay, stimulating spirit to the Salon. In addition to attending, flattering, and often bedding or being bedded by the more mature women, they became spokesmen for Lola's views on and off the campus.

Lola leased a home nearby as a clubhouse for them. I don't know when they studied. Almost every night they held wild drinking parties, which Lola often attended.

She did complain to Ludwig that not one of his ministers or senior civil servants frequented her Salon. She claimed that the Jesuits influenced his cabinet members, and she was correct. The Catholics were furious at Lola's usurping their power and control of the Education Ministry. Her lackey's first major change, dictated by Lola, was to include Protestant Church Schools in the Bavarian education system.

This pleased the King, a devout Catholic but a religious free thinker. It delighted Queen Theresa. She remained a fervent Protestant, and her church schools would now receive state funds. The city of Munich, ninety percent Catholic, did not appreciate change.

The English Consul visited. "You angered the Jesuits," he said. "Lord Palmerston admires that." He handed a purse to me.

"The Jesuits are always after me," Lola said.

"By controlling the Education Ministry you declared war on them," Favish said. "Bavaria inherited a large population of Protestants in settlement of the Napoleonic War. Many aristocrats supported the Jesuits. The thirty-nine German states combined into the Deutscher Bund. Its purpose, to replace the Holy Roman Empire as a buffer between Islam and Europe. However, the German States are divided between Catholic and Protestant.

The Jesuits want the German states and all Europe to be Roman Catholic. The individualistic personalities of the German people oppose them. After the Plague, the thirty-nine States turned to Ludwig as arbitrator. He brought order to the religiously divided, vibrant, but chaotic German economy."

"He succeeded," Lola said. "Bavaria and the Deutscher Bund are thriving."

"Ludwig's success makes him a target for Austria. He blocked Dutch incursions into the Germanies. He assigned military to guard against a Turkish invasion. Most important, he regulated German ports, shipping and shipbuilding. He expanded the Deutscher Bund merchant navy. The King is respected. With no territorial ambitions, Ludwig threatens no one."

"Except von Metternich."

"Exactly," Favish said. Then he asked a totally irrelevant question. "Can you access letters received or sent by the King?"

"He often uses my writing desk," Lola admitted. "He takes the open mail. Those unread letters or ones to be sent, remain."

"I mail them," I said.

"I must teach you to use this." He held up a thin four-inch sliver of bamboo, slotted two thirds of the way down its length.

"What is it for?" Lola asked.

"Extracting mail from envelopes without any one suspecting."

"How can you do it without breaking the seal?" .

"Is there a letter sealed by the King?"

I brought a letter to him. He sat me opposite and

looked at the front of the envelope. "It is addressed to his sister. Probably unimportant, but you can never tell." He turned the envelope over. Only the wax impressed seal held it together. "Notice, the seal holds down all four flaps where they come together in the center. I place the envelope before the lamp. Notice the outline of the letter inside. I insert this slotted bamboo in and up through the lower right corner flap. Fit the slot over the letter inside. I twist the bamboo, rolling the letter tight, then slip it out."

He unrolled the letter off the bamboo, read it and said, "His sister is quite dear to Ludwig."

He handed the letter and bamboo to me. "Try putting it back." I reversed his steps and untwisted the letter inside the envelope. Only the slightest wrinkle marred the envelope's corner. I smoothed it with my thumb.

"Good," the Consul said and turned to Lola. "Is it true you fired your pistol into a crowd?"

"They harassed me on the Boulevard."

"You might have killed someone."

"Of course. But I didn't aim at them."

"As individuals, Munichens are independent enough. As a group they can become violently unrestrainable. Do not alienate them."

Lola sipped her wine, held up the glass and said, "Our supply of the Pope's spirits is running low."

"Storms in the North Sea delayed your shipment. Our agents hear whispers the King may ask you to marry Lieutenant Nusbammer."

"What!" Lola shouted. "That's ridiculous! I prevented Ludwig from exiling Nusbammer to the Austrian frontier."

"The marriage would be a legal fiction. The idea is accepted among royalty. It legitimizes your status as a Bavarian citizen, takes away the peoples argument against you, and removes any embarrassment for Queen Theresa."

"The Queen and I met by chance in the Palace. We exchanged a few words. She is very pleasant. As for the Munichens, they can go to hell. Ludwig is King. He listens to me." Lola pointed at her desk and ordered me, "Bring those poems he wrote." She read:

> "Two rocks are we, against which constantly are breaking
>
> The adversaries' craft, the enemies' open rage;
>
> But scorpion-like themselves, they pierce with deadly sting.
>
> The sanctuary is guarded by trust and faith:
>
> The enemies' cruelty will be avenged on themselves—
>
> Love will compensate for all that we have suffered."

Lola looked up and said, "This second one he calls, 'Sonnet to Lolitto'." She read further:

> "If, for my sake, thou hast renounced all ties,
>
> I, too, for thee have broken with them all;
>
> Life of my life, I am thine—I am thy thrall—

I hold no compact with thine enemies.

Their blandishments are powerless on me,

No arts will serve to seduce me from thee,

With thee my earthly pilgrimage will end....

So, until death, with thee my being is blend-ed.

In thee I have found what I ne'er yet found in any—

The sight of thee gave new life to my being.

All feeling for any other has died away..."[9]

"The man is infatuated with you," Favish said.

"Ha!" Lola guffawed. And I realized she drank more wine than she could manage. She said, "You want a stable relationship? The King will do whatever I say. He worships me. The man kisses my feet." She looked at the Ambassador. "You seem surprised. He sometimes sucks my toes and does other things with his tongue..."

I took her by the arm. "It is late. The Ambassador will excuse us."

---

[9] *The Unknown Queen* by Ishbel Ross p. 19

# CHAPTER 18

## FRAU GANSER

Frau Ganser was recommended by Baron Pecham to manage our household staff and interpret for us. She worshipped the King. Lola's flirtations and sexual activities upset her. She viewed it as a betrayal of her Sovereign—and she reported it to Baron Pecham. "That woman is evil," Frau Ganser said. "Madam Montez is the King's consort, but sullies his name by sleeping with any man she meets. She beds the young student leader, Piesner, his two friends and Lieutenant Nusbammer."

Pecham clapped his hand over his mouth but Frau Ganser heard him gasp, "Together?"

"Sometimes the three students, but Nusbammer is always alone. There are others."

"God in heaven! The woman must be mad. Proof, Frau Ganser: I require proof."

The woman reached into a pocket of her house dress and produced a diary. In concise, unembellished terms were names, dates, times and places. "Frau Ganser," the Baron asked, "Would you be prepared to explain to the King what you revealed to me?"

"I considered that. It is too embarrassing for me, so I reported to you."

"Do you consider yourself a loyal subject of our King?"

"Yes! Yes!."

"Then it is your duty to inform his majesty. As a Bavarian, and Munichen, and good Christian woman in the service of our King, you are obligated to protect him. I will arrange a discreet meeting: you, my loyal Frau Ganser, I and the King."

Others approached Baron Pecham with stories of Lola's escapades. He disregarded most, believing them petty jealousies. She smoked cigars in public, appeared at shooting galleries and bowling emporiums—places where women were prohibited. She joined the betting, often embarrassing the men by winning. The newspapers related every negative incident, including Lola's arguments with vendors for unpaid debts. She forwarded the bills to the State Treasurer. What remained a thorn in the eye of most Munichens was her Bavarian citizenship. Legally, the Burghers had the privilege to confer nationality; It had been given without a vote in the Landtag by Ludwig. Whispers of dissent filled the streets, homes, and beer gardens.

Frau Ganser, a short, stocky, unobtrusive woman who said little and did much, also translated for us. She wrote our German correspondence and managed the household staff. It was only after the Nusbammer affair that we learned Baron Pecham headed the Bavarian Intelligence Service.

Both he and Frau Ganser were dedicated Jesuits. He set Frau Ganser to spy on us. Lola's meeting Lieutenant Nusbammer was accidental; it evolved into a controversy with the King.

A handsome, dashing, young cavalry officer assigned to the palace guard, he strolled Munich's main street. We became involved in an altercation.

It was my fault. Lola loves animals, and she pur-chased a dog. Turk was the largest Boxer I ever saw; I think his mother mated with a horse. He weighed more than I, and slobbered over everything. Standing on his hind legs, he put his paws on my shoulders and looked down at me.

Like all males, Turk loved Lola. I was charged with holding him on a long leather leash. He was obedient. When I stopped, he sat. He didn't pull. We stood on the street discussing the purchase of some paintings for the new palace with Frau Ganser.

I didn't see Turk wander toward a family nearby. The youngest was eating ice-cream in a sugar-wafer cup. The dog walked over, sniffed the youngster and ate the ice-cream, cup and all, in one big slurp. To add insult to theft, Turk slobbered on the little one. The child's eyes widened and he shrieked. The parents thought he was being mauled, but soon realized what happened.

They berated me until Lola stepped in and punched the husband, bloodying his nose. The wife stepped for-ward, and Frau Ganser translated, "You hit my husband because he is a gentleman and would not hurt you." Lola promptly knocked the woman down with a punch to the jaw.

A crowd gathered. Someone recognized Lola, and people became angry. The crowd grew larger. They shouted and threatened us. Young Lieutenant Nusbammer came to the rescue: he whisked us three and Turk into a passing cab.

Lola invited the Lieutenant to visit. He did. His visits became so frequent that Ludwig questioned Lola. "Oh, he's in love with me," she said. "I fear I'll break his heart if I send him away. The young fellow will be ruined." The King accepted Lola's explanation, and only asked that Nusbammer not be there when he arrived.

I went out every day to deal with the contractors, artists and craftsmen. Lola wrote detailed descriptions of furniture she wanted for the palace. Money came my way from all directions. If the road were not made of Belgium blocks, there would be a well-worn path to the money-changer. Cash came without my asking: workmen, contractors, craftsmen and artists applying for specific jobs.

If I granted it, they handed me ten percent of the total amount. I bargained well for the King, who paid the bills. The money flowed into my pockets. Sculptors, stone masons, carpenters and housing supply people paid it. I had no time to feel guilty. I left the apartment early and returned after dark.

From the servants I learned that Nusbammer visited regularly. I warned Lola he would cause trouble. One day the King and Nusbammer passed each other in the hallway, but Ludwig believed Lola's explanation of the young officer's infatuation. She alleviated the King's suspicions, but did not lessen mine. She was bedding Nusbammer in addition to the student leader. For what? Nusbammer came from a no-account family: no money, no business, and no future in the army. The three students must wait years to inherit independence, wealth, and significant titles.

Ludwig saw Nusbammer again, and he complained to Lola. I sat her down and wanted to know why this young officer attracted her.

"A bent tallywhacker," she answered. "He is normally endowed in length and girth, but his penis is bent up at the front end. It touches a place no one else reaches. I tell him how to stroke me, and he listens. Oh!" she said, and shivered, squeezing her thighs together. "The wine heightens the experience, but it is that upward thrust of his tallywhacker that makes him special."

"Special enough to give up your title, the palace being built for you, your annual stipend, not to mention an open account on the King's treasury?"

"I thought about it," Lola said. "I can convince Ludwig black is white and up is down. He loves me and accepts anything I say."

"I have read about this kind of infatuation. In Hindi it is called, 'Thunder Love'. It comes during the Monsoon season. I never witnessed it. Do you enjoy sex with the King?" I asked.

"I enjoy sex with anyone. Everyone! I like sex! It is a good thing you taught me to be a courtesan; otherwise I'd be a poor whore, paying others to lay with me."

"How did Nusbammer's thing get bent?"

"He said he woke up after a night of drinking, lying face down on the floor. He still had an erection, and was lying on top of it. It was bent. He tried tying it to a small board, but it never straightened. Thank God."

Two days later it happened again. Frau Ganser told me the King was so angry at seeing Nusbammer that he and Lola quarreled. Ludwig issued orders, and the Lieutenant was transferred to a distant outpost on the Austrian border.

I should have been alerted to Frau Ganser's access to

such information from a higher echelon. I spoke to Lola about Frau Ganser. She took my arm and marched me to the King's office.

Within minutes we were with the King. He sent two ministers, several noblemen and myself out of the room. He and Lola spoke in loud tones, and we in the ante-room heard. Because they spoke in Spanish, only I understood everything. These were intelligent men. By the look on their faces. they also comprehended. It became public knowledge.

The Duchess of Landsfeld, that evil Spanish woman, convinced our naïve King to rescind the order of banishment and allow Nusbammer to remain in Munich. Ludwig even allowed the Lieutenant to visit Lola—but never in his presence.

He did demand that Lola get rid of Turk. The animal was flatulent. Ludwig couldn't hear Turk pass gas, but we all smelled the noxious odor. When the dog broke wind, poetry, conversation, and reading stopped. I opened the windows and fanned the stench from the room.

Lola cried, but gave Turk to a farmer and his family. I often wonder if the farmer was able to feed the animal. Turk ate like his father the horse. I suppose I get silly every now and then.

It is time to leave Lola. I sent so much money to my Princess that she must be the wealthiest virgin in India. She is probably the oldest. It is time to go home—but my hand is caught in the jar. I am the monkey. I have seen poverty, and I can't let go of such wealth.

I will buy my Princess a Maharajah to wed, build her a palace: a large fairyland with many rooms. It will have a reflecting pool, with water lilies and colored carp. It will be surrounded by pure white stone arches and jasmine vines scenting the air. It will have a special kitchen to feed the poor, and places for them to shade under mimosa trees. I will build a theater and invite artists, traveling circuses, famous musicians and singers. If I can locate Guru Rama Singh, I will arrange a hostel for him and his followers.

These are my dreams. I often take them out and revel in them, then put them away for the future.

While I was dreaming of the future, reality came knocking.

Baron Pecham approached the King. "As your Chief of Secret Police, it is my duty to protect you. To accomplish this I must investigate everyone with whom you meet, preferably prior to the occasion. This was not the case with Baroness Montez. Sire, may I speak frankly?"

"You had better. We have worked together for over fifteen years. My confidence in you is absolute. You are one of the few people in my Cabinet who never uttered a word against my Lolita."

"I must now be placed in the larger category of The Baroness's detractors."

"My good fellow, don't look so perplexed. Do your duty."

"Sire, you must be aware of the confusion, arguments, and confrontations the Baroness had prior to arriving in Bavaria: riots in England, and France, almost a revolution in Poland. Where she goes there is trouble; this includes Munich."

"Save yourself the recitation of her encounters in our

city. She tells me everything."

The Baron cleared his throat. "She antagonizes your people. There is a hatred of this Spanish foreigner."

"That is only in Munich, and by those who would usurp my authority."

"The people love you. Munich is the capital of Bavaria and you are leader of the Deutscher Bund: thirty-nine German States."

"You forget that I made her a Munichen."

"Without permission of the Landtag. The people are irate. They query your actions with the Baroness, and they question her behavior in general."

"Specifics, Pecham. Give me specifics," Ludwig ordered.

"The Baroness speaks openly of Your Majesty's favors to her."

"That is nothing but petty jealousy, and resentment by those seeking my favor."

"It is further charged she boasts of her influence over your decisions in affairs of state."

"I am King. No one will convince me of that which I oppose."

"Sire, a week before you decreed the salary increase for teachers, Baroness Montez told people in her Salon that she convinced you to do so."

"Lolita spoke the truth. She always does. She presented the idea in the phrase, 'Nations will no longer be judged by the number of its population but by the level of its education.' I believe she is correct. And you, my dear Pecham, are not wrong. She should be more discreet. I will speak to her. But no one speaks of her good qualities. Do you know that wherever we go she feeds the poor?"

"Yes, Sire. Charity is a most desirable quality. If your Majesty will not take offense, I will make further use of your grant of total frankness. The entire city talks of Baroness Montez allowing men to visit her, during the day and at night after you leave – specifically, Lieutenant Nusbammer. Then there is the leader of the Alemaine student's corps, Piesner. And his two friends"

"Now, look—my God, that's nothing. I know. Lola tells me. I forbade Nusbammer to be there when I am. Do you have specific proof of Lolita's infidelity to me?"

"I do not."

"There you have it."

"Sire, you know of the affair on *Fruhlingstrafe*."

"You mean where the female Concierge knocked out the impersonator?"

"Impersonator?"

"Yes, my dear Pecham. Be assured, upon hearing of the incident I rushed to my Lolita. She sat as calmly as could be, reading Dumas' latest play. I prepared to banish the impersonator from the Kingdom, but Lolita with her kind heart pleaded with me not to disgrace the woman. The Baroness is a most forgiving person."

Baron Pecham emitted a frustrated sigh. "Sire, I would like you to listen to Frau Ganser."

"Isn't she the sculptor's wife?"

"Yes, your Majesty. I placed her in the Baroness' household to manage the staff and translate."

"And to spy?" Ludwig smiled. "Well, that is your business, spying. What has Frau Ganser to tell me?"

"I would rather you hear it from her lips."

"When will I meet her?"

"She is in the anteroom."

The King motioned for Pecham to bring the woman in.

Frau Ganser entered. She curtsied, bowed, and waited for permission to speak.

"Madame Ganser, a pleasure to see you," the King welcomed her. "Your husband's sculptures for Baroness Montez's palace are commendable."

"Thank you, Sire."

Ludwig recognized the signs of distress in the woman's face: tears brimmed her eyes, and she clutched a black notebook to her breast. "My dear Frau Ganser, I know you as a loyal subject..." Before he could finish, she fell on her knees and kissed his boots. She held up the notebook.

"What is this?"

"Betrayal, Sire."

"By whom?"

"The Spaniard."

"Not Lolita! Never!" He opened the notebook and perused the pages. He began to tremble, and collapsed on his knees with Frau Ganser.

In addition to assignations with Nusbammer, the student leader, and others, Lola bragged of influencing the King to replace a Provincial Governor and Minister of Transportation with her supporters. She wrote in a letter to Alexandre Dumas that she had isolated Ludwig from former friends and mistresses.

Baron Pecham helped the King to his feet.

Ludwig's sister—Charlotte Auguste, the Dowager Empress of Austria—happened to be visiting Munich. Ludwig went to her and poured out his heart.

"Happiness is not for this earth. I was happy here, but now I am thrown down from my heaven. The unbelievable happened. The years I have yet to live I had hoped to spend in exalted love with my Lolita. It was a dream... It is over now. But no undue haste. The bearer of this," he held up the black notebook, "The wife of the sculptor Ganser, presented this evidence. I invited Lolita here. If I break with her forever, I must see her once more. As King, I am ashamed. As a sixty-year old man, I am not." He wept on his sister's shoulder. "I honor and love the Queen, but her conversation is inadequate for my spirit, and my heart. I thought I found it in Lolita."[10]

His sister embraced him and said, "Stop torturing yourself. The Spaniard deserves your scorn. If she appears here, send her away. Never see her again."

"No!" Ludwig said. "I cannot condemn her without a hearing. Don't worry, I can reorganize myself. She deserves the right to answer the charges."

"Are you hoping she can refute this evidence?" She pointed at the notebook.

"She could be innocent," Ludwig pleaded. "Or possibly not as guilty as it appears in Frau Ganser's notes."

"Ludwig," His sister said, "My presence in Munich is not as casual as it appears. State leaders of the Deutscher Bund requested me to appraise your ability to rule in light of Countess Montez's influence."

Ludwig stepped back, stiffened. "I defeated an entire Army of Napoleon's finest divisions." He tapped the medals on his chest. "These awards attest to my ability in war. If my former comrades-in-arms desire to test my

---

[10] *Lola Montez* by Brice Seymour p 122

army, I will crush them."

"No one is threatening war. You and I are related to almost every royal family in Europe. But von Metternich is stirring the European pot. There are dangers. Berlin's intelligence reports that von Metternich and the Jesuits will attempt to bribe Lola to leave you and Bavarian politics."

"They already have. Metternich's agents offered her 250,000 francs. Lolita told them to go to hell. Now you see? What appears simple and clear has many facets." He waved the notebook, "Her faithlessness causes me much pain. However, I cannot condemn her without a hearing. That would be unjust."

"You know von Metternich is like a pit–bull. He will hound you."

"Baron Pecham and his people will protect me."

A butler entered. "Sire," he said, "Baroness Montez and her maid desire an audience."

Ludwig's sister, warned by Pecham that Lola often carried a stiletto or pistol, moved behind the sofa. Ludwig received Lola. He sat her down on the sofa and held up Frau Ganser's notebook. His sister said, "What must be said is confidential. Please dismiss your maid."

I left.

The following Lola related to me.

> "I sat on one end of the sofa, Ludwig on the other. The Dowager Empress stood behind. The Empress pointed at the black notebook in Ludwig's hand, and summed up a list of my supposed betrayals of her brother. In respect I remained silent. Then she said, 'The purpose

of this meeting is to make a separation between you and the King as amicable as possible.'

"She began to reproach me for purported,
despicable acts of infidelity resulting in public embarrassment to the King. 'Never! Never! Never!' I shouted. 'I would lay down my
life for my one and only love!'

"I realized Ludwig was on the verge of tears.
I jumped up, and threw my shawl and hat at
his sister. Words poured from my lips—I
don't recall them. It was shocking enough to
drive Ludwig's sister from the room.

"I went around smashing things and screaming at the King. His sister peeked in, and I
threw a Chinese vase that broke against the
door. I approached Ludwig. Poor old Ludwig
sat with his hands folded in his lap, eyes cast
down. I placed my fingers under his chin and
lifted his face. I stared into his eyes and said,
'Ludi, my Sovereign, and my love, I cannot
ask your forgiveness for things which never
occurred. I am innocent. I swear it by all that
is holy. I swear by my father's grave. Everything in that notebook is lies. You want me to
leave? Say it! I will be off to Paris this very
evening. Oh Ludwig, my love...'

"I stumbled about, tearing at my clothes. He
hurried to stop me, and the moment our flesh
touched I knew he was mine again. I wasn't

going to let him off that easily. I berated him for not trusting me, for setting spies on me, when I thought of him as a better person. His heart was torn between me and the notebook. I shed a flood of tears, and the contents of Frau Ganser's book were washed away.

"Ludwig spent a half an hour confirming his love for me, and we reconciled. I agreed not to leave Munich. Ludwig admitted that even if all the accusations were true, he would forgive me. He loves me more than life itself. On our way out his sister said, 'Ludwig, you will not see her again!' *'Au contraire,'* the King replied. 'I will compose a poem which I shall read this evening to my Lolita.'

"'Ludwig!' his sister shouted, 'Forgo pleasures of the flesh for the sake of your honor, your people, and the future of Bavaria!'

"'Enough!' Ludwig snapped. 'I am King. No one dictates to me.'"

I followed Lola to the carriage, and she told me everything. I thought she would take a nap after the confrontation. Instead, she went to her desk and wrote a letter to Alexander Dumas. Usually I scanned her letters for errors or grammatical mistakes, but.this envelope she sealed with her signet ring in hot wax and left it for me to post. I waited until she slept, took the slotted bamboo stick, removed the letter and read.

"Well dear Alexandre, I left Paris at the beginning of June as a lady errant and raced about the world and today I am Baroness of Landsfeld with the title of Countess! I have a lovely property which is just now being completed. Horses, servants, in sum, everything that could surround the mistress of the King of Bavaria.

"Here I am encircled by great ladies. Everywhere I go, all of Munich waits upon me, ministers of state, generals, great ladies, and I no longer recognize myself as Lola Montez. The King loves me passionately; he's given me an income of 50,000 francs for life and has already spent more than 300,000 francs on my property, etc. etc.

"I do everything here. The King publicly shows his great love for me. He walks with me, goes out with me. Every week I have a party for ministers etc. etc., which he attends and where he can't do me enough homage."

(Lola failed to mention Ludwig's order for ministers to attend Lola's Salon.)

"I know dear Alexandre you always wished me well and this news will please you. That is why I am writing, because although surrounded by all the glories and homage of my ambitious hopes, alas, sometimes I dream, I think of Paris. Dear Paris! In truth there is no real happiness in grandeur. There is much envy, so many intrigues. You always have to play the great lady and weigh your words to each individual! Alas! My joyful life in Paris!

"But I am resolved. I won't leave this world to which I find myself elevated as if by a miracle. The King has a true passion for me. He has never had mistresses before."

(What did Lola think the Gallery of Beauties was but a collection of portraits of his mistresses?)

"But my character pleases him. He is a man of remarkable talent. A true genius and one of the most elegant poets currently existing in Europe. My slightest whim is a command for him, and all of Munich is bewildered. They don't know what to say anymore. He loves me so much that everyone I like is immediately in favor.

"Give my regards to all our acquaintances. Oh Paris! There I suffered so much and was also so happy.

"Farewell dear friend. I send you a kiss. Thank God you are not here because I can have neither friend nor... Grandeur is so difficult!

"Your ever affectionate, Lola"[11]

---

[11] *Lola Montez*, Bruce Seymour p120, 121

# CHAPTER 19

## INCIDENTS

Lola's Palace appeared miniscule compared to the King's, but no less impressive in style and beauty. The cost ran twenty-five percent over the budget set by Ludwig.

The Minister of Finance complained. Cabinet members supported him. Jealousy inspired many, others honestly denounced the king's spendthrift ways. Ludwig signed for everything. How could he do otherwise? He helped plan, build and furnish the Palace.

The people dubbed it Lola's-Ministerium. It was located in the fashionable Barerstrasse neighborhood near Ludwig's Palace, the entrance landscaped with a formal English garden. The crushed mother-of-pearl, half-moon carriage way to the portico entrance framed a pool on the left with four marble dolphins spouting water. The Palace received the first plate glass used in Bavaria, which allowed for larger windows. The interior became more viewable from outside and sun-lit inside. The windows could be shielded by iron shutters. The massive front doors were made of oak. The finest woodcarvers in Bavaria created an integrated scene from the Black Forest. Bear, deer, wolves, rabbits and squirrels frolicked under carved wooden trees, through brambles, around bushes and waterfalls. Throughout the house hinges, doorknobs, window grips and French door accoutrements were cast in burnished bronze. Liveried footmen greeted the guests. Italian marble floors mirrored their footwear. One's gaze was drawn to the magnificent crystal staircase spiraling up to the mistress's bedchamber.

How could the King remonstrate with Lola about expenditures? He decided on much of the furnishings, the pure white matching marble mantles over fireplaces. He selected Italian and Spanish artworks, his taste impeccable—and expensive. He furnished the large kitchen close to the dining room with double swinging doors to reduce noise. On the second and third floors were numerous bedrooms, dressing rooms, and baths. Below, the magnificent dining room could be extended into the entranc-way to seat four hundred and fifty guests. Lola's Palace represented a stunning example of classical Italian architecture. Using modern materials, working through the nights by torchlight, with German efficiency and attention to detail, workmen completed it in only a few months.

Prior to our moving, a group of us walked from the theater to the hotel. We found a party in the lobby hosted by the hotel owner for his suppliers. The owner invited us to join them. Lola remained aloof, but many of our group joined the festivities.

One of our companions, a coarse fellow who worked as a croupier in the Munich Casino, argued with the hotel owner. The owner asked him to leave. He became boisterous. Two large waiters escorted him to the door and threw him out.

Lola observed the incident. She entered the lobby, slapped the waiters with her riding crop and shouted at the owner, "That man is my guest, and I am your guest. Be so kind as to treat us so."

The hotel owner remonstrated with her. She hit him with the riding crop. His son intervened, pushing Lola away from his father. Lola tore into the son. Members of our party pulled her off. The owner told her to leave his hotel. She turned to me and said, "Attend our move tomorrow!" The son summoned the police. Upon hearing this, Lola sent me to inform the King.

Ludwig woke, listened, dressed, and we returned to the hotel. Police and newspaper reporters waited. The King ignored the latter, and listened to the police officers. He soothed the hotel owner, and sent Lola and myself to our rooms. He ordered the police back to barracks. All the newspapers carried the story. This took place on Wednesday evening.

On Saturday afternoon Lola went shopping with her retinue of fawning office seekers, among them a tall, handsome young German sailor, an ordinary seaman but a fine specimen of a man. I never learned where she found him.

We approached the Fraunkirche Cathedral. A large beer wagon was being unloaded for the Priests. One huge, powerful man pulled the barrels off the rear of the wagon, and they landed on a large hemp pillow at his feet. With one hand he rolled the barrels to several men, who pushed them onto two boards leading through a basement window down into the cool dark cellar of the church.

A stray dog wandered over to the big man unloading the beer barrels and began nipping his legs. At first the man tried to shoo the animal away. When that failed, he planted his boot into the side of the mongrel and sent him sailing and yelping through the air. He landed in front of Lola crying in pain.

My mistress didn't hesitate. She went after the big man with her riding crop, the sailor right behind her. The big deliveryman crossed his arms in front of his face to protect himself from Lola's fury. He could have swatted her like a bug, but instead, he grabbed the sailor by the throat with his left hand, jammed his right hand into the seaman's crotch, picked him up and slammed him down on the hemp pillow. The seaman didn't bounce up as the barrels did. He lay limp, spread eagled over the bundle of hemp.

"You killed him!" Lola screamed. "He's dead!"

I saw his chest heave and his hand close and open. Passersby and people leaving church heard Lola. Word spread that the Spanish woman killed a young German sailor.

More people from across the street came. They milled around. Tempers grew. Men and women shouted at Lola. Friends whisked her away, but not fast nor far enough. The crowd pinned us against the shop windows. We now faced an angry mob growing larger by the moment.

We took shelter in a jewelry shop. The crowd outside numbered over three hundred. Lola's two military bodyguards, assigned by Ludwig, sneaked away through the mob. They made for the nearest police garrison. When ten officers arrived, five hundred people surrounded the jewelry shop, thwarting the police.

Outnumbered, the constables became spectators to a horde of angry Munichens attempting to break into the jewelry shop. The shop security door and its grilled protection of the large window prevented their entrance. The mood outside grew uglier. Word spread that the Countess of Landsfeld swore the Burgers of Munich would rot in jail before she would leave Bavaria. The crowd chanted, "No citizenship! No citizenship!"

Word of the confrontation spread throughout the city. More than a thousand gathered outside the shop. The Alemaine student corps attempted to come to her aid, but they couldn't get near. They went around the rear to the service entrance of a Guest House, borrowed a ladder, entered the rear of the shop and took Lola and myself out. We went down the ladder, through a guest house window, and by carriage to our new abode in Lola's palace. Ludwig sent mounted Hussars to disperse the crowd. The mood in Munich turned against the King.

The following day was Sunday. Lola said she must show herself to the people of Munich. She planned to walk the main street. According to her instructions I put out one of her more revealing dresses, certainly not a Sunday dress. We strolled the avenue. She timed our passing the Fraunkirche Cathedral as services finished. Most people looked away. Many harsh stares followed us. Not a word was spoken.

That evening Lola timed our arrival to her private box in the Royal Theater to coincide with the King's entrance in the box next to ours. The audience stood and bowed to the King. Lola made it appear they bowed to her. She infuriated many by nodding acknowledgement and bowing in return.

Lola went to the jewelry shop where she had sought

refuge to repay the owner for his help. She ordered a silver tea service for twelve, a crystal punchbowl with eighteen matching cups, and a porcelain dinner service for five hundred. Unbeknownst to Lola or the King, the Minister of Finance had circulated a letter to shops in Munich, saying: "Future purchases by the Countess of Landsfeld charged to the Treasury must be approved by this office." When Lola read the letter, she punched her fist through one of the glass showcases. The owner wrapped her bloody hand in his handkerchief and called a doctor. It took several stiches, and she never expressed even a peep of pain. The Finance Minister was reprimanded by the King.

Disparaging articles appeared in the Munich newspapers, railing against Lola's actions and influence on the King. The English Pictorial Times published an accurate description of Lola's background, tracing her life from Limerick, Ireland to India, France, England and Europe. They exposed her mariage to Lieutenant James of the East India Company and that she was separated, not divorced, from him. It related occasions in England and on the continent where her abusive actions led to police intervention.

All major newspapers throughout Europe translated and published the article. If she left this attack unanswered, she would be finished. Lola confronted them. We hired a scribe, and the three of us worked from afternoon until morning writing the same letter to major newspapers in England, Europe, and America's East Coast. They read:

*"Sir,*

*In consequence of the numerous reports cir-*

*culated in various papers regarding myself and my family utterly void of foundation or truth, I beg of you through the medium of your widely circulated Journal to insert the following:*

*I was born at Seville in the year 1823. My father was a Spanish officer in the service of Don Carlos, my mother a lady of Irish extraction, born at Havannah, and married for the second time to an Irish gentleman, which I suppose is the cause of my being called Irish and sometimes English, Betty Watson, Mrs. James, &,&."*

*I beg leave to say that my name is Maria Dolores Porris Montez and I have never changed that name.*

*As for my theatrical qualifications, I ever had the presumption to think I had any, circumstances obliged me to adopt the Stage as a profession—which profession I have now renounced forever—having become a naturalized Bavarian and intending in the future making Munich my residence."*

Lola showed Ludwig the letter. He approved—unaware that I had posted them earlier. The King forbade Bavarian newspapers from derogatory mention of Lola. He took up the pen and published the following poetic attack on the Jesuits, Conservatives and International Press.

"You have driven me out of paradise,

Forever have you barred it to me,

You have embittered the days of my life,

But you have not caused me to hate rather than love.

Steadfast is not yet splintered;

Although the years of my youth have drained away,

My youthful strength remains unabated.

Tremble, you who wished me your slave!

You, who oppose me, have no equal.

Your own deeds have condemned you

For ingratitude, the whole catalog of slander.

The clouds disperse, the heavens are aglow.

I hail that decisive moment

That destroyed your power forever."

—Ludwig, King of Bavaria, Duke of Franconia, Duke in Swabia and Count Palatine of the Rhine. [12]

Von Metternich's coterie of agents forged a document purportedly written by the Pope in Rome condemning the King's relationship with Lola Montez. It circulated throughout Bavaria—until the newspapers

---

[12] Bruce Seymour, *Lola Montez* pages 149 &150

revealed it as a forgery.

People's attitudes began to change. They thought better of Lola's distrust of the Jesuits. The majority still opposed granting her Bavarian citizenship.

I intercepted a letter to the King from his wife Queen Theresa, and using the split bamboo I removed it. From the contents it is easy to surmise that Lola pressured Ludwig to present her at court to the queen. The following is as I copied it:

> "From Theresa Charlotte Louise of Saxony-Hildbrughausen

> Queen of Bavaria.

> My Dear Husband Ludwig,

> "What a loving duty it is to me, under all circumstances of life, to maintain for you, untroubled, for your domestic happiness must have been proven to you during your final weeks of our stay in Aschaffenburg because at that time I found a notice in the official gazette of an event that I, with my knowledge of your character, had thought impossible, and by which I was deeply pained. Far be it from me to let you hear a reproach over this matter here. The purpose of these lines is nevertheless by means of a word candidly spoken in the present moment to prevent a further possible indulgence through which the peace of our family circle would be forever disrupted. I owe it to my honor as a woman—which is dearer to me than life it-

self—she whom you have raised in rank—
never under no circumstances, to see face to
face.—should she seek to gain admission at
court through a promise of yours, you can tell
her, you know it for a fact—you, from my
mouth: the Queen, the mother of your children, would never receive her.

"In this confusion, in order to prevent any future trouble, I see it as my duty to tell you
openly of my absolutely unshakeable resolve.
And now, not one word more, either written
or spoken, of this difficult matter. You will
find me as before, cheerful, grateful for every
joy you give me, and ever watchfully en-
deavoring to maintain for you, my Ludwig,
the untroubled tranquility of our home.

"Your Theresa"[13]

Lola pressured the King to admit her to the Queen's
court because she coveted membership in the Order of
Theresa founded by Ludwig's wife. Noble ladies so
honored were entitled to be called an *Ehrendame*—Lady
of Honor.

I replaced the letter. Lola was never presented to the
Queen. Neither Ludwig nor Lola ever spoke of this in
my presence.

I did not restrict my use of the bamboo slip to personal communications. Most mail for or from the King
dealt with expenditures, building projects and requests

---

[13] *Lola Montez* by Bruce Seymour page 166

for political appointments. These, and the few military correspondences, I reported to Consul Favish.

Lola and I were too busy to evaluate these letters. One thing became clear. Von Metternich considered England the world's leading power because she dominated the seven seas. Britain's empire occupied one fifth of the earth's land mass and controlled one quarter of its population. I also reported on inventions and discoveries in mathematics, metallurgy, biology, and electricity.

These technological advances went beyond my ken. Lola understood some of the implications, especially the consequences of refinements to steam engine condensers. This resulted in a more efficient use of steam to power ships, trains, and large mining engines. She discussed them with the King. They meant to utilize knowledge to benefit Bavaria. Lola correctly predicted the rise to power of Japan with the modernization of the country by the Meiji Emperor, but neither she nor anyone else predicted Japan's war with Russia taking the pressure of Russia's ambition off the German States.

A vehement opponent of the exploitation of child labor, she encouraged the enlightened labor laws of Bavaria. This influenced other German states to amend their industrial regulations. Germany became the most enlightened country in the world regarding child labor laws.

Still, anonymous posters appeared calling Lola Montez, "The Great Whore of Babylon. Mother of Prostitutes and Abominations of the Earth. Death your reward and the Devil your companion. To hell with the Royal House!"

Although the King forbade Lieutenant Nusbammer

to visit Lola without his permission, Ludwig walked in on the two while they were having tea.

Prior to that they were enthusiastically involved in gymnastic lovemaking. I can only attribute their vigor to the Pope's Wine. They broke the bottom bedpost supporting the crocheted canopy. The carpenter assured me he would replace it by nightfall. The Pontiff's elixir appeared more potent than usual. I use it occasionally before hiring a male prostitute and noticed more cocaine leaves in the bottles.

Ludwig expelled Nusbammer as a result of this last incident. Lola spoke for the Lieutenant. Ludwig recanted and returned him to duty, but with secret orders to his superiors: "Keep the Lieutenant busy and away from Munich."

The following episode took place Monday. Ludwig called the Landtag into session to decide on the naturalization of Lola Montez as a Bavarian citizen. He prepared for some opposition and chaired the meeting.

Former friends and colleagues of the dismissed Police Commissioner prepared to oppose Lola's Bavarian citizenship. Not one member of the parliament supported the King's request. Their spokesmen pointed to her undocumented citizenship of Spain. The hostility in the Chamber became palpable.

Ludwig closed the meeting. He ordered the members to convene tomorrow morning prepared to vote. Ludwig wanted time to gather his forces before imposing his Imperial will on the Assembly.

That evening Von Metternich's agents, using the University students' corps and Jesuits, organized a mass torchlight rally opposing Lola's citizenship. Thousands marched past Ludwig's Palace on the way to Archbishop Reisach's palatial estate.

On witnessing the torch-lit parade file to the Prelate's home, Ludwig quipped, "Let them bring light to where there is darkness."

Tuesday the Landtag met. A declaration by a Minister recommended Bavarian citizenship be denied to Lola Montez. He averred this was the public's view and opinion of the Assembly. "My King," he said, "we recognize your constitutional power to overrule, but you would be ill-advised to do so."

"Poll the Chamber!" he ordered.

The Sergeant at Arms provided every member in the chamber with one white cube and one black cube. He then returned to each member. He held a wooden box with a wooden funnel above and a closed drawer below. The individual held his fist over the funnel and allowed one cube to drop into it. The voting box was presented to the Secretary at the foot of the throne. The secretary opened the bottom drawer of the voting box stood and announced. "Sire, it is dark. The Landtag votes, no!"

Ludwig looked at the men who served him loyally for so many years, and said, "By Royal Decree I declare Countess Montez a candidate for Bavarian Citizenship."

The Secretary responded, "So it is ordered, so it is done!"

Ludwig stood and said, "Even if it costs me my throne, I will not abandon the Countess of Landsfeld!" He expected some protest. Only deafening silence came from the grim-faced men filled the chamber.

Later, the King received the meeting's protocol and was advised by his Minister of Justice that as a Bavarian citizen, Countess Montez was more liable to be arrested on charges of the altercation in the hotel. It was suggested she leave Munich until the incident could be smoothed over or the arrest warrant expired. Another legal advisor recommended an immediate decree making Lola Montez a Bavarian citizen. If she were to be prosecuted, she would come under Royal protection. Ludwig complied. Lola Montez became a Bavarian citizen.

Upon hearing the King's decree, all Ministers resigned. Abandoned by his parliamentarians, he sent for Lola. The King's eyes were red and rheumy, his face gaunt and his voice trembled. Lola poured a full goblet of the Pope's wine. He drank it to the dregs. She refilled his glass. Her words, petting and the wine calmed him.

Lola quoted Lord Palmerston saying, "Every problem presents an opportunity."

"My dear Ludi, rest is what you need. Allow me to return home and think of how we can turn this desertion by so-called loyalist friends to your benefit. You sleep. Allow me to think on the matter."

And think, Lola did.

The King retired. Lola and I, in violation of our agreement with Consul Favish, went to the British Embassy. Initially our reception was cold. Hearing Lola's explanation for the breach of protocol, Consul Favish became enthusiastic. He canceled all appointments and sealed the doors to his office. We spent hours selecting people to fill the vacated Ministerial positions. All selected were favorable to Lola, supportive of the King, and against the Jesuits.

Dinner was served in the office. After our initial selection of candidates, we chose alternates in the event Ludwig balked at the proposed nominees. The girl from Limerick, raised in India who adopted Spain, was appointing Cabinet Ministers of the most powerful German state in Europe.

She remained confident in her ability to influence the King. Her enemies played into her hands by resigning. With a few minor exceptions Ludwig accepted Lola's list of Ministers for his government. Among them was the first Protestant Minister in Bavarian history. Lola became Bavaria's unofficial, senior powerbroker in the kingdom. Her title of Countess meant little in comparison to the financial, political and social control she now wielded.

Seekers of governmental favors and contracts came to the Lolaministerium rather than to the King. Engineers, shipbuilders, educators, military suppliers, and those in search of local, national, and international government appointments filled our anteroom. I scheduled their appointments. What a windfall!

By happenstance I learned that when receiving *Baksheesh*, if I just looked at the money offered, made no attempt to take it, but raised my eyebrows, more money was forthcoming. My eyebrows became well exercised.

Negative news articles and posters against Lola continued. The following appeared in a letter to Munich's leading newspaper: "...Respect for the King is being destroyed in the thoughts of Bavarians and forceful dissatisfaction of the monarchy is heard. Bavarians thought we had attained self-rule only to find we are administered by a Spanish woman who is immoral, stateless, and officially illegitimate. She remains legally married to Thomas James. From the hovels of the poor to the citadels of the rich, Bavaria has become a European joke..."

Ludwig replied in an open letter to the newspapers: "The rule of the Jesuits is broken. I remain a staunch Catholic in belief and practice. But it is time to join with our Protestant brothers who we Bavarians adopted in settlement of the Napoleonic War. There are foreign elements attempting to disrupt Bavaria. Austrian agents using naïve Munichens disrupt our lives with lies and slanders. I personally granted Bavarian citizenship to Maria de los Dolores Porris y Montez. She is ever thoughtful of Bavaria and its people... Munich, February 11, 1847."

Ludwig did not reveal to the new Landtag members that Lola would live tax-free for life. He also granted her a generous yearly stipend from Bavaria's public coffers.

Reaction to Ludwig's letter and Lola's influence on the Ministerial appointments spurred Von Metternich to order his agents to treble their efforts in disrupting Bavaria—to destroy Lola Montez and King Ludwig. Austria's spy-master increased subversive activities. His men began in the University, and Lola's actions stoked the flames of discontent.

In Munich's Royal Theater she had me purchase specific theater seats for the Alemaine students. I placed them to eavesdrop on certain people. Lola appeared early to the theater, where she awaited the King's arrival. The Queen would not attend. Ludwig entered Lola's box. The audience stood and bowed—that is, everyone but Lola. She offered her gloved hand, which Ludwig kissed before sitting next to her. Such disrespect by the foreigner created a tense atmosphere. The King and Lola appeared oblivious.

This singular incident resulted in a plethora of news articles and rantings in the newspapers and broadsheets. It became the sole topic for discussion in beer gardens and brothels. Lola and Ludwig ignored them. They prepared to celebrate her twenty-second birthday on February 14th. Actually twenty seven years old, she projected the blushing color of youth. Her skin tone, physique, and scintillating blue eyes were of a girl in her teens.

The King's persistent rash disappeared. He joined with the Alemaine student's in song and toasts to Lola. New ministers and political appointees united in the birthday festivities at the Lolaministerium. Ludwig arranged a public fireworks display, carnival acts, and the Royal symphony Orchestra to perform. A joyous three-day celebration ensued.

At the University, faculty and students—influenced by the Jesuits, guided by Austrian infiltrators—artfully stirred resentment. Teachers and students enlisted in the self-labeled Army of God. The Jesuits convinced a noted Philosophy Professor to propose a motion at the annual Faculty Meeting; he recommended the faculty congratulate the Ministers on their mass resignation from the government. The motion passed. The faculty and students cheered. The Alemannians opposed the resolution and were driven from the campus. They retreated to their rented quarters near the Lolaministerium.

Ludwig correctly recognized this intellectual interference as a political move by conservative Catholics to assert their power. It initiated the opening of a partisan battle between the Crown and the Church. Ludwig acted on Lola's advice. The Professor who made the recommendation received a dismissal notice. Word circulated through the university. Five hundred students marched to the professor's home where they cheered him. They made speeches lauding the Professor and sang patriotic songs. Faculty members joined the gathering, and Austrian agents attempted to direct the crowd. They circulated leaflets and placed posters calling for a protest march to the Lolaministerium at four P.M., there to give Countess Montez a present! The gift, a euphuism for something shocking to cause ill feelings—in this case a *Blivit*, from the Swedish, meaning a paper bag of dog dung set on fire and placed on the front steps for the owner to come out and stamp on.

Ludwig ignored this student's prank. He took seriously reports from his agents in Munich and the countryside that Austrian provocateurs incited his people. They spread false rumors about Lola's behavior and his granting her citizenship. The Professor's dismissal lit the fuse of public discontent. Reports of plots to kidnap and murder the Countess of Landsfeld came to Ludwig's attention. He posted additional guards at her palace. The acting Minister of Police informed him that the Home Guard could not be depended on to act. Neither were the Army's Officer's Corps reliable. "They dislike the Countess as do the rank and file," his agents reported.

"What of my Palace Guard?"

"They are sworn to you, Sire."

# CHAPTER 20

## UPRISING

On the second floor of the Lolaministerium, chimes of a gold-embossed porcelain clock sounded the hour of four in the afternoon. Lola invited her guests onto the balcony to await the protesting mob. Her eyes bright, lips moist, she reassured her guests. They were apprehensive, but Lola reveled in anticipation of a confrontation. A primordial thunder of human sounds came toward us from the *Boulevardier Ludwigstraße*. The far end of the road filled with a sea of humanity. They marched toward us, and the lines of Gendarmes and soldiers were swept aside. Police and military abandoned their posts.

The crowd assembled under our balcony, shouted taunts, heckled and hissed Lola. I was amazed at so much hate from so many people. Lola raised her wine glass in a silent toast to them, and then threw the wine and goblet at the crowd. The people roared. Lola laughed hysterically. She lost control, but refused my advice to retire. She whipped out a stiletto from her waistband and brandished it at the crowd. She screamed a personal challenge to anyone man or woman.

Several she recognized, she called by name and threatened with prison. The *Blivit* was lit and placed on the doorstep, but Lola was informed and the servants told to ignore it. She ordered more wine, poured her own glass, threw the bottle at the crowd and raised her cup in another toast to the furious mob below. There was not a trace of fear in her. Her face became contorted in a mask of hatred, and she ignored all who approached her.

Two platoons of the King's Guard arrived. They were irrelevant in the face of the massive mob. The officer climbed into the palace from the rear, and came onto the balcony, and pleaded with Lola to go inside. She laughed in his face and ordered him to leave. Before he could protest, a rock whizzed by Lola's head. Another, then another followed, breaking the plate-glass windows. The officer grabbed Lola's knife hand, took her about the waist, and pulled her inside. She kicked, fought, and bit to no avail. Servants closed the metal shutters. The slamming of paving stones into the metal raised a horrendous cacophony inside. We in the room were frightened, but not Lola. She fought to go back out on the balcony while screaming for me to bring her pistol. "I'll kill those low-life sons of bitches!" she shouted.

The King was informed of the riot. His Chief of Police warned him not to venture out, but Ludwig, his prowess proven in war, remained unintimidated. He donned his top hat, jacket and took his cane.

He set out alone. The Chief of Police ran to catch up, and no guards accompanied them. At the entrance to the driveway of the Lolaministerium, the Army officer had succeed in posting pickets. He turned to see the King on foot followed by the Chief of Police, both striding unguarded to the rear of the wild mob.

His men could not make a path for the King through the milling sea of angry humanity. The officer did what he was trained to do; he shouted, "Hats off before the King!" His men echoed the order. The people saw their King striding toward them. From habit, fear or confusion the mob uncovered their heads, bowed and made a path for Ludwig to the embattled palace. Ludwig accepted the honor as his due.

Several additional platoons of soldiers arrived, and with police reinforcements they coaxed the mob from the street. They did not break the demonstration. It was redirected. University students, Jesuits, and Austrian agents kept it alive. The mob wandered the alleys and side-streets, smashing windows, robbing shops, and tearing down street lanterns. The Civil Guard was called to help. The Guard agreed to function in Munich, but not in protection of the Spanish woman's palace.

By midnight the streets of the city were quiet. Sweepers and street cleaners did their best to prepare for the morrow's work day.

Ludwig assured Lola the perpetrators would suffer. Lola called them revolutionaries. He asked her to think of his alternatives. He had to leave for a scheduled game of cards with the Queen. I supervised putting the house in order. Broken glass and paving stones littered the balconies and interior. The *Blivit* was removed from the front steps. I summoned glazers, carpenters, and gardeners for the morning, then drew a bath for Lola. She napped and had dinner served.

The following was reported in the morning newspapers:

*"Our King, Ludwig I of Bavaria, with a show
of unparalleled bravery quelled a riotous*

*mob single-handedly in front of the Lolaministerium yesterday evening. The multitude defied police and army, yet doffed their hats and bowed when our King appeared. He arrived unescorted and unguarded. The crowd dispersed. They did not go home. They vented their anger on our fair city of Munich. They disrupted businesses, looted shops and destroyed street lanterns. The King returned to his palace the same way he came, alone and on foot. The largest part of the mob congregated around his palace gate. They tested the palace guards by throwing stones. This time when the King approached the rear of the mob they hooted and jeered him. Any man who doffed his hat was pummeled with brickbats. A reluctant crowd made way for the King but hissed, heckled and catcalled him all the way to the door of his castle. He showed no emotion. Not a pebble was thrown at our Monarch but many paving stones were ready. How the mighty have fallen for the love of a woman. A foreign woman at that."*

At noon the following day Ludwig came to take counsel with Lola. He dismissed her concern about his safety but agreed to have a contingent of mounted guards accompany his coach. He gave his word not to walk about until these disturbances ceased. He came right to the point.

"I am considering several courses of action. I can have disciplinary action taken against those in the Army, Police, and Civil Guard who refused to participate in quelling the mob. I am able to censor the newspapers."

"But foreign correspondents will report?" Lola said.

"I will deem them *persona non-grata.* They'll be deported as undesirable aliens."

"It will only make the news more valuable and its information prized," Lola replied. "Money will buy anything, including forbidden news stories. We can find more subtle ways of influencing the press. Much of their advertising comes from the royal coffers. There may be moral journalists and editors, but moral newspaper owners are very few."

Ludwig kissed her cheek and said, "If the people could only hear you speak they would understand your beauty is matched only by your wit. What do you suggest?"

"Nip the problem in the bud."

Where is that blossom?"

"The University. Your agents report the Austrians and Jesuits inspired the students to revolt. Last night's fiasco started on campus."

"What do you suggest?"

"Shut the University for a year."

"They will riot."

"Two thirds of the students are from other German States. If your soldiers rout them from the dorms, they will go home. Of the remaining thirty percent, half belong to my Alemaine Corps. That will bring the Jesuits and Austrian agents into the bright light of day. They will be seen as war-mongering revolutionaries, pawns of von Metternich. When shown the truth, your people will rally to your standard. All Bavaria will unite behind their King."

"I am a religious Catholic," Ludwig stated. "I oppose the Jesuits because of their power and influence in political and public matters. They serve their own interests, not the people or the Pope. Franciscans, Dominicans, and other Catholic orders will not be expelled from Bavaria. The Jesuits will be banished from my Kingdom. They represent a theology by which every law, divine or human, may be broken and the Pope's decrees flouted if it promotes their agenda."

Lola rubbed her hands together as a glutton before a bountiful repast. She was mindful that Ludwig's act of facing down the mob had shaken him to the core. For more than fifty years as Prince, then King, he was admired, even adored by his people. Now they mocked him. A letter from Ludwig's sister deepened his distress. She appealed to his sense of honor, responsibility to his people, his family and his legacy to history. She begged him to get rid of that foreign woman.

Using the split bamboo I peeked at his response and was shocked. He did not rebuff his sister, but wrote: "I confess that my infatuation and obsession with this woman is over. I know you have my welfare at heart. And I heed your voice. Yet I have an obligation of decency to be gentle with her, for I am not blameless. Your Loving and Appreciative brother Ludwig."

I brought the matter to Lola. She canceled all meetings, and we consulted on a solution. The subject narrowed to the Pope's wine, whether to withhold or increase it to influence Ludwig on her behalf. Events guided us to do neither.

Lola was not only smart; she was lucky. The stress on Ludwig emerged in a flare-up of his psoriasis. It became worse than before: ugly red blotches on his face, hands. and scalp. It was even in and on his ears.

The Queen was repulsed. She did not visit her husband. Lola embraced her lover and visited every day, often all day and night. She read Cervantes to him in Spanish, Honoré de Balzac's *The Human Comedy* in French, and Chaucer's *Canterbury Tales* in English. They engaged in long discussions about politics, economics, local, national, and international foreign policy.

Most often they discussed plans to confederate the German States. Ludwig feared the possibility of an Austrian-Hungarian unification of the former members of the Hanseatic League. The Austrian House of Habsburg was the inheritor of the Holy Roman Empire in the west. With Hungary at its side Austria would become the most formidable military power in the world.

The two lovers planned the future of Europe. Ludwig refused to leave his rooms and forbade all visitors, and Lola became his liaison for implementation of his decrees and policies. For all intents and purposes during the King's affliction, Lola wore the Crown of Bavaria. I became the gateway to that power. I no longer exercised my eyebrows.

More and more money was offered for timely appointments or answers involving contracts, land acquisition, and building permits. Yet this power also created enemies. Those not favored often became offensive. Lola was fair and logical in bestowing her benevolence upon petitioners. Using the police and the Alemaine student's corps, she spied upon bidders to see if they fulfilled their contracts. She punished slackers, publicly and severely. By doing so, her gifts far surpassed imagination. We had to purchase two more jewelry boxes. I also benefitted.

It happened that Munich's small Jewish community petitioned the King to purchase a plot of land within their ghetto for a new synagogue, for the existing one had been condemned by the city. I placed their request first among the petitioners. The King approved.

Lola found it difficult to find a minister who would meet with the leader of the Jewish community. She assigned me the task. The name given was the same jeweler I did business with.

We enjoyed a pleasant and straight-forward meeting. The price being asked was exorbitant, even by Munich standards, but the Jews were willing to pay. They wished to hold a bazaar open to all Munich, to raise money. They invited me.

I told Lola. She said she would like to attend. It meant thirty or forty wealthy people who graced her salon, and members of the city government, would be in her party. I was overwhelmed by her generosity. She pledged one thousand guilders to the Jews. Five hundred was Ludwig's idea and five hundred hers.

The day of the bazaar, the Jewish community showed their gratitude by preparing a culinary feast for the King. This was unacceptable, for they were Jews. Lola accepted the food and fed her coterie without telling them the source. After lunch she led them to the bazaar. They spent significant amounts of money and ogled the bearded men and strangely dressed women, pasty-faced boys with long ear–locks, and girls imitating their mothers in dress, actions and speech.

The Germans were amused by Yiddish. They called it bastardized German, and proper for Yids to speak. It was the first time most had ever seen a Jew up close. At one point Lola's exclusive group set themselves apart and were whispering to each other. They appeared very serious. Lola sent me to find out.

When I told her the problem she went to the old jeweler. "Sir," she said, "Most of my people have never met a Jew. They think your men's hats and women's head-scarfs cover horns, and the long dresses and coats hide the tails."

The old rheumy eyes smiled behind the wire-frame glasses. He asked, "Do you believe it?"

"Not one bit. I lived amongst the Jews of Cochin for two months. My father was stationed in their town."

The old Jew paled. He gasped, "You saw the Black Jews of India?"

"Yes."

"I heard tell they believe they are from the tribe of Benjamin."

"No, the tribe of Menasha," Lola corrected. "They are black as any African, but have white features. They claim roots to King Solomon."

"Do you know the Munich Museum of History has two ancient copper scrolls attesting to their origin?"

"Have you read them?" Lola asked.

"It is forbidden to a Jew. Would it be possible for you to view these scrolls?"

Lola threw back her head saying, "You presume too much!"

"I do! I do!" stuttered the old scholar. "Please forgive me."

"Could you show my friends, your people have neither horns nor tails?"

"Right away!" the old man said and hurried off. Soon Jewish women, men, girls and boys were uncovering their heads and lifting their coats.

Lola's followers applauded.

She led her group from the Jewish Quarter to the Hofbräu House, where the Alemaine student's corps was waiting. Piesner took his seat next to Lola. Her hand slipped over his thigh and she grasped his tallywhacker. He stiffened, then smiled. Hot pretzels arrived with foaming steins of brown beer, and the party began. It continued into the wee hours of the morning.

Lola developed a sore at the right corner of her mouth. We thought she was infected by Ludwig's psoriasis, but the court physician assured us this was impossible; psoriasis cannot be passed on by any form of touching. He diagnosed it as a cold sore, which should go away by itself. He prescribed an ointment and suggested Lola cover the inflamed portion with a sham beauty mark. This we did. It worked well and added to Lola's attractiveness.

The English Ambassador was pleased with the information we sent to him. He said von Metternich writhed and grumbled at the appalling situation in Bavaria. The Austrian Prince had no love for the Jesuits; he deported them, imprisoned them, and confiscated their property. Still, they were useful in his campaign against Lola and the King.

Jesuit power in Bavaria was ended by Ludwig's decree. Some were imprisoned, most exiled, and church property was confiscated. This created a confrontation with the Vatican. The Pope claimed inheritance of the Jesuit's property; it should revert to the Church not the State. Lola dictated a response without Ludwig's knowledge. She asked the Papal authority if the Holy See would pay property tax on land, buildings, and serfs.

The answer was swift and unequivocal. "The Holy See has never paid tax in a Christian country. We are not prepared to do so in Bavaria. King Ludwig is known as a devout Catholic. He has always supported the Pope. If his dedication to Jesus Christ and the Pontiff is now problematic, please inform us. The Holy Father will act accordingly."

These last words carried the threat of excommunication. Lola had to bring it to Ludwig's attention. He became upset with her. She argued the Church paid taxes in the Turkish Empire, and should do so in Christian countries. The King remained adamant. He drafted a letter to the Pope transferring all properties, land, and serfs belonging to the Jesuits to the Holy See. He signed it, "Humbly, your devoted servant in the service of our Lord Jesus Christ, Ludwig, King of Bavaria."

This decision marked the turning point of his skin affliction. The silvery scales fell away. In days the ugly red blotches disappeared. The King attributed the cure to his action in favor of the Pope. He added another ten minutes to his morning prayers and a large donation to the Archbishop of Munich.

Once again the King received Ministers and petitioners. He even strolled the Palace gardens with Lola. The subject of leaving her was never mentioned. His sister questioned him, when he would be rid of this female demon? Ludwig told her to mind her own business.

After his skin problems disappeared, the King's first formal public appearance was at the Lolaministerium. This enhanced her already formidable reputation for power. Ludwig proclaimed Lola Montez Baroness of Rosenthal in addition to Countess of Landsfeld, described in the register of Bavarian nobility as Maria Dolores Porris y Montez.

He announced the title of Baroness came with a yearly stipend of twenty thousand florins and two thousand serfs. He then had Lola's portrait brought in. It was placed prominently in his new wing of the Gallery of Beauties. My opinion of the painting is similar to many others; it does not capture the true exquisiteness and emotional effect of being in Lola's presence.

Surprisingly, her public image improved. Word of her dedication to the King during his illness, her influence on modernizing the education system, and her impulsive helping of the poor were well received. Because of her self-appointed role as the King's proxy, Lola had less time in public. Her tirades took place away from the press and public. This was fortunate, as she was always accompanied by two handsome young men and sometimes the student leader, Piesner. This ceased when the King returned to public life. One of the first things Ludwig worked on with Lola was how to transfer funds for scholarships to the Alemaine Corps without raising a public outcry.

When Ludwig became incapacitated with psoriasis, Lola installed the student leader Piesner in private rooms and an office at the Lolaministerium. There, under Lola's supervision, he functioned as an informal government purchasing agency. He negotiated contracts and sold favors.

I had to caution young Piesner; he left money—*baksheesh*—in plain view. Still, he was devoted to Lola, and never took a guilder for himself. These donations I deposited in Lola's account.

When the King returned to public life, Piesner's position was abolished—but he remained in his suite, on call when Lola required his services for bed or business. Of course my money went to the old Jew. He questioned me about the Black Jews of Cochin. I politely explained that I thought them another displaced African tribe that had migrated to India.

Several things I did recall. They had aquiline features and refused to work on their Sabbath. The men wore fringed shawls with little black boxes tied to their head and left arm. This excited the Jew, but I could only shrug at most of his questions.

Before I left, he warned me of a student demonstration soon to take place. It happened on my return trip. The entire student corps and many professors filled the main street of Munich on their way to the King's palace. They held placards demanding the reinstatement of this banished Professor.

The Bavarian newspapers were kept in line by Ludwig's police, but foreign articles and journals poured in over the porous Bavarian borders. The educated Burghers paid well for them. This particular demonstration was initiated and funded by the Archbishop, the same Prelate Ludwig recently had favored with a large donation. Now the Prelate turned against the King. In a Church/Student affiliated newspaper he wrote:

> *"The hopping, skipping, twirling antics of the Spanish harlot Lola Montez can hardly be called dancing. This immoral temptress may be an emissary of Satan. She is certainly an agent and spy for England's Lord Palmerston. She claims to be Catholic but is bent on destroying our religion. And the King aids her."*

A French newspaper replied, tongue in cheek, "Why do you interfere with the amours of your good Ludwig? We don't say he should not have observed rather more discretion, or have avoided compromising his dignity. Still, a monarch, like a simple citizen, is surely free to love where he pleases. In selecting Lola Montez, the amorous Ludwig proves that he loves equality and, as a true democrat, can identify himself with the public. Let him espouse his servant girl, if he wants to. Personally, we would rather see the Bavarians excite themselves about their constitution than about the banishment of a royal favorite. The King of Bavaria turns his mistress into a Countess; his subjects refuse to recognize her; and the university students clamor for her head. Happy days of Montespan, of Pompadour, of Dubarry, of Potemkin, of Orloff, where have you gone?"

A troubled calm blanketed Munich. Then, on February 10th, the entire university students' corps gathered before Ludwig's Palace shouting, "Down with Lola Montez!" "Down with the King's whore!"

It was organized by the students with coaxing from

von Metternich's agents. Others joined in. They timed this demonstration to coincide with city laborers finishing work. Ludwig watched from his balcony. The front lawn and carriageway were littered with paving stones and refuse. He never spoke.

When the last protester was gone, he went to his desk and wrote an order as Lola suggested. He closed the university. The King ordered all non-Munichens, students and teachers, (two thirds of the university population) to leave the city in twenty-four hours. This resulted in serious repercussions. The decree affected Munich's economy. The deporting of over two thousand cash-paying customers from the best families in Germany had confrontational consequences on every business in the city. [14]

Lola's account of the incident is quite creative but untrue. She was not there. Her memoirs state, "They came with cannons and guns and swords, with the voices of ten thousand devils, and surrounded my castle. Against the entreaties of my friends, I presented myself before the infuriated mob. They demanded my life. A thousand guns were pointed at me, a hundred voices fiercely demanded that I should rescind the ill I had done. It was impossible for me to accede to such a request; what I did was for the good of the people and the honor of Bavaria." [15]

An English newspaper published: "The indignation

---

[14] *The Magnificent Montez: from Courtesan to Convert* Pages 134 & 137; Horace Wyndham

[15] Modified quote from, *The Magnificent Montez: from Courttesan to Convert Page*; 139, by Horace Wyndham

against King Ludwig on account of his scandalous conduct with Lola Montez has roused Bavarian tempers to fever pitch... King Ludwig, who possesses many good qualities, is, unfortunately, a very licentious old man... Neither the tears of the Queen, the entreaties of his sons, or the public's indignation, can influence the old monarch, who has become the slave of this most beautiful Spaniard."

Lola became a prisoner in her own palace. It was surrounded by students and Munichens. The students' corps defied Ludwig's orders; they occupied the dormitories, marched and formed ranks in front of Lola's palace, threatening to destroy the Lolaministerium.

The lovely Spaniard appeared on the balcony in a beautiful gown, holding a wine glass in one hand and cigar in the other. She raised the glass in a toast, drank, and told the mob to go to hell. They did. They smashed through the large ornate doors of her palatial estate. Only the Alemannian students inside prevented the mob from getting their hands on Lola. She did not help her defenders or herself as she attempted to attack the mob with dagger and pistol.

Her military bodyguards summoned assistance. Bugles blared, drums beat, and a squadron of Cuirassiers clattered up the Barerstrasse, their sabers drawn, iron-shod hoofs of their mounts sparking the paving-stones. They trotted forward in line. The rioters broke and fled with Lola's mocking laughter burning their ears.

An uneasy calm reigned for two days. Then the Alemannian Corps decided to celebrate. They hired a restaurant in the center of Munich. On their way to the party they encountered students from other Corps, and a fight ensued. A platoon of mounted cavalry took the side of the university students against the Alemannia, and chased them into a restaurant where they barricaded themselves.

Other University students, in defiance of the King's orders to leave Munich, came at the run to punish the Alemannians. The cavalry officer withdrew his troops.

Word reached Lola. Without regard for her own safety, she took a carriage alone to the site of the confrontation. She was recognized and chased through the streets – thus drawing away the student corps—to the Austrian embassy. There she sought sanctuary, but the guards were instructed to forbid her entry. She made good her escape, and took refuge in the nearest church. Ludwig found her there, with a pistol drawn and dagger unsheathed, and convinced her to return home in his carriage. He agreed with Lola's demand to use the Army to implement his closure of the University and expel the students from Bavaria.

He was unaware that Munich's burghers and leading businessmen were meeting with the university professors and students, who planned to defy the King. They had friends in government and allies in the Army and police force who joined the impromptu gathering. When Ludwig was apprised of this situation, he realized his only power was the Army.

He issued an order to disperse the conspirators and arrest the leaders. The Army officers, from middle level down, refused to act. The King's order was ignored. His generals appeared before him on bended knees, and apologized for their underlings. A message arrived at the King's palace informing him the Landtag would meet tomorrow morning to hear the King's request.

"You don't request!" Lola growled, "You are the King. Order those swine to obey."

Ludwig stood, took Lola by her shoulders, gently kissed her forehead and placed her in my care saying, "The Countess is not to go outside until I say it is safe."

The next morning Ludwig appeared before the Landtag. Every seat in the forum was filled. The Minister of Public Worship, the Treasurer of the Royal Household, and other office holders all appointed or sanctioned by Ludwig and Lola stared bleakly at their King. One after the other they spoke of the rioting, the disruption of normal life and business in Munich, the injuries, arrests, imprisonments, and mostly the closing of the University.

Princes, and the aristocracy of Munich, sensing the weakness of the King, left the hall.

The Minister of the Army spoke last. "Sire, we respect you and your Kingship, but believe you are ill advised by this Spanish woman. We, the members of the Landtag, respectfully and humbly request you exile Lola Montez and rescind your order closing the university."

Silence hung heavy in the crowded room. From his throne Ludwig eyed the rows of men on left and right. Their jaws were set. He stood. Everyone in the room bowed. In a clear, strong voice Ludwig said, "My Kingdom for Lola, my only true love."

Grim silence was the response. As one, the members of the Landtag stood and filed out. When the last man had exited, the King who had faced bayonet, musket balls, and cannon fire collapsed on his throne.

Word of what happened in the Landtag spread. Munich businessmen called a meeting in the Hofbräu House. Their purpose was to petition the King to rescind his order closing the University and exile Lola Montez. The city's employees, private and public, concerned for their livelihood, joined.

Five thousand people congregated before the Hofbräuhaus, far too many for the restaurant. The meeting was held outside. Speakers attempted to elect a delegation to petition the King. With the help of University professors and the Burghermeister this was accomplished, but then there was a problem. The crowd wanted to accompany the delegation to the King's palace.

At first this was rejected by the elected delegation as an affront to the King, but the organizers soon realized they couldn't dissuade the mob from attending. By now more than six thousand people were assembled. The organizers understood they would have to accede to the people's demand, but such a crowd would appear as a revolutionary threat to the King. While speakers maintained the crowd's attention, the Burghermeister quietly sent three professors as a delegation to apprise the King of the situation and of their request. They were met at the main gate by an officer who said the King would not return to the Palace until later.

Ludwig was with Lola in our palace down the street. He was informed of the three-man delegation, but did not respond. Lola encouraged him to stand strong. She compared the petitioners to dogs. "If they sense weakness," she said, "They will attack."

An hour before sunset the Burghermeister and his delegation arrived by carriage at the King's palace. They were followed on foot by an orderly crowd of thousands. The palace mounted guard and infantry formed ranks before the entrance's closed iron gates. The delegation requested a meeting with the King. Ludwig sent word that his response would be in writing, and he would not receive them.

The crowd remained silent and peaceful, but there was an undercurrent of tension as more people joined the protest. When the King refused a second request he added, "I will not be held hostage by thousands of blackguards. Disperse, and I will consider your request."

# CHAPTER 21

## REVOLUTION

To prevent an armed confrontation, Munich's Burghermeister suggested approaching the leader of the House of Peers, Prince Luitpold, Ludwig's son. The Prince and his wife sympathized with the students; They abhorred the King's infatuation with Lola and her disrespect for the Queen Mother. They agreed to present the delegation's request for an audience with the King, and the five went to the Palace. The Prince and his wife entered the Royal Audience Chamber, and the doors closed behind them. An argument ensued. The King's angry voice could be heard outside. The doors opened. The Princess in tears, supported by the grim-faced Prince, exited. He addressed the delegation, "You may enter. Do not expect sociable treatment."

Ludwig wore his military uniform with battle decorations. He ignored formalities. "You claim to petition me on behalf of my people, yet you appear before my doors with thousands of rabble threatening the monarchy. You will receive my official response to your petition in writing. Your request to reopen the University is denied. Your request to exile Countess Lola Montez is in the trash."

He slammed his saber in its scabbard on the hardwood desk. "You people do not recognize the beneficence of the Countess, nor my benevolence. You businessmen and so-called educators are a greedy, ungracious, bunch of rogues. I will never accede to your petition. I may forfeit my life, but it will cost you dearly. Attack the throne, and I will show no mercy. You Burghers worry about business? If I move the Capital of Bavaria from Munich, think of your empty purses then. The business center will follow me. You moralistic academics will be out of work. Know this: the University will reopen when and where I decree. If I move the capital from Munich, the University goes with me." Ludwig pointed to the door. "Leave! Take my answer to that horde of ungrateful wretches outside. Tell them, harm one hair on my loved one's head, and compassion and kindness will be forgotten words in Bavaria. This I swear."

The delegation did not convey the King's reply in his exact words, but couched his response in softer terms. They feared a riot, and were uncertain where the army and police force's loyalty resided. The King's complete reply would be given at the Hofbräuhaus.

The mood of the people turned ugly. At the Hofbräuhaus, the leaders delayed another two hours before speaking, assuming that many would leave for their evening meal. Finally, the King's explosive declaration was delivered. The royal proclamation set off a roar of outrage from the Munichens.

The organizers had assumed that those who left to eat dinner would go home. They didn't. They entered the Hofbräuhaus and nearby beer gardens. They drank too much and returned to hear the King's reply. The roar of dismay spread throughout the city. More people poured into the streets. The atmosphere became highly charged. The mob chanted, "Exile Lola! Exile Lola!" At the Hofbräuhaus the chant changed. Led by von Metternich's agents, it became: "Burn the Lolaministerium! Burn the Lolaministerium!"

People started for Lola's palace. Those in the lead tore up picket fences to arm themselves. People ripped up paving-stones from the street. Whatever was at hand they took for weapons. Policemen were swept aside or abandoned their posts. The Home Guard joined the protestors. Army units posted at intersections leading to the Lolaministerium withdrew by order of middle-level commanders. These officers felt the King dishonored the Queen by his public affair with Lola.

In desperation Ludwig called on several former Ministers and lifelong friends to advise him. Their advice, revise his order closing the University. Close only the summer session. In this way he might divert the mob from a confrontation with Lola. The King agreed.

He sent a platoon of Dragoons to direct the crowd to the Royal Palace. There Ludwig announced the temporary closure of the University. Rather than placating the students, this encouraged them; they sensed weakness. Enflamed by Jesuit and Austrian agents, distributing the following article from a radical writer in Frankfort, they provoked the crowd:

> *"The King of Bavaria wastes the sweat of the poor on mistresses and their followers. Everybody knows that the jewellery sic which Lola wore to the theatre cost 60,000 guilders; that her house in the Barerstrasse is a fairy palace; that the Cabinet, the Council of State,*

> *and the whole civil service are at her beck and call; that the gendarmerie and military are her particular escort; that the finest Catholic professors at the University have been dismissed at her caprice. For the people of Bavaria nothing is done."*[16]

The cry went up: "Lola out of Bavaria! On to the Lolaministerium!"

Ludwig had to be helped from the palace balcony. At sixty-two years old, in a country where life expectancy was forty, his years weighed heavy. He retired to his bed.

Lola responded with a letter of her own to the newspapers. She wrote: "Far more money came out of the people's pockets to the Church than was spent on me. I changed that. My reforms in education, praised by my detractors, are now forgotten. My concern for the poor is overlooked. I earned the King's favors by liberating the country from religious tyranny. Now is not the time to quibble. Your King has made concessions. Honor him. Honor Bavaria, do honor to yourselves. Respect the Monarchy."

Attempts at reconciliation came too late. Munich was in insurrection. Students and citizens armed themselves. Multitudes gathered before the King's palace. They filled the streets leading to the square, demanding the dismissal of Countess Lola and the immediate reopening of the University.

---

[16] [Pg 168] *Lola Montez* Edmund by Edmund B_ D"Auvergne A Project Gutenberg

The situation became dire when the King addressed his Council of State. These ministers chosen by Lola and approved by Ludwig were their only supporters. They too turned against him. Shocked at their opposition, the King listened to them suggest he accept the demands of the people.

In that instant, Ludwig, King of Bavaria, was broken. He never expected that those who owed their elevated positions to him would abandon the monarchy. They did.

The fault was Lola's. She chose each man primarily for his anti-Jesuit attitude, and convinced Ludwig to approve. The Catholic Army of God no longer remained a significant threat; they were expelled, incarcerated, or gone underground. The Jesuits were exiled from Bavaria, imprisoned and stripped of all wealth, their stifling bonds of anti-democratic rule shattered.

The democratic idea in England and France was sweeping Europe. The newly appointed ministers retained ulterior motives; they were set on forming a more liberal parliament where they superseded the monarchy. They would control Bavaria. They also desired to unite the German states as England had done with Ireland, Scotland and Wales. The Landtag, not the monarchy, would control the army, the government and treasury. These parliamentarians tasted power, and they had voracious appetites.

Slumped in his throne, abandoned by all, Ludwig glanced down at his ministers and saw not a receptive face in the room. Deprived of trusted advisors, friends, and his Lola, Ludwig's hands shook when he proclaimed: "Let it be as you say. The university will remain open."

"The Countess of Landsfeld?" they asked,

The old king emitted a great sob. "Write the expulsion proclamation."

Lola's expulsion and denouncement of her Bavarian citizenship were written prior to the meeting. The Lord Chamberlain presented it to the King with quill, wax, and royal seal. Ludwig signed and stamped it. He requested from the royal cup bearer, "A flagon of the Pope's wine."

"Sire, there is none."

Ludwig, King of Bavaria, covered his face with his hands. He must abdicate to preserve the Crown for his son. Worse than losing his throne, he lost Lola. She would never forgive him. He would be alone forever.

The King's acquiescence in the face of betrayal by his appointed ministers reached Lola. She refused to accept it. She swore the Jesuits plotted it. A special messenger from the King ordered her to leave Munich at once. To Lola, the dispatch was incomprehensible. She refused to believe the King had abandoned her. If only she could see him, he would rescind the order.

Informed that an audience with the King was out of the question, she realized that Ludwig's capitulation to the demands of his parliamentarians and the mob was true. The Munichians heard, and they danced in the streets. Munich's Beer Gardens tapped their kegs and sent waiters into the streets with foaming mugs of free beer.

A senior military officer appeared before Lola and informed her she must leave at once. She recognized Ludwig's signature and seal, but did not comprehend his submission without drawing his sword in her defense. She went out on the balcony. Not one soldier, policeman or Palace Guard assigned to protect her were visible. The mob remained below.

"Your protection has been withdrawn by order of the Landtag," the officer said. "I will make all arrangements and assure you safe passage. The King suggests you go to Switzerland. I am instructed to place you on the train to Augsburg. Please travel light. Your personal belongings will be shipped as soon as possible."

Lola stood alone with her back towards me, yet I sensed the change before she turned and nodded her acceptance of the order. My Lola appeared smaller, deflated. Her voice quavered. She ordered me to pack her valuables and traveling clothes.

"Inform Piesner to find two strong students as bodyguards." The crowd gathered closer around our palace doors. Those below stared up at Lola and she stared back. "We leave within the hour," she said.

Her composure regained, the inevitable accepted, Lola organized our departure. The crowd outside grew. Lola threw back her head, squared her shoulders and led us and the military aide downstairs, out the front door and through the angry people outside. They parted. Not a shout was uttered nor a stone thrown. We entered the carriage and left the driveway onto the main street to the railroad station.

Behind us we heard an animal-like roar. The people broke into the Lolaministerium. At first they looted. Then they smashed that which could not be carried. They tore paintings and drapes from the walls. They fired the building.

All this must have been visible to Ludwig from the balcony of his palace. He was an old broken man. In his worn bed robe, disheveled, unshaven and uncombed, he drifted out of his palace to the rear of the ever-growing mob in front of the Lolaministerium. People danced, looted, and set fire to the palace of his one true love. He went unnoticed. He watched paintings, sculptures, and works of art carried off by the exultant crowd. Someone struck him from behind. He fell to his knees. They hit him again. He felt hands going through his pockets.

A harsh voice grumbled, "The old bastard ain't got nothin'." Someone helped him up and brushed him off. He staggered past people running to loot the burning fairyland palace of his dreams. Not one person recognized their King.


I decided not to go to Switzerland with Lola. The time had come for me to return to my daughter. I wanted to fulfill my dreams of retiring as a wealthy widowed Maharani.

If Lola could impersonate a Spanish noble–woman, I had learned enough during the years to imitate a widowed Hindu Princess. I made up stories about my background, interwove them with the truth about my early education and meeting various aristocratic personalities throughout England and Europe. Of course I had observed these famous people as a servant. I practiced speaking and thinking of them as equals.

However, nothing comes easy. Lola had her own plans, and she had not given up. At the first station outside of Munich we disembarked from the train with the students and we rented rooms in the nearest hotel.

Lola, I and Piesner returned to Munich by carriage. We stopped at a homestead both Piesner and Lola used for *tête-à-têtes.* From there she sent Piesner with a message to the King, begging his indulgence for her to say good-bye. Lola was certain if she could just touch Ludwig's hand he would revoke orders of banishment. He would call on loyal Army men to fight the rebels.

It was not to be. I never saw Piesner again. Two large intimidating police officers returned in his stead. They informed us the King refused to see Lola, and they read a second order banning her from Bavaria. Lola became furious. Her beautiful face turned into a distort-ed mask of anger. She snatched the document, tore it, and threw the shreds at the officers. They let the torn bits of paper fall to the floor. Each drew his pistol and put it to Lola's stomach, saying, "We have orders from the King."

With my help and the unflinching demands of the police, Lola consented to leave. Escorted by the police-men, we returned to the hotel outside of Munich. There was a six-hour wait for the train. It was there I decided to leave Lola. and return to India and my daughter.

Suddenly one of the Alemaine students appeared with the strangest message. He had followed the police officers. He slipped into our bedroom and told an amaz-ing story:

The King had a mental crisis, and was a broken man. The clergy imposed their will on him by claiming he was a victim of Lola's witchcraft.

"Bullshit!" Lola shouted. "It's his ministers and peo-ple that have ruined him!"

The mental crisis weakened Ludwig's understanding.

He was persuaded by his new advisors that Lola's power over him was due to witchcraft. The Archbishop of Munich convinced the disoriented Ludwig that a black crow visited Lola's room by night to relay instructions from Satan.

Before the student finished his story the two police officers burst into our room. They clubbed the student unconscious, dragged him from the room and returned with new orders from the King. "We will not take the train," an officer announced. "We go by carriage to Weinsberg."

"What the hell is in that godforsaken village?" Lola demanded

"Justinus Kerner!"

We soon learned Kerner was the recognized exorcist for the entire region.

The following are excerpts from letters written by Kerner reporting progress in his treatment of Lola:

> "By the hand of Justinus Kerner February 18th 1848
>
> "Lola Montez arrived here the day before yesterday, accompanied by her handmaid and two Alemaine. It is vexatious that the King should have sent her to me, but they have told him that she is possessed. Before treating her with magic and magnetism, I am trying the hunger cure. I allow her only thirteen drops of raspberry water, and the quarter of a wafer a day. Tell no one about this—burn this letter."

To another correspondent Kerner wrote:

> "Lola has grown astonishingly thin. I mes-
> merized her, and I let her drink asses' milk."

That any man could control Lola was beyond my comprehension, but he did it. I witnessed hypnotism in India, but Herr Kerner was an expert.

He sat Lola before him, raised his forefinger before her eyes and told her to watch his finger. He moved it side to side like a metronome. He moved the finger upward until her head was bent back and her eyelids fluttered. Then he barked the command, "Sleep!"

Lola's head dropped until her chin rested on her chest and her shoulders slumped. He brought her down, down, down into a deeper trance. He then dismissed me, and I was never again to witness his exorcism or diet treatment.

Somehow, by her own will Lola broke whatever spell Kerner had over her. Although thinner, the light of decision glowed in her eyes. On the last day of February, Lola ordered me and the students to pack her bags. We were leaving for Switzerland.

It may have been a message of Lieutenant Nussbaum's death that decided her. He was killed in a minor skirmish with Austrian troops outside the town of Düppel. Lola never said a word about the news. Not so when I told her of my plans to return to India.

"How can you leave me at a time like this? The move to Switzerland will be terrible. I never lived without you at my side. You are the mother I never had."

I took her in my arms and we wept. I said, "You are the daughter I had, but have not seen. She is your age, and I have fantasized for years that you were she and she was you. But in my position as slave..."

Lola grasped me by the shoulders and held me at arm's length. "You were never my slave. You were my Nanny and surrogate mother."

"I was never freed. You never paid me a salary. Your mother purchased me from the English consul in Delhi."

"English law freed you some years ago. As for the salary, isn't the ten percent you take enough?"

My jaw dropped. Lola reached out and gently closed my mouth. "You'll catch flies with that beautiful mouth." We laughed. It was what I told her as a child. "Why are you surprised I know about you collecting ten percent? I and the King use the same Jews to exchange and send money abroad. The Jews in every European city are under surveillance of the secret police."

"Why didn't you stop me?"

"You always were fair and mindful of my interests. That was your salary. Bring my two jewelry boxes here."

Lola opened both boxes. They contained brooches, rings, pearl necklaces, and golden bracelets. Lola pointed and said, "Dip each hand into each box, and keep what you carry."

"I cannot accept."

"You must. According to you, you are still my slave—and slaves obey. Plunge your hands deep, for I truly love you."

We embraced and wept. Lola took my hands and thrust them into the jewelry boxes, then raised them up dripping with gold, diamonds, emeralds, rubies, and pearls. She dropped several fortunes into the lap of my sari. I choked on tears of gratitude. Her display of affection was deeper than I ever imagined. Lola whispered in my ear in Hindi, "You have well earned a respite from me. Go in peace, knowing I will always keep a place in my heart and my house for you."

My leaving was soul-wrenching, but the time was here. I parted from one daughter to be with another. I had not seen Princess for over twenty years. It was long past her time to be married.

I took a suit of clothes from one of our student escorts. Dressed like a man, I returned on the public stagecoach to Munich. There I made for the Jewish Quarter. At the synagogue I convinced a youngster to take a note to the old Jew. He had his wife clothe me in women's garb before he would listen.

I told him the danger my carrying such a wealth of jewelry. He devised a plan to send notes to Calcutta where I would be paid. I explained my plan to return to India acting as a wealthy, widowed Maharani. He agreed with my plan to return. Playing the part of a Maharani he made no comment.

"You require a suitable wardrobe for a Hindu Princess.", he said. "There are two people you should meet."

He summoned Jacob and Sarah. The color of their skin was brown like mine, and their almond-shaped eyes not European. The husband and wife were Jews from Peshawar, India. We conversed in Hindi. They had three children and couldn't stand living in Germany; the food was too bland, the language too guttural, and the weather too cold.

Jacob whispered to me that the Hebrew prayer service of these "Ashkenazim," as he called European Jews, "Is not ritually correct." He and his wife wished to return to India. They had been captured by pirates in the Bay of Bengal, ransomed by the Jews of Madagascar, and through a series of transfers arrived in Munich hosted by the Jewish community.

They asked if I would consider hiring them as servants. They would attend, guide, and protect me on the voyage home, and I would pay their passage to Calcutta and home to Peshawar. I agreed. They refused a second class cabin; they said it would appear suspicious and uncomfortable for servants to travel so well. They insisted on traveling steerage.

Sarah was very helpful. She designed and instructed the community tailors as to color, material, and how to fit Hindu clothing for me. The two accompanied me on shopping trips, buying presents for my Princess and her future husband. We chose quality cookware, porcelain, and items difficult to come by in the souks of India. They arranged for my first class cabin in the center of the ship, on the top deck of the port side.

We took passage on a river steamer to Marseilles. There we booked for Calcutta, and I sent a letter to Princess of my arrival date. We departed before an answer could be received.

I remained in my cabin for three full days. Apprehensive does not express the anxieties I suffered worrying about my impersonation. Sarah and Yaakov assured me that no Hindi-speaking passengers occupied first or second class berths. The Captain sent a message inquiring of my health and inviting me to dine at his table for dinner.

I felt somewhat relieved. I went out, but could not imagine how Lola tricked, lied, and bluffed her way for so many years. I decided to smile, say little, and listen more. It worked.

Not only was I accepted by the first class passengers, but was sought after to grace their tables during meals or at festive events. It was a gracious style of living.

On occasion I almost got up to serve the soup or take away the plates, but always caught myself. The life of luxury is an easy habit to acquire. I did not lie too much. I explained that after the death of my husband, the Maharajah, I traveled to England, France, Europe and Russia. When questioned, I dropped names famous and familiar to all. I had observed these people at close hand, and could add personal quirks. This one lisped, and that one liked young boys or the Cossacks" wild drinking parties.

I became a sought-after guest. No one ever questioned my lineage. I expected to be questioned, and spent most of my time preparing the answers. Then I realized, Europeans weren't interested in native Indian culture no matter how high the rank. To them we were all WOGS, Worthy Oriental Gentlemen – even the ladies. As a servant I had been invisible to them; as a Maharani I was shown off as an oddity, and my knowledge of current affairs was an aberration.

I speak English, French, Spanish, and Hindi, and understand some German. People asked me to translate between passengers. An English Colonel being posted in Rawalpindi mentioned something about a possible second Sikh Rebellion. My ears perked up.

He spoke at length about the importance of his new posting. Later, a wealthy French merchant asked me to interpret exactly what the Englishman had said. I explained, and the Frenchman questioned me at length. He was seeking information as Lola and I had done for Lord Palmerston. I wrote to Lord Palmerston giving the name of the Colonel and the information he had divulged.

I indicated that the Frenchman was interested in the shipping of cold-weather clothing for troops and animals. He spoke of a new type of cartridge for the Brown Bess, which I assumed was the name of a musket. The Colonel said the British Ordnance System converted these flintlocks into the new percussion system called the Pattern 1839 Musket. I posted this letter at the next mail buoy.

During the voyage I had a metamorphosis. No longer the servant, slave, or agent for the English, I was Inderjeet—one who wins the love of God. A cloak of caricature fell from my psyche and I became myself, a real person. I literally felt I could fly. I dreamt of rising up from the deck of the ship to scan those waiting for us on the dock. I searched for my little Princess and I became distressed. I knew she was there. I thrashed about and fell from my bed, and I lay on the floor sobbing and weeping. I did not recognize my own daughter.

Prior to docking in Calcutta, Sarah and Yaakov came to my cabin. I paid them as agreed, gave them presents for their children and several thousand rupees to begin life anew in India. I invited them and their families to visit me in Calcutta. They said they would see to my luggage, and we parted.

I went out on deck in time to watch the ship's hawsers tied to the stanchions on shore. The steam-whistle blew its last blast and the thumping engine stopped. A military band ashore played *God Save the King.*

I was so nervous that I ran to the cabin to relieve myself, then hastened back to the rail. As in my dream, I scanned the crowd of Hindus waiting off to the right where steerage passengers would disembark. Except for royalty, Hindus weren't allowed in the first class reception area. I waved both arms in the direction of the Hindu crowd. No one responded. I scanned those waiting for second-class passengers to disembark. There were few Hindus. None was young, female and beautiful.

I continued waving until the Captain approached. "Maharani," he said,"We will soon allow the second-class passengers to disembark. You are the last of the first class to leave us."

"I didn't realize," I said. "You have been so hospitable, it is difficult to take leave."

The Captain bowed, "And you have been so gracious, everyone sought your company. I bid you adieu."

I started down the whitewashed gang-plank with a parasol to shade me from the sun. At the bottom of the gangplank stood a tall, lissome, beautiful young Hindu woman. I gasped and stumbled. I was looking at my own image twenty years ago. It was like looking in a mirror but the reflecting figure, although the same, was acting differently. She ran to me, fell on her knees and wrapped her arms around my legs sobbing, "Mother! Mother! You've come home!" I fell to my knees and we embraced. We cried and hugged, kissed, and embraced until a tall handsome Sikh with a jeweled turban helped us to our feet.

"Mother," Princess said, "This is Sahib Bedi Singh, my husband. Husband, this is Inderjeet, my mother."

The tall young man smiled with a set of strong, even white teeth. "Mother," he bowed, "If you will allow me to call you that?"

I automatically replied, "Yes." The great shock that my Princess was married confused reality with my dreams. I tried to find something to say and blurted out, "Shouldn't we move on from this first class section?"

"Mother," Princess said, "We own this wharf, and are contemplating purchasing the ship you arrived on. Bedi is a member of the Nobility of the Sword. It is comparable to being knighted in England."

"How can this be?"

"Part of it had to do with the money you sent," Bedi said. "I invested it for you, and have kept careful accounts. You see that sailing ship? It is a grain carrier, and you own it. There are more properties in your name. I manage them for now, and will sign over managerial duties to you."

"Your English is better than your Hindi," I marveled, "Where were you educated?"

"In Cambridge."

"And before that?"

"My family is from Thailand, known in Europe as the Spice Islands. My great-grandfather was issued a charter from the Sultan of Brunei to trade. My father had five sons. He heard about Rothschild sending his sons throughout Europe to establish a banking empire. My father trained and sent us to the near and middle-east. We are forming an international trading company.

You, dear mother, are a great factor in our success."

"Mother," Princess took up the tale, "The guilder is worth 35 to 1 against the rupee. You sent us a fortune in credit through the Jews in Calcutta. Bedi invested your money with ours."

"As helpful as your money was," Bedi said. "Even more so was your introduction to the international money transfer of the Jews. My family now use them for most currency transactions. Your Jewish contact in Munich put me in touch with the Rothschild son in Berlin. We are having their shipping agents represent us in Europe."

"Do you know anything of a possible second Sikh rebellion?" I asked softly.

A significant glance passed between my son-in-law and daughter.

"There is talk of unrest in the mountains to the north," Princess said. "Although the Hindus speak of Sikhs as a military caste, we in Calcutta are merchants. The knife in my husband's cummerbund is ornamental."

"You remain Sikhs?"

"We are." Both said together.

"Why or how did you know to call me Inderjeet when we first met?"

"Guru Rama Singh is here," Princess said.

"Here in Calcutta?"

"He married us. He performed the ceremony just as he described it to you aboard ship."

I covered my mouth but was unable to stifle a sob, "The man knew you were going to be married."

"He never met me."

"I told him you were waiting for me to return so you

could be married. He answered with an English proverb, 'time and tide wait for no man'."

"You can question him when we return home. He will be waiting."

They led me to a large ornate carriage drawn by four white horses. I asked, "How did you recognize me?"

"I have followed Countess Montez in the newspapers, and some photos of her included you. We look more like sisters than mother and daughter."

"When I saw you, I thought I was looking into a twenty year old mirror."

"When I saw you, I thought, if that is what I will look like in twenty years, thank God."

"How long are you married?"

"Eight years,"

I was about to ask about children when a footman opened the carriage door. Out tumbled six: three boys and three girls. I swooned, and Bedi caught me. After a minute he introduced me to each. "Boys first," he said. "Our first son is seven. We have had a child every year until now."

"Isn't that enough?" I asked.

"I never had brothers or sisters," Princess said. "I want twelve. Bedi says enough. He worries about my health. I believe it is because our youngest girl smells up the house. He calls her Stinker."

Bedi held up the little baby in one hand over his head, and laughing said, "Here is my little stinker." He brought her down and nuzzled her. Child and father laughed.

On the trip home we drove the length of the port.

Princess pointed out two more wharfs, three docked ships belonging to the Singh Corporation, and several warehouses, stables, and blacksmith shops also. The carriage turned and we went up the hill, where the breeze off the water was most refreshing.

At first I thought we entered a wealthy suburb of Calcutta. Princess explained this was the outskirts of their home. The people worked the land, had reliable water, sewerage and their homes were compact, neat, and in blocks indicating the British influence of the grid design. Princess referred to 'the house'.

What lay before me was a palace larger and more beautiful than Lola's. It compared to Ludwig's castle. It had no fortified walls and was only two stories high. The long portico front was supported by large, pure white, fluted pillars. The main entrance was shaded by an overhang and balustrade. Two large Sikh warriors, in colorful red uniforms decorated with gold epaulets and sash, guarded the massive teak doors. The guards sported fierce handlebar mustaches and trimmed black beards. Their uniforms may have been for show, but these two would make anyone hesitate to force entrance. They each wore a saber, two pistols, and one muzzle-loading rifle in a stand near their right hands.

Is such security necessary?" I asked.

"Wealth draws the unwanted," Bedi said.

I busied myself with the children. I tried to learn their names but then Stinky lived up to her title. I handed her to Princess who held her at arm's length and passed the baby to Bedi, saying, "You wanted her. You have her." He scrunched his nose and held the Stinker away from him.

The Sikh guards opened both front doors, and there stood Guru Rama Singh. His white hair and beard framed his smiling mahogany face. He spread his arms wide and said "Welcome!"

Behind him were people dressed in festive clothing. Most were musicians playing drums, flutes, and other instruments. The song was one of welcome. The Guru embraced me saying, "I knew we would meet again."

"You also knew my daughter would be married when I returned."

"Not a mystical thing," he said wagging his head from side to side. "The apple does not fall far from the tree. I knew if your daughter looked anything like her mother she would be wed before you returned."

"What are you doing here?"

"I travel and preach. There is a significant Sikh population in Calcutta. I thought to visit your Princess. She was about to be married and asked me to perform the ceremony. I interviewed them. Her husband was quite wealthy before they met. They combined their fortunes, and you see the results."

"Is he as good as my first impression?"

"Probably better, but then, I am not impartial. You see, he established an Ashram for me. It is a small village down the road. Your daughter and son-in-law support our community."

"What is it you do there?"

"We work, eat, sleep, study, and meditate together."

"To what end?"

"To leave this world better than when we entered it."

"How can it be? We enter as a pure soul in the body of an infant."

"Because you are thinking only of the body," Guru Ram said. "I teach the improvement of oneself and his environment. We are a group having common spiritual goals who, instead of preparing ourselves for heaven as the Christians and Muslims do, we try to bring heaven to earth."

"You are asking for sainthood," I said.

Guru Rama smiled, "You are wise beyond your years. No one can achieve sainthood in heaven; there God rules. It is only on earth that we can do good in the face of evil. In heaven there is no evil. We will be judged by our actions on earth."

"I have seen so much of the world, and taken part in all manner of wickedness."

"Now it is time to change."

"I do not know if I have the strength. I am ashamed."

"Why?"

"Without me, my son-in-law and daughter turned out so well."

"Dear Inderjeet, Princess is your offspring. Your blood flows in her veins. You will always be with her. Your goodness is apparent in her actions."

"I would like to visit your Ashram."

Guru Rama placed both palms together before his face. "You give me the pleasure of anticipation."

I brought my palms together and said, "Khudu Hafiz—may God protect you."

# CHAPTER 22

## HOME

Three months passed in this palatial estate before I acclimatized to my new station in life. The shipboard experience was helpful, but there I was pretending. I dropped the title of Maharani. Being the mother in-law of Bedi Singh was more than enough respectability and honor.

I continued to rise early. The household help became upset when I put my room in order, folded my clothes and cleaned up after the little ones. I've restrained myself for their sake.

I no longer think of the Punkawallas working the overhead fans from ropes outside the building. The breeze is refreshing and makes sleeping a pleasure. The one area where I refused to relinquish my rights is in caring for the children.

Each one has a Nanny. I allowed the ladies to help me change nappies, especially with Stinky. If she matures as strong as she smells, she'll be an Amazon! She is Bedi's favorite. He tries to give equal attention to all, but because of his business it is difficult.

Princess and I do everything to give her husband more time with the family. One morning Bedi planned an outing for the entire family. He took us all to dockside. We pulled up to a beautiful white and blue transport ship. The paint was fresh, but there was no name on her.

"I am contemplating purchasing this ship," Bedi said. "I would like your thoughts on the matter."

"I suggest you hire a qualified shipwright to go over her stem to stern," was my thought.

"We've done that," Princess said. "As our partner in the Company, we are asking how you think she looks. Do you have a good feeling about her?"

"She is beautiful, clean, and steam driven," I replied. "Without paddlewheels, it means she has propellers. This is a major asset. You must hire a ship's master to ascertain her seaworthiness."

"We have," Bedi said. "Help us herd the children aboard, and we shall picnic on the quarter-deck."

Without the use of tugs, the Captain maneuvered from the mooring and out of the harbor into the open sea. A table was set on the quarterdeck. Fruits chilled by ice brought down from the Himalayan Mountains were served. A sumptuous meal followed, and we each took one of the youngest children to feed. The sun was warm, the breeze cool, and everything was right. "Oh, how God has blessed me," I sighed.

"You earned everything good in life," Princess said. "Now, what do you think of this ship?"

"What is the Captain's opinion?"

Bedi waved to the wheelhouse and the Captain appeared wearing appropriate gold braid on his sleeves, epaulets and cap. He bowed.

"Captain," Bedi asked, "What is your evaluation of this craft for use as a commercial carrier?"

"Sir," the captain replied, "She is a proper sturdy ship, well built, with twin screws. It is powered by the most reliable steam engine built in Scotland. Her hull was laid in Amsterdam, and those Dutchmen know how to build."

"Do you have any reservations about this craft?" I asked.

"Aside from small modern innovations for loading and unloading, none with the ship."

"What else is there?"

"The price. The owners are asking three quarters of a million rupees. Converted to guilders, it is a proper selling price in Europe."

"What is appropriate in Calcutta?"

"Six hundred fifty thousand rupees. Anything less would be a steal."

I smiled at him, "Let us see if you and I can steal her."

"My pleasure, Maharani."

"Inderjeet is my name. If my son-in-law approves, I will take his family name of Singh."

"I am honored," Bedi said, "But Princess and I would like to make this ship our gift to you. She will be named The Inderjeet, and incorporated into the family merchant fleet. You can direct her in trade and travel."

"I appreciate your good intentions. My life was dedicated to bring heaven to earth for my daughter. There is one more contribution." From my handbag I withdrew the largest diamond brooch given to me by Lola. "This is the Antioch Diamond. It is valued at more than half a million rupees. I would like to offer this in trade for the ship."

"Mother, how did you come by such a jewel?"

"I haven't spoken of my years with Lola Montez."

"We would like to hear," Bedi said.

"When the children are asleep. Suffice to say we spied for Lord Palmerston."

"My God!" Bedi burst out. "He's now Prime Minister of England."

"And the Queen hates his belly."

"You mean his guts," Princess said. "It's American slang."

"I met several Americans. They do not speak English as she is meant to be spoken."

"Mother," Bedi said, "If you are going to help us in business, you must learn American. They build the fastest ships, choose the most dedicated leaders, and are always looking to make or find something better."

"Bedi, you raised a subject I wish to discuss in private with both of you." Princess directed the nannies to take the children. We sipped mint tea and had wafer-thin sugar biscuits for desert. "You two spend too much time trying to convince me the money I sent was used wisely. Stop. I am overwhelmed. You two take me around saying I own this, and that. I wish more time with the children. I would like to do other things."

"Mother," Princess said, "We want you to be part of our family. The business is the greatest part of that."

"No, dear: the children are. I would like to put a rock on each of their little heads so they would not grow up, but then I'd deny myself the joy of witnessing their next steps in life."

"Are you saying we do not afford you enough time with the children?" Bide asked.

"Yes. And there are other things I wish to do."

"What are they?" Princess asked.

"I would like to visit Guru Rama's Ashram. I studied in western academic schools, but am ignorant of my own religion."

"Guru Rama will teach you here in the house," Bedi said. "We can hire the finest teachers in any subject."

"No, I wish to see the Ashram and study with other people."

"Mother, we are here to make your life as pleasant as possible. I know you love me. I think Bedi and the children have found a place in your heart."

""You all fill my heart to bursting. But please, stop trying to convince me that the money I sent was properly invested. What you two have done is better than I dreamed. I thought to build an Ashram for Guru Rama, and without knowing it, you two did that very thing. Your actions speak volumes. I do not wish to be involved in the business of making money. I may never become used to ordering people around, but life with the family is good."

"If you are saying that you no longer wish to be involved with the decision-making of the business, I can accept that," Bedi said. "Princess and I would like to be able to question you about global matters. The European world is a mystery to us. Our business is becoming involved there."

"My pleasure," I said. "I sense something else on your mind."

"Yes," Bedi said. "You acted as a spy for Lord Palmerston. It started me thinking. How might I utilize my shipping agents as commercial spies?"

"There is no definitive line between military, political, and commercial spying. One affects the other. I will guide you. Lola and I were two opposites in our approach to gathering information. She talked, talked, talked. When she stopped, the men jabbered away just to be heard. I barely spoke. To fill the silence, the men talked and talked. The most reliable intelligence is that which is paid for. Those who can't be bought cannot be trusted. There is a trick with a piece of split bamboo used on letters."

"What if we report to you once a month about the business, and we meet at a time of your choosing to speak of a spy system?"

"Let us call it a commercial intelligence committee,"

"Then it is agreed." Bedi said.

"There is one other thing. I wish to negotiate for the ship with the Antioch diamond as payment. The owners will carry it safely in a pocket to Europe, where it will fetch a higher price."

"Are you a good negotiator?" Bedi asked.

All the money I sent to you came from bargaining. I do a thing with my eyebrows..."

"I will accompany you."

"I prefer the Captain escort me."


The Captain and I met the ship's owners in a private room at the Alhambra Hotel. They were two Frenchmen. I had them watched and investigated prior to our meeting.

My people found they had come into ownership of the vessel in payment of a four-hundred-thousand Rupee debt owed by a Portuguese trader. They were both dissatisfied with life in India. One suffered a malaria attack, and both wished to return to civilized France.

Armed with this information, the Captain and I marched into the hotel room set aside for the meeting. I saw two Hindu men seated to the right. They had jeweler's loupes and small candles on the table before them. Pleasantries were exchanged. I withdrew the brooch from my handbag and unfolded the sparkling jewel on black velvet. That is how the old Jew in Munich presented his best pieces. "The Antioch Diamond," I said.

The stone always drew sighs of admiration. The two jewelers obviously knew of this titled stone. They tried to hide their excitement, but their eyes glittered and they leaned forward. The two Frenchmen casually looked at the stone in its gold, ruby-studded setting, then passed it to the nearest jeweler.

"This stone is more than a trinket," the Captain said. "I'm certain your experts know its history. Antioch on the Orontes was an ancient Greek city in Turkey. This stone is mentioned in 200 B.C. Am I correct that your asking price for the ship is three quarters of a million rupees?"

"That was the asking price," one of the owners said. "It is now nine-hundred thousand rupees."

"Why did you bring us here under false pretenses?" I asked.

"Madame, it is only the fair market value we seek. We have another bidder."

"The Antioch Diamond is not worth your new asking price."

"How much do you believe it is worth?" the merchant asked.

"Your asking price of seven-hundred and fifty thousand rupees," I answered. The merchants turned to the jewelers who shook their heads in the negative.

"What is your estimate of the value?" the Captain asked them.

One jeweler said, "Six-hundred and fifty thousand rupees."

The second jeweler said. "Between half a million and six-hundred thousand rupees."

"Nonsense!" The captain said. "Your men," he pointed at the jewelers, "Are quoting Calcutta prices. The Antioch Diamond is not known here. In Europe, where you two are going, and at the exchange rate of thirty-five rupees to a guilder, you will come out far ahead."

"How do you know where we are going?" one merchant asked.

"The whole city knows you are fed up with the heat, the food, and lack of good wine," the Captain answered.

"How can you expect Hindus, Sikhs or Muslims to produce good wine if they won't drink it?" the Frenchman said.

"Are you willing to come back to your original price and accept the brooch as payment?" I asked.

"Madame," the Frenchman said, "There is nothing but your word that the jewel is worth what you say, in Europe."

"Ask your jewelers. They know the European market."

"How do you know what they know?"

"My son in-law is Bedi Singh. I consulted his jewelers."

The owners acknowledged Bedi Singh's name with a nod of their heads. They extolled the virtues of their vessel while the jewelers lit the candle and took turns examining the stone in the flickering light. The first jeweler said, "I remain with my estimate of between half a million and six-hundred thousand rupees if sold in Europe."

The second jeweler said, "I upgrade the value in Europe. This brooch will fetch the equivalent of three quarters of a million rupees in Zurich."

The older merchant shook his head. "Not enough. We have an offer for nine-hundred thousand rupees."

"Then take it," the Captain said. "It is far more than you will receive from Madame Singh."

"The buyer lacks cash at the moment."

"I looked directly at the two merchants, raised my eyebrows and said, "When I don't have the money I will offer a million, then wait until the Calcutta heat weighs heavily and your malaria returns. You will sell for half a million. You two accepted the ship in payment for a four-hundred thousand rupee debt. I offer the brooch which your jewelers price at between six-hundred thousand and three quarters of a million rupees. Aren't you gentlemen being a bit gluttonous?"

"Madame, we are merchants. You refer to us in that unflattering term but we are honest men attempting to make a straightforward profit."

"Since you received the vessel in lieu of a four-hundred thousand rupee debt, and the median price of your two jewelers is at least six-hundred thousand, don't you think a profit of fifty percent is enough?"

"Madame, we are entitled to earn whatever we can. That is good business."

"Not with me," I said and stood. I swept the Antioch

Diamond into my handbag and took the Captain's arm. Both jewelers were agape as they watched us march out.

Two days later Bedi received a message to send his lawyers to complete the sale of the ship for the brooch.

"Mother," Bedi said, "The Captain tells us what a clever negotiator you are."

"The negotiations were simple, the results, a foregone conclusion. I hired three policemen to follow and learn what they could about the French merchants. The trick was finding which jewelers they would choose, and bribe them."

"You bribed both?" Bedi blurted out.

"Only one. The one who recommended Zurich."

"Mother!" Princess frowned. "That's dishonest."

"That's commercial intelligence. Bedi, Do you still wish me to help you in this underhanded, nefarious, scheming, endeavor of information-gathering that can save you a fortune?"

"Oh yes, Mother dear," Bedi said. "And I will explain the facts of life to Princess."


I developed a very comfortable routine. Rise early, make breakfast for the older children, dress them and send them off to the English Embassy School. They returned in the afternoon to do their homework. At dinner Bedi questioned them about their lessons. When the table was cleared the children were tutored in Hindi.

For breakfast I received the younger ones with clean nappies, ready to eat. Princess and I took turns feeding them. It was a constant joy. When the parents left for work, the three youngest were mine. I played with them until ten and handed them back to their nannies for a nap. I changed clothes and took an open one-horse carriage to Guru Rama's Ashram.

The first time I entered the Ashram I was shocked. Men and women walked about naked, or fully covered by an orange cloth. For reasons I do not know, many allowed their hair to grow wild. Others braided and plaited their locks. Some shaved their heads.

Guru Rama Singh explained, "There are many different approaches to worshipping God. In this Ashram all may express devotion in the way he or she wishes. Man is born and, having been gifted the human form at birth, if he does not attempt to extol God on earth he has lived in vain. 'Vanity of vanities,' said Shakespeare."

I had learned Shakespeare and seen his plays. My life had been lived in vanity. My sale into slavery must have been a necessity. Remaining as a servant was my choice. I could have escaped into the Indian mass of humanity. At the Ashram I decided to sample the smorgasbord of philosophy, meditation, yoga, Buddhism, the Vedanta and other disciplines being taught.

In the small thatched huts I listened, questioned, studied and attended Guru Rama's lectures. On one occasion he and I discussed certain questions about the future of the Ashram. It was now six months since I entered this course of study. It was time to discuss my future with Guru Rama. He sat in the rear of his thatched hut. It was larger than others but not large enough to accommodate those wishing to learn from him. He and I exchanged pleasantries. He asked, "Have you decided which path to take in serving God?"

"Yes," I answered. "You may be disappointed in my choice."

"Allow me to judge."

"The Vedanta School of thought appears to dominate your students and teachers. Buddhism based on the teachings of Siddhartha Gautama, Carvaka, and Ajivika follows as the preferences of many students. Buddhism, Yoga and Meditation can, and is being practiced by agnostics in your Ashram."

"Thank God for Agnostics!" Guru Rama said.

"When I entered your school you told me I had a debt to God for being born human. How can you praise those who doubt God?"

"In questioning God they are witness to his being. If you accept another person's word that God exists, whether it is from me, priest or Imam, then that person stands between you and God." Guru Rama pulled his beard and wagged his head. "The individual must experience the Almighty. Whatever path he takes in this quest is the correct one. It is the journey that counts."

"How then can you place two teachers in adjacent huts? One extols Carvaka; which is a materialistic approach worshipping free will. The other endorses Ajivika, denying free will, and is anti-materialistic."

"I purposely placed them close together. The only way we can draw the truth from our thoughts is to argue."

"You should meet some of the Jews I stayed with in Munich. They argue about everything."

"I would be interested in that. There is so much to learn and so little time. But tell me why do you believe I will be disappointed in your choice here on the Ashram?"

"You offer nothing I find practical. I believe serving

God is serving man. I owe a great debt to God. Your schools offer nothing that would satisfy me that I could please God."

"That is a problem," Guru Rama said. "Do you have a plan?"

"Serve man. An old Jew told me that man is made in the image of God."

"He is probably right," Guru Rama said.

"When I serve man, then I would be serving God?"

"It depends how you intend to serve man."

"Feed him, clothe him, and ease his pain. I learned this from Countess Lola Montez, who saw it put into action by Franz Liszt."

"The great composer and concert pianist?"

"The same. He is a good person."

"That is the most one can wish for. And where do you intend to begin?"

"With your permission, here on the Ashram."

"So then this Ashram will be of use to you?"

"In that sense, yes—but not in my beliefs, religious practices, or philosophy."

"Who knows the source of knowledge that enters one's heart in the search for truth?" Guru Rama smiled and the room seemed brighter. "What are your thoughts?

"To build a proper house, with a lecture hall large enough for you to accommodate those who wish to hear you. It will be impressive enough, befitting your importance."

"In my youth I thought to be rich, famous, and humble. Alas, dreams change. I am none of the three, and seek only the latter."

"My dear teacher, you are not a good judge of yourself. Rich you are, for your needs are so few they are easily satisfied. You want for nothing; you ask for nothing. Famous? Everyone who knows of you bows their head when your name is mentioned. And my dear Guru Rama, humble you are by nature—and wouldn't recognize yourself if your modesty were to enter and serve you tea."

"And, my dear Inderjeet, what makes you such a good judge of my character?"

"I personally benefitted from your wisdom, advice and influence. I own two merchant ships."

"Wealth may put you in a position to judge others, but it doesn't mean you are right. I hope you will not enter the American slave trade, or the English opium profession."

"I was a slave; I will not condemn others to that fate. There is enough money trading herbs and condiments from the Spice Islands where Bedi's family has roots."

"Please consider my recommendation before building a headquarters for me. Feed the people first. They are so thin, It hurts my heart to look at them."

"Yes, my teacher."

The following morning, after the children were off to school and the little ones napping, the Captain and I went to the souk in the Muslim quarter. There we bargained for three giant cooking pots, several smaller ones, and ceramic bowls by the basketfull. They were from China, brought along the Silk Road. We went to the Sikh market and bought two wagon-loads of grain and one of vegetables and herbs. We also rented four wagons to fill with wood and charcoal and flour.

"Shall we go to the Circassian market and buy meat?" the Captain asked.

"No, the Guru and I discussed this. Although meat is not forbidden to Sikhs and others on the Ashram, our religion stresses living in harmony with others. By eating meat in front of Hindus and those Sikhs who abstain, we would create tension." I fluttered my eyelids, looked up at the captain and asked, "Do you think we can send this convoy of wagons to the Ashram, while you and I return to the ship and your cabin to discuss sex?"

The captain began to blush, cleared his throat and said, "I thought of that subject since we first met."

"I would like to know your thoughts."

"And so you shall Madame Singh. So you shall."

# CHAPTER 23

## DIWALI

Throughout Calcutta, our big house, and the Ashram, everyone was cleaning. The streets were swept, garbage burned, even stray animals were washed. Diwali is the five-day festival dating back three thousand years. Lakshmi, the goddess of wealth, is honored. This also marks the end of November harvest season. Everyone counts it as the beginning of the Hindu calendar year.

Throughout the great land of India, Diwali is celebrated in different ways. Much like Guru Rama's teachings, the religious significance of Diwali depends on your philosophy, beliefs, myths and legends. But for all faiths it is a happy time. The wealthy provide fireworks. Where affordable, communal meals are served free to all.

The excitement was contagious. Each family member took part. Bedi was in charge of the overall preparation, including the fireworks and entertainment. I, Princess, and the three older children oversaw the purchase and cooking of food for five thousand meals during a three-day period. The remaining two-day feast of Annakoot was celebrated, with 108 different dishes. It was hosted by a colleague of Bedi. Those who worship Lakshmi request the benefit of her benevolence by doing good deeds. They wish to be blessed in the coming year with mental, physical and material well-being.

Hindus offer to various gods symbolizing music, literature, and scholarship. They gift the mighty ones for guidance in an ethical life and to be granted fearlessness in expressing the truth.

Diwali for Sikhs marks the incident when Guru Har Gobind freed himself, and the imprisoned Hindu kings, from Fort Gwalior prison. They were captives of the Islamic ruler, Jahangir. Gobind led the Kings to the Golden Temple in Amritsar. Ever since, Sikhs celebrate Bandi Choorh Divas, with the annual lighting up of the Golden Temple, fireworks and other festivities. The celebration is one long five-day period. No time is set for meals, sleep, dance, or storytelling. People do what they want, when they want. Fakirs, whirling Dervishes, magicians, snake charmers, musicians, and holy men appear from nowhere. Everyone enjoys the fire walkers, sword swallowers, and storytellers. What a pleasure to hear the new tunes of Hindu music, and to recall the old favorites. Bedi hired the best puppeteers and performers available.

Princess and I supervised the children. The oldest boy wanted to explode his fireworks in a cobra nest. We forbade it. Bedi heard the commotion, took charge, and said he would show his son how he did it as a boy.

By the time we reached the serpents nest there was a crowd following us. Bedi showed his son how to light the fuse and throw the fire cracker so he would know how long before it would explode.

More people gathered. Men brought long swords or rakes and hoes. Cobras are responsible for more deaths than illness. Bedi tied several fire crackers around a large one in the center. He encouraged people to light torches, and handed the explosives to his son, who walked fearlessly to an overhang covered with bushes. He lit the fuse, hurled the firecrackers into the nest and walked backward as his father instructed.

There was a frightening bang. Smoke floated out from the overhang. Four two-foot-long cobras wriggled out, followed by a seven-foot-long female. Men jumped in and killed the snakes. Other cobras slithered out of the smoking den to be finished off by the people.

I recalled Lola as an eight year old, exploding a firecracker on a sleeping cobra. She giggled and cut its head off with a kitchen knife. I hadn't thought about Lola in months, and was surprised at myself. She hadn't written. I decided to write her.

After the holiday I took the older children to mail the letter. While I was in the queue, the Post Master came out of his office and spoke to my oldest grandson. I questioned the boy, and he told me the Post Master asked if I knew a Maharani Manuela.

"That's me."

"But you are Grandma Inderjeet."

The postmaster handed over a packets of letters. All but one were from Lola. Lord Palmerston expressed his gratitude for the information about the talkative Colonel on the ship. He wrote "If the English government can be of service to you, please inform me or our Embassy in Calcutta."

I made a note to ask for a recommendation of an honest broker in England and Europe with whom condiments from the Spice Islands might most profitably be traded.

Always an imaginative and prolific letter writer, Lola did herself proud. She kept me updated. Her letters are a journal. With some work, it would make several interesting chapters in a book.

Although officially revoked, she continued to use the title, Countess of Landsfeld. The yearly stipend promised by Ludwig continued from his personal fortune. The Landtag rescinded all Lola's claims to Bavarian citizenship. Her dream palace, a burnt out ruin, was confiscated by the government. Ludwig's son was crowned King. Lola knew the young man. She assessed his intelligence as being "several pence short of a shilling"—certainly not a shadow of his father's stature.

According to newspapers in Europe, the King's abdication, set in motion a revolutionary movement throughout the continent. The common people enacted laws making the aristocracy responsible to an elected parliament. The thirty-nine Germanic States began serious discussions about unification. This was provoked by Prince von Metternich and the Austro-Hungarian Empire signing a military treaty. Von Metternich was poised to swallow up the Germanic states one by one. Throughout Europe, the people realized their power. Protests and riots in Warsaw, St. Petersburg, Italy, Romania, Amsterdam, Sweden and the Baltic States— aristocrats, mindful of the French Revolution, fled to Switzerland, Zurich the most popular destination.

In Switzerland Lola regaled in the center of the European cultural world. She had inadvertently ignited an American idea in the minds of Europeans: government by the people and for the people. She never believed in it. Lola insisted on rule by an educated aristocracy, but the power of princes did not match the will of the people. In Zurich she found herself pursued with invitations and hosted at the most exclusive gatherings, celebrations and yachting parties on the lake.

That is a summary of several letters, Lola wrote to me. Below is a copy of a letter she sent to Ludwig, which portrays a different picture of life in Zurich.

"My Dearest Ludwig,

"I seem to myself like a criminal in flight, even more so because probably, on your Ministers' advice, you involved the police in this scandal, and you'll see in the newspapers that I was forced to leave you by yourself and that the police escorted me away. I hadn't expected that from you my dear Ludwig, and I am very certain the cruel idea was not yours—but I am resigned to everything now. ...I'm in a deplorable state physically, and even more spiritually, because who knows, now that I have been separated from you, whether enemies and false friends will tell you lies about me—Now I know why the person unknown to me told you that infamous lie about the student Piesner, and you my dear Ludwig believed it. ...I beg you not to forget what I have suffered for my dear Ludwig, because I didn't want to deceive you like others, but always told you the truth about others even against my own best interest; that is not enough to assure you I love you infinitely but I am so unhappy now— although everyone here is very nice to me, I think that only in the tomb will I find rest ...don't confide in anyone, neither man nor woman—no one is completely sincere—to pass my time in exile, I want to study German. And in a little while I hope to write to you in your own language. But my dear Ludwig, I can't wait the whole time in Switzerland—in truth it is not possible, this country is so sad in winter and cold... I think with fear and horror of living in Switzerland—it's a terrible punishment—send me another passport with an English name—and I will leave with it on the instant for Palermo—I got my period yesterday and I am very indisposed. While I am here I do not intend to go out in order to avoid public curiosity—farewell, my Ludwig, until I get a letter from you and my shipment of personal belongings arrive. I'll wait here, from my heart I give you thousands of kisses from your faithful Lolita.                    Don't forget and don't be unfaithful to me."[17]

Lola remained consistent in her ability to project the image she desired to the person she addressed. Yet Ludwig had misgivings. A letter he wrote but never sent to Lola appeared in Bavarian newspapers. Lola sent a copy to me. I can only think someone else knows how to open letters with split bamboo.

"From the King.

---

[17] *Lola Montez* by Bruce Seymour p.206

"My Dearest Lolita, I was desperate, almost mad in this separation from you; if only you had been a faithful lover to me and even during the time you were here I was convinced you weren't; the separation from you has made me so, so unhappy! Your Ludwig is not subtle like Lolita. But he is no fool. I don't speak of the Jesuits or the nobles, they had other motives, but you have betrayed my love in public and made an enemy of it. Your infidelities have betrayed my heart, but I forgive you, and I repeat: the world is not capable of making me break with you, you alone can do that. Do you want this, Lolita? Oh, if only it were possible for you to be faithful to me in all things, or at least sincere a limitless sincerity..."[18]

He never completed nor sent this letter. Somehow it was exposed in the newspapers. Lola says this is his style of writing and I agree. He did send a shorter, more conciliatory, letter to Lola on the same date.

"Very Dear Lolita,

"You know it: the whole world does not have the power to separate you from me, you alone have it. The decisive moment has arrived. If a student travels with you, or joins you, you will never see me again, you have broken with me. Lolita, you inspire a love in me as

---

[18] *Lola Montez* by Bruce Seymour p. 207, 208

no one ever has before in my life. Never have I done for another what I have done for you. With your love, it would mean nothing to me to break with everything. My beloved, think of the past sixteen months, how your Ludwig has conducted himself in this time we have known each other. You will never find a heart like mine. Lolita has the decision."

She did decide, but did not share her decision with Ludwig. She dismissed the student Piesner and took his best friend as her lover. Two weeks later she dismissed him and took the last of the three students, a large blond fellow named Mussinan, for her companion. She took other lovers as she found them at parties and social gatherings. At one of the parties a Swiss professor of medicine commented on the cold sore at the corner of Lola's lips. She forgot to apply the beauty mark. The doctor questioned her and asked if she would be so kind as to visit an old man who appreciates beauty. Lola couldn't resist the flattery and agreed. She described the meeting in the doctor's office.

"He questioned me about the cold sore. I answered truthfully, and he asked other questions to which I responded frankly except when it involved my sexual activities. I told him I was not a frivolous woman.

"'Nevertheless," he said, 'You are afflicted with syphilis.'

"'Are you mad? I am Lola Montez, Countess of Landsfeld! It's impossible.'

"He stroked his chin whiskers and said, 'No, Countess. It is an irrefutable fact, based on scientific deduction resulting from the diagnosis. Sadly enough, I have reached this conclusion for princes, kings, and clergy. That is why the University conferred professorship on this old grey head.'

"'But you don't understand,' I shouted and thought longingly of you my dear Manuela. How I miss your comforting touch and sage advice. Alas, my choices are limited: either to treat my condition or not.

"The nurse offered tea or cognac. I took the bottle of cognac. I am unaccustomed to it and fell asleep in the doctor's office."

Lola decided to go ahead with the standard treatment. She described it as follows: "Holy Gum to chew. It is the sap of a certain tree used to restrain the spread of the disease. It is not unpleasant but tiring on my jaw. An ointment of metallic mercury mixed with coal tar and petrolatum rubbed into my skin several times a day for two weeks.

"In between the rubdowns I entered a process called sub-fumigation. It entailed bathing the body in sulfur and mercury fumes. This torture takes place in an over-heated room with an oven containing large rocks. Every so often the nurse enters, throws a bucket of mercury-water onto the overheated rocks and runs out before the blast of heat from the oven hits her. I sat and sweated.

"After two weeks I refused to continue. I lost so much weight not one dress fit. My breasts sagged. I was adamant. The doctor complied and prescribed mercury in liquid form to be taken daily, and the Holy Gum to chew. The doctor is uncertain whether the mercury treatments prevent the spread of the disease or not.

"He said, of future sexual relations, I should require

my partner wear a sheath. I told him I would, but to hell with it. Men gave me the pox. I'll return the favor. I tried to think of who passed this ugly disease onto me. The Professor said it is most common among soldiers. I believe Lieutenant Nusbammer is guilty. He was unfaithful to me on more than one occasion. It may not be polite to speak ill of the dead, but I wish that bastard burns in hell. Would you inquire how the Hindus treat this malady?"

I questioned Guru Rama if he knew how to prevent syphilis. He reached down and plucked a pebble from the ground, saying, "I remember your mistress aboard ship. She was sexually active." He placed the pebble in the palm of my hand saying, "Tell her to hold this between her knees."

"It is too late. Is there a treatment?"

"I know little of medicine," Guru Rama answered. "The Chinese use arsenic and lead without success. Acupuncture is unhelpful. Hindu charlatans use a combination of mercury and arsenic. I think they kill more than they cure."

"Is there nothing?"

"Not to my knowledge. But you can explain to Madame Montez that European medicine is greatly influenced by theology. Christian clergy view doctors as soldiers of God. Human beings are born in sin. Disease is considered Satan's influence. They believe an afflicted person should suffer. They encourage pain during childbirth. For them, illness is God's punishment and doctors must not alleviate pain. My opinion, any palliative is less dangerous to the Countess than the cures mentioned."

"Is there nothing you can recommend?"

"For ulcerations, the juice from the leaves of an Aloe plant. The life force in the body according to the Chinese is called 'Tchi'. They say, through contemplation, this Tchi can be directed to heal the body. Hindus use meditation and Yoga. I think either of these methods is less harmful than the medicinal approach. My philosophy is, we are born with both health and sickness. How we lead our moral lives determines our wellbeing."

I passed this information on to Lola. She appeared to be doing well in Zurich. The former Home Secretary of Britain, Robert Peel, invited her to Bern on the River Aare. He opined, it is now the center of world politics. A wave of European aristocrats, industrialists, and royalty fleeing the insurgencies, descended on Bern.

Robert Peel played on Lola's ego. He claimed her pithy critique of recent history, and grasp of implications on the future, would be most welcome in the salons and embassies of Bern. The Swiss Parliament convened here. It replaced Zurich as the center of international culture.

Lola first met Robert Peel in Paris, at George Sand's Salon. She encouraged his plan to form Britain's first police force. That is how British policemen came to be called Bobbies, a contraction of Robert, the Home Secretary's first name.

Soon after Lola's arrival in Bern, European royalty was rocked by news of a second revolution in France. King Louis Philippe and his Queen fled to Britain. The Orleans monarchy ended.

Political rumors and gossip ran rampant in the salons, cafes and embassies of Bern. This was a world made for Lola, a quick thinker with informal entrée of personal friendships to consulates and homes of the European powerbrokers. She thought a step ahead of most in her assessment of current events. Royalty, politicians, and businessmen sought her advice.

Never reluctant to state an opinion as fact, Lola held forth in grand style. I pictured her lecturing with certainty that captivated and influenced her listeners. She was lobbied by diplomats, aristocrats, and industrialists. The world of Bern, Switzerland became Lola's playground.

Then Robert Peel approached her, requesting to be reimbursed for helping Lola move—finding her a beautiful mansion, introducing her to the powerful and influential of Europe, and for a two thousand five hundred franc gambling debt she owed him.

Lola sent Robert Peel packing. She took a swing at him with her umbrella in the lobby of Bern's most prestigious hotel. She was the Countess of Landsfeld. All accommodations were her due as a Spanish Aristocrat and Bavarian Royalty. "Gentlemen," she said, "Do not discuss gambling debts with a highborn lady."

The following letters indicated a less than comfortable experience in Bern. She told how she implored Ludwig to send her money and an account she could draw upon. He answered, "Twenty thousand Florins a year is what I made available to you. You are terrible with money. There will not be more than promised. You would drain the Horn of Plenty."

Lola responded, "What have I done to you that makes you deny me a few francs to maintain my reputation? This is what I get after my expulsion from Bavaria. I hope these words touch your heart."

I cannot say what made Lola leave Bern for Geneva, but I suspect it had to do with debts. She contacted her young lover Piesner to meet her in Geneva. There she moved into the *Chateau de Imperatrice*. Lola described it as a splendid structure, expensive by any standard. Price did not stop Lola from renting it and hiring an architect to make alterations she desired. The following is a portion of a letter Lola sent to Ludwig. She was sick and bedridden.

".... It is all the same to me, life or death. I am ill and fear being thrown in debtor's prison. I fear you will be angry with me for I have had to spend more money than I have. My furniture was damaged on the trip from Bern to Geneva. I must have it repaired. The stables are a ruin, and I recall you saying a person is responsible for the dumb brutes who faithfully work in their employ. With tears in my eyes and death in my heart, I see your angry face and my heart is broken. What am I to do? Life without you is no life."

Ludwig sent money. He paid the outstanding debts in Bern. There was a box of jewels Lola left in Ludwig's keeping, but Ludwig could not find a safe way of sending it. He promised Lola that when they arranged a secret rendezvous he would bring the jewelry with him. The plan was to meet in the small Swiss town of Malan. Ludwig would travel to Innsbruck to visit relatives and slip away for a week to be with Lola. The reunion was set for August, then postponed until September.

Lola wrote: "Ludwig My Dearest, We shall make love with our bodies, our limbs and our lips on every part of each other. Nothing is forbidden us. I am more in love with you now than ever before. I request that you be faithful. My heart is yours, my cuno is yours, and all of my body awaits you."

Ludwig responded that he couldn't wait to take her unwashed feet in his mouth to show the depth of his feelings for her. Word of the assignation in Malan leaked out. The Landtag confiscated the jewelry and threatened Ludwig with loss of his pension if he met with the Montez woman. Furthermore, the Council stated that if he met her outside of Bavaria, he would be forbidden to return. He would live out his life in exile without a pension. If Madame Montez returned to Bavaria, she would be incarcerated.

Ludwig canceled the trip to Malan, but too late to inform Lola. She arrived only to be met by a courier who gave her two thousand francs and Ludwig's explanation. Lola wrote him, he was her only love. "It causes such great pain not to hold you in my arms again. Not to be held by those strong, sensitive hands and your mouth. The thought of your lips on mine ignites a fire in my heart." She kissed the letter leaving an imprint of her lips.

Ludwig responded: "I kiss your lips over and over. Your mouth has given me as much pleasure as your cuno. If you can send a representation of your cuno I will kiss it most lovingly."

Ludwig somehow repossessed Lola's jewelry and arranged to send it by a trusted messenger. She sold the jewels immediately to satisfy her most pressing debts. Ludwig had spies reporting on Lola, for in a fit of exasperation he wrote about the jewelry sale. "....You want me for money, Papon" (her new financial manager) "for conversation and that student Piesner to *besar* in bed."

At the time, Piesner was relegated to a small room in the rear of the Chateau. He saw how Lola squandered money, then dared her debtors to bring her down. Piesner had his own debts he had hoped Lola would pay. He realized that she couldn't solve her financial problems. Piesner packed his bags and left. Lola did not take it as a great loss.

Through one of the Alemaine students in Bavaria Lola was informed that her financial manager Papon was a spy for Ludwig. Papon sent weekly reports on her activities. She actually searched the Chateau for him, pistol in hand. He fled before she could shoot him.

Lola was in such grievous debt that she decided to answer Ludwig's letter about her having him for the money, Papon for conversation and Piesner for *besar*. She wrote: "....someday all secrets of this world will be opened before God and then, my dear Ludwig you will be persuaded of my faithfulness and the sincere love of your slandered Lolita. Dear Ludwig, I know Papon was your spy. I am pleased you watch over me. But there is death in my soul—without you I am disgraced in this world, without friends in a country as terrible for strangers as it is at Geneva. ...if you don't come to my aid, I will become the joke and ridicule of the world— my honor will be completely lost, what shall I do, it is too terrible and my health is always so fragile—but God is good, and my dear Ludwig you are too devoted to me to abandon me."

Lola knew which heart strings to pluck. Ludwig sent twenty thousand more Francs.

Despite her feigned illness, Lola remained active in Geneva. A wealthy barrister from England proposed marriage. She turned him down, saying her heart was promised to Ludwig. At the Geneva Theater Lola spied a handsome young man. Inquiry proved him to be Julius, Lord of Schwandt, and Count of Shliesen. His parents had died the year before, and he was in line for a large inheritance. Lola asked to be introduced. Eight years his elder, Lola charmed him. An intimacy developed. They often met in a fashionable hotel. The rooms belonged to a friend of Julius.

Lola wrote: "Lord Julius proposed to me. I discouraged him as gently as possible. I explained my love was not only pledged to Ludwig but that my heart and soul belonged to him. The poor boy left grief-stricken. It is a good feeling to be admired, but one can earn a reputation for casual romances that will be inscribed in historical ledgers."

I laughed out loud and woke the babies.

The Spanish press confirmed that indeed, Count Julius proposed marriage to Lola. On hearing this, his two siblings, aunt, and uncle rushed in and whisked him back to Cologne. Lola prepared to hunt Julius down. The German charge de 'affairs stepped in and made it clear, Lola would not be welcome in Cologne, nor would her Bavarian passport be acceptable at the border. According to the article, the charge de' affaires made a hasty exit. A pistol shot was heard and virulent female cursing from the Chateau.

How she did it I do not know, but the Geneva newspapers wrote that Lola went to Cologne and brought Lord Julius back to Bern. He was there no more than a week when the Swiss police questioned the young Lord.

They decided he was under the immoral influence of

Countess Montez, and put him on a train under armed guards to Germany. By Lola's immediate reaction, and information gleaned from the press, I surmise Lola was informed by Swiss authorities to leave the country. I do know that Ludwig advised her to apply for Swiss citizenship.

Lola balked saying, "If I did so, I must give up my Bavarian title as Countess." Now she was *persona non grata* in Switzerland. I expected her to return to Paris. Being Lola, she decided on England.

She always had her reasons. When she took time to think them through they were very logical. She turned to Ludwig for financial help to make the move. Just prior to the King's receipt of Lola's request, young Piesner appeared at the Palace seeking an audience. The King received the bedraggled debt-ridden student. Ludwig seized the opportunity to find out the truth about Lola. He questioned the young man closely and often. Piesner was destitute and headed to debtor's prison. He broke down and admitted everything. Yes, Lola consorted with him and his friends, often together. She took other lovers. He confirmed Lieutenant Nusbammer as her favorite.

Ludwig's heart was torn asunder. He kept his word, paid Piesner's debts and sent him on his way. Ludwig sat down and wrote the following poem:

> Had I never seen you!
>
> For you I gave my last blood,
>
> Torn apart by nameless agonies,
>
> For you, my life's brightest flame of love!

I set myself defiantly against everyone,

Trusting in your loving heart,

Let nothing move me, unshaken

In the restless storm breaking upon me.

What I always refused to believe,

That you were faithless, is really true,

Nothing could wrest from me my trust in you,

Yet now at last I clearly see your guilt.


A kingdom you wished to control

And boasted that you the ruler were,

You wanted to reign exalted over all,

And ever turned toward what was base.


With betrayal you have repaid my trust,

You wanted my money, you wanted my power.

What you achieved is that all raged against me,

Transformed my existence into night.

Deep within I was already broken,

Aggrieved, wounded, sickened by the world,

As villainous outrage revealed itself,

As faithlessness was added to ingratitude.


The years' long dream has now vanished,

I have awakened in a wasteland.

All that I sensed, all that I felt is no more,

And yet I am still bereft of my crown."[19]


After writing this poem Ludwig sent Lola the money she requested.

Prior to leaving Switzerland for England, P.T Barnum, the American creator of the Greatest Show on Earth, offered to sponsor an American tour for Lola. She wrote, her refusal was based on professional objections. With P.T. Barnum she would be just one of many acts, and he the star. She deserved singular recognition and prime billing.

He would not agree.

I found two letters, one from George Sand the other Lola's reply.

"Dear Lola, Lord Brougham passed through Paris on his way to London. He is no longer

---

[19] Pages 245 & 246, Bruce Seymour, *Lola Montez*

the Ambassador to Bavaria and will not be
the candidate for Lord Chancellor of England. He is disgusted with British politics and
is exploring ways of attaining French citizenship. He wants to run for Parliament here in
Paris. The French will never allow it. Politics
in France is at least as convoluted as in England, maybe more so, but Lord Brougham is
a dreamer. He purchased an estate here in our
fair city to establish residence. He still abhors
the men's clothes I wear and cigars I smoke. I
reminded him that President Andrew Jackson's wife smoked a corncob pipe. I think I
will ask the American Ambassador to purchase one for me. Would you care for one? I
introduced you to cigars and am told you
continue to smoke in public. Good Girl! To
hell with the elitists. Lord Brougham mentioned that you are no longer in the employ of
the British Intelligence Service. He says you
receive a sizeable yearly stipend from former
King Ludwig. He blames you for the King's
abdication. Brougham has no idea how
quickly you can spend money. He and most
of Europe hold you responsible for Ludwig's
abdication. Your fiery temper and inability to
accept situations gone awry is said to be your
downfall. I repeat a phrase you spoke when
you were my house guest. 'Every problem
presents an opportunity.' I am the bearer of
an unscrupulous proposition that can satisfy
your financial rapacity, sexual needs, and

stimulate your mental resourcefulness. My sources in Switzerland say you are the most sought after courtesan in Europe, that you have rejected several proposals of marriage which carried with them titles and wealth equal to yours as Countess of Landsfeld. Do you continue to assume the role of courtesan? The proposition I recommend is with a gentleman from Nepal. You are particularly suited for this undertaking. If I have piqued your interest, read on:

"Jung Bahadur is the monarch of Nepal. He is forty years old, loves beautiful women, and splashes money on them in the same fashion you spend it. He is handsome in an oriental way, well-tanned and well-muscled. The socialites refer to him as a WOG. It is an ethnic, derogative, acronym. The letters stand for Worthy Oriental Gentleman and it replaces the more offensive 'Nigger'. The reasons I recommend him to you is, his money, passion for beautiful women (you are unsurpassed), and he longs to speak his native language, Hindi. Brush up your Hindu language skills. No one else understands him. He speaks accented English, is a graduate of Cambridge and an ardent devotee of Napoleon Bonaparte's administrative skills, which he intends to bring back to his native Nepal. Best of all he believes himself to be a crack shot with a pistol. I recall you winning large sums with pistols, in the Champs Elysees shooting galleries, from the young blades attempting to impress you. It would impress him more if you lost. But that is not in your character. I am certain you will pique the King's interest. Your beauty, scintillating conversation and shooting skills assure it. What say you? Will you visit me here in Paris? King Jung Bahadur is now on his way from Berlin to St. Petersburg. He will return from Russia to Paris in the spring. Remember Paris in the spring. It is a romantic setting fit for an oriental monarch and you. George"

Lola wrote:

"My Dear George, What an honor to receive a letter from the world's most acclaimed woman author. Flaubert wrote, that those who do not appreciate your writing should read shopping lists for pleasure. He hails your words as scintillatingly combined in such a manner as to leap off the pages in your description of place, nature and people. Most valuable to me, even more so than my relationship with the world's most famous female writer, is that you call me friend. You understand my needs and have thought to help me. The offers of marriage you refer to were made by old men with no hair and teeth like stars. They came out at night! I was more interested in their sons and grandsons. However in most cases the older ones hold the purse strings. The correct title for Jung Bahadur in Hindi is Raja. I am definitely interested in meeting him and hope to be splashed with part of his fortune. In fact he and I met before. He visited Calcutta when I was a child. He was a prince and heir to the Nepalese throne. He enjoyed military displays. My father, who was a lieutenant in the East India Company Brigade, complained of having to stand on parade for the little monkey. I was about twelve and curtsied to him. My father, who died of malaria shortly after, introduced me. The Prince nodded and passed on. That was it.

"I like your idea of the shooting gallery. Most men respect my expertise with the pistol. On your recommendation I stopped carrying that weapon and stiletto, but openly tout a short riding crop which I use when necessary.

"I had difficult times in Paris. Yet I can only recall the wonderfully warm people. The marvelous climate (when April showers bring May flowers) and exquisite culinary delights. Morning walks on the Champs Elysees, meeting the world's most renowned playwrights, musicians, newspaper editors, artists and writers in the sidewalk cafes. Yes! Yes! Yes I accept your invitation. I thank you for thinking of me. Don't take this amiss, but I prefer my own apartment rather than impose on you. You are a most powerful woman. My last stay over was memorable but I am more interested in seducing Raja Jung Bahadur than being seduced by you. How long will the Raja remain in Paris? Please rent an apartment in my name, from April 14th until a week after he is due to leave. I will then continue on to London. I have an open invitation to appear at the Royal Theater. I cherish the pleasure of seeing you again. With All My Love, Lola, Countess of Landsfeld"

Lola's exploits in Paris were no less sensational. Jung was Nepal's King, and on a state visit to France. The two often chatted in Hindi and spent two months traveling together. She ignored those who derided her for consorting with a brown native.

+++

## *POSTSCRIPT:*

My grandchildren are growing. Princess is pregnant with her seventh child. The standard Hindi greeting to a pregnant woman is: "May you birth a thousand sons." I prefer girls. Especially Stinky.

We performed the Amrita for my oldest grandson. He took the solemn vow to keep the moral laws of the Sikh religion and to treat all as equals, no matter what his or her caste

Lord Palmerston's office responded to my request for a trustworthy shipping agent in the Spice Islands. Bedi's family in Indonesia had long sought an accommodation with this English company. They signed contracts to that effect.

My ship, named the *Guru Rama #1*, has made two profitable voyages.

With Guru Rama's guidance I feed those on the Ashram and visitors. Somehow my fortune is not diminished. Bedi and Princess sometimes accompany me to serve the people. I will soon open a free kitchen in Calcutta for the poor. Bedi promised a large warehouse. He and Princess are part of this project.

How could I complain about my life? Yes, I ached so long to be with Princess growing up, but I could not have made her a better person than she is. Bedi is a blessing as a husband and son in-law. I now have six grandchildren at all different stages of growth. A seventh will soon join us. Isn't it wonderful how God can give each of us the most beautiful children in the world? But what you do with that beauty determines your happiness. I pray that Lola will overcome her beauty and find true joy.

# WHAT LOLA WANTS

# LOLA GETS

# BOOK II

# *PROLOGUE*

## CODICIL

### *Lola Montez, Bern, Switzerland February, 12th 1850:*

Lola escaped Bern, unobserved. She slipped into Italy with plans for a clandestine meeting in Milan with Ludwig. German language newspapers uncovered the plan. Revelation of the King's intended assignation fomented riots. The Bavarian people took to the streets *en masse*. Lola Montez had insulted their beloved Queen, she had made a fool of their King. and she ridiculed Bavarians by claiming unauthorized citizenship. Lola stood accused of provoking revolutionary outbreaks all over Europe. The Landtag convened and voted to revoke former King Ludwig's title, impound his money, confiscate his properties and refuse to allow him to return to Bavaria if he met with Lola in any place at any time. While awaiting the forlorn King in Milan, Lola bedded an Italian Duke. He escorted her around the city. He showered her with works of art. Upon learning of the restrictions placed on Ludwig, Lola promptly sold the Duke's gifts and left for France, without paying her bills.

Traveling through the State of Piedmont, Lola took ill. She stopped in Turin, the capital city. The municipality was situated on the left bank of the Po River. Its university boasted one of the finest medical centers in Europe.

The Rector of the University, along with the senior physician and his staff, received her. Lola requested that the staff be dismissed. She confided her need for secrecy. The doctor and Rector listened to the diagnosis and treatment begun in Switzerland. They questioned Lola, examined her, and confirmed the Swiss physician's treatment with liquid mercury. The doctor suggested she stop the daily dosage for a week. If her condition improved, whe would reduce the prescription by half. To Lola's question of a cure, the doctor shook his head. "There is no cure for the French disease," he said. "However I must warn you. The mercury treatment can lead to disorienting mood swings."

Lola burst out in hearty guffaws that shocked both men. "Madam," the doctor said, "Syphilis is not a humorous matter."

Lola patted her eyes dry, controlled her laughter and replied, "My mood swings got me run out of England, France and Poland before the Pox. Mood swings are natural for me. What is natural is beautiful!"

Both men looked at each other and spread their hands. The Rector said, "Countess if those close to you begin to criticize your actions as being unseemly, please seek professional advice. There is an ongoing debate in the medical world, whether to discontinue the use of mercury for curing syphilis. Some believe ingested mercury causes more harm than good."

"Gentlemen," Lola said, "Is there no cure for the Pox?"

"Countess," the Rector said, "Our finest people are searching for a cure. We apologize for not being more helpful. If you wish to make a donation to the University to further our efforts to eliminate the Pox, you may entrust it to me."

"I do not reward failure!" Lola said and swept out of the room.

Ten days later Lola reached Paris. She was twenty-eight years old and claimed to be twenty-four. Her figure, complexion, and brilliant black hair contrasted by electric blue eyes gave her the appearance of a vibrant nineteen year old, fully developed woman.

At George Sand's suggestion for secrecy, Lola slipped into Paris unnoticed

George wished to make a surprise presentation of her famous courtesan, responsible for rebellions in a dozen countries. Even Lola's nemesis the Austrian Prince von Metternich fled Austria. From Vienna he sought refuge in London. The atmosphere in Paris was highly charged with expatriates from many countries, developing and planning counter-revolutions. Most of the schemes, plots and strategies originated in George Sand's Chateau, her Salon, and the center for European conspirators. Sand intended to introduce Lola into this pressured atmosphere by presenting her and Jung Bahadur, Ruler of Nepal, in her Salon on the same evening.

A second letter from George Sand arrived. It contained a list of subjects from her informant in the Nepalese delegation traveling from St. Petersburg to Paris. The King was collecting information to modernize and strengthen his backward country. Lola utilized every waking moment studying the recommended subjects and improving her Hindi language skills. She continued her dancing lessons without attracting public attention.

George Sand learned of King Jung Bahadur's official Paris reception itinerary. King Louis Napoleon II would parade the military corps in salute to the oriental potentate. Later, King Bahadur would visit the Jardin-Mabille Gardens in *Fauborg Saint-Honoré'*, Paris. George Sand arranged for Lola to perform her Spider Dance at the splendiferous, aristocratic play-land for the Raja.

Only the wealthiest could afford this dream-like adult amusement park, an enchanted garden built for the rich. Meticulously laid out paths wound through trees, flower gardens, and manicured lawns. There were secluded galleries and grottos for private use day or night. They contained a salon, bedrooms and baths. The park, equipped with three thousand gas lamps, could turn night into day. A Chinese pavilion with a multi-tiered pagoda marked the park's entrance. Placed around it were artificial palm trees, fish ponds, and a merry-go-round. The artificial trees, shrubs and vines were gilded in gold and silver leaf to enhance the fairyland atmosphere.

Prior to Lola's appearance on stage at the Chinese Pavilion, the Can-Can and Polka were performed by the chorus line. Then the theatre darkened. There was silence. The gas stage-lights lowered. Slowly at first, from out of the dark, the repeated tapping of Lola's heels clicking on the hardboard stage grew in volume and rapidity until it seemed impossible for any human to continue. The orchestra joined in building to a crescendo and then sudden silence.

In the momentary dark the only sound was the breathing of the audience. Slowly the lights went up and

Lola Montez stood illuminated in a form-fitting red silk dress. It was slit from the ruffled ankle to the inner thigh. She stood front, stage center, her hair like black fire, her large electric-blue eyes challenging every man in the theater. Her lithe, full-bosomed body arched from high heels to her proud head. Her left hand held the dress up high on her bare thigh.

The effect on the audience was audible. They sucked in their breath at the beauty before them. Lola turned stage left, whipped open her fan and bowed to Maharaja Jung Bahadur in a private box. He smiled, raised his eyes in an unasked question and bowed to Lola. She covered her smile with her fan and bowed lower revealing even more cleavage. The audience, witnessing the inter-play, erupted in cheers.

The music began and Lola performed her Spider Dance. Lola innovated and perfected the peasant Tarantella folk dance, thought to cure the spider's bite by dancing wildly until exhausted. Lola's version was transformed into a ballet done on her toes in the new fashion.

She portrayed a young lass walking through a meadow being attacked by one, then another, of the hairy beasts. Lola raised the hem of her dress to avoid the venomous creatures. She stamped on them, in time to the music, with her Flamenco heels. They invaded her petticoats, and she shook the vermin out, each time showing more and more underclothes, until at the height of the tension she finally won out over the deadly vermin.

The audience went wild. Raja Jung Bahadur, an aficionado of women, attempted to leap the railing from his private box onto the stage. His brother Dhir restrained him. Lola took three curtain calls and many floral bouquets.

Back in her room she received a note from George Sand's spy in the Nepalese delegation. It read: "Dhir, Brother of the King, dissuaded his majesty from meeting with you. He claimed you are a security problem. Dhir doesn't believe it proper for the King to be seen with you. He cited your frivolous reputation. The King is now at the Park's shooting Gallery, a few meters from you."

"Frivolous reputation, my arse!" Lola shouted. She stopped changing clothes. Still wearing her form-fitting red dance gown, she pulled down the front to reveal more cleavage and opened a polished long flat mahogany box on the dressing table. Two steel-blue Navy Colt pistols with hexagon barrels rested on green felt. She took one of the weapons, and loaded it with six balls and caps.

Hiding the pistol behind her fan she hurried to the shooting gallery. The Raja was surrounded by his retinue and French officials. His brother Dhir, always alert to danger, saw Lola coming and moved to stop her. He put out his hands, never expecting the woman to punch him in the stomach. He doubled up and she swept by, tapping Jung Bahadur on the shoulder. She said in Hindi, "I challenge the King to a target shoot!"

Shocked by the Hindi language coming from this most beautiful white woman, he composed himself. "Where did you learn Hindi?"

"We spoke once before," Lola said. "I was twelve and introduced to you on the parade grounds of the East

India Company in Calcutta. You inspected the troops."

"How poor my memory is. Alas, I cannot recall the incident."

"With the King's permission," Lola said. "I challenge you to a target shooting contest."

Dhir, having recovered from the blow to his stomach stormed into the crowd around the King. He grabbed Lola by the shoulder, shouting, "You will please leave!"

King Bahadur took his younger brother's hand off Lola's bare shoulder, cast an eye down her cleavage and said, "Not now, brother. This lady challenged me, and I accept."

He offered his pearl handled pistol to Lola. She placed her Navy Colt inconspicuously under her fan on the shooter's table, and hefted the weapon handed to her. She brushed the ebony ringlets from her right eye, and in one motion brought up the pistol and fired with a two-handed grip. She fired all six shots in quick succession. The smoke and smell of gunpowder wafted past them. Lola returned the weapon, handle first, to the Raja. A boy ran up the alley with the target, bowed, and presented it to the King.

"Three bull's eyes and three close fours," he said. "That is excellent shooting."

Lola patted the lad's head and said, "Send out six moving ducks."

The Raja nodded for the boy to comply and handed the revolver to his brother, ordering him to reload. Lola took her Navy Colt from under the fan, wiped clean the sights and raised the weapon shoulder high as six yellow metal ducks moved in a line. Lola fired in rapid succession, and all six targets went down. "My God!"

the King exclaimed, "That is fantastic! Miss Montez, would you try your expertise on the pendulum target?"

"They do not have .36 cap and ball ammunition in this Gallery."

"So you shot here before?"

"I practiced to impress you."

"You have. Your Hindi and shooting are both a pleasant and extraordinary surprise. Use my weapon."

He turned to his brother who completed loading the pistol. Dhir handed the weapon butt first to Lola. It fired as Lola's hand gripped it. The bullet creased Dhir's trousers, drawing a small amount of blood from his thigh. Enraged, he looked up at Lola, who smiled and said, "I hope the Prince will excuse me, but the weapon must have a hair trigger."

Before the enraged Dhir could explode, he was whisked away to be treated.

"A regrettable accident," Jung said. "Especially for such an expert."

With a twinkle in her eye Lola said, "I always hit what I aim for."

"Does Lola always get what Lola wants?"

"Yes."

"Then what do you wish our bet should be, for I cannot match your expertise with the handgun?"

Without hesitation Lola responded, "Little Lola would like you to escort her to George Sand's Salon tomorrow evening."

"Miss Montez, I enjoy speaking my native language. If I won the shooting competition I could ask no greater prize than to escort you tomorrow evening to the Chateau of George Sand."

Lola bowed and handed her Navy colt pistol to the King. "My present to his majesty. It is a prototype designed by the Texas Navy, and one of two given me by a representative of Colt manufacturers."

"Why would they give such a magnificent weapon away?"

"For publicity. They gave pistols to Wild Bill Hickok, Doc Holliday, Buffalo Bill and Annie Oakley. Would you like to receive a matching pair of pistols?"

The King's face brightened with childlike glee. "I would indeed. And when they arrive, I will return your gift—for pairs should remain together." He reached out and stroked her arm.

Lola knew she had optimized her impression. Anything more would be superfluous. The art of a courtesan was to part after the most positive effect. She bowed to the King and withdrew. His retinue applauded her.

Lola danced around her apartment singing, practicing her bows, nods and snubs. She selected a fine electric-blue felt gown that matched the color of her eyes. It had a low-cut bodice, framed by white Belgian lace to reveal and emphasize her cleavage. A thin, crafted silver belt accented her tapering waist and smooth rounded hips. Lola was most proud of her thick, ebony curls; they, more than anything else, gave her the appearance of a Spanish grandee. Behind her right ear she placed a pink tea rose. Her hair was skewered in the back with a decorative tiny silver sword that matched the belt buckle.

Raja Bahadur himself escorted Lola from her hotel room to the carriage, a coach with gold embossed on black-lacquered doors and wheels, and four matched black mares in polished harness. Two burly drivers and two more bodyguards stood behind the coach, with four outriders for security. The King's brother followed at a discreet distance in a second, less opulent, coach. It carried eight armed men.

Jung helped Lola into the coach, compressing the wire hoops under the gown so she could enter the narrow doorway. Once seated, he tapped the roof with his jewel-encrusted sword, and the carriage rolled forward.

"I thought the Raja would have stallions pulling his carriage," Lola said.

"In consideration of you, I ordered mares."

"Why so?"

"The males have large phalli swinging under their bellies."

"I like large phalli," Lola answered with a coquettish smile. "If you have it, flaunt it."

The King's cheeks reddened, and he changed the subject. "We are speaking Hindi, and you say we met in Calcutta. My brother Dhir asks, how is it you claim ancestry from Spanish Royalty if your father was an officer in the British army?"

"Hmmmmm!" Lola mused. She focused her mischievous blue eyes on his, placed the palm of her hand on his inner thigh and said, "I sometimes lie."

The King placed his hand over Lola's hand on his thigh. "You are not only beautiful, but a most intriguing woman."

Lola's hand slipped between his thighs and she gripped his penis It began to swell and she tightened her fingers. The King moaned. She released her hold, raised her hand holding his and kissed his palm. "Are you familiar with *Kama Sutra*?"

Jung let out a deep breath saying, "I am a devotee of the great Hindu sex manual."

"Thank God!" Lola smiled. "Maybe I will learn something new."

"We can study together. But if your hand keeps roving, I will say, to hell with George Sand and bed you in this carriage."

"That would be fine with me, but your loss. It is important for you to attend the Salon. George made extensive preparations for your highness to meet with some of the most powerful and influential men in Europe."

"My brother agrees with you."

"As head of state you will meet the aristocracy and planners of world industry, business, science, and military. The exponents of European art, music, and literature will be there. But only one King an evening. Tonight, you are he."

"Is it true that George bedded Chopin?"

"And Franz Liszt too."

"Her family must have an interesting historical background."

"Most certainly do. Her father owned a brothel and tavern. Her title of Duchess was conferred because of her talent as a writer, and her ability to seduce a Prince and Princess at the same time."

"I understand that George wears men's clothes and smokes cigars?"

"True, but she is bi-sexual. I learned smoking cigars from her. The men's clothes give her *entrée* to places not frequented by women. Before the men realize it, she is among them."

"But you bulled your way into the shooting gallery."

"That is my nature. I do not ask permission from anyone to go anywhere. I am Lola Montez, the Countess of Landsfeld." She took the King's sword and rapped with the hilt on the ceiling, calling, "Stop on the next rise."

"Why are we stopping?" Jung asked.

"As Raja, you should not be overly impressed by George Sand's Chateau. I will tell you about it."

The carriage stopped, and Lola pointed to a long row of lights pouring from many windows of the long two-storied building. They illuminated a half-moon mother-of-pearl driveway, with a fountain of cupid passing water into a scallop shell.

"You wouldn't expect such a large, luxurious place in the center of Paris," Lola said. "In addition to the formal gardens of flowers and shrubs, George employs a Japanese groundskeeper who manicures Bonsai trees. Each is a work of art. George not only has a title of countess and stipend from the French government, but she owns her own newspaper publishing company, and is heavily invested in building projects for the poor. The Chateau is her place of refuge. She controls everything within. There are twenty-seven rooms for guests to sleep or entertain, two libraries, a smoking room, and playrooms for adults and children."

"What can a playroom for adults contain?"

"Billiard tables, ten-pins, several dart boards, chess, checkers, and professional gambling tables with roulette. A part of every bet is donated to charity. The servant's quarters are behind the house, and close to the most elaborate and organized kitchen. The kitchen extends the length of the villa. Carts deliver to stalls behind the house. Refuse is burned or carted away to make compost for the gardens. Butchers for meat, fowl, and fish occupy separate stalls and ovens. Soups and vegetables have their own places, and there is a building for pastries and sweets. There are seven chefs and a Master Chef, a building for laundry and servants' uniforms. Women wear black blouses with white aprons. Men are garbed in either blue, green, or gold velvet waistcoats, knee-length black trousers, and buckled shoes with white silk stockings. Their shirts are white linen, ruffled to the chin. Everything is meant to blend with this theme of isolation from the outside. She wants her guest's attention,"

"Is she beautiful?"

She is a handsome woman with a good figure. Her personality is her most attractive feature. You feel power exude from her. She has a way of stepping closer to you when speaking that intimidates and excites. She is aware of this, and does it purposely."

"Why?"

"To put one off balance. Then she asks a direct question and demands an immediate answer with her eyes. It is her way of getting at the truth."

"Does she use any other ploys for interrogating people?"

"She is the most perceptive person I ever met. Like myself, George has no patience with ignorance or effeminate social grace."

"Enough about the hostess," the King said. He tapped the roof and ordered the driver onward. "In Nepal that chateau is the size of my outhouse. To keep your toilets inside the house is a disgrace."

Alerted of their arrival George stood at the entrance to greet them. "It's been two years," she said to Lola. "You are a busy lady. When you left Paris you were hunting for a Prince. You found a King."

They looked each other over and fell into a genuine, whole-hearted embrace. The King waited patiently until they separated. George apologized, led them into the ballroom, and introduced the King and Lola to her guests.

Word spread like wildfire through the large hall. The guests were abuzz with gossip: the savage chief of the Nepalese mountain tribes, and Lola Montez! The dancers stopped, the music ceased. George, the King and Lola became the center of attention. The crowd applauded. The band played the Nepalese Anthem.

Jung Bahadur did not understand French, the lingua franca of international aristocracy. Outwardly smiling amongst themselves, the snobs in the hall sharpened their verbal knives. In whispers they derided Lola for attending with the Nepalese savage. Everyone noted the immense ruby in the King's turban, his jewel-encrusted sword, diamond brooches flashing from the royal satin sash across his chest. Grudgingly the gossipers admired the King's conspicuous wealth. Jung Bahadur planned it so. This was not his first introduction to elitist European society. He adhered to the English idiom, "Money Talks."

It was an Englishman who made the first approach. Lord Brougham led the British delegation of military and businessmen to greet the Raja and his envoys.

Lola, who once spied for Palmerston, knew of Brougham's dislike for her and her morals. She detested him for terminating her spying contract. In her mind he was a pretentious egoist. He had suffered her temper tantrums on several occasions and was wary. He attempted to separate Lola from the King, but Lola was having none of it. She remained attached to the King's left arm. Jung chatted amicably in English with the British delegation. After several minutes of casual conversation, Lord Brougham broached the question of the evening.

"Your Majesty," he asked, "Will Nepal give succor to the Sikh mutineers in this their second rebellion?"

"An interesting question," the King said. "If I deny assistance to the Sikhs, I must fight them. If I grant them refuge, I must fight you."

"We put down the Sikh rebels two years ago," Brougham said. "We will do it again."

"Without Nepal's help, there will be a third rebellion in two more years." the King replied.

Lord Brougham took a glass of champagne from a passing tray, raised it in salute and said, "That may be. And we will win a third time."

"At great cost to Britain," Lola said. "England will also lose prestige and influence amongst both the Hindus and Moslems of India."

"Harrumph!" Lord Brougham exclaimed. He took umbrage at Lola's remark and sipped champagne to clear his throat.

Jung Bahadur said, "The Countess of Landsfeld correctly identified the problems."

"And what might they be?" Brougham asked.

"The price for both of us."

"I agree," Brougham said.

Lola signaled to George Sand who entered the throng around the King. Lola asked her, "Might you recommend a room to discuss serious matters?"

George straightened her cravat, opened the button on her double breasted jacket, puffed a blue cloud of cigar smoke above the listeners' heads and said, "The first room to the right behind the bandstand."

"A more distant room from the noise of the merry-makers, please?" Lola asked.

A look passed between the two women. "Follow me," George said, and led them down a corridor of rooms. The King signaled for his brother and two minis-ters to join him. They, Lord Brougham, and two repre-sentatives of the British delegation entered the last apartment in the Chateau. It was furnished with enough chairs for all and a large oval table. George seated the King and Lord Brougham at either end of the table, and excused herself from the room.

The King whispered in Hindi to Lola, "What was that look between you and George about the rooms?"

"The room George initially recommended has secret ports for listening and viewing. Be firm with Brougham. He is a difficult man."

The King smiled and said aloud, in English, "Lord Brougham, are you empowered to make decisions for England?"

"I am so designated to do so by Lord Palmerston. However, all international agreements must be ratified by Parliament. Given our present political situation, that is a formality. And you sir?" Brougham asked

"I am King!"

Brougham replied, "I wish your Highness long life. But in the near and far east there have been forty coups, assassinations, and overthrowing of rulers in the past thirty years. How can we be certain you will continue to rule Nepal?"

"That is my responsibility!" Dhir said.

"Where you are is where you are supposed to be," Lola added. "What the future holds is in the hands of God. That relates to the English as well."

""Lord Brougham," the King said, "You stated what you want from me. Now hear my terms."

"Yes, your majesty."

"My studies at Cambridge and travels throughout Europe are for one purpose," the King said, "To view and understand the modernization of the western world and apply what is beneficial to my kingdom. China, Japan, Korea, and all of Southeast Asia are resisting attempts at westernization. I conclude that Europe will lead the world into the twentieth century. I have about thirty years to position Nepal to lead the Asian nations into the future. If I am successful and we reach an agreement, England will have backed the future leader of Asia. That is more than half the world's population."

The westerners at the table sat erect. They looked with genuine respect at the Nepalese monarch. Lola, too, was fascinated by the foresight and preparation of the oriental potentate.

"Your Majesty," Brougham said, "It appears that your interests and England's converge. What is it you want?"

"If England desire's Nepal's help in putting down the

Sikh rebellion, we want the most modern weapons, ammunition, and advisers to train our people."

"Weapons and supplies are no problem, but I doubt we could find five English soldiers who speak Nepalese to train your troops. Where would we find trainers?"

"Not a problem," Jung's brother said, "The First and Second Gurkha Battalions."

"They belong to the East India Company," Brougham objected.

"And England owns the East India Company. If my King snaps his fingers, every Gurkha serving under the English flag will desert. There are two full regiments of Gurkhas. The King and I believe British control of India depends upon these Gurkha regiments. We request only two battalions."

"Young sir," Brougham said, "I know the importance of the Gurkha in India. My maternal grandfather, Sir Ralph Lilley Turner, served with King Edward's Own Gurkha Rifles. His letter of praise for the Gurkha rests in the British War Museum. He concluded that letter with the phrase, 'If a man tells you he is unafraid going into battle he is either crazy or a Gurkha.' You too must understand how important two battalions of your countrymen are to England and India. I will make every effort to have them transferred. That is the most I can do."

"Their transfer is necessary," Dhir said. "Inform your Foreign Office that with weapons, ammunition, and two Gurkha battalions, Nepal will guarantee the defeat of the Sikh rebels. Furthermore, we will stop the Sikhs from sheltering in the Himalayan Mountains or slipping into Tibet."

"With those assurances," Lord Brougham said, "I am confident you shall have your Gurkhas. What else is required?"

"Help in the modernization of Nepal," the King said. "Roads, bridge and steam-engine builders from Scotland: They produce the best engineers. We require bankers and industrialists from London to advise and direct a modern Nepalese economic system. Most important is your organization of national hygiene. The Europeans set up clinics, infirmaries, and trained doctors, and brought clean water to the cities after the Black Plague. You English perfected your national hygienic system. The average life expectancy in Nepal is twenty-six years. That must be extended for our country to progress. "

"You shall also require agricultural and educational advisors," Brougham noted.

"The Americans are sending farming experts. Accompanying them will be two hundred newly invented steel moldboard plows. This plow alone will open up twenty percent more of our rocky soil for cultivation. The Yankees will also send a shipload of grape cuttings. As for education, we decided the English system of lower education is preferable, German for higher education. It is most compatible with our Nepalese culture."

"Why not use French vintners as advisors? They are known for their fine wine."

"But every vine in France comes from America," Dhir said. "Several years ago a blight wiped out French wine growers. They imported a disease-resistant strain of vine from America."

"I was unaware," Brougham admitted. "Why haven't

you adopted the American education system instead of the English?"

"Americans are trying to form a classless society. You British have your Magna Carta and two houses of Parliament; your social order is severely stratified as is Nepal's. We can adapt your parliamentary system more easily."

"But this hodgepodge of different approaches will cause confusion."

"A little chaos can do Nepal much good," the King said. "Diversity breeds competition. Britain and France promote cultural Imperialism. I do not wish my country to be governed by yours."

"And the Americans?" Brougham asked.

"The Americans don't care about imperialism as long as they can make money."

"Your majesty," Lord Brougham bowed to the King, "You are the most astute and well organized leader I have met since Prince von Metternich."

"The King is also more pleasant," Lola quipped.

"Indeed so," Lord Brougham bowed a second time and said, "I understand his Majesty is returning to Nepal. My proposals shall be submitted in writing for your perusal. I would very much like to finalize an agreement prior to your departure."

"We shall cooperate," the King said.


Lord Brougham and his advisors left the room. Lola turned to Jung Bahadur and his brother. She curtsied in a flamboyant fashion, holding both ends of her gown out at arm's length, and said, "Your Majesties worked together perfectly. Was it planned?"

"Very much so," the King said. "Mostly by my brother. Dhir is a recognized genius. He astounded the Dons at Cambridge."

"Why don't you like me?" Lola asked the Prince.

Dhir turned away, and the King answered, "My brother is more prejudiced against whites than those aristocrats out there are bigoted against us niggers."

"Firstly," Lola said, "You are brown, not black. You do not have Negro features."

Dhir whipped around, his face contorted with anger. He pointed to the door and said, "Those who just spoke so respectfully and acted so properly are now referring to us as trained apes. Let me explain. While you Spanish, English, and French were scratching with sticks in the mud, Nepalese scholars were creating poetry, teaching mathematics and building structures that still humble your white civilizations. You praise this chateau. My summer home can accommodate two like this."

"You speak the truth about the past," Lola replied, "But unless you adapt to the present and plan for the future, Nepal will be scratching in the mud forever."

"You describe reality," Dhir admitted. "That is why King Bahadur is here: to modernize Nepal."

"Enough truth for one evening," the King said. "Dhir, ask Madam George Sand if this suite is available for the night." Before his brother could answer, the King bowed to Lola and said, "With your permission?"

"Of course," Lola said.

When Dhir and the Nepalese Ministers left, the King turned to Lola. "Before we retire to the bedroom, I wish to complement you on your behavior during the negotiations."

"I hardly participated," Lola said.

"Exactly. Your silence when you could have spoken was most effective. Lord Brougham kept glancing at you as if you were a bomb ready to explode."

"I have berated him on several occasions."

"It is also clear you negotiated as concubine to the King of Bavaria. I would like you to sit with us when we draw up our proposals for Lord Brougham."

"My pleasure, but right now I would like to make love."

"I prefer the Hindu way of a more leisurely approach to the art," Jung said. "Working my way through seven petticoats, a dress, and that wire frame underneath seems a needless distraction."

"The bedroom closets contain night clothes for our use," Lola said. "You change first."

"When Jung Bahadur returned from the bedroom, Lola lay stark naked on a large couch with royal purple silk pillows behind her head. The King gasped. His eye lids fluttered, and she smiled. He bent over her and kissed the nipples of her breasts. She caressed his face, untied the belt of his robe, and said, "In the carriage I felt that you are well endowed."

"I was trained by concubines all my life for this moment."

"The best sex is always the next one."

"So let us prolong our first endeavor."

"You are my King."

"Then allow me to slip under and behind you." He dropped his robe and set a pillow so he was in a sitting position, with Lola on top and between his hairy, muscular legs. She snuggled back into his embrace. He stroked her thighs and touched her pubic hair, massaged her legs and mound of her soft belly, saying, "We are not children. Tell me your most outrageous fantasy, and I will attempt to fulfill your dream."

"And will you allow me to do the same?"

"I require it," the King said, and his fingers massaged her stiff nipples. His voice was soft yet commanding. "Tell me what it is you dream about when you are alone in bed and masturbate."

"That is something I never shared," Lola said.

"Do so with me."

His hands moved over her silken skin. She hesitated to reveal her secret fantasies. She always controlled the men she bedded, but his voice urged her on and his hands lit a fire in her vulva. He coaxed it into a flame. She shifted and felt his erection on her spine. She shivered.

"Tell me," Jung insisted.

Lola heard her own breathing. She was panting with each stroke of his hands. His finger pried open her vulva, and he caressed its lips. She took his hand and pressed it into her and she shivered. "Put your finger in deeper," she said.

"Tell me your fantasies, your imaginary sex, your dreams."

"Touch me deeper," Lola begged.

"I want to know!" He leaned over her shoulder gathered both breasts in his hands and proceeded to kiss and suck both nipples.

Lola reached up and pulled his head down, and whispered in his ear, "I want to fuck. I love to fuck. I want to fuck until I am like a wet dish rag. Then I want to suck the cock the fucked me to death."

Jung pulled the pillow from behind him, slipped out from under Lola and placed the pillow under her buttocks. He kneeled over her and used his erection to massage her breasts.

"Put it in! For Christ's sake shove it into me!" Lola panted. Jung Bahadur raised up, spread Lola's thighs and plunged into the hairy black patch. She responded by wrapping her arms and legs around his lithe muscular body. "Oh, how I like to fuck!" she moaned. "Again! Again! Do it again!" she cried, "Up and down! back and forth! In and out!"

The King pounded her into the couch. He timed his climax with hers. He withdrew, and Lola moaned in disappointment. He reached down and turned her over, put the pillow between her knees and belly, then entered her from behind. His strokes were long and slow until Lola began to call out for him to do it faster and faster. They climaxed again, he slumped over her back and the sweat of their bodies intermingled. Lola whispered, "Do you have strength for me to satisfy your secret desires? Or should we wait until you reload?"

"I will reload now," Jung said. He arose from the couch and took a silver snuff box from the dressing robe pocket. He opened it and offered the white powder to Lola "What is it?" She asked. .

"An aphrodisiac made from the leaves of the coco plant and mixed with limestone powder."

"Do I eat it or drink it?"

"Neither. You sniff it."

"Up the nose?" Lola asked.

"With your right thumbnail take a little bit, then with

the forefinger of your left hand close the left nostril, sniff the powder, and repeat for the right nostril."

"You show me."

Jung Bahadur dipped his thumbnail into the powder and sniffed, dipped again sniffed. "Ahhh!" he exclaimed, "This is what I meant by reloading."

Lola copied him, and they sat cross-legged on the couch facing one another, watching each other's eyes dilate. Lola felt her nipples swell and the burning sensation between her thighs. "Fuck me again," she said.

"I will fuck you to death," the King promised, "But first you must pleasure me."

"Tell me," Lola demanded.

Jung explained.

Lola followed him to the doorway where he stood stark naked, arms and legs spread, touching the door jamb on either side. She then took a small cruet of sweet oil and while standing before the king massaged her body with the oil. She embraced him and transferred the oil to his body from hers.

She caressed and kissed every part of his body. He was shivering with delight and anticipation—but the moment he moved a hand or foot from the door jamb she stopped, picked up her horse crop and whipped him until he returned to the position. She returned to her manipulations until the man was convulsing in muscle spasms.

He cursed her in English and Nepalese. She took his ten-inch erection in her mouth and his hips thrust back and forth in paroxysms. She withdrew her lips from the swollen penis and sucked on his scrotum until one egg-sized ball and then another came into her mouth. She did as he had told her.

She sucked harder and harder until the pain was so excruciating he could no longer hold the door jambs. He released his grip. Lola, on her knees before him, could not see him reach out and pull the servants bell. He staggered and fell to the floor. Lola was still causing him excruciating pleasurable pain with her mouth on his scrotum. He attempted to crawl across the carpeted floor, dragging Lola. He collapsed. She released him.

He rested on his side, outstretched arm under his head. She rolled him over on his back and straddled him with her knees. She took his limp hands and massaged her breasts with them saying, "That fairy dust I sniffed made me hotter than a blacksmith's furnace. Now you will suck my cunt, then fuck me, as you promised?"

Jung Bahadur shook his head, "It is forbidden for the king to do a woman like that."

"Bullshit!" Lola snorted, "King Ludwig did it. He even sucked my toes."

"If it is a tongue fucking you want," Bahadur said, "She can help."

As pre-planned, George Sand responded to the butler's bell. She threw her shirt and cravat on the floor, and came forward naked except for a large black leather belt around her waist. She reached down and caressed Lola's cheek. George ran her fingers through Lola's thick black hair, then with a vicious pull dragged her off the King and pinned her left arm while Jung pinned her right to the carpet. Both leaned over Lola and kissed her face, her lips, her neck, and each took a breast, using their tongues to arouse the passion of Europe's most famous Courtesan. Lola fought them at first. But the effects of the cocaine and their manipulations took over. She begged, "George, you are my friend. Don't make me do it."

"You agreed to suck his cock," George said. "Satisfy him first, and we will talk." The King kneeled over Lola and she took his penis in her mouth. He became excited and thrust deep in her throat. George had to pull him off twice.

Then he exploded. He covered Lola's mouth with his hand and said, "Swallow. It will make you strong in every way. It is the seed of the Kings of Nepal."

He motioned for George to bring his robe. He took out the silver box, and shared the cocaine with George. They both held Lola and forced her to ingest through her nostrils. The two caressed Lola with their bodies, hands, lips, and tongues. She attempted to resist, but to no avail. She became sexually aroused by both. Her body and mind began responding to their caresses.

She sucked George's breasts, kissed her navel, then below the navel. George rolled over, spread her legs, and Lola crawled between them. "Lick her," The King ordered. He shoved Lola's head down into the brown thatch.

Lola decided to bite and free herself. She opened her mouth and with her teeth bit into the hairy nest. The short hairs caught in her teeth. She smelled George's musky odor. Involuntarily Lola's tongue came out. She tasted George, and the larger woman shivered and moaned. Lola tasted her again and again. George shivered.

Lola wanted to control the older woman. George was blessing her, holding her head down with her hands and giving instructions, "Point your tongue. Widen your tongue and lap like a dog. Slower now. A little faster, faster, faster. Oh God!"

George spasmed, and Lola felt herself being positioned as before, on her knees, by Jung. She thought he would enter her from behind, but he didn't. He entered her anal passage. He filled her. He had oiled his penis, and it slipped deeper and deeper. Lola found it difficult to breath. She gasped, "You bastards planned this!"

George raised up Lola's head with her two hands and kissed Lola full on the lips. They searched for each other's tongues. She tried to comfort Lola as Jung pressed himself deeper and deeper with each stroke. Lola began to gag. George shouted at Jung, "You are going to kill her with that cock of yours!"

"She wants to die fucking."

"Not in the arse," Lola gasped. "It hurts."

Jung quickened his pace, threw his head back and fell over Lola. George pushed him off her and lightly slapped her cheeks. *"Mon Cheri,"* George said, "I didn't know he would rape you."

"I never thought sex could be so painful," Lola whispered.

"That wasn't sex," George said. "That was unadulterated lust. Some people derive their pleasure from the pain of others."

"He's so educated"

"The educated ones are often the worse. They believe it their right to be cruel."

Lola looked over at the sleeping figure of the King stretched out on the floor, and said. "I would like to get back at the little bastard."

"I heard him say the king is not supposed to dine between a woman's thighs."

"You were listening?" Lola asked.

"And watching," George said. "I saw and heard everything."

"But I thought we were friends. Why did you help him rape me?"

"That wasn't planned. Since we met, I have had a burning desire to love you. I listened to your secret desires, and I can fulfill them better than that little bastard." She pointed at the sleeping figure of the King. "Let's use his cocaine for a little enjoyment. We'll get him aroused. Then we will make him violate that which is forbidden to Kings". She pointed to the thatch between her thighs.

"The little fucker deserves it," Lola said. "He's hung like a stallion. I can't sit down."


Two days later Lola got up from bed and took on the preparations for her trip to London. A messenger arrived with a varnished cherry-wood box about twelve inches square, its hinges and key plate of gold.

"Countess," The messengers said, "His Highness the King of Nepal desires to express his appreciation of your beauty, wit, and talent. He wishes you fond memories." The Messenger presented Lola with a golden key, and left.

She sat in a high, wing-backed chair and examined the box. It was impressive in its workmanship. Her fingers trembled as she inserted the key and opened the lid. In the box was a Meissen porcelain *carafe au lait* soup bowl, blue and white with gold trim. Lola thought it unusual to have a matching cover.

She removed the cover and her eyes were filled with the colors of precious stones; red, blue, green, yellow and pure white diamonds filled the bowl. There were two necklaces, two bracelets, and one brooch with a large blue white diamond sparkling in the candlelight. Lola cleared her writing desk, and one by one placed the precious jewelry in groups according to usage, and the unset cut stones according to color: seventy-six pieces. She took paper and quill and described each stone to the best of her ability. She ordered a carriage with two out-riders, a driver and two guards, to the south bank of the Seine River, in the Marias district, *Rue des Jouifs.*

"Countess," the driver said, "That's Jew Town!"

"I wish to see the tailor, Marcus Pincus."

Pedestrians hugged the buildings to avoid being struck by the large carriage in the narrow *Rue de Rosier.* Two outriders led the way into Jew Street, and stopped before an old sign advertising Marcus Pincus Tailor.

The burly guards shepherded Lola to the shop. She had them wait outside, two at the front door and two at the rear. To the shopkeeper she said, "I wish to ex-change jewelry for a voucher drawn on your Rabbi in Jew Town, London."

"Madam," the tailor replied. "You seem to know me or about me, but I do not recognize you."

"I am the Countess of Landsfeld. We never met, but my former servant Manuela was here many times."

Without acknowledging Manuela's prior visits he asked, "Where is Miss Manuela now?"

"With her daughter and grandchildren in Calcutta."

The smile on the tailor's face was genuine. "Miss

Manuela was always very nice," he said.

"She brought you much business," Lola replied. "That was my money you exchanged."

"Then you must be the famous Countess?"

"Exactly!" Lola snapped. "Now, to business. This will be the largest transaction you ever made. "

The tailor bowed, "Countess, I am honored to serve."

Lola explained to him how she wanted the jewelry appraised. Shortly, two bearded jewelers with long black coats and wide-brimmed black hats arrived. They each carried a case containing scales, weights, viewing lamp and magnifying glasses.

Lola arranged three small tables in the back room. The two jewelers sat on either side of the room with their backs to each other. Lola sat between them with the jewels and her list. She passed two jewels to the tailor, who then placed one in front of each jeweler. They each made their evaluation, wrote it on a slip of paper, and the tailor exchanged jewels to be evaluated a second time by the other jeweler. The notes and jewels were returned to Lola, and she then set the jewels on the highest written bid. This slow accounting went on until sunrise. When it was finished the tailor wrote out a note for two hundred and fifty thousand English pounds payable in London.

"Will the London Rabbi have enough money to cover this?" Lola asked.

"Yes, Countess. We act in the service of Baron de Rothschild. The Bank of England depends on the Rothschild's Bank. If you wish, we can deposit the money directly into either bank."

"You Jews served me well over the years. The Rothschild's Bank will do."

On her way home Lola shifted some pillows to ease the pain in her derriere. She thought, "A quarter of a million pounds can alleviate much discomfort."

# CHAPTER 1

## THE YOUNG LORD OF SHWANDT

A week prior to Lola's departure for England, George Sand invited her to Paris. The world-famous authoress owned a private box at the Paris Theater. There Lola espied a handsome young man in the most prestigious box in the theater. He was accompanied by nobility from several countries. George Sand explained, "He is Julius, Lord of Schwandt. His cousin is Count von Shliefen. They are Austrian. I know the Count. Would you care to be introduced?"

"What are the lad's financial circumstances?" Lola asked.

"Most desirable. His mother and father died of influenza. Julius is sole heir to a fortune that will make him one of the wealthiest lads in all of Europe. I thought you would ask about his age. He's only twenty, eight years younger than you."

"I like them young," Lola said. "Teaching them the art of love is exciting, thought provoking, and quite enjoyable. Why did you say he will be the richest bachelor in Europe?"

"In three months he reaches majority age. Then he receives unfettered access to the family fortune."

"In the meantime he must have money."

"More than most."

Ask the Count to introduce me." Lola smiled. "Keep

a watch on his crotch."

"Whatever for?"

"I am going to raise his erection when we meet."

"Bullshit!" George Sand growled.

"A bet?" Lola challenged.

"What is the wager?"

"The bill from my concierge. I win, you pay."

"How much are we speaking of?"

"A thousand francs," Lola said.

"I'll introduce you myself," George said.

"First I must prepare. Close the curtain to this box, please."

George attended to the curtain and Lola drew the drapes to the entrance. She slipped her gown off her shoulders and lowered her bodice. Her magnificent breasts stood proudly unsupported. She began massaging her nipples between thumbs and forefingers. George turned around. "Ohhh!" she exclaimed. "If I had a cock, it would be inside you and fucking your brains out. Let me kiss one of those."

Lola smiled, "Kiss both. Make the nipples hard."

George lowered her head, and her lips engulfed the pink tip of the near breast. She kissed, sucked, and lightly scraped the edge of her teeth on the nipple until it hardened.

"Do the other one" Lola said.

George manipulated the nipple between her lips and with her tongue. She reached down and pressed one hand into Lola's cuno. Lola shivered, but pulled George's hand away and pushed her back. Lola tore some material from inside her bodice, rearranging her dress so the stiff pink nipples were visible through the white lace. "Let's be off," Lola said.

"To hell with Lord Julius," George panted, "I'll pay your bills, just let me make love to you now."

"Come," Lola insisted. "You must introduce me."

"Introduce yourself!"

"I will," Lola said and walked off. She took a circuitous route so as to approach young Lord Julius from behind. She nudged his left arm with her right breast. He turned, bringing his face close to hers. He froze and inhaled Lola's perfume. His eyes fixed on her face, then followed her elegant neckline down to her cleavage. The rosebud nipples pressed outward from under the white lace. He gasped. His hands involuntarily came up, and his eyelids fluttered uncontrollably. Lola smiled, spread her fan, and covered her bodice. All conversation stopped.

"Pardon the intrusion," Lola said. "I was to be introduced to you by George Sand, but Countess Sand is momentarily indisposed. I am the Countess of Landsfeld, Lola Montez."

She moved the fan showing her cleavage. Her electric-blue eyes contacted his, and she held him with her gaze. Above his cravat a bright red blotch appeared on his throat, of which Julius was unaware. He stammered a near-incoherent introduction. The blemish on his neck grew. Lola stepped even closer so her right breast brushed his arm. The redness crept up both cheeks—and Lord Julius' cousin rushed to his side.

"My Lord, you must rest!" he urged, attempting to pull Julius away. The young man resisted until assured he would meet the Countess again. The red blotch now colored his cheeks. People around Lord Julius were aghast. Lola pulled her shoulders back, revealing her magnificent breasts beneath the flimsy white lace and said, in an affected tone with a wave of her gloved fingers, "Ta-ta! I must be off." She turned, and her shapely derriere undulated in such a seductive way that more than one husband received a pinch from his wife.

On return to her apartment, Lola cancelled her trip to England and made certain the concierge would send her bill to George Sand. Lola's apartment was bare but for a bed, clothing and traveling accessories, empty. and so was Lola's stomach. She ordered twelve oysters, steak and eggs with Les Frites—new style French fried potatoes. Lola was one of those rare individuals who enjoyed eating but did not gain weight. She never cooked, saying, "If God wanted me to prepare food, he wouldn't have made restaurants."

She ate, and slept well into the following morning and awoke in time to receive an invitation from Lord Julius Schwandt. The meeting was arranged against the advice and warnings of Julius's cousin and those traveling with him. The two rendezvoused at a small but exclusive hotel in Paris. Lola planned her approach to the young man with the cunning of a Chess Master.

She chose her most exotic and easily removable gown, to be taken off by an inexperienced lover. Her choice of perfume was subtle and evocative. She purchased two bottles of the Pope's wine at an outrageous price. This wine, an aid to the libido, contained coco leaves which turned into 12% cocaine during fermentation. She chose the dinner menu. Throughout Europe it was known as the bride and groom's *table d'ho'Te*. In addition to blood-red beef, lamb and chicken, bananas and asparagus represented the penis. Avocados (from the Testical Tree), figs when cut in half represent the female sexual organ. Garlic and oysters were served with almonds, chocolate and honey. Lola had the chef use dried basil to flavor the meat.

She met young Julius at the apartment door. He was so excited he tried to hand Lola his hat and cane. She demurred. The maid accepted the two items and he entered, his eyes fastened on Lola. His hand trembled as he took the aperitif offered him by the maid. Lola saw a spot of red blossom on his neck and thought, "The child will pass out before I bed him."

She beckoned him to follow her, and pointed out the wall paintings, tapestry and sculptures provided by the hotel. The redness passed, and they sat opposite each other at the oval dining table. Julius recognized the menu as the aphrodisiac-oriented bill of fare. He attempted to prepare himself for whatever questions Lola Montez would ask. He had not one answer prepared correctly. No, he had no knowledge of the *Kama Sutra*. Lola explained it was the ancient Hindu sex manual.

She asked forthrightly if he had much experience in sex. For this he answered, "I have had more than some, and less than most." He did not reveal that on two occasions with courtesans he ejaculated prematurely. His heart leapt into his throat when Lola asked, "Would you be adverse to me teaching you the ancient art of Hindu sex?"

He sipped some of the Pope's wine and said, "Yes, I mean no, I am not averse to learning. I would... Yes I will be an attentive student."

"Good," Lola said. "Eat! We will both need our

strength. I am going to love you as no one has or will ever again. When you think you have expended all your strength, I will arouse you and you will love me as a man should."

Julius's erection was ready to burst from his trousers. He bit off the tip of an asparagus. Lola reached across the table, took the asparagus tip from his mouth, put it between her lips and manipulated it back and forth. She whispered, "Have you ever had your golden wand done in this manner?" She swallowed the asparagus.

Julius blushed and wagged his head from side to side, gurgling, "Never."

"Think about it," Lola said and pursed her red lips. "Anticipate the pleasure." She filled both glasses with the Pope's wine and dismissed the maids.

Lola stood, came around the table, lowered her bodice, and placed her bare breasts on the back of his neck. He shivered. She reached over his shoulder and massaged his scrotum and erection. She grasped it and squeezed, and massaged it, and it swelled until rigid. He moaned, and she felt the penis pumping seminal fluid. They both looked down and saw the stain spread over his light grey trouser leg. She put her tongue in his ear.

He quivered, and she whispered, "I will make you explode several times tonight. It will feel as if you're urinating semen. Now I wish you to pleasure me. Kiss my breasts." She straddled his lap facing him. He lowered his head and suckled.

Lola relaxed and instructed him. Through the night and into the morning they coupled in the Toad, the Bandoleer, the Easy Rider, and Evening Delight positions.

They slept into the afternoon, bathed each other, ate lunch and returned to the study of *Kama Sutra*. Julius passed out while performing in the Grip position. Lola was invigorated. She recommended Julius return to his apartment and rest. They would meet later, tour Paris, and spend another night together.

A messenger arrived at Lola's apartment. She opened the seal and read, "Lord Julius of Schwandt presents his compliments to the Countess of Landsfeld and begs to enclose herewith a letter of proposal of marriage between our eminent families."

"Mary, Mother of God!" Lola exclaimed. "In Limerick they'd say, 'You got him by the short hairs, old girl.'"

This letter could be worth a million francs if he decided to renege. Lola's imagination kept her occupied. She weighed her options. To hire a barrister and try for a million, or marry the young whelp and take several million. She didn't like the ring of the title, Countess of Schwandt, but in addition to financial wealth, the Schwandt family properties were extensive. Lola wondered if he followed the Catholic or Protestant religion.

It could make a difference. She was legally separated from Lieutenant Thomas James, but not divorced. If Protestant, she might be forced to settle for a million. She believed Lord Julius of Schwandt had more money than King Ludwig, and no elected officials to oversee his expenditures. "My obligation as courtesan is to get as much money as possible. As Julius' wife I deserve more than a million. The boy is infatuated with me. He will pick me up at four this afternoon, hoping for a positive answer to his proposal of marriage. "Old son," Lola said aloud to herself, "You ain't getting; nothing but sex until we come to an agreeable marriage arrangement. I require another title, bestowed prior to the wedding."

Lola knew nothing of Julius' family. Would they object? How much interference could they be? Lola felt confident the lad would do whatever she requested. To antagonize the family made no sense—unless, of course, they came between her and the money. She had to find out what powers the family held over Julius, and what religion he was.

Julius arrived in an ornate carriage pulled by four black mares. Four outriders complemented two guards on the driver's seat and two in the rear. "Will you marry me?" Julius blurted out.

"Let us discuss this in the carriage," Lola said and kissed his cheek. In the carriage he asked again.

"I am not opposed to marriage," Lola replied, "But you well know there are many things to be discussed: titles, endowments, the religion of our children, etc. etc. Are you Protestant or Catholic?"

"Protestant," Julius said. "It would be difficult for my family to accept a change of religion."

"Not to worry, dear boy. Religion doesn't present a problem."

"But you do believe in God?"

"Of course I do," Lola said. "The Almighty has always blessed me, and I am forever grateful."

"I would prefer to return to your apartment," Julius said. "Making love with you is like... I never experienced anything like what happened last night. There was a moment when I thought my soul was coming out my penis."

"I promised you would ejaculate as if urinating. It is

a difficult climax to achieve."

"Did you experience the same thing?"

"No. In time I will teach you to pleasure me in such a way."

"I so much want to kiss your breasts."

Lola removed her right breast from her bodice. He leaned over and kissed, sucked and manipulated it as she taught him. Lola leaned back enjoying the sensations. She watched as they passed side streets and called, "Driver! Turn right and stop before the Church of St. Maria."

Julius' face shone like the morning sun. Lola straightened her dress and touched the inside of his thigh. She didn't want him staining his trousers upon entering the church. "I've been told it is a quaint old place," she said. "The Bishop's quarters are open to the public."

"We must ask if Protestants are allowed." Julius said.

Upon her questioning the caretaker, he replied, "There is no difference in this church. The Protestants worship the *Bon Dieu* and we Catholics worship the *Vierge. Eh bien.*"

"What about the Eastern Orthodox Churches?" Lola asked.

"Who knows what those heretics do," the caretaker said. "Their priests wear beards like Jews and are allowed to marry!"

The church was more exceptional from outside. Inside, a piscine at the entrance contained holy water. Rows of wooden benches marched down to a raised altar. There were Confessional booths on the left and plaster statues of saints in wall niches down both side walls. Lola had only stopped here to find out what she learned in the carriage. He was Protestant.

Far more impressive than the church were the Bishop's apartments. The two wandered hand in hand through the beautiful rooms. Master craftsmen of Europe had carved the furniture from exotic woods. Matchless paintings, and exquisite sculptures of bronze and marble, adorned the rooms and hallways. Elegant drapery and fine wall hangings from Turkey competed with matchless Persian carpets, upon which rested large porcelain vases from China.

Lola was lost in thought of building a new palace for herself, larger and decorated in the Spanish style. It would be more eloquent than the one Ludwig built for her in Munich. She felt challenged to surpass the exquisitely beautiful, and sophisticatedly furnished, home of the Latin Prelate. Lola realized Julius was saying, "It is time for us to leave."

"Please send the carriage back," Lola said. "I prefer to walk and think."

"Only if your contemplations will be on accepting my proposal of marriage."

"Nothing else occupies my mind," Lola said.

They walked the length of the *Champs de Mars*, onto the *Quay d'Orsay*, passing along the *Champs de Elysees* to her hotel. They spent two more days without leaving the hotel room. They planned to remain longer, but Julius' cousin appeared, banging on the apartment door. He burst past the serving girl and confronted the scantily-clad Julius, waving a telegram. "Our Aunties are coming!" he shouted.

"Why?" Julius demanded.

"I summoned them." He pointed to the bedroom door behind Julius. "I assume the Spanish witch is in there, half naked."

Julius gritted his teeth and said, "Cousin, it is none of your business and less of my aunties' concern."

"Until you reach majority age, it is. Auntie Martha appointed me your chaperone."

"To hell with you and my aunties! I love this woman. I'm going to marry her."

"She's nothing but a high-priced whore."

Julius' right fist connected with his cousin's nose, and blood spurted. The cousin lay outstretched on his back, and the blood from his nose filled his eye sockets. He opened his eyes but couldn't see. He cried, "I'm blind! I'm blind!"

Lola swept into the room buttoning a sheer nightgown, shouting, "What the hell is going on?" She took in the scene of Julius, looking down in awe at his cousin crawling around on all fours, blinking his blood-filled eyes and weeping hysterically, "I'm blind! Blind!"

Lola plucked up a water pitcher, used for the plants, with one hand and went to the crawling figure, grabbed him by the hair, raised up his head with her left hand and poured the water onto his bloody face. The young man sputtered, blinked his eyes and shouted, "I can see! Thank God I can see again!"

Lola handed the pitcher to Julius and tried to cover her laughter.

Julius reached down, helped his cousin to his feet and handed him a nearby doily to clean his face. After a few words he led his cousin to the door, took the telegram and slammed the door after him.

"Why so angry?" Lola asked. "Didn't you see the humor in it?" She imitated the cousin crying, "I'm blind! I'm blind!" She knuckled her eyes like a child and cried, "I can see! Thank God I can see again." Lola began laughing and Julius joined her. They laughed so hard they sat on the floor and fell into each other's arms. Lola felt Julius's erection pressing into her thigh.

She removed her nightgown and instructed him in the Rocking Horse position. She had him sit upright and cross his legs Indian style. She massaged his penis, stood over him and lowered herself onto his erection, facing him. They kissed. He kissed her breasts, and she manipulated herself up and down. She was watching his eyes. They dilated and the irises quivered. She held herself in check to make his climax and hers coordinate. She lost control and raised up and down in a fury. The two clasped and rolled around, locked in a spasmodic embrace on the carpeted floor.

After some time Julius said, "I must meet my aunties at the train station."

"Is it really that important?"

"Yes. There are three: Helen, Lily and Martha. They are my surrogate parents since the death of my mother and father, especially Auntie Martha. They deserve my respect."

"Where in France will they be staying?"

"La Rochelle. It is a Protestant enclave. They are religious women. They will object to me marrying a Roman Catholic."

"Don't concern yourself about that. I can overcome their objection."

"Would you convert?"

Lola was unprepared to reveal her Anglican baptism. "Do you trust me?" she asked.

"Implicitly," Julius said.

# CHAPTER 2

## KIDNAPPED

Unbeknown to Lola or Julius, the three sisters were already in Paris. Informed by Martha's son, the women sensed great danger to their nephew from the infamous Countess of Landsfeld. Aunt Martha hired two policemen to help her take Julius back to the family estate in Austria.

Julius arrived at the Paris Central Railroad Station in good time. He was pleasantly surprised to see his Aunties awaiting him, and didn't think it unusual that they arrived early. Train schedules were quite unreliable, after all. He hurried to embrace the elderly ladies.

He was about to ask how their trip was, when two large men grabbed him from behind and walked him to a gate advertising the Rhineland Express to Austria-Germany. Resistance was impossible. The two policemen hustled him to the platform, up the three steps of the first class carriage, and into a private room. Two burly men awaited him there, and they took charge of Julius.

He realized resistance would fare no better against these two. His Aunties had hired their own private suite. His struggles were useless. He slouched in the corner of the compartment and attempted to think his way out and return to Lola. He would rather die than be separated from her. "The toilet," he said. "I must use the toilet."

One man stood and motioned him to the door and followed him out into the narrow passageway. A conductor approached them, and Julius asked, "Where is the toilet?"

"It's at the either end of this car, but you cannot use it while we are in the station. Once the train starts I will unlock it."

"How long will that be?" Julius asked.

The conductor looked at his pocket watch and said. "Two minutes." He tried to pass Julius in the narrow corridor, but Julius bumped into him and slipped a gold sovereign into his hand. Their eyes met. Nothing was said.

As good as his word, as the train started up the conductor returned and unlocked the nearer toilet door. Julius contrived to slip him another sovereign, but said nothing until the conductor was several steps past them. Then Julius called, "Conductor! I might need some extra toilet paper. I have an upset stomach."

"Right you are, sir. I'll be back shortly."

The conductor returned, slid past the guard, and knocked on the bathroom door. "Come in," Julius called. "I can't get up." The conductor entered. The guard outside stopped the conductor from closing the door, but the door opened inward so he couldn't see Julius who, was sitting on the toilet with his trousers lowered. Julius signaled the conductor with his hands for something to write with. At the same time he said "Put the paper over here." The conductor handed Julius a pencil, received another gold sovereign, and Julius whispered, "See me later."

During the remainder of the trip Julius managed to

write a letter to Lola. He slipped another sovereign to the conductor, with the letter and Lola's address.

Two days later the letter arrived in Paris. It read, "My dearest Lola, Love of my life. We were betrayed by my cousin. I was kidnapped at the train station. It was a plot by my Maternal Aunt, Martha, and her sisters. I will be held under guard in the family chateau. If you love me as I do you, help me so I may return to your loving embrace. Excuse the paper upon which this letter is written; I am closely supervised. There are several people in our employ who are loyal to me; the most reliable is the Master of Hounds. Hire and send a group of men to break me out of the confinement in my own home. Loving You Forever, Julius."

Lola weighed her options, and considered several plans. In the end she adapted these to one course of action. The objective was to return with Julius, marry him, and enjoy life as the Countess of Schwandt. She required help. To recruit and transport a group of toughs by train would be noticed; they would be Parisian outsiders in a German-speaking community.

She recalled seeing Baron Theodore Heidrick of the Austrian embassy at George Sand's salon. She had worked with him before. He was her Austrian contact when she was in power in Munich. He was also a part of von Metternich's spy system. She once saved him from disgrace; he had bedded the wife of his Prince, ambassador to Bavaria, and was about to be caught. Lola had rescued him. It was time for him to repay.

Lola stepped off the train at the only station in Schwandt. She wore black clothes of mourning with a heavy veil, dressed to appear as a frumpy *fraulien* in mourning. The trip was a revelation. It was the first time she had worn a veil. Her face was the most intimate part of her beauty, but through the veil she could observe people without them knowing. They gave her scant attention. It was like being invisible.

Two men approached her on the station platform. One in proper evening dress, the other in a green velvet hunting jacket, high laced leather boots and canvas riding trousers. The latter remained respectfully silent. The former said, "Countess, I am Hans Kunen, representative of Baron Heidrick, at your service." He bowed and clicked his heels.

"Have you a plan for liberating Lord Julius from his chateau?" Lola asked.

"Yes," Hans answered. "This is Gustav, Master of Hounds and loyal to Lord Julius since birth. He and I will bring his Lordship to you at eleven tonight. The train to Paris will arrive at eleven fifteen. Here are two tickets." He placed them in Lola's hand. She asked, "And where will I stay until then?"

"I have reserved a room for you under the name Schoenfeld at the Inn across the street. I suggest you have a leisurely dinner and await our arrival."

"Will there be violence?"

"I do not anticipate the use of force." He patted a bulge under his suit jacket with his right hand, moved his left hand, and a vicious looking black leather sap appeared. "I'm prepared."

The Slippery Noodle Inn, was immaculately clean. Lola thought the food good, but then, she enjoyed eating. The Vienna Schnitzel was larger than the platter.

Potato dumplings and sausage with a Slippery Noodle pudding, and then Lola retired to her room and waited. As the church bell rang eleven, a carriage pulled up to the Inn. Fearing recognition of Lord Julius at the Inn, Lola took her overnight bag and hurried downstairs.

Yes, he was there. She and Julius hugged and kissed in the carriage. The driver pulled into the shadows beside the railroad station. The carriage shook and rocked as the two made frantic love. The train whistle warned the driver. He used the butt of his buggy whip to alert the couple, who had the sense to disengage and run for the train.

Lola and Julius made love in their private compartment, and they were in a gay mood when they arrived at the Central Paris Terminal. "Let us celebrate your freedom," Lola said. "A meal on the Champs de Elysees?"

"I have no money!" Julius exclaimed.

"I have," Lola laughed. "What is mine is yours."

"And what is mine is yours, my love," Julius said.

Lola thought, "I intend just that."

Each ordered oysters on the half shell. They looked into each other's eyes and smiled as they slurped the mollusks flavored with Mignonette Sauce. They both ordered Chateaubriand. Colorful vegetables surrounded the blood-red meat, and the waiter ladled a piquant gravy over all. The meal completed, Julius and Lola strolled arm in arm to her hotel.

The last words Lord Julius of Schwandt said to Lola were "It's the same two policemen!" Behind them towered a third figure who watched as the two slapped a velvet bag over Julius's head, tied his arms behind, and whisked him neatly into a waiting carriage. Lola reached into her cummerbund, but the very tall man restrained her. "Mademoiselle, I introduce myself: Inspector Gilbair LaClaire of the Paris Metropolitan Police Department."

He glanced down at her hand buried in the cummerbund and said, "If you were to withdraw a knife or pistol, I would be forced to arrest you. Understood?"

"Take your hand off me, you big oaf." She withdrew her hand, showed him it was empty, and asked, "Where are you taking Lord Julius?"

"Back to his Aunties in Schwandt."

"How could you know so quickly?"

"The telegraph. We followed you from the moment you stepped from the train. It would be a shame to allow those oysters to sleep alone tonight; I had the same menu as you."

Lola took a longer look at him. He was a virile man in his early forties. He undressed her with his eyes and said, ""You will be better satisfied by me than that man-child."

"Maybe so, but that little twit is worth millions."

"Auntie Martha says she will compensate you." He held out his right elbow, "Allow me,"

"Where are we going?"

"To bed."


Several days later Inspector LaClaire brought her an envelope containing one hundred thousand francs. It was less than expected, but Lola retained the note from Julius proposing marriage. It could be useful in future negotiations.

# CHAPTER 3

## CROSSING THE CHANNEL

Lola sent her luggage in three large drays from Paris to the port of Le Havre. She and her retinue took a paddle-wheeler on a leisurely trip down the Seine.

As a titled aristocrat, the Countess of Landsfeld was an honored guest at the Captain's table. He kept a tradition of circulating a subject for discussion prior to each meal. Lola approached these discussions as a contest, since she desired praise for her intelligence as well as her beauty.

Most people at the Captain's table were the nouveau riche or minor aristocrats traveling to Great Britain. First class passengers expected to be interviewed by newspapermen. Lola wanted the press to spread the word of her return to the London stage. When last she departed England, some newspapers claimed she was run out of the country for imitating a Spanish noble-woman, that she was born Eliza Gilbert, and baptized at the Anglican Church in Limerick, Ireland. Those aboard the vessel knew little of this.

They observed her sunning in a deckchair and thought she slept, but Lola's mind was always working. The subjects for discussion were given out prior to the meal; first she categorized it, and decided what position to take. A born contrarian, she chose the least popular theme, then set up an order of priorities for defending her stance. She prepared for each meal and every topic as if for combat. She memorized appropriate quotations and anecdotes.

Of the twenty ladies and gentlemen seated regularly at the Captain's table, only a doctor, the editor of the *Manchester Guardian*, and the publisher of *The Scotsman* were intellectually prepared to challenge Lola. Without them she would have had no sounding board to reflect her views.

Upon being introduced to the newspapermen, she planned to impress them. They were accompanied by their wives, who remained protective of their spouses. Lola was more concerned that her appearance at London's King's Theater should be mentioned than in bedding the husbands. She was to star in a one-act play, which she had authored, about Lord Palmerston, Lord Brougham, and her conflicts with Prince von Metternich of Austria and the Jesuits.

The first subject at the Captains table was the works of Louis Pasteur, specifically, his concept of immunology and vaccination. A doctor at the table was asked to describe the two ideas, which he did in a cogent and concise manner. "Professor Pasteur," he said, "Has saved innumerable lives with his pasteurization of wine and milk." One well-fed man replied, "Monsieur Pasteur can do what he wants with the milk, but I wish he would stop boiling my wine."

"It kills the germs in both liquids," the doctor replied.

"I never saw a germ," the man said, "And if I did see them in my glass I'd rather see live ones than dead ones floating around."

"The subject is Immunology and Vaccination," the captain said. "We can discuss pasteurization another time."

"Doctor," a woman asked, "You scientists and professors call this period the Age of Reason. Is it reasonable to think that, for one to prevent a disease, you must first give the person that disease?"

"When stated that way, no,"

"Listen to Pasteur explain it," the editor of the *Manchester Guardian* said. "My colleague, publisher of *The Scotsman*, and I came to France to interview Louis Pasteur. In simple terms, the scientist says, by introducing a very small amount of measles vaccine to the body, it allows the individual's natural immune system to overcome the foreign measles germ—and will forever protect that person from contracting that disease."

"But the French government insists our children be immunized first," a man said. Others joined in the conversation. The ship's Captain called for order. He was about to speak when Lola asked, in an authoritative voice, "May I attempt to answer?"

"Ladies and gentlemen," the Captain said, "I have the honor of introducing the Countess of Landsfeld, Miss Lola Montez."

Lola nodded and said, "The doctor agrees there are sometimes adverse effects from the vaccination. The side effects are usually a mild fever and possible headache, and those for only a day or two—far less dangerous than the disease itself. The reason the young receive immunization first is that they are the most vulnerable. In school or at play, they make physical contact with children who have the disease. Their bodies are smaller and less able to fight the illness. It is the young who are most likely to suffer death or physical damage from Whooping Cough and Measles. Pasteur reduced mortality among women at childbirth from puerperal fever. He created and proved vaccines for rabies and anthrax. These last two prevent certain, horrible deaths. I believe in vaccinations. The risk is worth taking."

"I would like to thank all those who participated in this discussion," the Captain said. "We shall conclude with dessert."

After dessert, the two newspapermen approached her. "Countess," the Publisher said, "You spoke most authoritatively. It was an edifying experience. My colleague and I would like to interview you for our respective papers. Would you share some of your time with us?"

"Had you not asked me," Lola said, "I would have sought you two gentlemen out." Both men bowed their appreciation.

"We would like to interview you before we reach London," the editor of the *Guardian* said.

"What will be the theme?" Lola asked.

"The *Guardian* will focus on your past," the publisher said, "While we in *The Scotsman* shall describe the present and speculate on your future."

"Let us begin," Lola said.


The cross-channel trip was pleasant and brief. The ship was powered by steam, with a new screw-driven propeller. Now, ensconced in her apartment, Lola considered the proper moment to make her London debut. It was determined for her by the morning article in *The Guard-*

ian *Newspaper* and the afternoon article in *The Scotsman.*

The *Guardian* editor wrote:

*I traveled to France for the purpose of interviewing the famous scientist and biologist, Professor Louis Pasteur. In yesterday's paper you read my article about his renowned discoveries in microbiology. He has opened new fields in the study of fermentation, pasteurization, the causes and prevention of diseases by vaccination. I was further educated on this subject by a most famous and unlikely person: The Countess of Landsfeld, known to all as the renowned dancer, Lola Montez. It is three years since Miss Montez departed from England's shores. At the time there were critics of her dancing and her attitude towards the public. I can only say that I never read a negative word about her beauty, nor of her wit. This woman held center stage at the captain's table on our voyage home. She did so by virtue of her intelligence. She never fell back on her title or her beauty to make a point. The first subject at the Captain's table was the Pros and Cons of vaccinations. The subject is prominent in all modern countries. Miss Montez took the pro side and was so effective amongst the diners that I will ask her to write an article on the subject for our readers. Even more impressive was her ability to take Pasteur's concrete proofs of sci-*

*ence and apply them to the abstract concept of God. It happened thus, the subject chosen by the ship's Captain for the diners was the recently published "Communist Manifesto" by Karl Marx and Frederick Engels. There being no English translation of the two German writers, guests were able to give a synopsis. It appears that while in Bavaria former King Ludwig himself had translated the Manifesto for Miss Montez. The beauty maintained her silence until one of the translators said, "How can a communist believe in God when he calls religion 'the opiate of the masses?'"*

*Miss Montez corrected the gentleman, and from memory quoted Marx from an earlier writing. "'Religion,' Marx said, 'is the sign of the oppressed creature, the heart of the heartless world, and the soul of soulless conditions. It is the opium of the people.'"*

*The gentleman in question asked, "How can anyone believe in a loving, forgiving, ever bountiful God when we see so much suffering, pain and poverty?"*

*"These conditions exist," Lola responded. "To say otherwise is a lie. To give a reason for such horrible conditions is to claim one knows God's mind. That, to me, is offensive. But for you to deny the existence of God is to violate this Age of Reason in which we live."*

*"Then provide us a reasonable answer," the gentleman requested.*

*Miss Montez did just that. She went on to present one of the most cogent arguments I have ever heard for the existence of God. She said, "Those who claim God doesn't exist, never existed nor will God ever come to be, must believe in spontaneous generation. That a combination of slime, chemicals and microbes all met somewhere and burst into life. But Louis Pasteur dealt this concept a mortal blow. His simple experiment of isolating an object, whether it be animal, vegetable or mineral, he showed it cannot produce microscopic life without germs."*

*How does this fact prove the existence of God? How do we know God is?"*

*From her beautiful lips came the following words: "It proves there is no circumstance that without microorganisms, or shall we use the term parents, life cannot come into being. Mankind was formed by our parent, God Almighty."*

*"You mean God is both mother and father at the same time?"*

*Now Lola relied on something her Nanny Manuela had been told in answer to a similar question by a Jew money changer in Munich. "In ancient Hebrew," Miss Montez said, "The Old Testament uses the plural for the name of God. Read the story of Adam and Eve. Adam was both male and female before Eve was created."*

*"Countess, I cannot debate your knowledge of ancient Hebrew" the gentleman answered. "I will read the story of creation more closely. Thank you"*

*Miss Montez was applauded. Everyone congratulated her, even an atheist at the table made his compliments public. Miss Montez (the Countess of Landsfeld) went on to say that, "Never will the doctrine of spontaneous generation recover from the mortal blow of Pasteur's simple experiment of isolating a specimen and preventing creation. There is no circumstance in which it can be confirmed that microscopic beings came into the world without germs, without parents similar to themselves. Pasteur is responsible for crushing the doctrine of spontaneous generation. He performed experiments which revealed, that without contamination, microorganisms cannot reproduce. Therefore mankind exists because of God."*

*I look forward to Lola Montez's appearance on the London stage at the Royal Theatre, in a play she wrote and stars in."*

### THE SCOTSMAN
### THE COUNTESS OF LANDSFELD

By John Ritchie

*As publisher of this newspaper I had the*

*pleasure to meet and interview Miss Lola Montez, the Countess of Landsfeld who is recognized as an accomplished dancer. She is celebrated for her appearance on the London stage and renowned for her interpretation of the Tarantella or Spider Dance. I was initially drawn to this young lady by her exceptional beauty. Superlatives are inadequate to describe such exquisite loveliness. Yet it was her intellectual astuteness which most impressed me. On my return trip from meeting with Professor Louis Pasteur, my wife and I had the good fortune to be seated at the Captain's table with Miss Montez. The captain chose a subject for discussion at meals. By virtue of her intellect and at the request of the diners, Miss Montez dominated the conversation. We were awe struck by her knowledge of past and present. Her observations about the future of western civilization are remarkable. Her relationship as courtesan to King Ludwig of Bavaria gives her a unique view of the imminent. She believes the former colonists in America are setting the guidelines for the future. They use a strong military to build an industrial infrastructure and protect the same. The Yankees do not wish to occupy foreign soil. They desire to control North America from the Atlantic to the Pacific Oceans. The phrase used is "Manifest Destiny". Americans believe they are destined by Almighty God to own the*

*Garden of Eden (North America). Miss Montez pointed out that Europeans have no concept of the immensity of America. The Yankees are still mapping territories they took from England, bought from France and confiscated from Mexico. The entire countries of England, Ireland, Wales, Scotland, France and Belgium could fit in the original state of Massachusetts. Alternately, they would also fit in the former French Louisiana Territory, or again in the recently acquired Mexican lands of Texas, New Mexico, Arizona and California." Miss Montez enlightened us. We never realized the vast American natural resource potential. For example, she described how immigrant families walk up the Mississippi River, with little more than an ax and rifle. They shoot the abundant game or fish the river for food. There are no lords or landowners. It is wild country inhabited by Stone Age natives. The family finds a stand of trees close by the river. They cut and trim the trees, making giant rafts upon which they build a hut. They launch the raft and float downstream offering the wood for sale at the many new settlements along the Lower Mississippi. With the cash earned from the sale they buy fertile farmland in the great Mississippi Valley. No one taxes their income. To be an American is to be free.*

*The Countess of Landsfeld praised Yankee*

*ingenuity. She held up a bent piece of wire. Then demonstrated several uses for what is called a safety-pin. She spoke of Cyrus McCormick and his invention of the "Mechanized Reaper". She talked about the steel-tipped "Moldboard" plow invented by an American blacksmith named John Deere. This plow will open up millions of hectares of rough prairie land for planting. It will enable Americans to feed the masses flocking to the colonies from all over Europe. An Englishman at our table quipped, "Those immigrants are the dregs of European society. They can't possibly organize and run a country. We're glad to be rid of them."*

*Miss Montez's eyes spat fire when she retorted, "That rabble you speak of defeated the French in the Indian Wars, defeated you British in their revolution and again in 1812. Santa Anna conceded defeat in Mexico City to the Americans and their Marines cleared the pirates from Tripoli. Their merchant marine competes with Europe for the China trade. The Sea Witch just set a record for the China Run. This newly designed Clipper ship took only seventy-seven days from Hong Kong to New York."*

*No less startling was Miss Montez's grasp of global politics. She predicted the Russian Czar would declare war on the Turks. She claimed the Czar sees the Russian Orthodox*

*Church as the protector of subjugated Christians in the Ottoman Empire. The Ottoman government requires all non-Muslim males (mostly Christians) to pay dhimma. It is a derisive tax under Sharia Law, allowing infidels to live among Muslims. Miss Montez is rumored to have been on intimate terms with the Czar while in St Petersburg. The countess's prediction of war between Imperial Russia and the Turks raised far more than eyebrows. The dining table was abuzz. Listeners attempted to assess the effects of such a war.*

*Lola Montez had little patience for her audience's concern about a Russian-Turkish war. Three sheets to the wind, she sailed into her next subject, Railroads. She began with Cornelius Vanderbilt and other American industrialists. "These visionaries," Lola said, "were shocked into action when the English steam locomotive, the* Blue Mallard, *made a test run at one hundred and twelve miles an hour.*

*Cornelius Vanderbilt pointed out to the members of Congress that every capital city in the world was located on a river. It was so for two reasons. The river provided water for the population and a means of travel through the wilderness. Later roads were developed alongside the river banks. They followed the meandering rivers. Railroads of the future will carve straight lines from one point to another. If we can't go over the mountains," Vanderbilt said, "We'll go through them." Vanderbilt asked Congress to enact a law referred to as Eminent Domain. It gives the railroads right-of-way by virtue of enacting laws "That, property may be taken for use or by third parties, who will devote it to public or civic use for economic development." "European governments," Miss Montez insisted, "Must help the railroads acquire the right-of-way to build railroads on the European continent. If not, the industrial groundwork of Europe will be forever retarded."*

*I believe Miss Montez is overly impressed with the New World. What is new is not necessarily better. England commands the Seven Seas and rules one quarter of its population. France dominates European culture and the Germanic States lead the world in science. Lola Montez's bright mind, quick wit, and sometimes fanciful predictions are a welcome breath of fresh air. The Countess may be wrong but she makes people think.*

*Lola Montez is also the most beautiful and impressive woman I have ever met. I look forward to seeing her performance in a play of her own writing skills. If it is as entertaining as her talks at the Captain's table, attendance will be well worth the price of admission. The play is about the Countess' as-*

signations as a courtesan with aristocrats in England, France, Russia and Bavaria. I wish this extraordinary lady well, in her premier presentation of "Whatever Lola Wants Lola Gets" at London's Royal Theater.

# CHAPTER 4

## RETURN TO ENGLAND

Elias Piesner, senior student of the Alemaine and one of Lola's lovers, appeared in Munich destitute. He petitioned an audience with former King Ludwig, and Ludwig granted it, for he recognized it as an opportunity to learn the truth about Lola. Rumor had it the lad had been Lola's paramour, something she always denied.

Ludwig conducted an intensive questioning of Piesner. He was destined for debtor's prison, and broke under Ludwig's interrogation. He admitted Lola consorted with him and two of his friends, often together in the same bed. He confirmed she took other lovers, Lieutenant Nusbammer being her preferred partner. He named other transient lovers, some distinguished, others not. "Why," Ludwig asked the young man, "Why in the world did you remain under such demeaning conditions?"

"I loved her. My soul loves that woman." Piesner fell to his knees before Ludwig and wept, "Of all the people in this world, I thought you would understand. She is bewitching."

"I know," Ludwig whispered.

The King's heart was torn asunder. He kept his word, paid Piesner's debts and sent him on his way. Then the former King sat down and wrote bitter poetry to Lola.

The poem from Ludwig was delivered with his monthly stipend to Lola. The King recognized a moral obligation to support her. He added, "You should feel free to marry, as there will be no opportunity for you and me to be together again. Your Loving, Ludwig".

"My Dear Ludwig," Lola wrote, "Pay no attention to the lies and insinuations of people such as Piesner. They are cruel, jealous, misfits who attempt to bring others down to their level. Believe me, since we first met there has never been anyone but you. It may be impossible for us to meet again under the constraints of the Landtag, that gang of fools, but this congress of blood-suckers has no dominance over our thoughts. Allow your feelings for me to fly upward and there intermingle with my imaginings of you. Hold me in your strong, virile arms, and let us make love through the night. What a lover, what a man, you who are always in my thoughts. You walk through my dreams and leave your footprints in my heart. You stimulate my imagination to the point of physical distraction. Oh Ludwig, my love! We may never again meet in this world, but if God is fair, we shall spend eternity together in heaven.

"May the Lord bless you and keep you. May He shine His countenance upon you, and may all the works of your hands and desires of your heart be blessed. Until we meet again, you are my King. Your Loving, Lolita"

Lola found out that British theater managers and agents had very long and vivid memories of her violent outbursts and past, public antics. She was persona non grata in the London theater district.

However, Lola cornered the director of Covent Garden. He read her play. He was more impressed with the names of royal lovers from England, France, Russia, Poland, and Bavaria mentioned in the play. The director realized Lola's life depicted on stage as a courtesan to such famous personalities would pack the theater. It would surely restore his standing at Barclay's Bank. The play was called, *"Lola Montez, ou la Comtesse d'une Heure,"*

For the same reason the director wished to produce the play, Britain's Lord Chamberlain rejected it. Lola told of boudoir intimacies with living European royalty, most of whom were related through the House of Hanover—all still very much alive. The license was refused.

Without the projected income, Lola sought less expensive accommodations. She rented at 27 Half-Moon St. in fashionable Mayfair. She organized acquaintances into a small but stylish salon. Through this clique of prigs, prudes, and plutocrats she hoped to attract one wealthy enough to marry. At age thirty-two Lola desired stability.

One young man caught her eye. He visited her gathering on two occasions. She flirted with him by a glance and a flick of her whalebone fan. He blushed. She dismissed him as being too young; it was older men who controlled the wealth.

Lola went daily to a professional dance instructor. If she couldn't find a wealthy man, she would have to return to the stage. Ludwig's stipend, generous by normal standards, did not meet Lola's needs..

One day on return from her dance lesson, a man stopped her carriage and asked to speak with her. Lola recognized the man as an English-speaking spy in the service of King Ludwig. She allowed him to enter the carriage and asked, "To what do I owe the honor of the King's dog sniffing around?"

"It is true, your Highness," the man said. "I am in the employ of former King Ludwig. I wish you no harm."

"Good for you," Lola said, pointing a small pocket pistol at him. "Now what is this about?"

"You are being followed, every day from your home to the dance class and back. Look through the rear portal of this carriage. See the small two-horse brougham? Tell your driver to continue and you will observe it follows."

Lola did, and it was so. She ordered the driver to take the Hyde Park path and the brougham followed. Satisfied the man was telling the truth, she questioned, "Who is in that carriage?"

"I can find out."

"It will be well worth your while."

"Payment is not necessary, Your Highness."

"Ludwig pays you?"

"He sent me to protect you."

"And report my love affairs?"

The man looked away, saying, "There have been none in England."

Lola thought, "You are right, old son, and I'm getting restless between the thighs." She said, "Do inform the King of my chastity. You may leave now."

Every day for the next three days, the brougham carriage followed Lola wherever she went. The third evening, at a gathering in her salon, Ludwig's spy appeared at the servant's entrance and spoke in private with Lola. "The young man following you is George Trafford

Heald. He is a Lieutenant in the Life Guards."

"What about his family?" Lola asked.

"He bought his way into the most famous regiment in the British military."

"So his family is wealthy?"

"Yes, with more to come. He will soon inherit everything: estates, businesses, and two banks. His mother died years ago, and he will inherit her fortune and his recently departed father's fortune, as the only male heir. The father died of cholera, a wealthy, highly respected, Chancery barrister."

"How old is George Trafford Heald?"

"He'll come of age for inheritance on January first of the New Year, eighteen-forty-nine."

"That's a month away." Lola massaged her forehead, thinking, "I'd be robbing the cradle again." She asked, "What does he look like?"

"Everything about him is military. He is tall, slim, with straight blond hair, and affects a light downy mustache. He is trying to grow chops but... It will take some years. He drinks a bit too much, but most military men do. He is a loner."

"What is his choice of liquor?"

"Ten year old, single malt whiskey. Young Heald is considered by the well-bred young ladies of London, and their mothers, as the most desirable catch in the kingdom."

Lola's forehead wrinkled. There was no doubt in her mind she could trap this infatuated adolescent. She walked over to the wall and shifted a painting aside. She peered through an eye hole, then beckoned Ludwig's spy. "Is the blond in uniform George Trafford Heald?"

"Yes, Countess."

It was the same young man she had flirted with. She walked to her desk, removed a silk purse heavy with silver coins and tossed it to the King's spy.

He bowed. "Thank you, Your Highness."

"How can I contact you?" Lola asked. "I may have need of your special talents."

"At your service, always."

# CHAPTER 5

## IN PURSUIT OF A GROOM

Lola had gone fishing for a Prince and hooked a King, only to lose him because of a revolution. For her, the European aristocratic waters were muddied. Royalty avoided the Countess of Landsfeld. This young lad would have to do.

Her experience as a courtesan gave her a sense of absolute certainty. She meticulously planned her approach. It took place in broad daylight on the riding path through Hyde Park. The brougham followed her carriage. At a sharp bend she instructed the driver to block the road. The brougham pulled up. Lola's driver approached the coach and said to the occupant, "The Countess of Landsfeld extends an invitation to join her."

George Trafford Heald stepped out, tugged his uniform jacket straight, and marched to what he feared would be the end of his fantasy. Lola's driver opened her coach door. She crooked a lace gloved forefinger, beckoning him to enter. He sat down across from the most beautiful woman in the world and held his breath. "Lieutenant Heald," Lola lowered her voice as recommended in the *Kama Sutra*. "For some time now you have followed me wherever I go. What am I to think?"

George Heald had envisioned this moment, practiced and honed his responses to potentially delicate questions, but now he stammered. Lola asked, "Do you intend to harm me?"

"Oh, no! Never!" he cried. "The furthest thing from my mind! I love you!" He appeared more shocked than Lola at having spoken the words of his heart. He burst into tears, slipped off the seat opposite her onto his knees, and begged, "Forgive me! Please forgive me! I planned to approach you in a far more dignified manner. I confess my undying love for you. Please, please do not send me away."

Lola had planned to do just that. She hoped to build up his desire, but it exceeded her expectations. She dabbed his wet cheeks with a lace handkerchief and said, "Sit up. We shall talk."

Heald's brougham returned to the stables without its passenger. The couple retired to Lola's apartment on Half Moon Street. They enjoyed a week together without leaving the apartment. They imbibed the Pope's wine, used cocaine left by the Maharaja Jung Bahadur, and studied *Kama Sutra*.

Sex and exploring each other's mind and body were supplemented by exquisite meals and excellent conversation. George Trafford Heald was schooled in Britain's finest institutions, but he was no match for Lola. Although she didn't perform her Spider Dance, she spun an unbreakable web around the young man.

He proposed.

She accepted.

On July 19th 1849 they married. Leaving the London church with her new husband, she tucked thoughts of past adventures away. She anticipated a sedentary life of propriety, wealth and influence.

To her dismay, their honeymoon was unceremoniously interrupted by the police.

George Heald's spinster aunt, Susanna Heald of Horn Castle, hired private detectives to search for her nephew. They found him, but too late to stop the marriage.

Early on the morning of August 6th, London police detained Lola. They charged her with bigamy. Auntie Susanna signed the complaint. Her detectives unearthed unsavory stories about Lola and her fictitious aristocratic, Spanish lineage. Lola legally retained her title as Countess of Landsfeld, but she held no valid passport to prove her nationality. Birth records from the church in Limerick, Ireland showed her baptized Anglican: her family name, Gilbert. At age fifteen she married Lieutenant James, now a captain. Several months later they separated, but were forbidden to divorce by the Anglican Church. Auntie Heald set the wheels of English Law in motion against the newlyweds. Once again Lola fought a battle with a guardian aunt over the fate of her youthful nephew.

A reporter described the couple's appearance at Marlborough Street Police Court.

> *"At half-past one o'clock, the Countess of Landsfeld, leaning on the arm of Mr. George Trafford Heald, her present husband, entered the court. They sat in front of the bar, Mr. Heald appearing nervous, the Countess of Landsfeld very much at ease. She smiled, made remarks to her husband, and answered whispered questions from reporters. The po-*

*lice sheet indicates her age as twenty-four. According to the Limerick birth records her correct age is thirty-one. The Countess, dressed in black silk with close-fitting black velvet jacket, displayed the figure of a twenty year old beauty. She wore a plain white straw bonnet trimmed with blue, and sheer blue veil. She is beautifully proportioned and of middle height, dark complexion, and symmetrical features, set off by a pair of unusually large blue eyes with long black lashes. Her disputed husband, Mr. Heald, sat with the countess's hand clasped in both of his. He periodically gave her hand a fervent squeeze. As evidence was presented by the complainant's advocate, he whispered to her and often pressed her hand to his lips."* [20]

A reputable barrister, a friend of George's deceased father, recommended the couple post bail and flee to a foreign country. The barrister explained that the overly protective aunt invoked an outdated prohibition to divorce. Her excellent legal representation assured a decision in her favor. Their flight would entail loss of 2,000 Sterling bail money. Lola selected Spain.

They fled to Folkstone, on the southern coast of England, known as a smugglers harbor, a haven for pirates and scavengers where honest citizens came to buy tax-free. The main sales area for illegal goods was a

---

[20] Abridged, from *Lola Montez*, Edmund B. d"Auvergne p.184.

field alongside The Warren Inn.

Folkstone's captains had a reputation for charging high prices but assuring safe passage across the Channel. With help of the Inn's owner, George negotiated passage for both to Boulogne, France.

They toured Europe on their way to Spain. The newlyweds often argued, sometimes in public. Just as often, they made up in wildly passionate love-making. On several occasions Lola had to pull him from a carriage or guide him down a gangplank.

George Trafford Heald drank. He drank his meals. He drank in between his meals. Lola, who rarely imbibed, often found him passed out in an armchair or on the floor. After one episode he made up by purchase of a diamond necklace, earrings, and bracelet. They cost ten thousand sterling.

Some friends believed Lola encouraged the fights to receive the prize of apology. George always came crawling back to her bed.

On another occasion he and Lola sat for a portrait. At a party in Barcelona, where the painting was first displayed, George got falling down drunk. He and Lola argued publicly. He tried to slash the picture in half, saying he wanted no part of her. She in turn pulled a stiletto and stabbed him in the arm. The police commissioner was one of the guests. He cautioned Lola, that the next morning the police would serve her with an arrest warrant.

"But you saw my husband pull the knife first."

"But he threatened a painting. You stabbed him. There are those here tonight that hate you."

"They don't even know me."

"They know of you. Your beauty antagonizes most women and excites their men. The women do not like that."

"Is there a way for me to remain in Spain?"

"I want to lie and say yes so I might take advantage of you."

"Commissioner," Lola said, and stepped closer. "You are a handsome man. Power exudes from the very pores of your body. The advantage would be mine."

"Oh my dear Countess, how I regret saying this, but the alternative to your leaving is spending time in our jail waiting for the court to hear your case. At the trial you will be found guilty. You fled bail in England; it will not be granted in Spain."

Lola left Barcelona that night. She took with her everything of value, including George's personal jewelry. She returned to Paris, where she hired two policemen to report on George's activities. He was drinking even more than before, avoided company, and went sailing with a case of whisky. He sometimes returned to port days later when the whisky ran out.

Lola kept a low profile in Paris. Then, one dark moonless night, when pirates and smugglers do their best work, she hired a boat round trip from Boulogne to Folkstone. She was the only passenger to the English port.

In The Whistling Pig Tavern she met King Ludwig's spy, the same man who had informed Lola of being followed by George Heald. The man realized that some kind of proposal would be made. The Countess had invited him in secrecy; it would probably have to do with spying. She only had a couple of hours before the tide changed, and her boat must leave for the return trip to Boulogne. He listened to the Countess rant against prudish English laws, framed by dogmatists and administered by idiots, which condemned a woman to lose her conjugal rights and threatened imprisonment. Lola pushed her plate aside. She looked at her lapel watch, leaned forward and whispered, "Discretion is most important."

"Madam, my training in the service of King Ludwig has been a lifelong lesson in propriety."

"In your career serving the king have you ever eliminated anyone?"

"No, Countess. We have specialists for that. Would you like me to introduce you?"

"No, no. I want you to handle it. And not in France. In Barcelona."

"May I be so bold as to ask who?"

"My husband. It must be done soon. That wicked aunt of his is trying to annul our marriage."

There is an excellent man in Barcelona. He is Spanish and works for the church."

"They employ the best," Lola said.

"He doesn't come cheap."

"We are not bartering in the fish market," Lola hissed. "How much?

"Five hundred sterling."

"Providing it appears as an accident."

"It will."

"How can you guarantee this will be done in the manner I wish?"

"I take full responsibility," the agent said. "Withhold payment until the mission is accomplished to your satisfaction."

"Agreed. Tell your man in Barcelona, my husband goes sailing almost every day. He is known to drink while cruising alone. Everyone expects an accident to happen."

"That is most helpful. How and when will I receive payment?"

Lola took a slip of paper from her purse and handed it to the agent. "When the deed is done, that will get you five hundred pounds or the equivalent in francs from the Jew money changer. He is a tailor, at that address in Jew Town, Paris. I will notify him when to pay you."

"I don't go near those filthy Jews."

"If you want the five hundred sterling, you will. And keep in mind, this accident must happen soon. Auntie Heald is petitioning the courts for an annulment of my marriage and any possible inheritance."

The return cross channel voyage inspired Lola's creativity. She wrote Ludwig in Berchtesgaden. "I have been burgled by one of my servants in the service of some unscrupulous people. I am destitute. Unable to pay my bills and have to sell my clothing to eat properly. Worst of all, she stole the collection of the king's personal writings with all your intimate thoughts. I received an extortion note demanding fifty thousand francs in return for the letters. Alas, my dearest Ludwig, I do not have the wherewithal to pay them. I fear not for myself; it is for you, my dear. Your well-deserved place in history could be compromised. These vicious, unscrupulous blackguards threaten to sell the entire collection to the press. Your Loving Lolita"

Ludwig understood Lola's story of the theft as a fabrication, but his letters did exist. They would cause him extreme embarrassment if publicized. Yet he sent her a year's allowance in advance, and told her to put the blackmailers in touch with him. He would negotiate with them. He concluded with the following poem.

"Through you I lost a crown,

But I do not rage against you for that,

For you were born to be my misfortune,

You were such a blinding, scorching light!


Be happy so my soul calls after you.

Into the ever receding distance;

Now at last chose the path of salvation;

Vice brings only ruin and shame.


The best friend you ever had,

You shoved faithlessly away,

The gates of happiness were closed against you,

You simply followed your lascivious long-ings.


For life we remain divided,

And never again will we meet face to face,

> Leave me my heart's so painfully won peace,
>
> Without it life is such a burden. [21]

Sometime after the delivery of Ludwig's generous yearly allowance, a well-known Irish concert pianist, Frank O'Brien, appeared at the King's residence in Berchtesgaden. He delivered a package. It contained all of Ludwig's stolen writings. There was no explanation. O'Brien, when questioned, revealed he was hired by a Jewish tailor in Paris to make the delivery.

Relieved to have the letters, Ludwig sent two thousand more francs to Lola.

She in turn wrote Ludwig, "My dearest Ludi, I am physically alive but spiritually dead. You will never be troubled again by me. My heart is broken, but I will attempt to finish this life in peace with my fellow man."

Lola's broken heart was soothed by carefree spending. The bill collectors soon reappeared. She was forced to return to the stage to pay her debts. She began three hours a day practice with dance master, Monsieur Jardin Mabille. At the dance studio she met Mr. Edward Williams esquire, a theatrical producer from New York.

He requested a private preview of Lola's performance. After her recital, he hosted Lola at a fashionable restaurant on the Champs de Elysee. During dinner he proposed she appear in a play he had purchased. Impressed with the man's family background of four generations in the English and American theater, and his offer to pay her passage to New York, with a salary based on box office receipts, she requested to meet

---

[21] P. 275, *Lola Montez*, Bruce Seymour

again in two days. This time she made the proposal saying, "Lola Montez will never again work for anyone. They will work for her."

"How do you suggest to do that?" Williams asked.

"You represent me. You do the theater bookings, performance dates, my practice sessions, monetary negotiations, travel, everything."

"I would then be your agent?"

"Exactly."

"That is unheard of in theater. Actors negotiate their own contracts."

"Let's change that. You are well grounded in the theatrical business. You know New York and the American theater; I do not. Who better to represent me? Besides you are the first man under seventy who has not tried to bed me."

Williams smiled, brushed his pinky over his eyebrow and pulled up his cravat saying, "You are the most beautiful woman I have ever met, but..." He raised his eyebrows and Lola understood he preferred men.

She smiled and said, "Fanny Ilssler and Jenny Lind succeeded on the American stage. If they did it, so can I."

"That is why I made the offer," Williams said. "There is much to be gained. Americans have been anticipating your arrival. They read about Lola Montez's exploits. Soon they will pay to see you in person." He put out his hand and said, "You will be the first Spanish grandee and European countess to grace the boards of theaters in the New World."

Lola shook his hand and said, "You'll be the first theatrical agent in history. Let's go make a lot of money."

While organizing the voyage to America, Lola received an envelope with a death notice from a Madrid newspaper. "We regretfully notify the public of the death of English citizen George Trafford Heald. The death is ruled an inadvertent boating accident. His craft was found overturned and his body in the cabin. The Heald family is represented by his Aunt, Susanna Heald of Horncastle, England, who is Heald's legal executor. She will administer the body's relocation to England. Miss Heald is the sole facilitator of the Heald estate, appointed by the Horncastle Court. This same court annulled the marriage of Mr. George Trafford Heald to the Countess of Landsfeld, Miss Lola Montez. All claims against the estate of the deceased should be made within thirty days."

"Claims!" Lola exploded. "That bastard married me. I should be awarded everything." She raged through the apartment, cursed Susannah Heald, and threw whatever she could pick up. The lighter items she hurled at the portrait of her and James. She was about to cut the portrait in half as James had tried to do, but stopped, thought and decided to forever hang the painting in her bedroom—facing the wall.

"A husband," she would say,"Should not see everything his wife does in bed, nor with whom."

# CHAPTER 6

## AMERICA

Lola's agent, Edward Williams, was a very animated man. He ran, not walked. He babbled, not talked. Unless controlled, he took one's breath away. Lola called him Fast Eddie, and she controlled him. In England he introduced her to James Benet, editor and publisher of the *New York Herald*. Impressed by the Andalusian beauty, Benet championed her arrival in America. Other newspapers around the world picked up the story. For most it was the glitter and vitality of the New World attracting the best of the Old World.

But not everyone favored Lola's debut. The *New England Press*, guardians of American morality, led by Boston's Protestant blue-bloods, vociferously objected.

Boston Newspaper Editorial:

### *LOLA MONTEZ, THE COURTESAN*

*"This supposed Spanish aristocrat speaks several languages, none better than English. Her other languages also have the intonation and peculiar lilt of "Lace Curtain Irish". She may claim aristocratic Spanish heritage, but even the Hidalgos give her short shrift when she expresses herself in their language. Lola Montez was born Betty Gilbert in Limerick,*

*Ireland. Lord Brougham once referred to her as being, "...as Irish as Paddy's Pig." He could have added, she has about the same morals as a greasy porker. She cost European nobility dearly. King Ludwig of Bavaria lost his throne over her. Prince von Metternich missed the opportunity to become Emperor of Austria-Hungaria, Ivan Paskievich, Viceroy of Poland, had to put down a revolution she instigated, and the Jesuits saw their power dissipate in many Germanic states because of Lola. She is credited or dis-credited with starting the wave of revolutions throughout Europe. The Countess of Landsfeld (her legitimate title) is considered persona non-grata by church, state and European nobility. Her last theater appearance in London was four years ago, and she was heckled off the English stage. Miss Lola Montez, Countess of Landsfeld, Betty Gilbert of Limerick, Mrs. James or Mrs. Heald, however you wish to call her, wearied the possibilities for a European courtesan. The fish in those waters are no longer interested in the bait. She will now try angling for a rich American. (I meant that as a double-entendre). She is not only fishing for a wealthy husband but also desirous of maintaining her title and performing the lewd Spider Dance. We Americans, who fought German George and his English royalty for freedom from ostentatious aristocratic rule, often*

> *pay homage to the lowest titled Europeans. It is an anathema. I will not deny the woman's beauty. It is also a fact that she can articulate most eloquently on many subjects. However, if you expect erudition, sophistication and the intricacy of modern dance, look elsewhere. Miss Montez leaps around most athletically. She does this in the new fashion, on her toes. She is no gazelle. I liken her to a raunchy she-goat. She is morally adrift when measured by American society's view of propriety. The Europeans are fed up with her. Now, she comes hunting for a wealthy husband in the New World."*

The *New York Times* wrote: "...We shall be sadly disappointed if this creature (Lola Montez) has any degree of success in the United States. She has no special reputation as a dancer. She is known to the world only as a shameless and abandoned woman."[22]

However, Daniel Webster, the great Senator from Massachusetts, commented, "The Countess of Landsfeld's religious affiliation troubles me not. Her beauty piques my interest. The newspaper pictures are less flattering than the intriguing descriptions by her most avid detractors. I would pay to see this phenomenal woman in person."

James Benet of the *New York Herald*, and other newspapers influenced by him, countered with articles praising the Countess. Benet labeled her, "...an astute

---

[22] P. 278, *Lola Montez*, Bruce Seymour

witness and activist in the political, economic, and military affairs of present-day Europe. She appeared on the stages of Europe's most prestigious theaters. Lola Montez was hosted in the capitals of Europe. The Countess is renowned for her performances before royalty in England, France, Belgium, Bavaria, Poland, Spain and Russia. If you desire morality over entertainment, go to church. If you aspire to see Lola Montez perform her Spider Dance in a two-act play written by her, about her life as a courtesan to some of the most powerful and influential men in the world, purchase your tickets early."

Both articles inspired public interest. The demand to see the Countess of Landsfeld on stage was overwhelming, the opportunity to learn the boudoir secrets of aristocratic Europe, irresistible. Theater managers from New York, Boston, and as far away as Washington D.C. awaited at Pier 21 when the *Humboldt* docked.

A bidding war broke out on the gangplank by those vying to book Lola Montez for their theaters. Fast Eddie Williams took advantage of the situation and signed with the Broadway Theater.

Fast Eddie coached Lola to meet the press. "Americans are more interested in patriotism than sex," he said. "Shove a flag stick up a dog's arse, parade him around, and you will get applause. Carry an American flag, and no one will insult you."

"But I'm not American."

"The only true American are the Indians, and they don't count."

"Why not?"

"They don't buy theater tickets," Eddie said. "Listen

to me: you are beautiful. You've used that beauty to excite the animal passions in men. It worked with European audiences. Here in the United States, like Catholicism and Protestantism, Americanism has become a religion. If you wish to succeed, you must bow at the altar of xenophobia."

In every pre-arranged newspaper interview, in addition to her horsewhip (reporters and the public always hoped to witness her use of the short riding crop), Lola carried an American flag.

Fast Eddie did not rely on props alone. He had seen Lola dance, and generously rated her ballet efforts energetic but mediocre. He hired America's premier dance master, George Washington Smith, of Philadelphia, to train her and choreograph her play. Smith adapted her music and polished her inspirational improvisations to suit American audiences.

Lola never tired of exercise, rehearsal, and voice strengthening workouts. She had a good, but thin voice; it did not carry well in a crowded theater. Smith worked around that. He found Lola totally dedicated to her art. He rated her a mediocre danseuse but adept at memorization. With only two weeks to prepare, Lola and the company of thespians set a grueling schedule of rehearsals. Always on time, she never complained about the work schedule, but harangued and harassed those who did.

The Broadway Theater held over three thousand patrons. Opening night was chock-a-block. The theater manager called it "The Night of the Penguins". Only men attended. All dressed in black suits with white shirts and black bowler hats. Women did not attend; the play was considered too risqué. Smith anticipated this and choreographed out the blatant sexual innuendos to creative titillating flirtations. It left the spectator to imagine his own truth.

In the New York Theater, competition was fierce for the publics' dollar (the normal cost of a theater ticket). You could hear William Makepeace Thackeray lecture on comedy in the English language. One magician sawed a lady in half, pulled silver coins from people's ears and live rabbits from their hats. P.T. Barnum promoted Tom Thumb as his leading attraction. But Lola packed the house every night. Word spread that Lola's presentation was less racy than originally thought. It disappointed the men, but women were intrigued. They attended, boosting ticket sales, which led to ticket scalping.

When sales leveled off at the end of December, Smith offered a new playbill: "Diana and the Nymphs". This time Lola insisted on designing all costumes for the nymphs. The dancers were practically nude. She fought with Smith, Fast Eddie and the theater manager. She beat the manager and Fast Eddie with her riding crop until they fled the theater. Smith and Eddie arranged an accommodation with the theater manager. Lola's costumes would remain, but each nymph carried an American flag covering part of her nudity. The theater manager advertised the nymphs as French ballerinas, since French thespians were given more moral latitude in America. Actually the young women were from The Bowery Follies in Brooklyn.

Most serious assessments of Lola's performances were unflattering. Those linked with Benet's New York

Journal, were lukewarm in their praise. Still, Lola and Williams made money—more money than any actor or actress ever made in the same time period on a New York stage.

Lola's lifestyle exceeded her fabulous income. Fast Eddie warned her, but she contributed to every poor actor who requested help. She hosted parties at hotels, put on benefit programs for the fire departments in New York, Brooklyn and Staten Island, free of charge. She continued the habit learned from Franz Liszt of personally donating to local charities—except the police. She didn't like policemen.

Lola socialized with the wealthy as with the poor. She was a guest of Commodore Cornelius Vanderbilt, exchanged stories with newspaperman Walt Whitman of the Brooklyn *Eagle,* and hosted every editor and publisher she could button-hole. Lola understood the power of the press, and used it well.

Of all the fascinating people Lola encountered, the most impressive was Adah Isaacs Menken. Born in Louisiana, by virtue of her many talents as actress, dancer, poet, artist, and writer, she was the foremost female star in America. For Lola, meeting Adah Menken was like gazing into a living mirror. Menken was compared to George Sand in literature and Jenny Lind in theater.

Comparisons were made in the press between Lola and Adah as dancers. They were both out-spoken, smoked in public, had volatile tempers, and did not adhere to the dictates of social norms for women. The two struck up an immediate friendship.

The vivacious, talented Menken had one fault; she

was a Jewess. More than that, she flouted her Jewishness. Like Lola, she spoke her mind—and in an argument, she didn't slap or scream; she swung her fists like a mad Cajun. She too smoked, and often wore men's clothing. When she met Lola, she had been married four times and lost two children to influenza.

One evening between rehearsals the two women met for dinner. Lola led the way to an upscale hotel nearby. The maître-de stopped them at the entrance; it was improper for ladies to be unescorted in the evening. But he recognized the two stars, and he would make allowances. He said, "Miss Montez, you may enter."

"And why not Mrs. Menken?" Lola demanded.

The maître-de politely held a napkin to his lips and mumbled.

"Speak up man!" Lola growled.

He pulled away the napkin saying, "She is a…MOT."

"What in the hell is a MOT?" Lola demanded.

"It stands for a Member of the Tribe," Adah explained.

"What tribe is that?"

"The sons and daughters of Moses," she said and touched her nose. "Can't you tell? We children of Moses have Jewish noses."

"You son-of-a-bitch!" Lola pointed at the man. "How would you like to go flying through those swinging doors behind you?"

Both women looked at each other. Simultaneously they reached out, grabbed him by the shoulders and turned him around. Each took a grip on his collar with one hand, and grabbed up between the back of his legs to his scrotum with the other hand. He leapt into the air, screaming and waving his arms.

They heaved him through the dining-room doors.

He sprawled flat on his face in the center of the floor. The two ladies turned and left for another restaurant.

Word of the incident reached reporters in Pfaff's underground tavern. They rushed to the scene, and then to interview the two most famous ladies in the country.

Police arrived soon after. The reporters slipped the policemen a few dollars, Adah Menken used a piece of charcoal from the hearth to sketch one policeman's profile on a linen napkin. Lola signed another napkin and put the imprint of her lips on it. The police left with their treasures while the reporters plied the two women with questions.

In response to a journalist who called her a convert to Judaism, Menken replied, "I was born a Jew and live like a Jew. Through my religion I have found great well-being and blessings."

"Is it true," the reporter asked, "That you cancelled your appearances in Philadelphia because of the Yom Kippur holiday?"

"Of course," Adah Menken said. "It is not a festive holiday, but the holiest and most solemn day of the year."

"I wish we had more time together," Lola said.

"I'm scheduled to appear in Philadelphia, Chicago, St. Louis, and then off to the California gold fields."

"That sounds like a tour I might like to make. Please keep in touch. Let me know what happens."

George Washington Smith anticipated a drop in revenue because of the lukewarm reviews and level of theatrical competition. He suggested a different play to show off Lola's talents. This was the drama everyone had been anticipating: "Lola in Bavaria." She was the star.

The story worked around King Ludwig. With no House of Lords to stop her, the play included portrayals of Prince von Metternich, the Czar of Russia, Franz Liszt, Alexander Dumas and the Prime Minster of England, Lord Palmerston. Freedom of speech was an inherent right in America.

George Washington Smith choreographed the play so Lola was never off the stage for more than three minutes. It became her most physically demanding role. She played the danseuse, a stateswoman, a countess, a political radical, the king's courtesan, and finally a beleaguered fugitive from aristocratic Europe.

Her opening appearance on stage was of her arrival in America waving the Stars and Stripes. This assured applause. But no level of jingoism could obscure from press and public "her deficiencies as an artiste or dramatist". After two weeks the play closed.

On the 27th of December she appeared at the Broadway Theatre in the title role of *Betly the Tyrolean*, a musical comedy written especially for her. It was expected that she would prove a powerful attraction, and seats for the first performance were put up to public auction. It was not to be. The play was withdrawn on the 19th of January. Lola's voice couldn't carry through the theater.

Fast Eddie secured an engagement at the Walnut Street Theatre, in Philadelphia. It was a mild success.

She returned to New York in May, and reworked the original version of *Lola in Bavaria*. Lola had earned more than any other actor or actress in the same amount of time, but she spent it even quicker. Fast Eddie came up with a scheme. To his surprise Lola agreed.

She organized receptions at a table on the sidewalk outside the Broadway Theater, to which anyone paying a dollar shook her hand, gazed upon her beauty, and conversed with her in English, French, German, or Spanish. The function was hardly consistent with the Countess's dignity, but it revealed in a striking manner Fast Eddie's knowledge of the American character and Lola's ability to adapt to it. She made a lot of money.

Eddie was right. To shake hands with a well-known, beautiful, titled personage is esteemed by your average Yankee a greater privilege than visiting the Acropolis or wading in the River Jordan – perhaps partly because such creatures are so rare in America. The line of men waited patiently with dollars in hand. Her mastery over men was due not only to her physical charms, but to her intellect. It says much for her shrewdness that she, who had hitherto found it safest to appeal to men through their passions, perceived that the cold Yankee was most vulnerable through so artificial and dispassionate a sentiment as patriotism.[23]

Critical American theater-goers shared their opinions in clubs, taverns, and newspapers expressing their disappointment in Lola's voice, dance, and stage presence. Yet she earned four thousand dollars in one week, more than any artist in the history of American theater.

---

[23] P 196-197 *Lola Montez*, Edmund B. d"Auvergne, abridged.

The combination of Fast Eddie's publicity and Lola's flood of letters to editors of newspapers drew audiences. Editorials against Lola's avaricious Spider Dance drew even more ticket seekers. There appeared nothing to stop her.

Then she took ill. Her doctors stopped the mercury treatment. Her hair began to fall out, and she lost her strength. She explained to Fast Eddie about her use of the Pope's wine, which contained cocaine, and its medicinal properties. He went to Professor Muff Abrahamson, graduate of the Royal College of Surgeons, in London, the most reputable pharmacist in the United States. The doctor was familiar with the Pontiff's wine, and promptly blended cacao leaves with dolomite powder in a barrel of wine. As soon as he judged the cocaine properly developed, he gave Lola the wine. In twelve hours Lola stood up. In twenty-four hours she walked from her room, and no hair fell out. In forty-eight hours she was on a train to the Walnut Theater in Philadelphia. She was so successful there that they held her over for a second week.

Then she went on to Baltimore and Washington D.C. for three performances. She heard of the new Photographic Emporium and decided to see what a photograph portrait would look like. She and King Ludwig were never quite satisfied by the court artists.

At the photo-studio a delegation of Indian Chiefs, who had just met to sign a treaty with President Fillmore, were having their photographs taken. The Cheyenne, Sioux and Arapaho Chiefs had their pictures taken with Lola. The Cheyenne Chief, Light in the Clouds, named Lola, 'Little Mischief Maker'.

Lola returned to New York for five performances and then to challenge the center of American moralism, Boston, Massachusetts.

The first article in the Boston papers described Lola chasing a Conductor out of her car when he tried to prevent her from smoking a cigar. Numerous articles appeared in the New England press criticizing Lola's indecent behavior in Europe, her nudity on stage, and lack of public morality.

Fast Eddie could not have been happier. Lola replied to these articles with letters to the editors. She was a prolific writer, and had learned from her lover Dujarier how to manipulate the European press. She utilized her experience on the over-confident Yankees. Instead of blatant sensational acts, Lola presented a demur, chaste image to the public and press. Benet, in his *Daily Journal* wrote, "Lola required only Church sanctification and a pair of golden wings to make her an angel." That was a bit overstated, as attested to by those in her entourage—whom she supported at great expense. She took new lovers as often as she changed theater appearances. She cursed like a trooper at the slightest mistake in rehearsal. On one occasion Lola insisted that the first violin and the bassoon players were Jesuits sent to disrupt her performance. On advice from her doctor and insistence of Fast Eddie, she retreated into seclusion for a week and stopped the mercury medication completely. Seclusion for Lola meant not appearing on stage. She was seen riding about Washington D.C. in open carriages with government dignitaries such as Congressman Polk, brother of former President Polk of Tennessee, and Senator Sam Huston of Texas.

Lola proclaimed her morality and cited the benefits she had arranged for the firemen of Baltimore, New York, and Washington, and her support of aging actors and the poor common people of those cities.

Fast Eddie said, "It matters not what they say about you, as long as your name and the date of your next appearance are spelled correctly."

Lola had an argument with teacher and chorographer George Washington Smith, and she socked him in the jaw. He was more stunned than hurt, but left the company.

Lola did change the costumes and some of the more sexually suggestive parts of *Lola in Bavaria*. The New York critics appreciated her compliance with American morals.

By the fifth night, more women attended than men. Again Lola's income exceeded her previous record.

Boston posed problems. The trouble arose from the Nob Hill Brahmins.

After her stage appearance at Boston's Howard Athenaeum, one of the city politicians invited her to tour Boston's public schools. They were the pride of the young nation. Lola dressed appropriately, and reporters described her actions as exemplary. At the Wells School for Girls she was introduced as the Countess of Landsfeld. She quietly observed the modern teaching methods. At the English High School she entered into a conversation about American literature with the students. Her question to them was, "Why is almost all American fiction about America and not the countries the authors immigrated from?" The initial answer was, "That is why it is called American literature." But the countess went on to say, "American writers always seem to be examining America and Americans. European writers examine everyone else." The students concluded, America was so young, it was just finding out about itself. Teachers and students applauded.

In the Latin school, Lola conversed in Latin with the students and asked, "Why do most Americans, English, and Europeans refer to the Native Indians in American literature as Noble Savages, and the Blacks as Bloody Niggers?" This led to a heated discussion. One student from Texas told the countess that where he lived it was the Indians who were Bloody Red Niggers and the Blacks were Texans. A lively discussion ensued which brought up the subject of ending slavery. The countess spoke emotionally, and received hearty approval from students and teachers when she pointed out that England, France, and Spain had all eliminated slavery, and it was high time America joined the human race.

This innocent educational visit set off a ranting from the elite of Boston society. The bone of contention being that such an undesirable person as a courtesan shouldn't be paraded around in Boston's public schools as an example of how to succeed. "Shame on Boston!" editorials clamored.

The press battled it out in the morning and evening editions. Fast Eddie couldn't have been happier. Box office receipts increased. Lola, who never withdrew from a fight, joined the battle. She wrote a passionate letter to the editor of the *Boston Daily Evening Transcript*:

"Believe me, there is often more impurity in

the mind of the critic than in the object of his criticism. There are men who stand before the Venus of Medici and the Apollo of Belvedere and see nothing but their nudity... I speak of Jesuitical lies... They say I tamed wild lions and horsewhipped policemen, shot flies off bald-headed aldermen, fought duels and threw old ladies overboard to feed the sharks. Now sir, do you see the sly, Jesuitical, infamous design in all this? It is simply a plan to unsex me—to deprive me of the high, noble, chivalrous protection, which is so universally accorded to women in this country by generous men... I bow, silent, content and happy before the only successful realization of a principal to which I have devoted my life. And now when I, as a stranger, wish to pay a visit to those nurseries or your noble statesmen—your Websters, your Calhouns, your Clays—you cry out against me as an intruder! Fie on you, sir... Above all, if you have the character of an honest man, never give circulation of aspersions of the character of a lady of which you know nothing. These aspersions which are false in themselves, and which, for my own part, I defy any man living to prove. Lola Montez, Your humble servant, Countess of Landsfeld,[24]

---

[24] *Lola Montez*, P 287, Bruce Seymour, abridged

# *CHAPTER 7*

## CONFLICTS

From New York Lola exchanged letters with Adah Menken in California. Adah described San Francisco as bursting with energy and gold. It was a boiling, bubbling cauldron of nouveau riche buying its way into fashionable society with nuggets from Sutter's Mill. The mining towns were rough and tumble affairs. They paid unqualified entertainers twice New York salaries, and legitimate ones two and three times that. Adah suggested Lola put together a road show, tour the South this winter, and make San Francisco in the spring. Her appearances would be sold out. "America is waiting to see Lola Montez. The Countess of Landsfeld is often mentioned in the papers, journals, and conversations."

For Lola, life in New York had become routine, the men who attended her, boring. The Gold Coast sounded exciting. She wanted to see the wild mining camps, and play to the adventurers who came to rip their fortunes from the ground. It would also supplement her bi-annual stipend from King Ludwig. Lola's expenditures were far greater than the King's annuity. The idea of touring the United States motivated her. She had Fast Eddie read Adah Menken's letter, and ordered him to make arrangements for a southern tour and California bookings.

Lola's final appearance on Broadway took place on December 1$^{st}$, 1852. The following day she joined the

New York Fire Department on the docks to distribute free Christmas trees and hot meals to the needy.

Fast Eddie made plans for Lola and her retinue to travel west by way of the southern states. The winter weather blocked the northern route, and the center of the country was threatened with the same. They boarded the Norfolk Southern railroad at Central Depot in New York City, and rolled away.

Lola played twice a day to packed houses in Columbia, North Carolina: Charleston, South Carolina: Macon, Georgia and Mobile, Alabama. Prior to her appearance at Placida's Varieties in New Orleans, Fast Eddie expressed his concern about this deeply religious city in the heart of America's Bible Belt. Negative articles about Lola's past were circulated by various religious denominations, such as this:

*"Occasionally some distinguished passengers passed on the upward and downward tides of ruffianism and rascality that swept periodically through Cruces. Came one day Lola Montez, in the full zenith of her evil fame, bound for California with a strange suite. A good-looking, bold woman, with fine, bold eyes and a determined bearing, dressed ostentatiously in perfect male attire, with shirt collar turned down over a velvet lapelled coat, richly worked shirt-front, black hat, French unmentionables, and natty polished boots with spurs. She carried in her hand a handsome riding-whip, which she could use as well in the streets of Cruces as in the towns of Europe; for an impertinent American, presuming, perhaps not unnaturally, upon her reputation, laid hold jestingly of the tails of her long coat, and, as a*

*lesson, received a cut across his face that must have marked him for some days. I did not see the row which followed, and was glad when the wretched woman rode off on the following morning.*"[25]

With Lola's approval and assistance in writing and mailing, Eddie proceeded with a plan to make her morally acceptable to the churchgoers of the largest city in the Bible Belt. New Orleans held a mixed population of old Spanish, French home-grown Creoles, and Cajuns. Immigrants from around the world, using the sea route to and from the gold fields of California, also populated the city. Fast Eddie sent out a stream of press releases. From these the Louisiana press reported:

*"The Countess of Landsfeld, Miss Lola Montez, had distributed alms to the sick and needy on the east coast of the United States. She did this in repentance for a squandered youth. The Countess would soon take the vows of a novitiate in one of Louisiana's Catholic religious orders."*

Eddie and Lola sent other articles and letters to the editors of the Louisiana journals to improve her image. No one questioned that theater bookings were already made for the date the Countess would supposedly enter the Cloisters. Fast Eddie put out the following press release: "The Countess of Landsfeld, who recently arrived in America, was distributing alms in abundance to the poor, the sick, and the captive in the southern cities

---

[25] *Lola Montez*, P 200, Edmund B. d"Auvergne, abridged.

she toured, to make amends for her misspent life."

On the day Lola was to take her vows, Eddie issued the following press release: "Senora Lola Montez, yielding to that instinct of inconstancy so strong in her sex, is announced to have chosen the Opera instead of the Cloister."

The Hispanic and French aristocracy of New Orleans, Creoles, Cajuns, and those passing to and from the gold fields, packed the theater. The manager printed more tickets than seats. People stood, kneeled, and hung from supporting columns. Not even a straw could be slipped in between the spectators. Receipts were beyond expectation. Lola was ecstatic.

Then she received a letter that proved she was God's chosen. The Rothschild Bank of London affirmed thirty-thousand sterling in her account, from the will of former husband George Heald.

Yet, even with the money, the accolades and positive public attention, she was described by one New Orleans reporter as "...disillusioned, sore at heart, and world-weary; her restlessness bespeaks a mind ill at ease." The reporter could not have known of the effects of syphilis and mercury medication. He wrote, "She has no home, no familial ties, and no kindred. The noble Countess has a massive following but she is alone."

Much of this was true, but Lola was rarely physically alone. She held court with her retinue like a European monarch, lying in bed with thin silk sheets revealing her shapely body. Food, wine and strong spirits were served continuously. She selected a lover for the night, but the party continued. Some of the finest families of the aristocratic south were represented in the Countess's bed.

Several became syphilitic, but none ever attributed it to Lola. On stage Lola captured the hearts of both southern men and women. More women attended her last show than men.

Fast Eddie had moralized the play and drilled into Lola the idea of holding her temper in check. She promised to keep her lips sealed when it came to the issue of slavery and state's rights. She no longer displayed the American flag, for the subject of States Rights and Slavery was the topic of the day in newspapers, taverns, and on the street. For once she did as promised.

In private, she expressed a view similar to the congressman from Illinois, Abraham Lincoln; no man should be a slave to another. Lincoln agreed that the Black man was inferior mentally, but physically superior in warmer climates. She differed with Lincoln on States Rights, and felt the South should have the prerogative to secede from the Union. In 1852 this was the opinion of many Southerners. Those who condoned secession, rebellion, and war were considered extremists. Lola was not.

Lola's opening at the New Orleans Varieties Theater was a resounding success. Fast Eddie's publicity worked. Ticket prices were raised again and sold out again. Thoughts of morality concerning the Spider Dance were rarely mentioned. Southern theater critics responded well, which helped ticket sales. On the third night Lola endeared herself to the rough men from the goldfields and the more genteel local gentry.

It took place during the first act of *Lola in Bavaria*. A group of young rakes had a private box near the stage. They were drinking and speaking loudly, even shouting.

The audience realized their actions were disturbing the actors on stage. There ensued words between the audience and the group of young men—until Lola stepped out of character.

Moving to the right wing of the stage closest to the noisemakers, in a firm angry voice she said, "Ladies and gentlemen, it is an honor for me to appear before you, but if there is a clique against me for appearing on this prestigious stage, I shall this moment withdraw." The audience cheered, and the young men were shamed into silence. Later the group sent an enormous wreath of flowers with an apology.

Lola filled the house for twenty-eight straight nights. She was then engaged by the Orleans Theater for two performances. She had planned on taking ship to California, but was persuaded to remain in New Orleans for Mardi Gras.

The Biblical proverb, "Idle hands are the devil's workshop" suited Lola. During this respite from her hectic work schedule she arose late, ate, had a massage, and attended dance class. Afternoons she interviewed and rehearsed, evenings were for either hosting or being hosted. Nights were passed with a lover.

The first incident disturbing her leisure involved Lola's servant. The woman's contract guaranteed a paid ticket from whatever city where she left Lola's employment to New York. The woman enjoyed New Orleans, and more so a boyfriend from the French Quarter. She wished to remain and be paid the value of a ticket to New York.

She and Lola argued. Lola used her riding crop and beat the woman. Unlike European servants who suffered the anger of their masters with little recourse from officialdom, this woman went directly to the sheriff.

Two policemen were dispatched to escort Lola to the stationhouse for questioning. She used the riding crop to chase both from her apartment. They returned with a senior officer. Lola's full entourage was in attendance when the policemen arrived. The friends endeavored to dissuade the police from serving a warrant. The police were adamant.

"Enough! Enough!" Lola screamed. "An artiste cannot live in a world so meager and unsympathetic to the performer's place in society!" She raised the back of her right hand to her forehead, and drew a dagger from her waistband. The police thought she was going to attack them. Her friends thought she was about to use it on herself.

One policeman moved behind her and grabbed her arms, and the senior officer disarmed her. There ensued an argument between friends of Lola and the police. Two judges, a number of lawyers, and politicians in the apartment convinced the police they would be responsible for Lola's appearance at the courthouse the following morning. Lola had no intention of going.

When the appointed time for her appearance at the courthouse had passed, the judge sent the sheriff, the police Captain and two officers to bring her in. It was eleven in the morning when the group of court-appointed officials arrived at Lola's apartment. Once again her followers packed the rooms. The crowd parted. The sheriff approached Lola with the arrest warrant held aloft. Lola took a defiant stance, pointed at the sheriff and said, "You don't really think you can arrest a peeress of the realm?"

"I most certainly do," the sheriff answered. "This is America. We don't recognize titles. I've put several Barons, Dukes and Duchesses in detention for gambling debts. I will take you to court to answer the charges."

"What charges?" Lola demanded.

"That you did severely beat your maid about the head and shoulders. That you drew a dagger to strike two police officers who approached to serve this same warrant."

"The woman was a servant, who attempted to rob me. I am only familiar with the European attitude to servants."

"You are in America now," the sheriff said. "You will abide by our laws."

Lola ignored the reply and said, "I did not intend to harm your two policemen. Please accept my apologies for frightening them."

"Why did you draw the dagger?"

"To kill myself. They were about to drag me away to a squalid prison cell. I am the Countess of Landsfeld, Miss Lola Montez, star of the Broadway Theater. And now I will finish what I originally intended."

Lola made for a side table against the wall. On it was an apothecary bottle labeled in large letters "POISON". She removed the cork, put the bottle to her lips and in her best theatrical presentation said, "I shall now be free of all further indignity!" She drank and crumpled to the floor.

The startled Sheriff and court officers were slow to react. Lola's friends rushed to her side. People shouted for a doctor. One man slapped Lola's cheeks and a reporter swears she opened her eyes and said, "Don't hit so hard."

Her retinue of admirers was in various stages of remorse, anger, and guilt. The mood turned ugly. An apothecary tried to administer antidotes but all were rejected by Lola. She awoke, smoked a cigar, and passed out again. Angry followers and admirers backed the Sheriff and his men into a corner. They reached an agreement that Lola would definitely appear the next morning at the courthouse.

Her appearance never took place. One of the lawyers in Lola's entourage negotiated a settlement. He paid the servant, and she dropped the charges. Lola was soon up and about with no signs of ill effects from the toxic drink. But it was too late for her to be included on a playbill benefitting a local retired actor. An actress named Du Barry, whom Lola had helped, appeared on the bill.

Lola thought she would like to see her perform without staying for the entire show. She made her way unobtrusively to the stage door of the Varieties Theater where she had performed. Permitted entrance, she made her way to the right wing of the stage behind the curtain. George T. Rowe, the Prompter of the evening, used this place behind the scenes.

He prepared to raise the curtain and asked Lola to leave the area. He added, she should know she was violating the theater's rules by being there. Lola casually ignored him. He in turn refused to open the curtain, but insisted Lola leave. He reached out and touched her shoulder. She swung about like a wildcat. With fists, fingernails, and vicious kicks she attacked, screaming insults at the frightened man.

Fast Eddie had accompanied her, and he took the Prompter and threw him out the stage door. The battle was so loud and raucous, the audience was not interested in what was about to happen on stage but what was going on behind the scenes. The theater manager tried to make some sense of what took place. Lola shouted, "A common prompter tries to throw Lola Montez out of a theater! The audacity of the man!"

The theater manager requested Lola leave. She turned on him, calling him a damned liar, thief, and "a low-life son of a bitch who could walk under a snake wearing a top hat". The audience heard enough to make that phrase immortal.

Lola did appear in court to face the charges. She disrupted the proceedings when she accused the theater manager of walking around backstage in a woman's negligee. Then she accused the Prompter, Rowe, of making ungentlemanly advances to her. "This is why I kicked him out of the theater," She said. "These two so-called grandees of the acting world have never seen Paris, London, or Broadway, and couldn't spell it if they tried." That phrase spread too.

The newspapers sold out. Even those with new steam-operated presses could not keep up with the demand. One satirical journalist rhymed a piece called:

**"The Rowe Kick**

That you should raise your pretty foot to kick
the old man Rowe,

> Is more than e'en I thought you would at-
> tempt to do, I vow.
>
> The foot was made to dance a jig, to draw the
> vulgar eye,
>
> And that's the reason why, methinks, you lift
> it up so high."[26]

Lola's lawyer attempted to negotiate an out of court settlement with the theater manager and Prompter. Lola refused to pay. The lawyer had covered her expense once, but. he was not prepared to do so again. Lola's followers formed a committee to raise the money.

In the meantime, Fast Eddie made arrangements for Lola's California tour. Whether the syphilis or the mercury caused it is unknown,but Lola took it into her head that Eddie was stealing from her. He entered her boudoir, and without a word she hit him across the nose with the handle of the riding crop. Eddie fell to his knees. When he looked up even Lola was shocked at the size of the swollen nose. He muttered, "Why did you hit me?"

"You thief!" Lola shouted. "I trusted you with all my accounts. Blackguard, you took advantage of a lonely woman!"

"Bullshit!" Eddie said, "And you know it! I am not attracted to women, and certainly not that sewer between your thighs. I have kept honest accounts, and am prepared to prove it."

Eddie staggered to his feet and retreated from the

---

[26] *Lola Montez* by James F. Varley, P 91

                    

room with Lola cursing him. He went to the police station and filed a report. The Sheriff was only too pleased to serve the court order himself. By the time he found a judge to sign the warrant, Lola, the lawyer and Eddie had reached an agreement by which the lawyer would examine Eddie's books and accounting records. He would then make a decision as to who was in the right. The summons was held in abeyance. The lawyer employed an accountant, and the two men worked through the night and the following day.

Lola was due to sail for California. The lawyer brought Fast Eddie and Lola together in her ship's cabin. He stated in unequivocal terms, "I hereby attest to the meticulous and detailed accounting records of both Countess of Landsfeld's records and an equal meticulous accounting of Mr. Edward Williams's business and personal records. There are justified receipts regarding all transactions."

"Are you telling me I am wrong?" Lola demanded.

"As the referee in this dispute, that is my conclusion."

Eddie looked from behind his swollen nose and expected a tirade from Lola. Instead, her smile lit up the cabin. "I am so pleased," she said and approached Eddie in a conciliatory manner. "We have worked so well and long together, it hurt me to think badly of you. Will you kindly accept my apology?"

"Only if it is accompanied by a substantial amount of money," Eddie said, and pointed at his crooked nose.

"You are absolutely right." Her blue eyes sparkled as she asked. "Will you accept our mediator's decision on the amount?"

"Only if it is above one thousand silver dollars," Eddie replied.

"And only if you will turn over all the booking information for my California tour," Lola said.

For a minute Eddie felt he had lost, but he didn't know what it was that was gone. The settlement seemed fair, the lawyer unbiased, but Lola was being too compliant and it didn't fit her character. What was she planning? Then the lawyer said, "One thousand five hundred in silver shall be the settlement. Do both sides agree?"

Lola and Eddie nodded. Lola withdrew a check from her bag and filled it out. The lawyer examined it and passed the check to Eddie, who also examined it and put it in his shirt pocket. "Lola," Eddie said, "I am sorry it had to come to this. You are the most exciting woman I have ever known, also the most dangerous and unpredictable."

"I too regret our parting," Lola said, and raised her right hand to wipe a teardrop from her eye. But there was none. The words and motion Eddie recognized from the play, *Lola in Bavaria*, when Lola takes leave of King Ludwig.

It disturbed him, but not to distraction. Yet he was still uneasy as he walked down the gangplank to the dock and made directly for the bank. He had forgotten this was siesta time, and the banks and other businesses would open at four in the afternoon. He went to his hotel.

At four he left the hotel and strolled to the bank. He waited several minutes for the clerk, and heard the steam whistles of various ships leaving on the outgoing tide.

He was called into a booth, and produced the check. The banker examined it, and asked, "Do you wish this amount in silver, or would you like to open an..." He stopped in mid-sentence, then recovered and said, "I see this check is written by the Countess of Landsfeld, Miss Lola Montez."

"Is there anything wrong?" Eddie asked.

"Yes sir, there is." The clerk held the check for Eddie to see, and pointed to the date. "This is made out for nineteen-fifty-three, not eighteen-fifty-three. The Countess wrote another check with a similar date. Our manager is now with the sheriff. The countess closed her account this morning. It is empty."

Eddie snapped the check from the man's hand and flew out the bank door, toward the courthouse. He hadn't gone far when he saw the sheriff, the bank manager, and two policemen running to the docks. He caught up with them on Henderson Street as they boarded the port's pilot boat. Eddie jumped aboard. The sheriff shouted to the pilot who was also the Harbor Master, "I have a warrant to serve on a passenger aboard the steamship *Philadelphia*. Can you catch her? "

"If it's worth my while," The pilot responded. "Just guided her and several other boats out into the delta."

"One hundred silver dollars if you catch her," Eddie said. "Nothing if you don't."

The Pilot reached up and blew the steam whistle, then shouted to his crew, "Off your asses and on your feet! Cast off. Shovel number nine coal until the boiler is about to blow." He put the handle forward to full speed. With the help of the current of the mighty Mississippi, the tiny tug raced downriver into the delta.

"How can you tell which one she is?" The sheriff asked. "There are a dozen steamships heading out to sea."

The pilot pointed. "See that one with the twin red smoke stacks? That's her."

"They all have double stacks."

Yes, but her starboard stack cinder-cover is tilted. That's the *Philadelphia*."

"Sheriff," Eddie said, "You now have two warrants against that Spanish witch. I am reactivating mine."

"Good!" The sheriff said. "This time I'll put her in jail for a month of Sundays. No judge, priest, or politician will get her out. On that I swear."

The tug's furnace turned cherry red. The water boiled and steam drove the pistons while the crew oiled the bearings on the drive shaft. They began passing the slower steamships but the *Philadelphia* was still in the lead.

"Fire a rocket!" the pilot ordered. "Make signal to the *Philadelphia,* to hold position and prepare for inspection."

Lola had the most expensive suite aboard the *Philadelphia*. She was standing outside her cabin at the rail on the upper deck when the ship slowed. It then reversed its engines to hold position against the river's flow into the Atlantic Ocean. She watched as a seaman left the quarterdeck and hurried with two flags to the fantail of the ship.

He signaled to a smaller craft wending its way between steamships toward the *Philadelphia*. Lola walked forward, and requested permission to enter the quarterdeck cabin. "Sir," She asked the captain, "What is taking place?"

He put his binoculars down and said, "Countess, the sheriff of New Orleans and the Harbor Master request that I hold station until they can board and remove one of my passengers."

"Did they name the passenger?"

"No."

"May I borrow your binoculars?"

He handed her the glasses. Lola adjusted the lenses. She recognized the Sheriff and Fast Eddie standing in the bow of the oncoming craft.

"Is this legal?" Lola asked.

"Technically, no," the captain said. "The sheriff's jurisdiction ends at the confluence of the Mississippi and the delta. The Harbor Master gives up his rights when he guides us from the harbor and returns ashore, but in practice we adhere to his wishes."

"What would it take to have you disregard those wishes?"

"I assume you are the one they are seeking?"

"Your assumption is correct. "

"...I have been away from my wife for a month now, and it's seven days to Panama City."

"Would you like my company in your cabin," Lola asked. "Or may I extend the courtesy of my cabin to you?"

The captain reached up pulled twice on the whistle cord, took hold of the speaking tube and shouted, "Engine room: forward engines. Give me full power, flank speed." He undressed Lola with his eyes and said, "That pilot boat may catch us, but the sheriff will never board."

# CHAPTER 8

## CALIFORNIA BOUND

Three sea routes existed to San Francisco and the gold fields of California: around the Horn, by the poor travelers, by ship to Nicaragua, or to the port of Aspinwall on the Isthmus of Panama and overland to the Pacific, the latter being the most convenient and expensive. It didn't mean luxurious.

Panama had the only railroad in Central America: twenty-five miles of track through the steamy, malaria-ridden jungle to a point where a bridge would eventually span the No Name River, a donkey ride to canoes, paddled by the passengers to the nearest portage point. Again they mounted donkeys and traveled a path to the port in Panama City.

Lola weathered the conditions better than most men. Some came down with malaria and dengue fever.

Two nights prior to their arrival, the travelers sat around a camp-fire talking. A refined gentlemen from New England decided to relieve himself in the bushes rather than the fetid, makeshift outhouse. He wandered into the darkness of the jungle. The group heard him shout for help. A gunshot sounded. The New Englander bolted from the trees, trying to raise his trousers and flee at the same time.

Lola pulled her pistol from its shoulder holster, and marched into the darkness without a word. The men looked at each other but no one followed. Two shots rang out. A man screamed. Lola emerged into the fire-light, smoking pistol in hand. "Wounded one," she said, and went to her tent.

Two newspapermen amongst the travelers pounced on the story. Upon reaching Panama City, they sold their richly embellished articles to the English papers. The Spanish, French, and German papers translated and copied them. Crowds gathered to see the gun-toting Countess.

The steamship *Illinois* made Panama City a day before Lola's arrival. Among the passengers were a U.S. senator, two congressmen, wealthy businessmen and more newsmen. Among the latter was Patrick Purdy Hull, senior editor of the *San Francisco Whig*. Lola would have sought out the newspapermen in any case, but because of her shooting exploit, they attended her.

She and Patrick Hull became fast friends. They boarded the side-wheeler *Northerner* for a two-week voyage to San Francisco. The couple became a familiar sight together. He spent several nights in her cabin and she in his. Hull had the good fortune to back the Whig Party in the recent Presidential election won by Franklin Pearce; for this he gained a contract to conduct the California Census. Lola described him as handsome, tall, powerfully built, with a good sense of humor, and a natural storyteller. It did not bother Lola that he lacked commonsense; he was wealthy.

Early on the morning of May 21st the signal mast atop Telegraph Hill flared up. The fire-bell sounded, and San Franciscans poured into the streets. It was the *Illinois*, coming to dock with 2,000 bags of mail and the

Countess of Landsfeld, Lola Montez.

Initially, the mail was the center of attention. Patrick Hull explained it wouldn't matter if the Pope and King of England were aboard; the mail came first.

San Francisco had grown from a regional town of 200 Whites and ten Blacks (Chinese were not counted), to a population of fifty-thousand people in four years. The gold strike of 1848 brought hundreds of thousands from all over the world through this city.

Now, in 1853, more people left than came to the Golden Gate. The good mining claims were all staked out, and the more successful formed into companies. They, in turn, consolidated the remaining mines into corporations. The city's economy changed from a precious-metal based income to a diversified agricultural, manufacturing, and shipping one. San Francisco became America's gateway to the Far East. The city developed a classless society, its hierarchy judged by the amount of cash available rather than family, history, color, or religion. The Chinese, unnoticed, quietly built a shadow economy of their own based primarily on agriculture as more of them bought up small land-holdings outside the city.

Five days after arriving, Lola opened at the American Theater. She charged five times higher than east coast prices. *The School for Scandals* packed the house.

Lola did not dance the first night. She knew, with all the publicity from Patrick Hull and other newspapermen aboard the *Illinois* she would draw a crowd, and she held the Spider Dance in abeyance. Then she doubled the ticket price. The public paid. A newspaper article read:

> *"The Spider Dance draws them like fleas to a hound. Despite increased prices, the audience is most enthusiastic with Lola Montez's performance. The infamous/famous Spider Dance adds another page in our young city's history. "The dance is perhaps not for respectable ladies to witness. The danseuse is obliged to search for the spider in her skirts "rather higher than proper in so public a place."[27]*

On May 30th, the production of *Lola in Bavaria* opened to a full house. The reviews were generally good. Even with the ticket prices at a premium, her shows were well attended. One astute editor wrote: "Lola performs with energy and wit to compensate for deficiencies in strength of voice, lack of dance expertise, and a weak plot. The play represents Lola as a coquettish, wayward, reckless woman intent on no good. It does not portray her as the wily diplomat, the able leader which she truly is, as represented in history. She counsels the King with all the enthusiasm of a Red Republican sophomore, and with as much discreetness. History pays her higher compliments than does her own play."[28]

Lola spent much time with Patrick Hull in his offices at the *San Francisco Whig* and the *Commercial Advertiser*. He taught her how to set type, considered a man's job. She set print backwards quicker than some of the younger, more experienced men. She also edited.

---

[27] P. 313, *Lola Montez* Bruce Seymour, (abridged)

[28] P. 314, *Lola Montez* Bruce Seymour.

Some say she married Hull to become an American citizen, retain her titles, and solve the problem of an international passport. Others claim she wanted to settle down in this wonderful vibrant city he called home. On Saturday, July 2nd, a select group of guests met at the Mission Dolores for the wedding ceremony. Lola signed as Maria, Dolorosa, Eliza, Rosanna, Landsfeld, Heald.

She claimed to be twenty-six when actually she would soon be thirty-four. They honeymooned aboard the river boat, *New World*, then enjoyed a leisurely trip to Sacramento, where Lola scheduled an appearance. The newlyweds took the premier suite in the Orleans Hotel.

On July 5th, her opening night at the Sacramento Theater, everything went well. It is possible to attribute what happened the second night to the mistaken impression made by the hotel and the theatergoers of the first night.

The first audience was sober after the July Fourth celebrations. The hotel itself was less than a year old, and beautiful. Some used the word opulent to describe the lodgings. A gay, light, informal atmosphere surrounded the newlyweds.

What Lola didn't know was that the town's men outnumbered the women twenty to one—mostly miners, gamblers, and adventurers. They had dirt under their fingernails, and if it rained, considered themselves bathed for the month.

Yet contrary to popular belief, this rough and tumble lot had been exposed to the best theater America had to offer. The men paid more for tickets than at any place else in the world. They drew the finest entertainers of their time. The San Francisco men took their money and entertainment seriously.

Those attending the second night were different. The majority of ticket holders were on a three day drunk. They continued celebrating Independence Day in the theater. Famous Hungarian violinist Michael Hauser was booked to prepare the audience for Lola's appearance. The crowd knew Hauser, and he knew how to handle the rowdy crowd.

He played and received an enthusiastic applause, then he bowed, and the curtain went up. Lola strode out of the wings to center stage on her toes. Then absolute silence. She struck a ballerina's pose, lifted her chin and challenged the men with those sparkling blue eyes. She nodded to the First Violinist, and the music began. She danced back and forth across the stage, and the audience sat in awed silence.

Then a spectator in front started to laugh. Others joined in. They became so loud that the clicking of Lola's castanets could not be heard. She froze in mid-pirouette, came down flatfooted, and signaled with a sharp motion of her right hand to stop the music.

She strode to the footlights and glared down at the offenders. On rare occasions, with similar incidents, she had confronted the disrupters and was applauded for doing so. "If my presentation offends you," she said, "I shall retire. Behave yourselves, and I promise you a theatrical treat few others have enjoyed."

On previous occasions the audience had cheered. In some cases the offenders were run out of the theater. That did not happen. One man shouted, "I'd enjoy you on your back with those beautiful legs spread wide!"

Her face blazed with anger. Her eyes shot fire and her mouth spit brimstone. She called the men dogs. She shouted, "I have more respect for Californians to credit these inane creatures and their stupid laughter with any meaning. You animals do not appreciate the finer arts."

According to Violinist Hauser, Lola specifically insulted the heritage and intelligence of the audience. They had been entertained by the best thespians in America. They knew what quality was. Lola was looking down at them. They didn't hesitate to make it known.

Actors pulled her off. She fought her way back. The inebriated crowd shouted their anger. Someone had bought a basket of eggs from the greengrocer next door, and he sold them for throwing. Unable to find more eggs, he brought back vegetables. Other greengrocers heard, and stormed the theater with as much produce as they could carry.

Ducking the flying omelets, the theater manager and Hauser dragged Lola backstage. Fights broke out in the theater. Lola was restrained by two stage hands. She showed not the slightest fear, only intractable fury. She wanted retribution and cursed like a parade ground drill-sergeant.

The theater manager begged Hauser to go on and quiet the crowd before they destroyed his theater. Hauser bargained for six hundred dollars if he accomplished the task. He walked onto the stage playing *Yankee Doodle Dandy*. The spirit of July Fourth was still in the drunken revelers, and the audience began to sing and then to harmonize. Chairs and benches put upright. The men sang *Camptown Races, Nelly Bly, Sweet Betsy*

                    

*From Pike, What To Do With A Drunken Sailor....*

The crowd quieted, but remained dissatisfied. Many demanded their money back. The theater manager reached an agreement with them. If they would behave, he would have Miss Montez perform the Spider Dance.

Music filled the theater, and Lola skipped to center stage. There was some muttering but general acceptance. Several bouquets of flowers were thrown at Lola's feet (paid for by Lola's new husband). As in all of her performances, she stomped on the spiders with her heels. She always made certain at least one bouquet was always on the floor for her to stamp to pieces. The audience misinterpreted this act. They took it as a sign of her anger at the audience by crushing the bouquets thrown in her honor.

Shouts drowned out the music. The audience hurled more vegetables at Lola. She struggled to confront them. The manager and Hauser again pulled her to safety. The police and fire department arrived. They struggled with the crowd to prevent more damage. Eventually, they cleared the theater, forcing the unruly mob into the street. The bars on Main Street emptied out to join the fight.

Things turned ugly. Fire, always a primary concern, had destroyed large parts of San Francisco on two previous occasions. The Fire Chief, with the Mayor and Police Chief, decided the only way to prevent a full-blown riot was to quench the crowd's thirst. The Fire Chief announced through his bullhorn that the four largest saloons on Main Street would be serving free beer and lunch for one hour, courtesy of the Mayor. A deafening roar of approval accompanied the men from the street into the bars.

Realizing they had an hour's grace, both the police and fire departments' marching bands were summoned from their beds. When the bars closed, the bands struck up their Fourth of July repertoire. Once the crowd joined in singing, the Drum Major led the band and people from the business district to the nearby sports field. The mayor had four kegs of beer waiting. Both bands took turns playing martial music. They intended to serenade the mob until they dispersed or fell asleep on the grass.

This plan might have worked, but when they tapped the beer kegs there were no glasses. The men crawled under the spigots and opened their mouths. The crowd grew. Fights broke out. The four beer kegs soon emptied. Restless men looking for excitement defrocked the Drum Major. They decided to give Lola a Pike County Serenade and forced both bands to the Orleans Hotel.

The new resort was lit up front to back by large, modern kerosene lanterns from Poland. The approaching crowd armed themselves with improvised noisemakers, and surrounded the front of the hotel. Lola's new husband had succumbed to a bottle of Jameson's Irish whiskey, and slept in a lounge chair of the hotel's lobby. The noise outside did not disturb Patrick Hull or others strewn about the carpeted lobby floor.

Lola in her room heard the din outside. She went onto the balcony and the crowd hooted and howled. She disappeared into the room, and returned with a pistol. She fired into the air. There was silence. Her voice carried into the torch-lit night. "You lowlife sons of bitches wouldn't make a pimple on a real man's arse! I dare anyone of you to come onto this balcony and face me bare knuckles. I'll rip off your head and shit down your neck!" And she added more terms she had learned as an army brat in India.

One little wiry fellow accepted the challenge, leapt onto a trellis, and climbed up to the first floor balcony where Lola stood. He leaned over the railing and blew out the oil lantern. Lola hit him in the forehead with the butt of the pistol. Her finger jarred the trigger. The pistol fired. The man went over backward into the arms of the crowd below. At first everyone thought him dead. Suddenly, he shouted, "I love that woman!"

Lola shouted down. The crowd shouted up. The Drum Major had retrieved his baton and most of his uniform, marshaled the two bands into one unit and marched toward City Hall. Most of the people followed. The hotel staff dragged Lola inside. With no one to vent their anger at, the crowd followed the band.

The morning newspapers condemned Lola's actions. Her husband Patrick listened while she planned to win over the hearts of San Franciscans. First, she had to convince the theater manager to let her go on with her show. It took much shouting, cajoling and threatening. Lola finally agreed to give a written guarantee for possible damages. She rented the theater for one night and doubled the ticket price. They sold out before the Police or Fire Chiefs could object.

It was a packed house; you couldn't fall down if you wanted to. On this one night, Lola took in more cash than any entertainer ever earned in a week. She hurried the money to the bank prior to show time, in the event of another riot.

The police and firemen appeared in force. No eggs, vegetables, whisky or drunks were allowed. Many outside chewed spearmint leaves and licorice purchased from a nearby apothecary to hide any hint of alcohol on their breaths. If they could stand at attention and breathe in the face of a policeman without knocking him over, they could enter.

The theater manager convinced old John Sutter, on whose land gold was first discovered, to attend. The mayor escorted him in. The crowd came to its feet, giving him a big round of applause. Before Lola appeared, the orchestra played a medley of popular songs. The audience applauded, yet everyone sat on the edges of their seats waiting for some spark to set off the expected explosion. The theater manager stepped to the kerosene-lit foot lights and announced, "Ladies and Gentlemen—"(few ladies were in attendance) '—Before this evening's presentation, the Countess of Landsfeld, Miss Lola Montez, wishes to make a formal acknowledgment of personal fault and error last evening."

The danseuse appeared in costume. She made her way to footlights on her toes, with eyes lowered, chin down and fingers interlocked at her waist. A nervous smatter of applause rippled through the theater. The audience waited in hushed anticipation.

Lola said, "Last evening there was an occurrence in this theater which I regret. It is a small theater. I am alongside of you, and the sound is not always distinctly understood. I am subject to palpitations of the heart, and since I have been in California, I have suffered with it very much, which makes me at times feel very bad. While I was dancing I stamped my foot several times upon the stage and someone laughed, as I supposed, to insult me. I have many enemies who have followed me from Europe, and offered me insults, and I supposed it might be some of those who followed me with those intentions.

"I knew it was no American, because I have been moved and cherished by the Americans wherever I went... I can't always find the spider when I hunt for it—it can't always be seen—I can't always put it to the ground; and when I stamped it was only a joke. It is customary for my friends to sometimes throw bouquets of flowers for me to trample. It is meant to represent the spider, as it is not always convenient to find a real spider... I will wipe out from my memory what occurred. It was unworthy of me, and I shall speak of it no more. Ladies and gentlemen, if you wish me to go on with my dance, you have only to say the word."[29]

Two seconds' silence hung heavy in the theater. Then, as one, the (sober) audience came to its feet with a thunderous round of applause. Lola lowered her head, curtsied, and tiptoed behind the curtain. The manager announced that, in honor of John Sutter from Austria, Lola would perform her first dance from the *William Tell Overture* by Rossini. Led by John Sutter himself, the crowd cheered.

They cheered before Lola appeared, and even more so at the conclusion. She finished the show with the Spider Dance. This received a standing ovation, even more so as an encore when she stamped the bouquets covering the stage floor. There would have been more

---

[29] P149, *Lola Montez* by James F. Varley

than five curtain calls, but she requested to address the audience.

"You," she pointed at the audience, "Are the reason I wanted to come to this country. I love America, and I love Americans.

The rough, tough miners roared back, "And we love you!"

The morning newspapers overflowed with accolades for Lola. Her apology was accepted in print, in the pub, and from the pulpit. They acclaimed her a genius for having changed an atmosphere of hate and anger to love. They dubbed her, "The Irresistible Countess".

Much of the public affection was due to the respect for Lola's husband, Patrick Hull. Newspapermen held him in high esteem, not because of his journalistic expertise but because he usually picked up the bar tab.

Lola sold out five more nights. The sixth night she did a benefit show for the Fire Brigade. It was a rousing success. The firemen covered the stage with bouquets for Lola to stamp on during the Spider Dance. The Brigade band led the crowd to the Orleans Hotel. A week ago they had hooted and taunted Lola; now the band and crowd saluted her. Patrick Hull thanked the audience for treating his wife in such a good American way. He then opened the Orleans bar free of charge for all Firemen.

Patrick attempted to bed Lola, but she wished to join the Firemen at the bar. A fight ensued. The two threw anything at hand. Furniture and windows were broken. It became a knockdown, drag-out brawl which spilled into the hallway. The police were summoned. Only the Fire Chief's intervention prevented the Police Captain from arresting both husband and wife. Patrick Hull refused to spend the night with Lola. He found other lodging and female companionship.

The following afternoon, the Fire Chief arranged a tenuous peace between the couple. It was suggested they take a leisurely hunting trip in nearby Grass Valley.

# CHAPTER 9

## GRASS VALLEY

Patrick Hull packed two cases of Jameson's Irish Whisky for the trip to Grass Valley. Lola bought a new 12-gauge shotgun and rifle. She cleaned her navy Colt pistol and stocked enough ammunition for target practice. Hull spent most of his time drinking in the tent or at the campfire, trading stories and jokes with the guides.

In this area, where men traveled in pairs for safety against predators both animal and human, Lola often went hunting alone. She became addicted to the silence of the forest. The beauty of sun filtering through the trees and the tameness of the animals captivated her. She sat for long periods watching nature.

Lola slept and felt better. She determined to find a bear cub and raise it as a pet. Her Indian guide discouraged this as too dangerous; the mother bear would track her baby until either she or Lola was dead. Lola continued her search but she never found a cub.

On one of her hunting trips she met a German doctor named Adler, a well-built, intelligent man and experienced hunter. Lola did not return to her husband's camp.

Two weeks later Adler accidently shot himself while stalking a deer. He died.

The sheriff questioned Lola and found the death accidental. Some in Marysville wondered how an expert woodsman could make such a beginner's mistake

Lola's confidants thought she would soon leave California, possibly return to Chicago or New York, but the tranquility of Grass Valley worked its magic. Her desire for sex subsided. Lola stayed.

The miner's town of Marysville stood at the entrance to the valley. It boasted false-front stores, bars, and whorehouses, made of canvas, supported by wooden frames, the third busiest place in town being the assayer's office. There miners found out how much their toil in the mountains earned. The Valley itself swept several miles into the lush foothills.

Two miles up the dale, a community of families took root. Mostly professionals and businessmen, they were drawn by the area's lush botanical beauty, abundance of game, and fresh clean water from the snowcapped Sierra Nevada Mountains. Fifteen new quartz-crushing mills had opened, and two small gold strikes nearby provided work. The town was called Grass Valley.

The people wished to raise families away from the rough and tumble mining town of Marysville. They graded and laid out macadam streets, built a school, church and cemetery. They constructed a kiln to make bricks for fireproof houses. A guard walked the streets at night to frighten off inquisitive bears and wild pigs. Crystal clear water flowed in from the foothills. The townsfolk erected a sawmill using the river for power, to hew the 100-foot tall Lodgepole Pine trees into useable lumber.

Lola rented a cabin, took long walks in the forest and surrounded herself with pets, wild and domestic. Men did not interest her. Patrick Hull stayed in

Marysville. The sheriff said Hull had told him, "It's a good thing the Dutchman shot himself. I was going to do it."

Hull auctioned off his belongings in front of the Red Dog Saloon, bought drinks for everyone, then rode out of town. Lola never inquired of him again. On the outskirts of Grass Valley she caught, bought, and cared for a menagerie of pets.

A correspondent for the *San Francisco Herald* visited her there. On December 18th, 1853, he wrote about the Countess of Landsfeld "...living a quiet, and apparently cozy life, surrounded by her pet birds, dogs, goats, sheep, hens, turkeys, pigs, and her pony. The latter seems to be a favorite with Lola, and is her companion in all her mountain rambles. Surely it is a strange metamorphosis to find the woman who has gained world-renowned notoriety, and played a part upon the stage of international life with powerful potentates, and with whose name Europe and the world is familiar, to be settled down at home in the mountain wilds of California."

Another dispatch from Nevada City, dated 20th, January, 1854 said: "The merry ringing of sleigh bells has been heard for several days past in our city. Several sleighs have been fitted up, and the young gentlemen have treated the ladies to some dashing turn-outs. On Tuesday last, Lola Montez paid us a visit by this conveyance and a span of horses, decorated with impromptu cowbells. She flashed like a meteor through the snowflakes and wanton snowballs, and after a tour of the thoroughfares, disappeared in the direction of Grass Valley."[30]

---

[30] *Lola Montez*, Edmund B. d"Auvergne p.203

Gentlemen callers were always found at Lola's cabin. However, she made certain to invite respectable married couples when she entertained, and all left her place at the end of an evening. No man from Grass Valley, Marysville, or Nevada City remained overnight.

Lola's reputation was further enhanced when she agreed to a benefit performance for the town of Grass Valley. The show sold out before the tickets left the print shop. The venue was above the Grass Valley Saloon, and small enough for her voice to be heard. The people were ecstatic.

It may have been that night that she decided to purchase the cabin and settle in Grass Valley. She had plans to add to her number of animal residents. She also wished to furnish and expand the cabin to her taste. She drew up the changes, hired a manager, and left Grass Valley before the winter snows closed the roads.

She took a stage to Sacramento, and steamer downriver to San Francisco. There she purchased made-to-order furniture and what would become the most talked about musical instrument; a player-piano with enough rolls of music to enjoy without constant repetition. To her menagerie of animals she added several birds, including a parrot who sang with Lola, a wildcat, two hounds, a pony and her most sought after prize, a grizzly bear cub.

Lola also bought suitable flower seeds, vine cuttings, and fruit trees. She read stories about John Chapman—Johnny Appleseed—a devout member of the Swedenborg Church, and an American pioneer nurseryman. He introduced apple trees to large parts of Pennsylvania, Ontario, Ohio, Indiana, Illinois and West Virginia. He lived as a vagrant from choice, for he was quite wealthy, with two large nurseries in Pennsylvania. He planted, and gave trees and seed free of charge to one and all. He loved animals, and this gentle man did everything he could to protect them.

He introduced apples to many areas of the northern United States. What amused Lola about John Chapman was his religiosity and negative stance against whisky as a blight on the human race. Johnny Appleseed did not believe in grafting as a means of propagation. Because of this, his apples were of irregular flavor, and preferred more for making cider than eating.

People pressed the apples and fermented the juice to make hard cider. This alcoholic drink became so popular that in the state of Pennsylvania average consumption reached thirty-five gallons per person per year. The people also made a special cider, with less alcoholic content, for children. Lola bought enough apple trees for a small orchard, enough to guarantee a substantial supply of hard cider for her guests and herself for the foreseeable future.

Lola returned to find her cabin transformed into an elegant cottage. It soon became the center of social life in Grass Valley. Entertainers passing through Marysville visited regularly. They always found a warm welcome, a meal, and on occasion slept over in the bungalows she had built for that purpose. On most days Lola could be found outside the house playing with her pet bear. She wore a simple calico shirt with denim frock, and was sunburned as a field hand. Her ebony black tresses framed a glowing exotic face from which startling blue eyes shone as if they were lit by this new electricity. The common reaction of visitors was: My God, what a beautiful woman.[31]

Lola's sedentary life was disturbed by two letters, one from George Sand. George wrote that, although she had not met King Ludwig, Lola's former lover and financial benefactor was ill. Facts were difficult to come by, but his illness might include dementia. The second letter arrived from a New York actor, informing Lola that Patrick Hull had died in a drunken stupor—from syphilis. Lola was unmoved by the latter but concerned about Ludwig, for she held him in high regard. They had shared many poignant times, their personal dreams and fantasies, without inhibition.

Lola may have felt responsible for Ludwig's condition, but she had a way of compartmentalizing bad news. She relegated it to a place in her mind oblivious to everyday life. She busied herself with the animals and perfecting the cabin. People referred to it as a villa.

The new, covered veranda encompassed all four sides. She held a special Christmas party for the local children. She said she loved children and regretted not having any of her own. She became a confidant of John Southwick, owner of one of the more successful commercial gold mines. He did not become a lover, but rather a helper. He served as host when she entertained. He also convinced Lola to purchase stock in his mine.

Lola's bear cub had grown, and was kept chained in the front yard. Adults and children often came to play with the bear. Her Indian guide warned Lola to beware if the animal became cantankerous. He said it should be

---

[31] P.322 *Lola Montez* Bruce Seymour

hibernating for the winter. Lola disregarded the advice.

In the spring of 1854 Lola went out to give the bear a lump of sugar. He bit her hand, then mauled her shoulder. A neighbor came to her aid. He bit the bear's nose until it released its hold, and he beat the animal away from Lola with an ax handle.

The next edition of local newspapers in Nevada City, Marysville, and Grass Valley held an advertisement: "For Sale—one young Grizzly bear." Everyone knew the story. No buyers appeared. Lola eventually donated the animal to a man in Nevada City who hoped to start a city zoo. Editor of the *San Francisco Chronicle*, Frank Soule, wrote a poem about the incident.

"One day when the season was drizzly,

And outside amusements were wet,

Fair Lola paid court to her grizzly,

And undertook patting her pet,

But ah it was not the Bavarian,

Who softened so under her hand,

No ermined king octogenarian,

But Bruin, coarse cub of the land.

So all her caresses combatting,

He crushed her white, slender hand flat,

Refusing his love to her patting,

As she refused hers to Pat. (Hull)

Oh, had her bear been him whose glory

And title were won on the field,

Less bloodless hap ended this story,

More easy her hand had been Heald!

But since she was bitten by Bruin,

The question is anxiously plied,

Not if tis the Countess's ruin,

But whether the poor bear died?"

After a few lively letters to the editor, a short poetic apology appeared from the bear.

"When Lola came to feed her bear,

With comfits sweet and sugar rare,

Bruin ran out in haste to greet her,

Seized her hand because it was sweeter."[32]

During the spring and summer Lola occupied herself with her apple orchard, flower gardens, and animals. She took leisurely forays into the Mountains. On one of these outings she urged her horse to jump a stream. His rear legs didn't clear the far bank, and he slid backward down the embankment, breaking two legs and throwing Lola into the water. Fortunately the water broke her fall, and was shallow enough not to drown her. She used the Navy Colt to put the horse down, and walked back to Grass Valley.

---

[32] *Lola Montez* pages 173 and 174, James F. Varley

Not long after, she led a party of seven into the Sierras. Three days out, the animal carrying their food wandered off. It took the party two days without food to make it back to Grass Valley.

On another occasion she took a group of local dignitaries for a weeklong camping trip. During this venture into the mountains, two lakes were named for her: the Upper and Lower Lola Montez Lakes, recorded in the U.S. geographic survey of 1854.

She received offers to appear in Boston, New York, Washington, and New Orleans as a lecturer, but refused. She was completely happy in Grass Valley. Lola had never asked prices; she ordered things and, in her European past, often walked out on the bills, leaving lovers and friends who vouched for her to cope with the situation. She wasn't about to endanger her paradise in Grass Valley.

The cost of furnishing and renovating the cabin, stocking and supplying her menagerie, orchard, and extensive flower gardens became excessive. She also donated to local charities, paying little heed to her accounts. The purchase price, including transportation of items from Sacramento and San Francisco to Grass Valley, was restrictive for most. Not for Lola: what she wanted, she bought.

She made a decision to settle in Grass Valley and, for the first time in her life, consciously decided to improve her reputation. She planned meticulously. People came from far and wide to catch a glimpse of the world-famous aristocratic actress playing with her animals or tending her gardens. She often wore a man's strap overalls, plaid shirt, straw farmer's hat and high boots. She always had a lit cigar, and would puff smoke rings for children to poke their fingers through.

There is no doubt the Countess of Landsfeld's presence In Grass valley contributed to its growth. With three thousand energetic inhabitants, the town was blossoming. It was rated the fourth most populated town in Nevada.

The California climate, its flora and fauna and the pioneering people of Grass Valley, influenced Lola. She began to step out of her invented role as a Spanish aristocrat. For her it became an enjoyable experience. She read books on spiritualism. These led her back to the Bible.

This time she read it as an adult. She had questions, and unsuccessfully sought answers among the local clergy. For instance, the two versions of creation of man: why? Did Noah's son Ham really rape his father? If Abraham argued with God to save the sinners of Sodom and Gomorra, why didn't he protest the sacrifice of his son, Isaac? How could Judah be made King of the Israelites when he fathered a child with the wife of his dead son? Her inquisitive mind led her into frustrating intellectual blind alleys. Strangely enough, her unanswered questions strengthened her belief in God, the Son of God, and the Holy Spirit.

During Lola's tour of the south on her way to California, she had openly supported those promoting States Rights. It was not lost on prominent southern secessionists. A clandestine meeting took place in Lola's villa where only initials, not names, were used. This group of industrialists, wealthy merchants, and two staff officers from the American Army and two from the Mexican

Army all desired to see California secede from the Union and return to Spain.

They approached Lola because of her royal title and aristocratic Spanish birthright. The Spanish natives of Texas, Arizona, New Mexico, California, Oregon, Utah, and Nevada remained angry at the loss of so much land to the Americans by Santa Anna. Large portions of this vast unmapped territory had yet to be explored. Stories from trappers and Indians told of great mineral wealth, and powerful rivers to be harnessed, full of salmon, trout, bass, and beaver, vast uncountable miles of timber stretching to the ends of the earth. This wealth of nature Mexico had ceded to the United States.

Native Mexicans far outnumbered Anglos in these areas. Indians were not counted. The revolutionary plotters believed the Spanish speaking population would rebel. The insurgency would entail simultaneous uprisings in San Francisco, Los Angeles, and Stockton. Then Mexico would recognize Countess Lola Montez as Empress of California. They hoped to influence the other seven Spanish-speaking states to join them, in confederation with the Southern states led by North Carolina, and thereby dissolve the Union.

For years Lola had spied for Lord Palmerston of England. She contributed to and participated in military coups, political, negotiations and European plots. Astute enough to realize the impossibility of organizing and accomplishing such a bold strategy as this one, she held back. The plotters had no interior lines of communications and supply. She knew the population. She spoke Spanish. The plotters did not.

They depended on two distinct groups for success:

the minority, educated wealthy Hidalgos who saw themselves as Spanish, and the much larger group of unlettered poor who considered themselves Mexican. With her knowledge of the people and language, she believed it impossible for the two groups to make a viable alliance. She remained silent.

She did contribute a symbolic sum of money to the $50,000 war-chest. She received no further communications from the group. In Europe, Lola had learned to work both sides of the clandestine street. In London, Paris, Warsaw, St. Petersburg and Munich she had participated in similar meetings. Politicians and historians credited her with the fall the Austro-Hungarian Empire and Prince von Metternich, the Catholic clergy's loss of power in the Germanic States, and the abdication of her lover, King Ludwig I of Bavaria. She was wary, and took steps to protect herself.

Not long after the meeting, San Francisco newspapers reported that the two American staff officers who attended that meeting abruptly announced their early retirement from the army. Several California businessmen lost valuable government contracts. Lola never heard a word from either the American or Mexican authorities—although, as a matter of record, she received her American passport and citizenship shortly thereafter. Some believe it was for services rendered to the American government.

By June 1854 the gold in the Sierra Nevada Mountains petered out. Only wealthy miners using modern recovery equipment could sustain a profit. A general recession took hold in California. It forced many in Grass valley, Marysville, and Nevada City to close shop. All banks but Wells Fargo declared insolvency. One of the failing banks was Lola's.

Another of California's natural blessings soon turned traitor. The shade of tall trees and refreshing summer winds from the snowcapped Sierra Nevada Mountains became a curse to the towns of Grass Valley and Marysville. The dry mountain air prepared the littered forest floor, blanketed with tinder-dry branches, for the lightning storm that started the fire. The initial blaze topped the tall pine trees and raced toward the mining camps in the foothills. Then the lower tree trunks, heated by the fire above, squirted flammable resin to set the underbrush alight. The suction from the conflagration created its own firestorm. It whirled through the pine-covered foothills, destroying everything created by God and man.

Before abandoning her home, Lola set free the animals. She barely escaped with two pack horses and her ponies. The leveling and clearing of the grounds around the house for her large flower garden, the apple orchard, and the ceramic tile roof saved her main building. Everything around it burnt to a cinder. The apple orchard became a stand of small, thin, charcoal silhouettes. None of her animals were recovered. She prayed for their safety.

Lola contacted her friend Johnny Eastwick, owner of the mine she bought shares from. He advised her to continue collecting on the shares but not to sell them, as gold prices were at rock bottom. Lola received her bi-annual stipend from King Ludwig and a return on French stocks in a Paris theater willed to her by former lover Alexander Dujarier. It wasn't enough. She sold her custom-made furniture for a pittance and traveled to San Francisco. The saying of her former nanny and mentor in the art of becoming a courtesan, was constantly in her thoughts, "Every problem presents an opportunity."

Try as she might. Lola saw no viable prospects.

# CHAPTER *10*

## THE OPPORTUNITY

Lola returned to San Francisco with several trunks of clothing, fifteen hundred dollars, and her collection of jewelry. The seventy-nine pieces of gold, silver, diamonds and pearls were earned by her from European aristocracy.

She placed the entire collection with an auction house in San Francisco. Because of depressed business conditions on the west coast, she only realized twenty thousand dollars from the sale. It was estimated to bring close to a quarter of a million dollars in New York.

Lola did not have time. She planned to perform in Australia, where the economy thrived because of a gold strike. She would establish a framework of a theatrical company in San Francisco, to be filled out by local Australian actors.

A couple she once did a benefit for in New York had just returned from a two-year tour Down Under. They earned one hundred thousand dollars in two years. The couple convinced Lola she would be a sensation.

"Australians," they said, "Avidly followed stories of the Countess of Landsfeld in their newspapers."

Lola began to raise herself from the doldrums. She scouted for talent, re-visited old friends and entertained new ones. She marked a young man who arrived with the cast of a San Francisco show. When introduced, he acted shy and retreated. She noted that he was well built, tall, with fair skin, blond hair and clear blue eyes. He retired to a corner of the room. Friends called him "A wallflower".

Lola inquired about him. Ten years her junior, he had left a wife and two children with his sister in Cincinnati, to join the California gold rush. He failed. Until recently his father had supported him with money from a wealthy wife. When the father emptied her coffers, he abandoned her—and his son.

Noel Follin never struck it rich. He had basic schooling but no profession. He took a job in the theater selling tickets, and ran errands for the actors to other theaters. He sometimes heard of openings for actors, informed them. and was tipped for the service. He also filled in minor parts for missing actors. He was introduced to Lola by a leading man from one of the theaters. The actor exaggerated, saying, "My young friend Noel is a first-rate agent. He secured a lead role for me."

"I am seeking an agent for my Australian tour," Lola said. Noel's heart melted. Her electric-blue eyes sparkled. She stepped closer to him. He looked down into that deep beautiful cleavage. He blushed.

Lola offered her hand, and across the dance floor he followed her to a dimly-lit room. She ordered him, "Close the door. Lock it."

When he turned to face her, she reached out with her right hand and squeezed his penis. He started to double over, but her lips met his. She forced her tongue into contact with his. Like a magnet, his body clung to hers. She pulled his head back by the hair, exposed her breasts and whispered. "Chew on these, you horny bastard."

The two never returned to the party. Noel did things and assumed sexual positions he had never known existed. Lola had been some time without a man, and directed him. He satisfied her, and she brought him degrees of pleasure he had never before experienced. They did not sleep until the sun had risen.

Noel Follin found true love. He became Lola's agent. This was easy, since theater managers sought him. Noel helped her regain her spirit, sense of adventure, and acumen for planning.

She set Noel the task of arranging six weeks booking in San Francisco, then to plan and initiate an Australian tour. When Sidney's theater agents in San Francisco heard that Lola Montez was open for bookings, they flocked to Noel with offers. He had only to select the most prestigious theater, paying the highest price. Lola passed word to San Francisco's thespian community that she required performers for the Australian tour, and she had her choice from amongst the best in the city. She set Noel the task of booking her group on a major tour of the Pacific Islands, Hawaii, and Canton. Noel dedicated his life to her.

When negotiating for Lola, he shed his mantle of reticence. His shyness disappeared, and he became a veritable tiger. He took it as a personal mark of honor that he negotiate the best contracts and agreements possible. Lola in turn responded with amazing vigor, in bed and in her work schedule.

Her daily routine consisted of physical exercises, voice training, and rehearsals that would have daunted most men. She also attended business lunches and dinners, entertained, designed costumes for the cast, and frolicked with Noel. She was elated: he, exhausted.

One night when he was fatigued and she needed him inside her, she introduced the younger man to the dildo. She strapped it on him, rolled him over on his back, and mounted the large rubber phallus. He just lay there, fascinated by the joyful expressions on her beautiful face. She sucked his nipples vigorously, and suddenly he had an erection. He ripped off the dildo and tried to force her back onto the bed.

Lola insisted on measuring his erection against the dildo. They were the same length at ten inches, but his girth was larger. She put her hands on both his shoulders, shoved him back down and took him into her mouth, sucked for a few moments, then mounted him. Noel became so frenzied, while still coupled, he flipped her over. She was now under him, and he pounded her into the mattress. He threw his head back and climaxed. He withdrew, and Lola gave a disappointed moan. With one hand under her back, he lifted and turned her until she faced down, and entered her doggy-fashion from behind. Her cries of joy were muffled by the pillow. She felt he would drive her through the wooden headboard. Then he collapsed. His body spasmed, and she wriggled out from under him.

He missed two morning appointments. Lola kept all of hers.

On occasion Noel questioned their morality and sins against God. "I believe in the Almighty," Lola replied. "But alas, since childhood, my mother and others said that I was blessed with beauty from God, but my soul belonged to Satan. In India, outside my father's army base, I would dare cobras to bite me. Even the Hindu Fakirs called me the Devil Child."

"But God is gentle, loving and forgiving."

"You repeat what they preach in church. In the real world, God doesn't give a damn. Yes, I believe God exists. He created everything, and He created man to subdue and manipulate His creations. He gave us wheat, and man makes bread. He gives us trees, and we builds homes. But the Lord keeps His hands out of our dirty messes. Go down to the dock. They are shanghaiing drunks for two years' forced voyages, selling young boys and girls as sex slaves. Everyone knows, including the good church people, the sheriff, and politicians—but no one does anything about it."

"Can't you bring yourself to trust God?" Noel asked.

"My belief in the Almighty is absolute," Lola said, "My trust in him is not. Satan is more reliable. I don't have to ask if you enjoy sex with me; I know you do. Those in the pulpit say our joy is Satan's inspiration. If so, I'm all for Satan. I need sex. I love sex. I think I'll start a new church devoted to sex."

"What will you call it?"

"Saint Agnostics."

"What would be your creed?"

"Sex is good for the body and good for the soul; if you are lucky, you can fuck 'til you're old. Good or bad doesn't matter; we all end up dead sooner ir later. Saint Agnostics would buy and sell burial plots and real estate, then apply for tax exemptions. I learned that from the Jesuits."

"What about personal taxation?"

"Wash your mouth with soap! God forbid the government should start taxing individual income. A man's home would no longer be his castle; the government could walk right in, without a by-your-leave, and dictate to you."

"I guess you're right. We fought the Revolution because of taxation without representation."


Noel Follin did not mind remaining in the background at parties large and small; he was comfortable out of the limelight. He wanted to serve Lola.

He made arrangements for the cast and props to sail to Australia. The evening prior to sailing, a select group of friends joined Lola and Noel in her apartment. Among the guests was actress Laura Keene. She had just returned from a successful tour of Australia, and proved an encouragement to all.

On June 6$^{th}$, 1855 the sailing ship *Fanny Major* left San Francisco Bay on the outgoing tide. A goodly crowd wished Lola bon voyage. Performances in Hawaii and the Philippines were postponed until the return voyage.

The first day at sea Lola had trouble. A cabin boy delivered the noon meal, and her pet miniature poodle attacked him. He kicked the bit of fluff across the cabin, and Lola pulled a stiletto from her waistband. He fled. The lad no longer served her, but a week later the dog disappeared.

On July 17th the *Fanny Major* re-supplied in Samoa. They had been more than a month at sea. Although Lola held daily rehearsals and her troupe put on skits for the crew and passengers, the actors were bored. Noel helped Lola pass the time in bed, and with puzzles, and playing cribbage.

A month later, their arrival in Sidney's Port Jackson Harbor came as a great joy to all. The *Fanny Major* dropped anchor. The last part of the journey had been difficult; it was mid-winter Down Under. Wind, rain, and even snow had battered the vessel as it tacked back and forth around the Horn. After months at sea, passengers and crew required time to get their land-legs back.

There being no telegraph to Australia, Noel found that his ship arrived before others on which the Australian agents sent news of Lola's coming. No one expected her. Noel and Lola thought her investment lost.

However, her surprise appearance in Sidney became even more sensational. The Australians knew of her through their very active press; Lola Montez was famous Down Under, her arrival considered a blessing. Noel secured immediate booking at the prestigious Victoria Theater on Pitt Street, for the play *Lola in Bavaria*.

She bolstered her acting troupe with well qualified local actors. Sidney was no longer a rough-and-tumble mining town; to Lola it resembled Edinburgh, Scotland. The people acted more English than the English. The streets were wide, laid out in a grid pattern with alphabetically sequential names of trees, famous people, and places. The buildings were tall, solid structures made of dressed stone, with large windows to capture the sunlight.

Sidney's citizens dressed properly, but underneath the broadcloth, starched collars, and white shirts beat a proud, rustic Australian heart. A cocky group, the Aussies: Americans found them compatible to Yankees—

fiercely protective of their country and proud of their achievements. They had their own nasal twang and idioms. On the dock there occurred two incidents.

One of the dock workers approached Noel and Lola asking, "Hey cornstalk, can I have a fag?" The cigar almost fell from Lola's lips. Noel blushed and the man said, "I'll hump your swag for half price."

The two were astonished into silence until an Englishman stepped up and explained, "Madam, please don't be offended. This Banana Bender is using idiomatic English to ask for one of your cigars. He complimented you by calling you a cornstalk, actually a good-looking woman—and he is Nuts On about that."

"Why did you call him a Banana Bender?" Lola asked.

"His accent is from Queensland. Most of them sit around and bend the bow shape into bananas. Please give him one of your cigars; otherwise my explanation will boomerang, and I shall be likely punched in the nose."

Lola presented the stevedore a cigar but asked the Englishman what the word boomerang meant. "It's an angled piece of smooth wood, used by the natives for hunting. When thrown correctly, if it misses the target the boomerang returns through the air to the thrower. We use the term to mean that something we did will 'boomerang' back on you. I must be off. Welcome to Australia."

"Can you recommend a proper restaurant?" Noel Follin asked.

"Makes no difference," the man called back. "They're all the same."

The Americans never got used to Australian eating habits. No matter which restaurant or what time of day, breakfast, lunch and dinner was the same: cold beef or mutton, a huge loaf of bread, a cutting board and one knife. It was served three times a day, with rum or porter. Another peculiarity of restaurants; you had to dress to eat, even in boarding houses. One had to be properly attired in jacket, hat, polished boots, and cravat to sit in any dining room. Others were shunted to the kitchen.

During the *Fanny Major*'s two months at sea, the Australian economy had dipped dramatically low. You could no longer smell the dynamics of money in the streets. To complicate matters for Lola's theater group, Irish singer Catherine Hayes, known as "The Sweet Swan of Erin", captured the city's heart from the stage of the nearby Prince of Wales' Theater. Lola packed the house the first two nights, but the third evening the attendance dropped off.

Noel Follin realized that the two actresses in competition hurt each other. They had a limited audience to draw from, and the country's financial condition created a critical situation for both theaters. Noel learned that Miss Hayes had only three more performances. With Lola's tacit agreement, Noel arranged for Miss Hayes to be ill two nights, and Lola to be ill on two alternate nights. The third shows did not conflict. Both actresses played to full houses.

As usual, Lola held the Spider Dance in abeyance to build interest and draw the larger audiences at higher prices. On the 27th of August, Lola and her troupe presented a new play, *Yelva, the Orphan of Russia*. She had translated the play from French while aboard ship. She also performed two skits in a benefit for Australian actors. The build-up for the Spider Dance was intense. Tickets sold out. However, critics in the press challenged Lola's artistic integrity.

The correspondent from the *Argus* newspaper of Melbourne wrote of *Lola in Bavaria*:

> *I am compelled to say that I differ entirely from those who think Lola has any talent for histrionic art. Her appearance is good; her voice is, if not bad, deficient altogether in flexibility and sweetness, at least when raised to the pitch calculated for the stage. She is sometimes graceful for a moment or two, but coarseness and vulgarity is sure to follow upon such glimpses of a better spirit. Her grand effect is as a "postures." The manner in which she can conceal the exquisite proportions of her figure, and then to some extent deform them and then suddenly reveal them, in a burst of passion or an attempt at tenderness, in all their magnificence, is doubtless a study for the artist. She dresses her parts well—rather showily, but in taste; and takes very good care that no part of her beautiful figure shall be exhibited more than necessary. From one solitary glance of her foot during the whole piece, I should say it must have been some strong effort of female resolution which could induce her to keep it so studiously concealed. Her features are interesting but not regularly beautiful, and, to*

*my taste, not pleasantly expressive. The role she played in... Is about the greatest piece of trash and humbug ever introduced before an English audience. There is no indecency in the acting, but the whole tenor of it socially, politically and religiously, is profligate and immoral in the extreme. Lola Montez, if I mistake not, will find her visit to Sydney to turn out a failure.*[33]

The critic was shocked to hear Lola was enraged at his impudence. He thought his appraisal of her art was honest. In addition, he included conciliatory remarks about her work not being lewd or lustful, as portrayed in the San Francisco press. This he felt would induce the ladies and "proper gentlemen" to attend. He recognized what Lola and Noel did not; Australians held higher Victorian morals than their forefathers in England or American cousins. Aussies were prudes.

Lola wrote to the newspapers and challenged the critic to a duel. She offered pistols, knives, or a poison pill: he could choose. He ignored the challenge. This infuriated her.

While they were strolling Sidney's main street, fate brought them together. The newspaperman was pointed out to her. He entered a hotel bar across the street. Like a barracuda, Lola went for him. She burst into the bar and whacked him with the butt of her riding crop. He whirled around to fight, and saw Lola. He was so stunned, she got in two more whacks to his head before

---

[33] *Lola Montez,* Pages 332 and 333, Bruce Seymour

he punched her in the nose. She staggered back, stopped, touched her nose, threw the riding crop at his head and in the same motion leapt upon his chest, nails clawing his face. Her weight on his chest made him fall over backward. His head hit the bar rail. Incapable of fending off her punches, he tried to duck. She hit with her fists like a man.

Other patrons pulled Lola off, and rushed her from the bar. Accounts of the incident appeared in all Sydney's newspapers. The Aussies loved it. They enjoyed a good punch-up. Theater tickets were scalped at twice and three times the original cost. An extra show was scheduled, and it sold out.

In these two shows she performed the Spider Dance. The first night she was heckled off stage. The audience was offended at her showing so much leg and undergarments. The second night was a repeat of the first. Although paid for, only half the seats were filled. The show closed. Lola did not lose money, but her ego was trampled.

Noel made arrangements for her to appear in Melbourne. The seven permanent members of the cast learned they were not booked for passage with Lola. They challenged her to pay their fare back to San Francisco; it was written in the contract. Lola refused. The group hired an attorney who went to the Magistrate's Court. A writ was issued by the Judge to Sheriff Brown. Lola was notified to appear before the court on the morrow, but Lola was already aboard the steamer *Waratah*, prepared to weigh anchor for Melbourne. Sheriff Brown rowed out to the ship.

From the railing of the upper deck Lola heard

Brown identify himself to the deckhand above. "I am Sherriff James Brown, here to serve a warrant on the Countess of Landsfeld, Miss Lola Montez."

He clambered up the Jacob's ladder, and Lola made directly for her stateroom. She took off every stitch of clothing and stretched out on the couch. Shortly, there was a pounding on her cabin door. A harsh voice called, "This is Sheriff Brown acting upon the directive of Sydney's Magistrate Court. I have a warrant requiring you to accompany me to the aforementioned court. Will you comply?"

"Hell, no!" Lola knew that English law required the husband to stand good for his wife's debts. She shouted back, "I am a married woman."

The Sheriff also knew English law. "So I've been told," he replied. "You've had four husbands, none of whom are in Australia."

"Only two are alive."

"You appear to have a bad influence on your mates. But as they are not in our country, I must take you in."

"The door is unlocked," Lola called out, "But I am resting stark naked on my bed. If you want to drag me out unattired, and haul me back in your little row boat to the Sidney docks before one and all, be my guest."

There was no sound from behind the door for a long momentd, then Sheriff James Brown said, "Countess, I cannot believe you would expose yourself in such an unladylike manner."

He slowly opened the door and peeked in. "Holy Dooley!" he shouted. "I'll be stuffed! Naked as a jaybird." He slammed the door. After several more seconds, his voice was forced and far more contrite.

"Countess I have been appointed to carry out the order of the court." He pleaded, "Will you please dress and come out, as any respectable woman should?"

"You will have to carry me out as I am!"

Lola heard him mumbling, then the sound of his retreating footsteps. The Sheriff went to the quarterdeck, handed the captain the warrant for Lola, and went down the Jacob's ladder to row home alone.

The side-wheeler weighed anchor and steamed to Melbourne.

# CHAPTER 11

## MELBOURNE

### September 15th 1855:

Melbourne reminded Lola of a large California mining town; the city grew from a population of seventy-five thousand to four hundred thousand—mostly men—in just three years. These were adventurers, fortune-hunters, and many undesirables, from all over the world. They came to strike it rich.

Lola felt right at home; she believed they were her kind of audience. The ticket line went around the street. The theater sold out—but the first show almost did not take place. The manager and Lola engaged in a fierce argument. But for Noel Fallon's physical intervention, the man would have been horsewhipped.

Lola claimed artistic relevance to everything in the show. The manager knew his audience, and with Noel's help convinced her to remove the more risqué movements from the Spider Dance. The effect was positive; it earned her extra curtain calls and repeat performances. It also assured Lola's appearance in Geelong, a smaller mining town.

Before she arrived, the Gelignites—influenced by European papers—campaigned against Lola's appearance on moral grounds. The write-ups from Sidney, and more so from Melbourne, pacified most of them.

Lola was booked at the Theater Royal. The manager there, being more compliant, bowed to Lola's insistence that she perform the Spider Dance in all its splendor. She did and was heckled by the audience for showing too much leg. She stopped performing, went to the footlights and told the crowd they were a bunch of uncouth pig farmers who slept with their sheep. This comment brought as many cheers as it did debris upon the stage.

Lola challenged her hecklers to a duel or a fist fight. One inebriated patron clambered onto the stage, and she flattened him with a round-house right. Everyone cheered.

That is, everyone but Dr. Milman. The good doctor wasn't even there, but that did not stop him from protecting the morals of the Gelignites whether they wanted protection or not. He stormed into the Mayor's office, demanding a warrant for Lola's arrest—the charge, lewd and mischievous public conduct.

The Mayor convened the town's magistrates, all of whom had witnessed the performance, to render an opinion. They decided no warrant would be issued, as Dr. Milman had not actually seen the show. The good doctor ranted and raved, threatening to call the magistrates themselves as witnesses, but by that time they had fled City Hall.

Lola wrote a letter to the editor of the *Era*:

"Self-appointed defenders of outraged public morality, such as the good Dr. Milman, are no different anywhere in the world. They condemn without seeing, judge without hearing, and convict without knowing the art of the danseuse. At my own expense I traveled a great distance to bring the latest of culture from Europe and the new world of America only to be denigrated by those who cannot face the changing times and meanings. Art is the *avant-garde* of society. "

Ticket sales fell and the show canceled.

Not all newspapers were hostile. *The Geelong Advertiser* wrote:

### *Illness of Lola Montez*

*Owing to severe indisposition, this talented actress is unable to appear before a Geelong audience. When competent to perform, her reappearance will be duly notified. Madame is suffering from severe cold and bronchitis, and is now under the care of Dr. Thompson, of Melbourne. To previous indisposition was superadded a severe attack induced by exposure to the thunderstorm on Saturday.*[34]

Undeterred, Lola went on to play in many of the roughest, toughest mining towns on the continent. Although praise was sparse and complements rare, she sold out to audiences who wanted to hear her tirades from the stage and interaction with moralists in the audience. At Ballarat there was a fistfight between Lola, a theater manager, and a newspaperman. She took on both of them. Using her riding crop she chased them from the bar into the dust-covered street. The miners applauded the fight, but not the Spider Dance. The public loved to watch her brawls, but was morally shocked by her display of legs, thighs, and undergarments.

---

[34] abridged, from *Lola Montez*, Edmund B. d"Auvergne p.212

In a letter to the editor Lola wrote:

> "Yesterday's fracas with the editor and your misguided theater manager at the *Ballarat Times* is now well known to all. I drove these two cowards into the street and later sent a challenge to both. I would meet them with dueling pistols. However they heard of my shooting expertise against the Czars Cossacks in St. Petersburg. These two, weak, ineffectual rodents feared to reply."

The editor of the *Ballarat Times* responded in an article:

> *"Ballarat's theater manager and I abstained from engaging in fisticuffs with a woman. Notice I say woman, not lady. For the Countess of Landsfeld or Lola Montez, does not enjoy that classification and honor we Australians give to our ladies. The theater manager's wife, Mrs. Crosby saw the lash marks on her husband's face, took her buggy whip and went to the Ballarat Hotel. There she laid into the dark-haired danseuse who challenges Australian morals. That is why there will be no more Spider Dance or Lola Montez appearing in Ballarat or any other Australian town for a while. The Countess of Landsfeld is recovering from a thorough hiding by a proper lady. "*

Lola was a mystery to herself. When calm, she could reason. Her creativity and intelligence were obvious;

she had the willpower and strength of mind to reach her goals. Others found it difficult to oppose her dedication to an idea or concept. She also had a moody side. At these times she wanted to be alone with her animals that were no more.

When angry, Lola was capable of committing mental suicide. Her thoughts and actions were often unrelated to reality; she just had to be right. In her own mind she used her altruistic nature in helping the needy to justify her insistence on being right. The danseuse's tour, managed by Noel Fallon, was a financial success only because she abandoned her troupe, canceled the shows in smaller towns, and annulled her proposed Asian tour to India, the middle-east and Pacific islands.

Lola blamed Noel for her poor reception. He knew it was her insistence on a full performance of the Spider Dance that antagonized the prudish Australian public. The following is a typical article from a newspaper critic of *Lola in Bavaria*:

> *We do not quarrel with the version of those Bavarian events which culminated in the European Revolutions of 1848...Lola is a lady and therefore her veracity is unimpeachable...All we complain about is that the drama entitled "Lola in Bavaria" is utterly destitute of either plot, incident or situation; that the dialogue is made up of stilted and clap-trap appeals ad-populum, stale witticisms and exploded puns. The jokes were indeed so bad, that the audience, laughed at them contemptuously, the clap-trap was so palpable, that*

> *the most democratic individual present snig-*
> *gered at it derisively.* [35]

Lola's last performance in Australia was in the mining town of Bendigo, where she and her troupe were
performing a skit called *The Little Devil*. The theater
had a corrugated metal roof and wooden side boards.

During the third act a thunderstorm swept into Bendigo, not an unusual occurrence. Rain and wind rattled
the building, but the show went on. Suddenly a thunder-
bolt exploded through the metal roof with a thunderous
crash.

The lightning assumed the shape of a luminescent
ball the size of a wagon wheel that floated over the
heads of the stunned audience and actors. The air
smelled of ozone. Screams filled the theater. People
fainted. The lightning ball floated gently down toward
the stage where it hovered in front of the stunned actors,
then divided into two smaller balls.

They both hovered in front of Lola. She remained
unmoved, staring into the illuminated spheres. One ball
sped off through the building's wooden wall backstage,
where it blew a ten foot hole in the wall. The glowing
ball of lightning in front of Lola disappeared.

The thunderstorm stopped. The rain ceased. The audience stood in shock. Lola walked to the front of the
stage.and spoke, loudly and clearly, "I hope you ladies
and gentlemen will not be afraid. I am not."

While she spoke, actors and prop men behind her
extinguished the flames of stage settings which had

---

[35] *Lola Montez*, p. 269, James Morton

caught fire when the ball-lightning blew out the rear wall. "I do hope you will remain for the conclusion of *The Little Devil*," Lola went on. "We never before enjoyed such pyrotechnics in our presentation of that malicious imp. It will take but a few moments to put our scenery in order."

Not one person left the theater. Those who fainted were revived, and the show concluded with several curtain calls.

Despite Lola's heroic action to stem the panic and continue the show, all further appearances in various towns were canceled due to unfavorable press and moral public outrage. Some claimed the lightning attack was God's displeasure. Lola interpreted it otherwise.

For the first time in her life she saw God as a reality, as a force that took physical shape and was capable of rewarding and punishing. Her status as the Almighty's favored one, which she conceived from childhood because of her beauty, was challenged. She felt fear.

She stood before a full-length mirror and stared at herself. Her image looked back at her without pity. Lola approached even closer, speaking aloud to her reflection, "I am almost forty years old. My figure is still good. I do use more make-up at the corners of the eyes and lips to cover my age lines." She pulled down the bodice of her gown and her breasts swelled.

"Men," she said aloud, "Do not care about facial age lines when I show them my breasts."

She plucked two strands of gray hair from above her right ear. They came out without the slightest pain. She picked up the hotel Bible and read,

"In the beginning...."

Lola and Noel made their way back to Melbourne, where she attracted the brother of the Duke of Wellington. She spent several nights with him while shunning Noel. He was distraught.

Lola booked their passage on a three-masted sailing ship, the *Jane A. Falkenberg,* for the return voyage to America. She ordered separate cabins for her and Noel to San Francisco. Soon after boarding, he became ill with a fever and rash. He saw the ship's doctor.

That same evening before dinner, he forced his way into Lola's cabin and dismissed her maid. Lola was surprised; he never acted so assertively. More curious than concerned, she smiled and waited for an explanation.

"You are cruel to me," Noel said. "The only people you open your heart to are the destitute and unredeemed poor. Since that incident with the lightning, you are calmer—but it hasn't influenced your morals."

"Whatever are you speaking of?" Lola demanded.

"The Duke's brother! You abandoned me, and slept with him. I love you. You know I am married, and respect my obligations as a husband and father."

"You can't be so dedicated if you slept with me."

"I love you with all my heart! It is wrong, I know, but I cannot help myself."

"What do you want from me?"

"Have pity on me."

""A man who begs for pity isn't worth it!"

"Take your pistol and put a bullet through my head!"

"Now it's you who is being theatrical. Why would I shoot you?"

"As a favor, to save my family from pain and disgrace."

"Whatever are you talking about?" She held out her handkerchief for Noel to wipe away his tears.

He dried his eyes and said, "When I questioned your mercury medications, you told me it was for a woman's condition."

"So what does that have to do with the price of tea in China?"

"It has to do with the treatment of syphilis. The doctor recommended it for me."

Without a blink of her bright blue eyes or tremor in her voice Lola demanded, "What makes you think you got it from me?"

"Other than my wife, whom I have not seen for three years, you are the only woman I ever slept with."

"Oh! I knew your lovemaking was immature, but I had no idea you practiced celibacy. It sometimes takes years for the disease to display itself. Could it be your wife is at fault?"

Noel flew across the room and grabbed the shoulder straps of Lola's gown to throw her to the floor. The straps broke, and her breasts leaped out in all their magnificence. Noel froze. He buried his face between the beautiful mounds and wept until he fell to his knees at her feet begging, "Please, put a bullet in my head. I love you. I hate you. I, I, I...Please kill me."

Lola hefted her ample breasts in her hands and said, "I sometimes feel the same way about myself, but damned if I'll go down on my knees to anyone."

She lit a cigar, blew a stream of smoke at the head of the humbled man on the floor and said, "I learned to live with syphilis. You can too. I am going now to change my dress. When I return, I want you gone." Lola swept by Noel and slammed the bedroom door. He heard the lock snap into place.

Noel struggled to his feet and went outside to the lower deck. There he stood watching the sea for long moments. Finally he walked to the fantail and gazed at the ship's wake spreading out behind. He lifted his right leg over the rail, then his left leg. He sat for several moments, hoping someone would come and save him. Then he pushed off.

It was well after dinner when Lola queried if Noel had taken food in his cabin, and learned that he hadn't. Lola looked for him and didn't find him. She notified the captain, and the search began. The ship turned about, but no trace was ever found of Noel Follin. He was listed in the ship's log as missing at sea.

His disappearance sent Lola into deep depression. She blamed herself for his suicide, certain he had takem his own life. Hadn't he come to her begging for a bullet to end his misery? His desolation was of her making. Her problems were her own fault. She had no one to blame but herself.

Alone in her cabin, Lola began to write. Sometimes her writings were recollections of the past. Others were essays on life, morals, where and when and how to seek help. Lola started a diary. She wrote: "Once I lived for and from the world. I committed all its fearful sins and deceptions. I then loved that world. It was my all. I kissed and worshipped its chains that fettered me. And why was this? Because I lived out of myself depending on it for my happiness, then for my very bread from its vices. Oh, it took me years and years to rise out of its degradations. I loathed myself, I loathed sin. I tried to reform, not in outward show, for I never was a hypocrite, but from inward drawing toward the light which is truth. My state was a wretched one, oh fearfully wretched. I began to see what a monster in spirit I was." [36]

On the long voyage to America the ship's doctor was called to Lola's stateroom. Lola had fever and a rash, and she found clumps of her hair on the pillow. She thought it was the disease. The doctor determined the cause to be the mercury medication. He discontinued that treatment.

By the time they left Hawaii the rash was gone, and some of her hair grew back. With the aid of a hat she attended the captain's table. But it was a different captain; the original captain blew off his head while lighting Fourth of July fireworks.

Lola made the acquaintance of two couples at the Captain's table, Protestant missionaries who had just completed five years' service in the Hawaiian Islands. She spent much time with these men and their wives, discussing religion and the reason for being. She incorporated their thoughts into her essays, and they supplied Lola with religious reading material.

At the reverends' request she wrote two papers for discussion at the captain's table, which were well received. The two ministers encouraged Lola to publish these papers, and gave her a letter of recommendation to

---

[36] Diary of Lola Montez

the editor of their church journal. The two wives attempted to convince Lola to attend religious services. "You know something of my background," Lola told the women. "Much of the seedy part is true. Right now I feel like the Biblical Jacob who is wrestling with God. I would be a hypocrite if I walked into the ship's chapel, got down on my knees and prayed for forgiveness. I need more time."

"Would you object to kneeling with us now, here, alone in your stateroom?"

Lola thought, then answered, "That would be alright." The three women held hands and knelt on the hardwood floor. "Lola," one of the wives said, "You can remain silent with your own thoughts, but I would like you to ask the Lord to forgive you. Say it out loud: 'Jesus, save me. I am a sinner and need your help."

Lola looked at the two women whose hands she held. Their faces glowed, and tears streamed down their cheeks. Lola tried to speak. She choked, realized she too was crying. She lifted her eyes upward and gasped, "Jesus, oh Jesus, if you can forgive even a part of what I have done, I will be forever grateful." Lola released her grip and covered her face with her hands, moaning, "Please leave me. I must be alone."

When the door closed, Lola fell face down on the floor weeping. Her heart was filled with pain and beauty. It swelled against her lungs until she could hardly breathe. She hadn't the strength to rise. She feared to lift her head because she was in the presence of the Lord God Almighty.

Lola awoke lying on the floor. "Countess," a voice called from outside the stateroom door, "Will you be coming to dinner?"

Lola gathered herself and sat up. "Please ask the Captain to excuse me this evening," she replied.

"Shall I serve in your rooms?"

"No, just a pot of tea, please."

"Yes, Madam."

Lola supported herself on the large Morris chair and stood. She then collapsed into the soft leather cushions. She was still contemplating what had happened when the steward arrived with the tea. She lathered the crumpets with marmalade but had no desire to eat. Her world was upside down, and she didn't know how to cope with it. She struggled to understand.

Later, in a conversation with the four missionaries she commented, "You believe in God. I don't believe; I know God is. I experienced him as a child, being blessed with physical beauty. I used that beauty in the most divisive ways. Men who came close to me either died or are terminally ill. More recently it was a ball of lightning that manifested itself." She told the story. "Now you have brought Jesus into my soul, and I don't know what to do."

"What is it you learned about God?" the missionary asked.

"Nothing!" Lola broke down and wept. "I know nothing more about God now than I did before, except that he exists. He is real."

"And that," said the missionary, "Makes all the difference." He reached out his hands and the five people took hold in a circle, knelt on the upper deck in the sunlight, and prayed.

Often Lola knelt in her stateroom, alone with God and asked for his guidance. Certain questions she asked went unanswered. Others were answered in her thoughts, even before she finished thinking them. They were in the voice of her father—not exactly his voice, but the phrasing was what she remembered of him as a little girl.

When she questioned about employing a certain San Francisco gentleman as her manager, the reply was an emphatic "No!"

She was shocked. She and others held him in the highest regard. Inadvertently she thought the question, "Why? Why not him?"

The answer was immediate; "He is a deceiver."

"You mean a liar and cheat?"

"He deceives himself."

Lola asked other questions on the subject, but the only other response was that she manage her own affairs. In time, all her questions went unanswered. The voice never responded again. When the ship docked in San Francisco Bay, Lola was once again alone with herself. She made a generous donation to the missionaries, and gave them the two articles to be considered for publication.

She rented a modest apartment in a fashionable part of town, and set aside money to be donated to Noel Follin's wife and two children. In addition she had a lawyer sign over her shares in a Paris Theater willed to her by former lover, Alexander Dujarier, the funds to be used for the education of Follin's children.

She was pleased to learn that the gold shares she bought while in Grass Valley were paying a respectable dividend. Although she had not heard from former King Ludwig, he continued sending his bi-annual stipend to her. That and the income from the gold stocks met most of Lola's expenses.

The mercury-induced illness aboard ship had taken away some of Lola's sparkle and strength, but she signed a contract with the American Theater for a two-week run. On August 7th she opened to a packed house. Newspaper critics were far kinder to her; they praised her acting ability and dwelt on how much she improved since her tour of Australia.

The only negative critique was of her dancing. It was considered a result of her age. "The Countess is forty years old and not as flexible and agile but still the most beautiful woman to grace San Francisco's stage," The critic of the *New Californian* wrote, "If to her lot some trivial error fall, look on her face and you'll forget them all."[37]

Lola tired more easily. She reduced her practice time and shortened some of her stage routines. On more than one occasion she had to be revived and refreshed back-stage, but always made her curtain call, albeit a little late. She inspired others with her determination and sheer grit to give the audience what they came to see: The Spider Dance.

Although she hadn't been to Europe for years, there was no lack of imaginative journalism on that continent. Lola wrote the following letter to the journal *Estafette*:

"The Belgian newspapers, and some French

---

[37] *Lola Montez*, P. 351 Bruce Seymour

ones, asserted that the suicide of the actor, Mauclerc, who, it is reported, has thrown himself from the summits of the Pic du Midi, was caused by domestic troubles for which I am responsible. This is a calumny which M. Mauclerc himself will be ready to refute. We separated amicably, it is true, after eight days of married life, but urged only by our common and imperious need of personal liberty. It is probable that the tragedy of the Pic du Midi exists only in the imagination of some journalist on the look-out for sensational news. Trusting to your sense of fairness to insert this explanation in your excellent journal, I remain, yours, etc., Lola Montez."

This letter was published in many periodicals until the man who was supposed to have leapt to his death from the ten-thousand foot mountain wrote the newspapers;

"Sir, I read in your issue of the 7th, a letter from Lola Montez, wherein there is talk of a suicide of which I have been the victim, and a marriage in which I have been principal actor. I am a complete stranger to such catastrophes. I have never had the least intention of throwing myself from the Pic du Midi, or from any other peak, and I do not recollect having had the advantage of marrying—even for eight days—the celebrated Countess of

Landsfeld, Yours, etc., Mauclerc."[38]

Lola accepted an invitation to appear in Sacramento. She thought it a good opportunity to visit her homestead in Grass Valley.

She fell ill on her visit to Grass Valley. It may have been the shock of seeing her beautiful home, garden, and hot house overrun with weeds and destroyed by fire and neglect.

She made a courageous effort to appear at the Forrest Theater in Sacramento with Junius Booth, brother of John Wilkes Booth, as her leading man. On her return to San Francisco she appeared at the Metropolitan Theater with the middle brother, Edwin Booth. That evening she addressed the audience from the stage, saying, "I am contemplating a life-style change, and I foresee it will be most adaptable in New York. I wish to express my thankfulness to all Californians who made me so welcome in your wonderfully beautiful state. I bid you farewell."

---

[38] *Lola Montez*, P. 214, Edmund B. D"Auvergne

# CHAPTER 12

## THE VOYAGE

The most convenient method of transportation from California to New York was by steamship and railroad. Lola booked passage on the screw-driven *Orizaba*, which would sail the Pacific to San Juan del Sur, Nicaragua, then an overland crossing of the peninsula by train to the Atlantic. From there refuel in Havana, again at Norfolk, and on to New York.

Aboard ship were the wealthy and powerful returning to the east coast. The passenger manifest included three congressmen, a senator, several wealthy businessmen and industrialists. Among them was the famous writer of military and minstrel music, Stephen Foster, and his wife Abby Kelley.

Foster organized a series of ad hoc discussions in the ships lounge. The first of which was, "The Problems of Marriage." Foster stated that marriage was the result of nature's inequality between men and women. He claimed, "It is biologically natural for man and woman to desire one another, but they are not equals. Man is the provider, protector, and fountain of future generations. Woman is a place where man's seed is placed and nurtured. Woman cares for man in cooking, cleaning, clothing and bearing his children. She is moveable property. If women believe they are in a difficult situation, let them consider the following. Man is responsible for the failure or success of his family. On him rests their safety and reputation. The community who sees his wife as socially wanting, ostracizes him. Once wed, the man takes on this responsibility the moment he says, "I do". If his wife is slovenly, slow of wit, and not a breeder of sons, the man is called into question, not her. Woman has no equality with man. There is no alternative to the holy bonds of matrimony between a man and a woman. I do not, and will not, condone the Free Love movement of Mrs. Leif."

"Sir," Lola said, "You portray every man as a tyrant in his own home, that his wife is a breeder of slaves obligated to the man of the house."

"You have dramatically stated my position," Foster answered. "Until such time as society itself changes, this will remain my locus. I consider Mrs. Leif's proposal to forgo matrimony out of the question. It would break down the whole moral fabric of our society."

"Mr. Foster," Lola asked, "Aren't you confusing Free Love with Lust?"

"No Countess, I am not. Think about the wedding ceremony. Two people put everyone on notice when they are engaged, then again when they stand before their friends and neighbors in a public proclamation of their obligations to one another. If any man or woman attempts to put asunder what God has brought together, they should be shunned because it is despicable. I will now relinquish the podium to Mrs. Leif."

A tall, thin, stately woman, stylishly attired, with silver grey hair tightly bound at the back, stepped to the lectern. "I appreciate Mr Stephen Foster's martial music, and his melodies for minstrels start my foot tapping to his brilliant tunes. However, I do not condone his archaic view that women be listed with the farm animals, machinery and foodstuff. It is degrading. Most of us abhor slavery." Guffaws and negative sounds came from some in the audience. "We may soon go to war to free the black people. Spain, France and England unfettered their slaves. Yet in these same countries and the United States of America the female population is considered chattel. Women are legally enslaved to the male head of the household by state and federal law. Most men and even many women agree with these laws."

"Because they are applicable" a man said. "The bedrock foundation of America is not its governmental institutions but the family. And in every family like any business, it is, was and always will be the male who makes the decisions."

"Sir," Lola interceded. "You contradict yourself."

"How so?"

"First you say that the basis for a strong America is the family unit, not the government. Yes?"

"Correct."

"But you rely upon laws passed by government to keep women in submission."

Lola received a round of applause.

"Countess, you are correct," the man admitted. "My face is red. I did not intend to express myself on this subject, but rather on the Free Love Movement of which Mrs. Leif is the chairlady."

"Sir," Mrs. Leif said, "The title, Free Love, is a misnomer."

"Madam, how then would you call your organization?"

"Utopians is a more accurate term."

"But in your Utopia anarchy prevails. Anyone may do as he or she wishes."

"The title Free Love was tarred on us by our enemies. It carries the connotation of wanton and thoughtless sex. No intelligent person would promote that, and we do not."

"By whatever name you call yourselves, yours is a social movement that rejects matrimony."

"We do not reject matrimony. We reject the legal interference of church and state in the personal affairs of individuals."

"Madam, you claim marriage is a form of bondage."

"I do, and it is: social, financial and physical bondage. The initial goal of legalized marriage was to separate the state from personal matters such as birth control, and adultery. It purported these matters be left to the people involved, certainly not the government. But today, every state in the union legislates the do's and don'ts of sex in the privacy of our homes."

"Madam, is it true you believe a man can be convicted for raping his wife?"

"I most certainly do," Mrs. Leif said. "God gave woman her body, and she should have complete control over it."

"Doesn't that include homosexuality, birth control, abortion and prostitution?"

"I do not deny these actions. Our organization advocates women using their bodies in any way they choose; it is not the government's business. Women must rise from the position as ministers to the passions of men, and become their equals. Women must attain equal status as independent individuals. Women should be the companions of men from choice, never from governmental dictates."

"Mrs. Leif, you advocate unmarried couples living together. You condone birth control, adultery, divorce, prostitution, homosexuality and abortion. All these are abhorrent to most people."

"Then most people, given free choice, will not do them. Besides, sir, you contradict yourself. You say I am against marriage, yet refer to me as Mrs. Leif. In truth, I am married. I support marriage when the terms of matrimonial agreements are fair to both male and female. The couple should be able to work out their erotic passions any way they choose, so long as no one is abused. We talk of freeing the slaves—"

Someone in the audience said, "Not all of us."

Mrs. Leif ignored the remark and continued, "In reality, if we succeed in emancipating the Negroes, only half will be free. The female Negro will join her white sisters in legalized bondage."

Stephen Foster stood and announced, "Ladies and gentlemen, the Chief Steward informs me that dinner is served. I thank all, especially the speakers, and invite everyone to our next gathering. The subject will be Spiritualism. If you are interested in taking part in a séance, please register at the podium. We require twelve people."

Lola was enthused by Mrs. Leif, and agreed with her premise that women should control what they do with their bodies. When she expressed this thought to a female passenger, the woman retorted, "What about the homely, ugly and socially inept woman who cannot find a mate except through a traditional marriage arrangement?" She pointed to Mrs. Leif, "Mrs. Satan over there, nor you have considered us."

"What the Free Love people are saying," Lola replied, "is that both men and women enjoy the right to sexual pleasure without social or legal restraints."

"Countess, you who are recognized as the most beautiful woman in the world can say that. Americans see the family home, with a man as the master, being the basis for stability in this uncertain world. Gender roles are strongly defined and should remain so."

The woman walked off, and Lola registered to participate in the séance. She had dinner served in her stateroom.

Among her guests was a woman who read Tarot Cards. She found the readings interesting as they gave a glimpse into other people's lives. Lola's personal reading was more specific than others; the cards indicated a pleasant return to the east coast, the renewal of friendships and business associates. The Tarot card reader also claimed that Lola would change professions, yet continue to appear on stage. This sounded contradictory, and Lola had her doubts.

It did help her to form questions for the lecture on spiritualism. She wanted to know if her religious experience of God's presence meant something specific, and if the voice that answered her thoughts was truly that of her father. Could she communicate with him? Lola often daydreamed that he, in ethereal form, hovered close by – prepared to help or influence her. She was concerned if he had observed her sexual activities.

The evening of the seance, the passenger lounge was

rearranged according to the medium's directions. Where the podium had stood was now an oval table with thirteen chairs. It was situated lengthwise to the rows of seats for the audience.

The oil lamps on the large chandelier were extinguished. The room was dimly lit, by candles on the table and wall lamps. Silk blue curtains replaced the heavy white lace used on voyages. In the semi-darkness the audience filed into the room.

Those volunteers for the séance, including Lola, took pre-determined seats at the table. The lights were turned up by stewards, and a pleasant-looking woman in her thirties, wearing a starched grey dress belted at her thin waist, white crocheted collar, and up-swept auburn hair held in place by a Spanish comb, entered the room. She stood behind the empty chair at the head of the table, facing the audience.

She surveyed those at the table and said, "I am Mrs. Leslie Hogan. I am an Irish Gypsy. My parents and their parents were Gypsies."

The woman had cream-colored skin, and her cheeks were tinted a healthy natural rose color. Her auburn hair was worn like a queenly crown. Her hands moved in elegant flowing motions emphasizing her words. Her voice had that musical quality of the Irish accent, and Lola felt a rare pang of longing for her birth-land.

Mrs. Hogan asked, "How many in this room have never participated in a séance?"

The majority raised their hands.

She continued, "I am a medium. My mother and her mother before her were mediums. One doesn't choose this profession; it is bestowed by God. Spiritualism is a belief that the dead communicate with the living. The afterlife or 'spirit world' is not a stationary, unchanging place. It is an environment of learning, a place where the soul grows in quantity and quality. Often I am told by the spirits not to bother them because they are learning. However, when they do respond, you will be privy to a higher form of intelligence. They can guide you in decisions about the future. As a medium, I become the conduit or channel to the spirit world, through which they communicate. They use me to speak to you. I do not influence the message, nor do I control the form of communication."

Stephen Foster asked, "Mrs. Hogan, will you please explain your last statement?"

"I will go into the meditative state of mind, then into a trance. Sometimes I am oblivious; I do not recall what you asked or they answered. Also, the message from the spirits is not only by voice. Sometimes it is by knocks, breaths of wind, or movement of objects, but most often it is through me. You will ask a question, and if the spirit is with us, that soul may answer and I will tell you what he or she said—or they may speak directly through me. Sometimes the spirits have an unpleasant attitude, and you may not like what they say. I do not control them. In my experience, I've found that spirits retain their character traits in the spirit world. Jovial people remain so. Sarcastic or angry ones do not change, at least not right away. So, without further ado let us begin."

Mrs. Hogan pulled out her chair at the head of the table, stepped in front of it, poured a glass of whisky from a cut glass decanter, took a candle in her right hand and waved it. The stewards turned down the lights. She took a mouthful from the glass, and her pink cheeks bulged. She brought the candle up and spat the whisky over the heads of the people sitting at the oval table. It became a fountain of flame twelve feet long, and burst over the heads of the participants. Shocked silence permeated the room. Leslie Hogan began to hum.

In the flickering candlelight she was seen to be swaying left to right in her chair, with her eyes closed. She stiffened, and a man's voice in an English workman's accent came from her location. "Hey, love, you back again?" the voice asked. "Last time you couldn't find anyone for me to talk with."

"You have no one," Mrs. Hogan answered.

Lola was quick to notice that, when the man spoke, the medium's lips did not move. When Mrs. Hogan spoke, they did move.

"Well, ducky," the man's voice said, "There are a lot of people waiting here to speak with your friends, and I ain't giving anyone a chance before I gets my say."

Mrs. Hogan's brows furrowed, and she asked, "Can you help me interview those on your side to make connections on this side?"

"Yeah! Then I gets to talk with someone, even if it's just you."

"Are there many spirits waiting?"

"Enough. The first one wants to know if there is someone in your bunch who just lost a child."

Mrs. Hogan remained silent. She did not repeat the question. In the darkness several women said, "Yes!"

"Does the Letter 'M' have meaning to anyone?" he asked.

Two women replied in the affirmative. One said, "I would have named her Miriam." The other woman said, "My daughter's name was Marsha."

"Which girl was born closest to New Year's Eve?" the male voice asked from Mrs. Hogan's lips body.

"That's my Marsha! She was born five minutes after mid-night, and died in my arms."

"Well ole' girl, Marsha has a message for you."

Suddenly the voice of a child came from the medium's mouth, but her lips didn't move. "Mommy! Mommy! Please don't be sad. I had just one mission in life: to be born. I fulfilled that task, and returned. I will be waiting for you."

The mother wept, called out, "Marsha!" and collapsed. She slid off her chair onto the floor. Stewards carried her from the room, and without interruption the séance continued.

Lola was disappointed that she was not called upon by the medium or someone from the spirit world. She had hoped to hear from Dujarier, her former French lover who died in a duel with pistols. On her way out of the lounge, Lola stopped the Chief Steward and asked, "Do you know what the word TIPS means?"

"Yes Countess. It is an abbreviation for the words, To Insure Personal Service."

She placed money in his hand and said, here is your, TIPS. See that Mrs. Hogan comes to my stateroom prepared to give me a personal reading."

# CHAPTER 13

## A PRIVATE READING

The following day Mrs. Leslie Hogan and her husband entered Lola's stateroom. The chief steward arranged the parlor as requested by the medium. He replaced the heavy lace curtains with silk ones, added two candelabras and one small circular table with two chairs. Lola objected to the husband being a witness.

"No problem," Mrs. Hogan said, "He will wait outside. Did you attend yesterday's séance?"

"Yes, and was disappointed not to have communicated with anyone from my past. Most of my former friends were powerful personalities."

"Souls on this side of the veil may change on the other side. There is a constant intellectual and moral growth in the realm of spirits."

"It hasn't appeared to influence your Limey friend from the other side."

"It happens. God breathed into each of us a soul. He gave us freedom of choice. The Limey's name is Ted Barkins."

"Do we come back to live again?"

"You are questioning reincarnation?"

"Yes."

"There is no clear answer," Mrs. Hogan said, "No proof of rebirth, only anecdotal evidence. I and my mother have spoken to spiritualists who see an aura around certain people. That ambience, they say, represents a personality from the past."

"What do we do now?" Lola asked. "How do we begin?"

"Similar to yesterday."

"There is a bottle of whisky on the side table."

"That is not necessary," Leslie Hogan said. "The fire breathing is an old carnival trick, used to focus the audience's attention on me."

"I am pleased you admitted it," Lola smiled. "Fakirs in India use it for the same purpose."

Leslie Hogan sat down and placed her fan on the table. "Countess," she asked, "Whom would you like to contact?"

"My father, Noel Follin, Alexander Dujarier..."

"Three is the most I can physically tolerate. The supernatural interaction drains me. I will call them in relation to their age, the oldest first."

"My father, Dujarier and Noel Follin."

Leslie Hogan darkened the room except for a candle between them. She took her seat, placed her hands flat on the table, and leaned back in her chair. She began to hum, "Ohhmmmm...Ohhmmmm…Ohhmmmm..." Her body stiffened. Her lips moved, and she said, "Mr. Barkins, Mr. Barkins, listen to me. I cannot have you interrupting this discussion. Now be a good fellow, and leave. Yes, I will contact you. Would you please request, from the group, Countess Lola Montez's father? …No, I do not know his name."

Lola was about to volunteer the answer, but thought it would test Mrs. Hogan's validity.

The medium said, "A handsome man in his thirties is

approaching. He claims to be your father, but his name is Edward Gilbert. He is in uniform."

"Daddy! Oh Daddy!" Lola burst into tears. "I miss you so much."

"He says he knows you love him. He is sorry he couldn't be with you to make your life easier. He asks you to forgive your mother. She is an unhappy woman, jealous of your beauty and intellect, but she gave you life. Respect her."

"Can I speak directly with him?"

"I do not choose the means of communication. Time is of the essence. Do you have questions?"

"Daddy, is it you who guides me? Are you looking out for me like a guardian angel?"

"He says, 'Yes.'"

"Daddy, is it you who answers my questions in my thoughts?"

"Yes."

"Do you see me when I bathe, or in my bedroom with my husband? Is he aware of my affliction?" she asked.

"He is gone!" Mrs. Hogan said.

"I have more questions to ask!"

"Messier Alexander Dujarier is speaking to you, but he can't talk. He has a wound in his throat."

"From the duel," Lola blurted out. "He was shot defending his family honor."

Mrs. Hogan raised her hands above the table, and the table started to rise. One leg of the table struck the floor. She said, "One knock indicates yes, two knocks, no."

"Oh, Alexander," Lola sobbed, "You should never

have fought that duel! If you would have only allowed me to take your place, I would have killed the son of a bitch where he stood."

The table rose up, and one leg struck the floor. Leslie Hogan's sweet Irish face broke into a beautiful smile. "He is smiling. He loves you. He says you are doing the right thing by giving the shares in the theater he willed to you to Follin's wife and children."

"It is really you!" Lola gasped. "Oh, what a different life I would have led had we remained together."

"He says, 'It was meant to be. Do not try to escape fate; it will always be waiting for you.'" A frown crossed Mrs. Hogan's face.

"What is wrong?" Lola asked.

"Alexander is pulling a younger man forward to speak with you."

"What does he look like?"

"Spirits do not always maintain a physical form. His aura is good. Do the letters F N mean anything?"

Lola's brow crinkled in concentration. Her head came up and her eyes snapped open. "Not F N," she said. 'It is N F, Noel Follin."

"He is reluctant."

"I need his forgiveness."

Although the doors and windows were closed, Lola was struck by a burst of fresh air. It startled her and she cried out. She explained.

Mrs. Hogan said, "The answer is, 'No'. He will not forgive you. He acknowledges your vow to help his wife and children. For this he thanks you. Having taken his own life, he is condemned... "

"Condemned to what?" Lola shouted.

Mrs. Hogan opened her eyes and looked bewildered. Again Lola demanded, "What is Noel condemned to?"

"Countess, you are speaking to me in French. I do not understand the language."

"We've been speaking French since Dujarier entered. He rarely spoke English."

"I speak no French," Mrs. Hogan said. "The spirits speak through me. You were conversing with them, not me."

Lola stood and lit the oil lamps. "Do you recall anything?" she asked.

"Yes, you spoke to your father in English. I had the feeling he left before you finished your questions."

"I wished to know if he could see me when I bathe, or in my bedroom with my husband. Is he aware of my affliction?"

"The first two are common questions women ask about their fathers. It is my understanding that parents do not observe the intimate lives of their offspring. I cannot explain. In reference to your affliction, do you wish to tell me what it is?"

"No," Lola answered.

"If it becomes life-threatening, your spirit guardian will be with you."

The séance was concluded. and Lola asked, "What is your fee?"

"There is no fee. A contribution to the Charity of Progressive Spiritualism will be appreciated."

"What does your charity do?"

"We support spiritualists and those who promote spiritualism. We look for gifted men and women to train in our art."

Lola held out her purse and said, "Take it all."

Mrs. Hogan bowed and accepted the purse. Lola asked "Will you be crossing the Isthmus with us?"

"No, I am retained for séances in Nicaragua, and then on to Santiago, Chile."

"I hope our paths cross again," Lola said.

The accommodations at the Regents Hotel, in San Juan del Sur, were a far cry from the tents provided on Lola's outbound trip to the west coast. Everything in the hotel was new. Local people were hired and trained for service work. Two French chefs supervised the kitchen; they also stocked the hotel's wine cellar. A train instead of donkeys, and a bridge for the train, replaced the canoes to cross the river. The journey to the Caribbean Sea was quite pleasant.

On November 20th, 1857, Lola boarded the steam ship *Orizaba* for the United States. Upon landing in New York, she set up in a discreet hotel, and contacted Noel Follin's widow to set up the fund for her and the children.

Susan Follin rejected any contact whatsoever with the Countess of Landsfeld. Lola persisted until it was clear she was blamed for Follin's death. The widow hinted that with Lola's violent nature, she may have pushed Noel overboard. Lola did feel guilty, but for other reasons.

In spite of the widow's rantings, Lola made a vow to God and intended to keep it. She contacted Noel's mother. The woman was also a widow, and raising a daughter. Noel had shown his little sister Miriam's photograph to Lola. Lola was so fascinated by the girl's beauty and aspirations to become an actress that she sent money for her education in dance and voice training. The girl reminded Lola of herself as a youngster.

Noel Follin's mother responded immediately to Lola's offer of money for Noel's children, and eventually agreed to a meeting. When Lola was certain Noel's mother would distribute the money fairly, she outlined the fund she would set up. This included a stipend for Noel's mother. When Lola thought the conversation concluded, his mother presented her daughter Miriam. The girl had been waiting outside in the foyer.

She was more exquisite than her photo. She was sixteen, but appeared more mature. Her golden curls poured down both shoulders to rest on a well-developed bosom. Her grey eyes were stunningly beautiful, and she did not look away when Lola stared into them. Noel's mother said, "I thought you might like to see the results of the lessons you presented my daughter Miriam, Noel's sister."

"A pleasure," Lola said, "But there is no music."

"I will sing while dancing," Miriam replied. She removed her waistcoat, positioned herself before Lola, and sang. Her lithe body moved in time to her melodious voice. At once Lola was fascinated by this youthful beauty. The girl's movements were natural, graceful, but unprofessional.

Lola said, "When you put out both your arms to express the music, do it to the very tips of your fingers. Keep your toes pointed toward the audience. Your chin, a little higher please. Can you show those beautiful teeth when you smile? That's better." Lola turned to the mother. "The lessons have been worthwhile, but Miriam is not yet on a professional level. That will require serious training."

"Miriam," Noel's mother said, "Please wait outside."

When the door closed behind the girl, Noel's mother turned to Lola and asked, "Would you be willing to teach my daughter?"

"The thought occurred to me," Lola said.

"My daughter needs a strong hand."

"I have no time nor patience for a troublesome child."

"Countess, I hope you will understand. Miriam is dedicated to becoming an actress. She has natural beauty, and she is creative. Sometimes, like most youngsters, my daughter can be difficult. Without a man in the house, I find it challenging to rein her in."

"I don't train horses," Lola said. "If I decide to take her on as a protégé, she will either do as I say or go home."

"I agree."

"It is not for you to agree, Mrs. Follin. Miriam must understand my terms and swear an oath."

"May I bring her in?"

"First tell me the girl's real problem. I sense something else going on here."

"Your intuition is correct." Tears welled up in the woman's eyes, and Lola handed her a handkerchief. Noel's mother looked at the floor while speaking. "My daughter has been promiscuous."

"With many men?" Lola asked.

"Only one that I know of. I forced the man to marry her; the child was aborted."

"Miriam has a husband?"

"In name only. He legally relinquished all conjugal rights, the marriage was annulled, and he went west."

"You are certain he will not be a problem?" Lola asked.

"It would cost his family too much money. His father is a skin-flint."

"I grew up without a caring mother," Lola said. "My Nanny was her proxy. I also made mistakes." Lola paced the room, then said, "Bring your daughter in here."

Miriam entered with her hands clasped before her waist, head bowed. The girl's natural beauty radiated. Together in one room, the two beauties filled it to overflowing. On stage they would make a stunning couple. Lola asked, "Do you know what we were discussing?"

"Whether I could live and apprentice myself to you."

"Do you wish to do so?"

"I do! I do with all my heart."

"The theater is a serious business. Slovenly work ethics are not tolerated by audiences, critics, or me."

"I understand," Miriam said. "I swear to be faithful to you and the art."

"If I tell you to pirouette or leap, your only response must be, 'How high?' Understood?"

"Try me," Miriam pleaded. "Give me a chance."

"You must also improve your diction. Use the word opportunity instead of chance. I will expedite occasions for you to excel. You must take advantage of them. Your beauty will cover a multitude of mistakes before men, but not to me.

"Your mother tells me you had an abortion. That is the past. You made a mistake. Know that many men collect actresses as a hunter does pelts. They'll be sniffing around you. I want your word that not one of them will get a smell of what is between your legs. If you wish to go out with someone, I must approve!"

"Yes, Countess."

"I hope you are as intelligent as you are beautiful. If so, you understand that many of the risqué accounts of my past are false. Your brother would not stand for it, and he was my manager. A finer man never lived."

"Yes, Countess."

"I have become somewhat religious and will expect you to attend church with me."

"Yes Countess, but I am not Catholic."

"I am attracted to Methodism. Is that a problem?"

"No, Countess.

"I expect you to continue your education while you are with me. There is nothing more pathetic than a thoughtless beauty, and nothing more powerful than an attractive woman intellectual, who can manipulate men. I will teach you."

"Yes, Countess."

"Henceforth, address me as Lola."

"Yes... Lola."

"Good." Lola turned to the mother. "Have your daughter's clothing and personal items sent here. She will take the smaller bedroom. It has two closets; one will be for everyday wear, the other for training and stage costumes. We begin practice in two hours. Off, now, both of you."

# CHAPTER 14

## A CONFIDENCE BETRAYED

It became immediately apparent that young Miriam was more talented than Lola thought, though the girl lacked self-discipline. Lola looked on her as a little sister, and came to love her as such.

The January 23rd edition of the *New York Times* in 1857 gave Lola's place of residence as 13 Stuyvesant Place in New York City. The reporter was introduced to Miriam as the younger sister of the Countess of Landsfeld. He wrote, "Lola Montez, and Minnie Montez, as Lola refers to her sister, can fill any room, no matter the size, with their beauty. It would be enough for the two most beautiful women in the world to stand on stage and be admired. They both sing and dance. It is the combination of beauty, movement and voice that casts a magic spell over the spectator. The sisters will be a welcome addition to New York's theaters. Countess Lola returned from Australia with a small fortune. She increased her earnings by $25,000 dollars in California. More importantly, Lola has forsaken her spendthrift past. She no longer buys without questioning price. She has become sagacious in personal finance, more frugal in life-style and generous in charitable donations. Two of her articles on living in God's Kingdom have been published by the Methodist Journal of Idaho. A group of missionaries aboard ship from California to Nicaragua persuaded her to write them. She has since received requests to lecture to women's groups, church congregations and abolitionists societies. Having booked these appearances it is improbable the Countess of Landsfeld can do both."

On February 2nd, 1857, Minnie Montez appeared with her older sister Lola at the Green Theater in Albany, New York. Two nights later, both performed in *The Cabin Boy,* an abolitionist play. Minnie was put on the auction block as the beautiful young slave, and rescued by Lola from a life of sexual abuse and servile bondage.

Minnie's performances were not up to par with the other actors, but as predicted by Lola, the girl's beauty covered her mistakes. The youngster was a natural thespian; she learned her part for *Lola in Bavaria* in three days. This feat of memorization gained the respect of everyone on the set, and the theater critics.

Lola and Minnie made more headlines when on February 9th she and Minnie were to appear in Troy, New York, located on the west bank of the mighty Hudson River. A difficult winter froze the river, but two nights prior, higher temperatures and a great rainstorm broke up the river ice. The Hudson overflowed its banks. Ice, some in blocks the size of a double Dutch barn, moved inexorably downstream. All traffic across the waterway was discontinued.

Lola brought Minnie to the town dock where people had gathered to watch the mighty river. Lola commanded everyone's attention by offering $100 each—a year's salary—for any two boatmen to transport her and Minnie across the river. Two river men finally came to Lola.

They demanded payment in advance, which they handed to their wives.

They used two sturdy Nova Scotia sea skiffs lashed side by side. One man rowed on the right side of the upriver skiff and the other on the left of the downriver skiff. Lola and Minnie were seated on the downriver side. A crowd gathered, photos were taken, and last words exchanged. A Minister prayed. They pushed off into the ice-filled river.

Immediately they were struck by a slab of floating ice and turned halfway around. The two oarsmen managed to head the craft across the river while dodging other ice flows.

Minnie sat silently with her eyes fixed upon Lola. She drew strength from the older woman's calm demeanor.

They made it two-thirds of the way across when a jagged piece of ice cracked the ribs of the upstream skiff. The boatman jumped up, oar in hand, and was able to stand on his seat as the water rushed in. Lola took the oar from him as he unlashed the boat and hopped into their skiff.

The broken boat went under the jagged ice floe, and the two men worked their oars furiously to get away from it. There was a shout from the shore ahead of them and a thin line came whistling out of the night. The boatman caught it, tied on, and they were pulled safely to shore. Most of the costumes and some scenery were lost in the other boat, but the publicity of two daring women crossing the ice-packed Hudson at flood-tide made national and international headlines. It guaranteed sellout performances for months to come.

Minnie questioned Lola. "I watched you closely," the girl said. "You were not the least bit frightened during the crossing! It gave me and the boatmen courage."

"As a little girl in India," Lola answered, "I questioned a Hindu Fakir who played a gourd flute for three deadly King cobras. I asked if he was afraid. He told me that one of the most useless things in this world is fear. It may serve the simple needs of animals, but it paralyzes human beings just when they most need to think clearly. He said cobras do not hear as humans do; they sense vibrations. People, he said, do the same. If they sense fear, they attack. Fear not, my little Minnie, and you will be better served."

Spring came early in 1857. Prior to the opening of the theater season John Hunter and William R. Travers, two of the wealthiest men in New York, invited Lola and the cast of *Lola in Bavaria* to perform at Spa City in Saratoga, New York. It would be an early opening for their racetrack: four days of enjoying the mineral springs and entertainment for the rich and powerful from New York to Boston.

Commodore Cornelius Vanderbilt arranged special trains to Saratoga. Thomas Durant of Massachusetts organized three ten-car trains from Boston.

Lola and Minnie were John Hunter's personal guests in the President's Dining Car. John Hunter was a soft-spoken man with thatched grey hair that refused to remain in place. He liked to tell stories and surprise his guests. He could eat apples off his wife's head.

She was a petite woman who disliked attention, loved her husband and was the most ardent female abolitionist in the United States. An avid supporter of John Brown she promoted his policy of armed insurrection to overthrow the institution of slavery.

The little woman sat quietly. Her husband, a natural raconteur, dominated the conversation with interesting anecdotes. He spoke of the history of New York, political problems with Tammany Hall, and the railroads' need for right-of-way laws to service the mass immigration west to the Great Plains for wheat and cattle, north for minerals and timber, and South for the cotton. He asked what was meant to be a rhetorical question, but Lola answered, "The Erie canal is the greatest contribution to the economic welfare of the United States. It is also what has made New York the trade center of the New World."

Jack Fargo of the Wells Fargo Company said, "I believe the telegraph and steam boat contributed more to America's economy."

"For you that is a logical conclusion," Lola said. "You own the most successful stagecoach line in the country. Do you know that the Erie Canal employs 50,000 people? It opened up the west and north of America for the pioneers. The mineral wealth and timber of the Appalachian and Allegheny Mountains comes floating out of the great Lakes, down that three hundred and sixty-three mile trench from Buffalo to Albany, into the Hudson River and on to the Port of New York." Lola broke into song. Minnie joined her and the two beautiful women combined in sublime harmony.

"I got a mule and her name s Sal,

Fifteen miles on the Erie Canal.

She's a good ol' worker, and a good ol' pal,

Fifteen miles down the Erie Canal.

We've pulled some barges in our day,

Filled with lumber, coal, and hay,

And Sal knows every inch of the way,

From Albany to Buffalo.

Low bridge! Everybody, down.

Low bridge, 'cause we're coming through a town.

And you'll always know your neighbor,

You'll always know your pal,

If you ever navigated on the Erie Canal."

Everyone in the dining car applauded. The men stood, shouting, "Bravo! Bravo!"

Lola and Minnie acknowledged the accolades. John Hunter stood, bowed to Lola and said, "Countess, you are the first person ever to correctly answer my question." He turned to Jack Fargo. "The lady is right. Because of the canal, the Port of New York surpasses the combined shipping tonnage of Boston, Baltimore, and New Orleans."

"If I had the vote," Minnie said, "I would vote for DeWitt Clinton for president, rather than that backwoodsman from Illinois."

"First, my dear," Jack Fargo said, "Clinton is dead, and Abe Lincoln is nobody's fool."

"People speak of him as if he fell off the turnip wagon," Minnie said.

"Those are anti-abolitionists who invested in southern cotton, but I have a question for our host." He turned to John Hunter at the head of the table. "Why did you invite me and the Boston Brahmins so early in the season? There is still snow on the ground."

"Because I want the Wells Fargo Bank to invest one million dollars in my purchase and expansion of the Canadian-Pacific Railroad."

"You are going to have to give me a damn good reason."

"That is why I broached the subject of the Erie Canal. In a few years it will be outdated. The railroads will take its place."

"Ladies," Jack Fargo said, "Will you excuse us while we speak business?"

The women got up to leave, but John Hunter indicated that Lola should remain. He passed around Cuban cigars to everyone. Lola puffed away with the men, helping to create a colorful blue cloud above their heads.

When the discussion concluded, Jack Fargo committed to an investment of one million dollars. Others pledged to lesser, but significant sums.

When business was finished, the dining car was empty but for John Hunter and Lola.

"I wished to speak to you alone," Hunter said. "It is about your so-called sister, Minnie." Lola started to protest but Hunter held up his hand and said, "My dear Lola, I respect your beauty, intelligence, and talent, but I know more about you than most people in this world."

"Why is that?"

"Because I had you investigated."

"I take offence at the invasion of my privacy."

"Everyone in this car was investigated. My wife is under threat from anti-abolitionists. There have been attempted assassinations of persons in the movement, and two were successful. I will do whatever it takes to protect my wife."

Lola looked thoughtfully at the older man. "You do what you must to protect your family."

"That is not what I wish to discuss; it is your so-called sister, Minnie. She is Noel Follin's sister."

"Yes," Lola said. "I felt an obligation to help his family. She is a talented girl."

"A noble gesture, and she is beautiful. But she is not sixteen years of age; she is twenty."

"Her mother gave me her age."

"Her mother lied. Minnie is twenty; she will have her twenty-first birthday on May sixth. She is also quite promiscuous. My investigators claim she has had one abortion. My wife found out Minnie will soon have a scandal, and it is certain to affect you."

"I know about the abortion," Lola said. "What else is she up to?"

"She has been sleeping with the male members of your cast, including stagehands and delivery boys. She now has her hooks into a New York City Alderman named Ed Kiley. He is building a private house for her, with money he filched from the city."

"Who knows about this?" Lola asked.

"Walter Whitman, a reporter from the *Brooklyn Eagle*. He hasn't the whole story yet, but he is persistent."

"Members of my cast have hinted to me," Lola sighed. "I ignored them. I didn't want to believe Minnie would betray me," Lola mused. "I must let her go, but only when we have performed for you and returned to New York. I promised you a great show, and that you shall have."

John Hunter kissed Lola's hand and said, "Thank you, Countess."

"It is I who thank you. It would be an embarrassment for me if this comes to light. It would mean trouble. In some quarters my reputation is already in question. To be accused of corrupting a minor would be unthinkable."


On return from Saratoga, Minnie found her clothing and personal items packed and outside the apartment door. "I told you what would happen if you defied my wishes," Lola said. "You will make your way in this world by yourself from now on."

Stunned at first, Minnie recovered and replied, "I will make it with my own manager, Mr. Edward Kiley. You need my beauty more than I need yours. Countess, you are getting old."

"You ungrateful little bitch!" Lola shouted, and punched Minnie in the jaw. The girl stepped back, smiled and said, "I read there was a time you could knock down a grown man." She shook her head. "Those days are past."

Lola charged the girl but was stopped in her tracks by the stronger youngster, who pushed her away and hailed a passing cab.

Shocked at her inability to overpower Minnie, Lola

went into the house and stood before the full-length mirror in the foyer. She recognized the age-lines around her eyes and corners of her lips. For a long time she stood gazing and thinking. The flickering gas light cast unnerving shadows on the wall.

Minnie went on to moderate success with Edward Kiley as lover and manager. In a short time she stopped advertising herself as Lola Montez's sister. There had been a plethora of newspaper articles revealing her true name as Miriam Follin.

# CHAPTER 15

## SEEKING ADVICE

Lola went from success to success while taking up the slack for Minnie. However, friends, fellow actors, and critics cautioned her against overwork. In late spring of 1858, Lola fell ill. She passed out twice in rehearsals. Her shows in Pittsburgh, Louisville, Cincinnati, St Louis and New York had to be cancelled. Her mental acuity was sometimes called into question.

Doctors offered no cure for syphilis. She turned to a spiritualist. Lola sought advice from her former lover, Alexander Dujarier. Leslie Hogan, the spiritualist from the *Orizaba*, recommended Rosemary Bory of New York. Miss Bory was well respected by prominent people in the east—including Mary Todd Lincoln, whose husband Abraham was a candidate for President of the United States.

In her quest for the spiritual Lola forged a friendship with Reverend Hoyt, an Episcopalian Minister and Rector of the House of Good Shepherds Church in New York. He and Lola spoke of religion, philosophy, and moral issues. He was vehemently opposed to a séance. "You, dear Countess, have been privileged to be born again," he counseled. "Do not waste your time with swindlers and quacks. Open your heart to Jesus. Through the ball lightning you heard our Lord whisper in your heart. Turn to him with your questions, and He will answer you."

"Not you or Jesus can help me."

"Our savior is always waiting for you with his love."

"Reverend, I appreciate your advice and do take you seriously, but I wish to change the subject."

"Please do."

"Parts of this Church were destroyed in the big winter storm. The roof and walls of the main building collapsed from the weight of the snow."

"Yes, and the stables and toilets are gone, too."

"I understand you require five thousand dollars to complete the repairs?"

"Correct."

"Had I the funds, I would write a check this moment."

"Countess, you have been generous."

"I often raise funds for the poor, unemployed actors, and the fire department. I am physically unable to perform at the moment, but I could give a lecture. I can always draw a crowd. The entrance fee would go to your church, and I hope to attract a philanthropist or two."

"A marvelous idea, but are you up to it?"

"Talking is my forte. You read my two articles in the *Methodist Journal*."

"Yes, if you could do something like that, we might be successful."

"I will write up the lecture and submit it for your approval."

"And I will clear a date with the Bishop."


Lola was at her desk working on the lecture when there

was a knock on the apartment door. A young man there requested to see the Countess of Landsfeld. He introduced himself as an associate of the Pinkerton Detective Agency, currently employed by John Hunt and Cornelius Vanderbilt of the Canadian Pacific Railroad.

"What can these two men have to do with me?" Lola asked.

"Madam," the detective said, "They sent me to warn you against this spiritualist you are about to engage."

"How could they know about that?"

"I told them."

"And how do you know my private affairs?"

"Miss Bory is involved in a scam to bilk hundreds of thousands of dollars from two potential investors in the Canadian Pacific Railroad. I am an undercover agent. While in her employ I learned about her interview with you. I investigated your sister Minnie. I also informed Mr. Hunt of your intention to employ Miss Bory. He sent me here."

"So you and Mr. Hunt believe Miss Bory a fraud?"

"That is a fact. I am employed by her to make some of the ghost sounds, feats of levitation, and movement of the curtains."

"Will you be at the séance?" Lola asked.

"No, yours is a simple reading. She will handle the deceptions herself."

"Look here," Lola said, "I too was skeptical about spiritualism. I had a reading of Tarot cards aboard ship. The woman predicted I would stop performing but remain on stage, but not as an actress; and now it may come true. I have been asked to give lectures. I will no longer have to depend on others, renting theaters, hiring and firing etc. At the time, I didn't know what the woman was speaking about. My health now precludes dancing and the rigors of the theater. If I regain a modicum of health, I am considering this opportunity. That is why I want the advice of a spiritualist."

"I regret your present illness, Countess. I can sympathize with your attempt to seek answers to your future, but you won't get them from Rosemary Bory. She is a fraud and swindler."

"You said, you assist her. How?"

"She uses my skill as a ventriloquist. I can throw my voice so it appears to be coming from someplace else. I do this without visibly moving my lips. I levitate tables, make pens move and curtains billow as if a spirit is entering the room."

"How can you do all these things without being noticed?"

"I come into the room as a participant in the séance. It is not unusual that two or three employees of Miss Bory participate."

"How can you make a table levitate?"

"I cannot do it without your help."

"Prove it."

The young man held out both his hands and Lola put her hands in his. "You have cold hands," he said, "That means a warm heart."

"And what if my hands were warm?"

"That means a warmer heart. Do you feel my hands trembling?"

"Yes."

"A spirit has arrived."

"But you don't believe in spirits."

"The trembling is done by expanding and relaxing the muscles in my forearms. You sense it through my hands. Now release your grip and place your hands above the table, as I have. Now concentrate on the person you wish to meet."

"Must I close my eyes?" Lola asked.

"Only if it helps you to see the spirit."

"I see him with my eyes open."

"Good. He says you have achieved the epitome of accolades in the theater. It is time for you to move on to present a more moral image to the public."

"I really didn't wish to contact my father."

"I do not believe this is your father. I cannot see him clearly. I mean his shape and form are ethereal."

"Is he happy?"

"Concentrate, and the table will answer."

Lola concentrated, and the table floated up several inches. The young man said, "One knock is for Yes, and two knocks for No." The table wobbled in the air then one leg slammed the floor once.

"I'm so pleased!" Lola gushed.

"Pleased at what?" The detective asked.

"At Alexander Dujarier being happy."

"Countess," the detective said, "You are what they call an easy mark. This is a cold reading, and you fell for it."

Lola regained her composure and asked, "How did you know it was Alexander?"

"You told me it was a man, and then you gave him a name."

"I didn't."

"Oh yes you did."

"But he made the table float upward."

"I did that."

"How?"

"Turn up the lamp." The detective held up his hands and under each palm was an offset piece of metal that ran up his sleeves, inserted into harnesses on his fore-arms. "With these I lifted the table without touching it with my hands."

"But aboard the ship we were twelve people at a long heavy table. No one person could lift it."

"Three or four of those twelve people were shills. They worked for the spiritualist. Mrs. Leslie Hogan is one of the best in the business. She does a trick with a pencil. We know she uses a long strand of hair to make it move without seemingly touching it. What is unique is that she can make the pencil stand and write."

"Why did you require my help to move the table?"

"I didn't. I needed you to suspend your belief in the laws of nature. You did that by asking me questions. Each question you asked was loaded with information. I used the information to convince you we were com-municating with the spirit world. What ship were you on when you had this reading?"

"The *Orizaba*."

"That was from San Francisco to Nicaragua?"

"Yes."

"And the spiritualist who recommended Miss Bory was Mrs. Leslie Hogan?"

"How could you know that?"

"Either I am a spiritualist or a good detective. Miss Bory is a younger cousin and protégé of Miss Hogan." They worked the ships and land crossings to California and New York, taking gold from those who found it, and telling those who sought it where to look. Pinkerton took them off the run to and from America."

"How can I prove she, or spiritualism, is a fraud?" Lola asked.

"A cold reading depends on the 'Bird' giving suffi-cient information."

"What do you mean, Bird?"

"Have you heard the saying, 'A little bird told me so?' You, Countess, are the Bird—the person who is going to be plucked."

"How can I avoid giving her information?"

"By answering yes or no to her questions. Do not volunteer names, places or dates—especially if strange voices come from her mouth. I am a good ventriloquist; Miss Bory is better. If you and the spirit share a foreign language, ask the spirit questions in that language. Miss Bory knows French, Gaelic, Rumanian, Italian, and Spanish. She already has information about your tragic love affair with Dujarier. There is much information about you in the newspaper archives. These Gypsies are not stupid; they have their own intelligence network and language."

"Please thank Mr. Hunter and Mr. Vanderbilt. Still, I am not convinced all spiritualists are frauds. I saw the curtains billow in the ship's lounge when a spirit was asked a question. I felt the spirit pass by me."

"That is accomplished by one of the participants working for the spiritualist. He or she holds a small bellows between the knees and aims it at the curtains, which have been changed to achieve the effect or he aims the burst of air at you when the spiritualist says the spirit is moving in the room."

"I cannot believe I'm so gullible. I must prove it for myself."

The detective stood, bowed, and said, "Countess, consider yourself warned. Take care. When confronted, Miss Bory can be dangerous. She carries a knife."

Lola pulled a four-shot pocket pistol from her skirt. The detective smiled and bowed.


At the recommendation of Reverend Hoyt, Lola went to see Dr. Hugh McKune, the head of Bellevue Hospital's Internal Medicine Department, a powerfully built man with short cropped gray hair and a cigar clenched between two rows of straight white teeth. He took the cigar offered by Lola and put it in his shirt pocket. "I'll enjoy this later," he said. "Countess, at present syphilis is incurable. That may change with advances in medicine."

"Where are the most promising experiments being done?" Lola asked. "I'll go anywhere in the world."

"It's too late. The disease and mercury treatments have done their damage."

"Can the effects be reversed?"

"The human brain remains a mystery to the world. Every person has one, but we know little about it."

"Are you saying my brain is addled?"

"Manual dexterity tests indicate that your short term memory is affected."

"How so?"

"You forget recent events, and hallucinate."

"My Nanny always said I would lose my head if it wasn't stuck onto my neck."

"Interesting you should mention your Nanny. Manuela is her name?"

"Yes. She was my real mother. My birth mother was very young, and saw me as a competitor for the attention of younger men."

"You recently received a letter from Manuela?"

"How do you know that?"

"You told me."

"I did no such thing."

"Then how do I know Manuela has her first great grandchild? You told me."

Lola was stunned into silence. She stood, started to turn away. Doctor McKune stopped her by saying, "You revealed that a man from upstate New York proposed marriage. Is that true?"

"Yes, it is."

"I think it proper you inform him of your medical condition."

"I cannot think of him now. And you have no place giving me personal advice. You say I'm losing my mind, but that is all I have left. The young men no longer turn their heads when I pass." Lola looked at him with tear-filled blue eyes that once stopped men at twenty feet, and she wailed, "What am I to do?"

"Accept growing old gracefully," Dr. McKune said, and offered his handkerchief. "For your mental deterioration, you might consider a live-in caretaker. If this is not possible, seek out friends to be your advisors. Discuss with them what you intend doing before you do it. Most of all, listen to them—especially when you believe they are completely and inexplicably wrong."

Lola put the doctor's handkerchief back into his

hand, took her umbrella from the stand in the corner of the room, opened the office door and said, "Since I paid for your advice, I will now tell you where you can shove it."

"That won't be necessary, Countess." Dr. McKune shook his head. "Sadly, many others have already rec-ommended that storage area."

Lola stormed out of the hospital. On the carriage ride to her rooms she tested her memory by naming places and streets before she reached them. Convinced that Dr. McKune was a bigger charlatan than the spirit-ualist she would meet tonight, Lola prepared for the séance. It would be just her and Miss Rosemary Bory.

Miss Bory had a healthy blush of beauty to her fair skin. Her features were so much like the spiritualist, Leslie Hogan, that she could have been mistaken for her younger sister. The spiritualist was modestly dressed, and met Lola's eyes with open frankness. She helped Lola arrange a small pie-top table between them, with chairs facing each other, and an oil lantern in the center of the table. All other lights were extinguished and Miss Bory asked, "Is there someone specific you wish to contact who has crossed over?"

"Yes," Lola answered.

"Please give me the name."

"Manuela."

"This is a woman?"

"Yes."

"Does she have a last name?"

"Not that I know of. She was a slave, and my Nan-ny."

"Countess, you do understand that people on the other side are always learning. They dislike interruptions for frivolous questions."

"I do not speak lightheartedly. I wish her advice on my future."

"You are asking her to be your guide?"

"Yes."

"Then let us begin. Put your hands in mine. Close your eyes and envision Manuela as you last saw her."

Lola felt the woman's hands tremble but said nothing. Miss Bory released her grip on Lola's hands and said, "There are several spirits who wish to come forth." The spiritualist opened her mouth and a man's voice echoed above Lola's head asking. "Who is it you wish to speak with?"

Using her best stage presence Lola gasped, "Manuela. I require her guidance."

"In the realm of spirits there are no slaves," the voice said. "Her soul is free to accept or reject your invitation."

"I ask her as a friend."

"Manuela!" The male voice called out. "Manuela, will you come forward?" Lola felt a breeze on her legs. The spiritualist said, "A woman is stepping forward. Her image is not clear. She may be wearing a Spanish dress, and her hair is upswept, held by a tortoiseshell comb."

"Oh Manuela!" Lola cried, "How can you be in the spirit world, when you're very much alive?" Lola saw Miss Bory go pale, but she continued. "Manuela asks about your health."

Lola replied in Hindi.

Miss Bory said, "I am not familiar with this language."

"But Manuela is."

"Place your hands above the table," the spiritualist whispered. "Manuela, if you can hear and understand me, please raise this table and knock once." The table shuddered, then levitated. One leg banged the floor. Miss Bory said, "Countess, Manuela is so very pleased to see you. You may ask questions requiring yes or no answers."

"How can she communicate as a spirit when she is not dead?"

"Countess!" Rosemary Bory snapped. "If you are trying to trick me, I will leave now. When was the last time you heard from Manuela?"

I received a letter two days ago."

"How long ago was it sent?"

"It took a month to reach New York from Calcutta."

"Then I am sorry to inform you that your former Nanny is dead."

Lola slammed her hands on the table top, and Miss Bory arms were jerked downward. Her hands came up, revealing two pieces of metal under her sleeves.

"You," Lola pointed, "Are going to jail."

"The hell I am!" Miss Bory shouted. She pulled the metal bar from its harness on her arm and lunged at Lola. It missed Lola's face by a fraction of an inch. Lola fired her weapon into the tabletop between them, then pointed the revolver at the young woman, saying, "I'm an excellent pistoleer. At this range I could take out both your eyes."

"Why would you kill me?"

"For trying to kill me."

"Your word against mine. We are not in Europe where titles tip the scales of justice."

"You are a clever little girl."

"Clever enough to know that I cannot prove the spirit world in a courtroom, nor can you disprove it. I did not ask you for money or investments or jewelry. What will be your complaint to the police? That I told you fantastic stories? It will take a month to send a letter to this Manuela and another month to receive an answer. By that time I will be gone."

"Then go now!" Lola said. "If you come near me again I will shove this pistol up your arse and pull the trigger."

Rosemary Bory left, quickly. Lola collapsed in her chair and covered her eyes wondering where she could attain spiritual advice.

The one name that came to mind was The Church of Good Hope.

# CHAPTER 16

## LECTURES

Lola recalled Nanny Manuela saying, "Every problem presents an opportunity", yet after hearing Reverend Ralph Hoyt's problem, she found no opportunity. The Presbyterian Minister offered no solution. The Lecture was due to take place on October thirteenth, its title, "Roman Catholicism".

Reverend Hoyt advertised the upcoming event beyond the confines of Yorkville. Objections came in letters to the editors, then full-blown articles by respected church people. They opposed help from someone as disreputable as Lola Montez. The Episcopal Bishop forbade Reverend Hoyt to accept Lola's aid. Reverend Hoyt apologized to Lola. Her detractors did not offer to help fund repairs to the church.

This reaction started a fire in her belly that swept upward, igniting her heart. She slammed her fist into the palm of her hand and said, "These Holy Rollers have no idea who they are dealing with! I am Lola Montez, Countess of Landsfeld." She pointed at Reverend Hoyt and said, "I'm going to war with your Bishop."

The moment Lola sat down at her writing desk she was back in her own element. She selected religious newspapers, and those for the general public whose editors she knew. The essence of Lola's letters was simple:

"The idea of a clergyman in the selfish times we live in, giving food and clothes to the freezing and starving, instead of "feasting" them on "tracts" struck me as being most unheard-of conduct in a minister, and I felt a strong desire to give my mite and help to rebuild a church which is to be used for a very novel but true Christian purpose. Nor did I for a moment imagine that there was to be found even in the benighted regions of clerical bigotry and intolerance, one so stupid and so shameless as to find fault with a truly philanthropic clergyman (Reverend Ralph Hoyt of the House of Good Shepherds) for his willingness to receive a donation from me to feed and instruct the poor. I did remember that it was the doctors of theology and the pious folk who crucified the Master... But I am content to leave it to the thinking minds to say who the better Christian is, myself, or the cold-hearted Pharisee who would crush me or anyone else for doing good... And, to my lecture on Rome, I shall add a postscript in relation to anti-Christian and anti-American bigotry and intolerance, which may, also, as it appears, be used to rob the poor and divest man of his natural rights."

The secular and religious press carried Lola's message on their front page. A tidal wave of support for Lola and repair of the church erupted. The pious and the populace spoke out for her and the charity. Pressure mounted on the Presbyterian Bishop. He withdrew his objection, and the lecture went on as scheduled. It was well attended, and the financial goal to repair the building was surpassed before Lola started speaking. The Good Shepherds could again feed the hungry and clothe the poor of Yorkville.

With her lecture on Romanism, Lola gave up all pretense of being Catholic. She dropped her Spanish-accented English. Her clothing was more in keeping with a Methodist Church lady, and her tone of voice modulated to propriety.

Several newspapermen commented in their columns that the voice of the former danseuse was a source of pleasure. Her unique command of the English language more sophisticated, eloquent, and delivered with proper motions, enhancing the content and making a lasting impression on the audience.

They claimed her lecture was not a direct attack on the Catholic Church, but rather an oblique foray into the negative aspects of Roman Catholicism on the Protestant public. She accomplished this by comparing and contrasting Protestant communities in Prussia and the Cantons of Switzerland with those Catholics in Austria and Switzerland. In Catholic areas, she noted, education was restricted to the clergy and wealthy. Without education there could be no strong middle class. Lola claimed these Catholic communities were socially, economically, and educationally retarded—and they would remain so while under Pontifical rule.

The Countess said the industrial revolution required a minimum of seven years education in reading, writing, and arithmetic. She chose these geographical locations because the people came from the same biological stock, lived on similarly fertile earth, enjoyed or suffered from the same weather conditions—yet the Protestants had a higher standard of living and education, and longer lifespan, than Catholics.

A widely-reprinted article read:

> "The countess advises those of us who travel to Catholic countries such as Spain, Italy and South America to stand on a mountaintop and view the cities and towns below. You will always see a large beautiful church, with a golden dome, surrounded by squalid huts and shacks of the uneducated. For Catholicism to thrive, the people must remain ignorant. They do not learn Latin, therefore have no idea what is being said at Mass. Most people in these countries cannot read or write. They receive oral instructions and believe the trustworthiness of the Pope and his priestly representatives was bestowed by the Master; that the Roman Catholic Church has never erred, nor will it err to all eternity.

> "This is not true, Lola says. In the year 1087, Pope Gregory VII forbade anyone from judging the Pope. The countess pointed out that when a law forbids something it means it was taking place and should stop. Churchmen did and still do question the Pope. At this time in the Vatican there is a movement to make the Pontiff absolutely infallible. This will not happen so quickly. There remain men with

common sense among the cardinals and bishops who refuse to relinquish absolute power to the Pontiff. Yet most Catholics believe a directive from the Holy See is irrefutable. It is not. About six hundred years ago the Pope wished to help the fishmongers of Italy. He made eating fish on Friday and during Lent a religious obligation. The fishmongers were happy. The fish were not. Lola says, 'for most Roman Catholics, the Bishop of Rome is the preserver of apostolic truth. No one can supersede him. Nor can they question his decisions. The Pontiff is now working on making himself infallible. It will take a few years until the older Cardinals and Bishops die off.'

"America does not yet recognize how much she owes to the Protestant principle. It has given the world the four greatest facts of modern times, steam-boats, railroads, telegraphs, and the American Republic!"[39]

Other descriptions of Lola's presentation were more academic. Audiences attended expecting to hear a fire-and-brimstone speech from the first lady of stage; they were treated to a beautiful woman, forty years of age, dressed modestly without dagger, whip or pistol, carrying an American flag in one hand and a Bible in the other.

"As an actress it was her beauty and movement that

---

[39] *Autobiography of Lola Montez*, Lecture on Romanism, p. 292.

captured one's attention. Now her voice dominates. The beauty remains and the eloquent gestures emphasize the words. Lola Montez's diction is flawless, her phrasing as eloquent as to overpower the audience's common sense. On one hand she deplores the artifices utilized by the Church fathers and then extols the use of a woman's sexual appeal to men to attain their rightful place in society.

"All things considered, the Countess of Landsfeld gave the audience their money's worth. P.T. Barnum who was attracting crowds opposite Miss Montez, has a formidable competitor for public attention. The following are lectures scheduled by Lola Montez, the Countess of Landsfeld:

"'Beautiful Women', 'Gallantry', 'Heroines of History', 'The Comic Aspect of Love', 'Wits and Women of Paris', and 'Romanism'. Any dullness of academic facts are colored by the eloquent presentation. A flash here and there of Lola's personal reminiscence enlivened her speech. But the volcanic personality that once ruled American theater is not to be found in these lectures. And although no one would say so, I believe everyone came to hear the more saucy aspects of Lola's life as a courtesan in Europe. A more chastened church lady you cannot find. The Countess of Landsfeld is no longer the quick-tempered figure she once was. As a moralist this is a good thing. As a hedonist...? She is still controversial and draws a crowd. Lola gives the audience their money's worth."

Lola began her lecture tour from New York, to Washington and up into New England. Chauncey Burr and his wife accompanied her as manager and advisor.

The tour was a financial success, the audiences appreciative, the Burrs competent, efficient. and patient with Lola. No longer did Lola rant and rave, but she often forgot. On occasion she misremembered. The Burrs put this up to the strain Lola was under. In addition to her public speaking, she promised a publisher to produce an autobiography, with her lectures included.

Lola never lost her fastidious work ethic, rising early, exercising, and writing five hours a day. She had lapses in her health and returned to Dr. McKune, who was pleased to hear of Mr. and Mrs. Burr and a lady from the Church of the Good Shepherds named Mrs. Buchanan, who helped and advised Lola. When he questioned as to her wedding plans she appeared confused. Only when the doctor mentioned, "The Gentleman from upstate New York," did Lola's face brighten and she said, "We are to be married in Paris. I shall be leaving soon for France."

Dr. McKune refused to accept a fee, saying, "You disregarded my advice last visit. I expect you will do so this time."

"Correct on both counts," Lola replied, "But I understand you help feed the poor at the back entrance to Bellevue Hospital. Please accept this token of my gratitude to your charity." She placed a purse in the doctor's hand.

He smiled and said, "Countess, whatever they may write about you, in my thoughts you are a real human being. Don't overwork yourself; physical stress increases mental strain."

Lola revised her lectures to include her former lover, King Ludwig of Bavaria. She claimed he was one of the finest poets in Europe, a very clever and brave leader in war and in peace. He had immersed himself in the art of Italy and Spain, and established Munich as the cultural capital of Europe.

It was after the first presentation of this revised lecture that the following article appeared in the *Philadelphia Press:*

> "We have to state with much gratification, that this is the close of Madam Lola Montez's career as a public lecturer. We break no confidence and do not intrude on the secrecy of private life by mentioning that this fair and gifted woman is on the eve of a very brilliant matrimonial alliance. She proposes in ten days from this time to be en-route to Paris. Her return to America may be expected in the spring."

The Burrs were shocked. They questioned Lola about the upcoming marriage. She revealed the bridegroom to be the Austrian, Prince Johann Sulkowski, whom she had met thirteen years ago in Berlin. Lola never mentioned having seen him since.

The Burrs and Mrs. Buchanan questioned why she had not shared this wonderful news with them. Her answers were evasive; her directions were specific. The Burrs could accompany her and she would pay their fare to France. They would make all traveling arrangements. The wedding would be organized by the Prince who was already in Paris.

"Where does the Prince live?" Herman Burr asked Lola.

"At present Prince Sulkowski has a home and commercial farm in upstate New York. He fled the 1848 revolution in Austria. He is there now reclaiming his European estates."

The Burrs and Mrs. Buchanan tried to question Lola further, but she was evasive and claimed to be busy meeting a publishing deadline for her autobiography.

One bright cub reporter for the *New York Times* buttonholed Lola on the street and asked, "Countess, your second husband James Heald is dead, but your first husband Captain James is very much alive, so how can you marry again?"

"Young man," she replied coolly, "My first marriage was forced by my mother. I was very young, and it is not accepted as legal in England." Lola used the tip of her parasol to take off the young man's bowler hat and fling it into the middle of the rutted street. She walked off without another word.

# CHAPTER 17

## THE WEDDING

***December 12th 1857:***

Lola and her entourage sailed from New York on the steamer the *Robert Fulton*. She arrived in the Port of Le Havre on Christmas day. The Prince was nowhere to be found.

Inquiries were made. Lola employed a French private detective agency, retired to her hotel room, and locked herself in. The Burrs were charged with receiving the investigators' reports and keeping newspapermen from her door. Lola ignored invitations from Victor Hugo, Alexander Dumas, George Sand, and other old friends of importance. The headlines of Europe's journals appeared in extra-large type: "COUNTESS OF LANDSFELD JILTED".

The private detective agency gave a full written report to the Burrs. They in turn summarized it for Lola. Herman Burr said, "Prince Johann Sulkowski does exist. He lives in Lewis County, upstate New York."

"Of course he exists!" Lola exploded. "Why the hell would I travel all the way to France if he didn't?"

"You never told us about your meeting with Dr Hugh McKune of Bellevue Hospital?"

"Because it was no one else's business. How did you find out?"

"Pinkerton in New York was engaged by your French detectives. They spoke with Dr McKune. He did not divulge your medical records but..."

"But what?" Lola demanded.

"The doctor questioned you about this marriage to Prince Sulkowski. He felt, at the time, you could be hallucinating."

"Hallucinating! Hallucinating?! That mustachioed lying bastard of a Prince got down on one royal knee, took my hand in both of his and proposed marriage. He begged me to marry him!"

"When did this happen?" Burr asked.

"About two months ago."

The Burrs looked at each other and Frieda burst out crying. Lola went to comfort her and offered her handkerchief. "What is wrong?"

The woman pointed to her husband. Herman Burr said, "The Prince, his wife, and their five children have been touring the Southern states for the winter. At about the time you say he proposed, they were in Atlanta, Georgia."

"What on earth were they doing down there?" Lola demanded.

"Many businessmen are going south," Burr said. They wish to finalize contracts before the upcoming war. Prince Sulkowski ships train loads of apples every year."

"You say he is married?"

"With five children."

"That despicable cad!" Lola shouted.

Now Frieda Burr went to Lola and said, "We know you stopped taking the mercury medication. We know what it was for. The combination of the disease and the harmful medicine has caused you memory loss and infrequent hallucinations. Dr. McKune explained it to you. That is why Herman and I are in your employ. To advise you."

Now Lola wept and Frieda comforted her. Herman left the room. Sometime later Lola sent Frieda away. She pulled up a chair in front of a full-length mirror and sat looking at herself, thinking, "If this is to be my life, and I won't know fact from fantasy, what is there to live for? There are enough detractors to make fun of me without reason. Now I will be portrayed as the village idiot. Imagine their glee when they find out."

She continued to stare at her image in the mirror. Then she stood, walked stiff-legged to her vanity and took a beautiful redwood case from the drawer. She opened it. Inside there was one Navy Colt pistol and an empty place for another one. She had given it the other to the Maharaja of Nepal. She took one bullet from the case, inserted it into the cylinder, stepped back in front of the mirror and played the game the Czar's Cossacks showed her. She spun the pistol's cylinder several times and put the muzzle to her temple.

"Old girl," she said to her mirrored image. "Now you will find out the truth: heaven or hell." She squeezed the trigger—and the hammer snapped on an empty cylinder. Lola broke out in a sweat. She patted her face dry, returned to the vanity, inserted another bullet, went to the mirror and repeated the exercise. The hammer slammed down—on an empty cylinder.

Lola trembled. The sweat caused her make-up to run. She began to giggle. She looked upward and said,

"God, am I that bad you won't even send me to hell?" Faced with her own image and silence from the mirror, she stepped unsteadily back to the vanity. With shaking hands and numb fingers she loaded a third bullet in the six-chamber cylinder, and snapped it closed. She spun the cylinder several times, put the muzzle to her head, and jerked the trigger. It snapped on an empty chamber—and Lola passed out. The weapon dropped, hit the floor—and fired.

The sound brought the Burrs and hotel staff. Herman Burr assessed the situation and dismissed the staff, cautioning them to remain silent. Rather than call a doctor, he and Frieda attended to Lola.

When she regained consciousness, Lola admitted to the suicide attempt. Burr explained that the pistol fired when she dropped it, Lola went white. Her pale lips trembled. At first she couldn't speak. She eventually composed herself and explained. "This pistol was one of a set given me as a personal gift by the Colt Gun company. It is one of the finest weapons ever crafted. *It never misfires.*"

"It only misfired because you dropped it," Herman Burr said.

"I am an expert pistoleer," Lola said. "For this weapon to have fired by being dropped it would have had to rotate to the next cylinder. That is impossible. What happened is called a 'hang fire'. The hammer strikes the shell casing but it does not ignite the gun powder – not right away. After a second it fires. I should be dead."

"What does it mean?" Frieda asked.

Lola gathered the Burrs to her and kissed them saying, "It means Jesus Christ wants me where I am, as I am, and to continue my lectures." Lola's face glowed, her blue eyes sparkled. "Can you arrange a lecture tour for me?"

"I don't have connections here in France, but I will book appearances in England."

"I would like to return to the land of my birth," Lola said. "Do you have contacts in Ireland?"

"Many," Herman answered. "Then Ireland it is. But I must think of something to tell the press about the wedding."

"I will take care of that," Lola said.

"What will you say?" Frieda asked.

"The truth," Lola said. "It's about time I started revealing the facts. I am now confident that Jesus has chosen me to spread his word."

Lola wrote a letter for the newspapers, and incorporated her explanation about the failed nuptial with Prince Sulkowski into her lectures:

> "It is one of the romances of life that after so many years, the Prince should in this far-off Republican land seek and obtain the promise of the hand of one who had seen enough of the vices of nobility to have reasonably disenchanted her of all the baubles of honor. But every woman has the right to be a little foolish on that subject of marriage and Lola Montez, (I hope she will forgive me for telling family secrets) did engage herself to marry Prince Sulkowski; but alas for constancy, or in-constancy, of human love, whilst the

Noble Prince was furiously telegraphing kisses three times a day to his affianced bride, he was merrily traveling through the South with a celebrated singer. Putting his own name and title in his pocket and conveniently assuming that of the Prima Donna, they booking themselves as plain Mr. and Mrs.—at hotels."[40]

This letter by Lola disturbed the Burr's. It was written in the third person about herself, but since Lola's behavior was otherwise exemplary and her outlook on the future positive, they said nothing. Herman used his friends and business acquaintances in Ireland to schedule the lectures. They arrived in Galway, aboard the American steamer, *Pacific.*

It was twenty-five years since she had left Ireland as the fifteen-year-old bride of ensign Heald. The Irish came out in the hundreds to see her. It promised to be a highly profitable tour.

One bump on this road of re-acquaintance with her country of birth was an article in Dublin's, *Daily Express.* The editor revealed that Lola was born Eliza Gilbert, in County Limerick, Ireland. In fact this was no startling revelation, as Lola had now dropped any pretense of Spanish birth. She continued to claim her mother was of royal Spanish blood, but from the survivors of the Spanish Armada washed up on Ireland's coastline in fifteen-eighty-eight. Lola did take umbrage at aspersions of her character as courtesan to Alexander

---

[40] Autobiography of Lola Montez

Dujarier, French newspaper owner/editor, and King Ludwig of Bavaria.

Lola wrote a rebuttal to the newspapers claiming to have been engaged to Dujarier, and that she was a platonic friend, confidant, and political advisor to King Ludwig. She quoted the monarch as saying, "If you wore trousers you would be one of my cabinet members. The world is not yet ready for a woman finance minister." She claimed a close friendship with Ludwig's wife, the Queen. Lola claimed that the Queen wept when she was forced to leave Bavaria.

Rebuttals came fast and furious, many from eyewitnesses to the aforementioned events. Especially were the comments harsh about Lola's description of her friendship with Ludwig's wife, the Queen. As in the past, Lola's written response to the journals evoked an outpouring of supporters and detractors, all of whom increased her notoriety in the public eye. It assured sold-out lectures.

Lola was intelligent enough not to attack the Jesuits in Ireland, and they in turn ignored her.

Writer Mary Clemmer Ames of the *Independent Newspaper* reviewed Lola's lecture on The English Character, John Bull. She wrote, "Not an element of popularity was missing in this lecture. Wit, satire, sarcasm double-edged yet sheathed in smiles, history, politics, religion; quotations from Scripture; anecdotes of society, all followed each other in brilliant succession. She mixed in her careless gossip a strange quantity of sagacious thought, and of earnest humane reflection. Rarely a man, and very rarely a woman, holds so complete control over the modulation of voice as did Lola.

Ever changing, her intonations were perfect and sweet as they were infinite. In her physique, in the perfect abandon of her manner, in her voice, were hidden the secrets of her power. The rest was centered in her head, rather than in her heart. She had a most subtle perception of character, a crystal intellect and any quantity of sangfroid. The delicate skill with which she played upon that harp of many strings, a popular audience, proved her to be the natural diplomat. She carried the audience with her completely; and when at last the velvet robe, the laces, the bouquet of radiant flowers, and rarely radiant face made their curtsying exit it was amid the most enthusiastic applause."[41]

Lola's most successful lecture was titled: "The Art of Beauty, or, Secrets of a Lady's Toilet, with Hints to Gentlemen on the Art of Fascinating". Lola submitted this and two other lectures for publication prior to leaving New York. By the time she reached Ireland, the original printing sold out. It went to a second edition.

Although not a vegetarian like the acclaimed Reverend Sylvester Graham, an American dietary reformer and inventor of the Graham Cracker, Lola recommended moderation in eating: no fried foods, fresh fruits and vegetables, avoidance of whatever is unnatural. Also, avoid most commercially prepared cosmetics. She supplied her own formulas for skin creams, hair washes, and waxes for hair removal. She stressed abundant sleep, fresh air, and exercise. Most of all she emphasized hygiene, using John Wesley's quote, "Cleanliness is next to Godliness." She also provided her own formu-

---

[41] *Lola Montez*, James Morton, P 312-313

la for tooth powder, and recommended brushing after each meal.

Lola's fifty recommendations to men were in the negative, what they shouldn't do to win a fair lady. She informed her female readers and audiences that men were as fastidious as women in their preparation to rendezvous. "Women," Lola said, "Should be like a hackney cab. Let the men chase you until you catch them."

Lola appeared in Dublin's Round Room, and in addition to her lecture, she responded to several newspaper articles claiming her relationship with King Ludwig was immoral and she should be condemned. Lola answered: "I will not and do not reply, it being my determination to patiently leave the events of my life to history, which I leave my calumniators to that God who has ordained an especial act of punishment for "all liars "and who will I fear, find the next world a good deal hotter than they have made this one for me..."[42]

The audience was so large, and so many were seated on the stage of the Round Room Rotunda, Lola had little place to stand. Her monologue on the American character was well received. She claimed that American men were not half as romantic as Englishmen. The Americans were more interested in money than sex, and the United States would continue accepting immigrants until they were overrun.

"The Americans had not learned how to accommodate foreigners, who even in their second generation call themselves Irish Americans, Italian and German Ameri-

---

[42] *Lola Montez*, Bruce Seymour, P 378

cans. There is bound to be a race war. The United States will soon become an anarchy; just look at bloody Kansas, and other states with their Vigilance Committees. I have been confided in by men of power and wealth who will support a Constitutional Monarchy in America. Most people are unaware that a powerful lobby tried to confirm George Washington as King of America. He would have none of it. He, like this Abraham Lincoln of Illinois, was a constitutionalist. I was approached to become Queen of California. I gave an emphatic no as my answer. You see, I believe in Government by the people and for the people. But which people? To say everyone is born equal is rubbish. Some are stronger, weaker, more intellectual and creative than others. Equality does exist in the United States. The determination of who is more equal than others depends on the amount of money in your pocket. Not everyone has freedom. To vote in America you must be a freeman and landowner and have the money to pay a poll tax. It is not your ancestry in America that determines your status. It is money. This makes America the most dynamic country in the world. Everything is based on speed and price. We call it the New World. And it is. Most of the country's interior has yet to be mapped or surveyed. Railroads stretch out along the coast. Steamboats ply the rivers. Most every state capital in the United States is located on a river. There are few paths through the wilderness. The distances are too great. The one state of Idaho is larger than Ireland, England, Scotland and Wales combined. Thirteen years ago the state of Texas entered the Union. The entire republic of France could fit inside Texas with ten thousand square miles to spare. The native inhabitants are stone-age people who have no concept of land ownership or forging metal. Americans take advantage of the Indians. The United States would do well to learn from English law in Canada, how to treat its native population.

"Hard working immigrants who venture out past the borders of Kentucky and Kansas into the continent's interior can make their fortune. They will have to work for it. But it is possible. Respect is gained by making money."

Lola gave two more lectures in Dublin. She lectured twice in Cork and in Limerick. The Burrs booked her for Belfast and Waterford, but she was exhausted. Later, she drew full houses in Glasgow, Edinburgh, and Sunderland. Her health returned, and she sailed for England.

On her forty-first birthday, February 14th 1859, Lola spoke in Manchester. Then she went on to Sheffield, Nottingham, Leicester, Birmingham, Wolverhampton, Lamington, Worcester, Bristol, and Bath. With tickets at a premium, she had full houses. Lola outdrew Charles Dickens and charged three shillings, while Dickens charged only two. The press was quite favorable, the only complaint being that her lectures were too short.

Lola lost none of her spirit. On occasion she stopped her lecture to reprimand a boisterous patron or silence a talkative person. The London press and public received her with open arms. She spoke to overflow crowds, and received substantial financial rewards.

Lola in turn donated considerable sums to charities. She gave on the condition that the recipients of her largess be unaware of where the money came from. This was consistent with her recent concept of *"Imitatio Dei,"* the imitation of God. Lola now firmly believed that since God created everything and gave it to mankind to care for, the way for humanity to thank God was to imitate Him: give without the will to receive. After several months of touring and lecturing, she rested with friends in London on Weymouth Street. Her friends quoted excerpts from her letters that revealed her new spiritual nature:

"Oh blessed be God's holy name forever. I have found what nothing else can be compared to, what no one can give either by sympathetic advice or kind words. That the love of God was so great to the most depraved sinners that he gave his Son, His divine Humanity, that He might come into the world and take all sin from the world and die for us, that through his death we may have eternal life... Think what a sinner I was, how impossible it once seemed to me to become better, and it is only by His constant care and love and by my fervor and sincerity of heart that He has accomplished this miracle... I am a frail sinner in myself. I only breathe truth and peace because I prayed Jesus to come and dwell in my heart. I feel very humble. I have myself renounced much money and am poor as far as money goes. I did the right thing for the love of my God."[43]

Lola's dedication to religion and truth played on the background of a lifetime of ignoring the truth, lying, and verbal bullying. Combined with the effects of her illness, she sometimes disregarded reality, even in the most absurd situations.

---

[43] *Lola Montez*, Bruce Seymour, P 382

In one case, at one of her evening soirees, Lola said that a good friend of hers lost his leg in a battle with the Zulu in Africa. The man's sister was present and informed Lola that it was a carriage accident that took place in Calais. Lola remained adamant that her version was correct. The sister took offense, and Lola shouted her down and out of her suite. The Burrs put this up to hallucinations, but it was a remnant of the old Lola; she had to be right.

After her final lecture in London, the Burrs amicably settled accounts with Lola. They returned to attend family matters in America, but Lola decided to remain in London. The final bit of advice the Burrs rendered cautioned Lola not to lease a furnished home in Mayfair, at 26 Park Lane. Lola wanted to rent rooms to fashionable guests and insure a steady income while continuing to explore religion and do charitable works.

"Lola," Herman Burr said, "You are not a well woman."

"I will only take in proper ladies and gentlemen, and hire housekeepers to do the work."

"You must pay the help, supervise them, and discharge them when called for. It can be a daunting task."

"I see the future perfectly in my mind," Lola said. "You two return to the land of opportunity, and give my love to our mutual friends in New York, especially Mrs. Buchanan. I will be quite well here in London. God also visits England. He will see that I am taken care of in my retirement."

Lola purchased the lease.

# CHAPTER *18*

## RETURN TO AMERICA

From the beginning Lola's plans for the boarding house went awry. She calculated her success based on her public image. Lola believed her name and fame would draw a fashionable, wealthy clientele; from these she would select the cream of the crop. She envisioned hosting a salon for intellectuals, the affluent, and influential.

However, the Burrs' prediction proved accurate. People did not flock to 26 Park Lane. Lola's questionable reputation was a double-edged sword. Her style of management upset her patrons and antagonized the help; it entailed giving conflicting orders. Her forgetfulness resulted in confrontations with staff and guests. She lacked experience in house management. Arguments with employees were frequent and vitriolic. Some workers left.

Prominent boarders were not easily found. She couldn't pay her staff, and the workers took out liens against her property. To make good the debts, Lola arranged for two lectures. They were well attended, and to the audiences she appeared lucid and insightful.

These speeches took place prior to Lincoln's election as president. She correctly predicted the War Between the States; seven southern states, led by North Carolina, had already disavowed the union. "The south," she said,

"Has the true love of freedom. They desire state's rights. They do not want an imperial, federal autocracy governing their lives. On the other hand, the more numerous northern states have the wealth. Money will determine the outcome of this war. The north has the industrial infrastructure and sophisticated amalgamation of lines of communications and transportation: the telegraph and the railroads.

"The north and south both have their religious outlook on the union, but in the end, money will win. To you English traders in southern cotton, get as much yarn as you can before hostilities break out. The American Navy is certain to blockade the rebel ports. The south will lose, and the north will win—not only because of the money, larger population, and more developed manufacturing facilities, but because there are many good Christians in the south who know in their hearts that slavery is wrong.

"They may enlist in the Southern war effort, they may go to fight, but will know in their hearts, slavery is immoral. Immorality is not restricted to one people or nation. There is enough to go around. England has a good share of her own wickedness; I speak to those investors in Southern cotton. They pay silver and gold for the white fluffy stuff. Without that money, slavery in the United States would be finished. Fifty years ago these same English families voted to end slavery in Great Britain. Today they support slavery in America."

*The London Evening Journal* took offense. The rebuttal read: "For Lola Montez, The Countess of Landsfeld, to lecture the English on morality is the height of hypocrisy. The only reason people flock to her lectures is in hope they will hear some naughty tidbit about persons past and present. No doubt this woman is a talented presenter. Within five minutes of her speaking she holds the audience spellbound. Her physical presence, verbal presentation, diction, eloquent gestures and varied tone of voice is captivating. For me it matters not what she says, it is how she says it. But this woman is the last one who should be lecturing Englishmen on righteousness. Her principles were learned in the European, aristocratic, gutter. She throws enough dung against the walls of people's minds and some of it must stick."

In bygone days Lola would have exploded verbally, physically, and in writing a scathing letter to the editor. Now she looked outward to God and inward with Jesus.

While dealing with the problems of closing down the house and selling the leased property, Lola began a written account of her religious experience; "I found in God the love I once held for men. The perfectness of the invisible God cannot be faulted. The almighty entered my heart through Jesus. In my heart, wonder replaced disgust. The memories of my relations with men became abhorrent and translated into repentance for my sins. Christianity offers me new worlds for the old, promises new joys and zest for the old, and assures me and every human being of the tremendous importance of our own destiny.

"Oh, I dare not think of the past! What have I not been? I lived only for my own passions; and what is there of good even in the best natural human being? What would I not give to have my terrible and fearful experiences given as an awful warning to such natures as my own! And yet when many people, even my mother, turned their backs upon me and knew me not, Jesus knocked at my heart's door. What has the world ever given to me? (And I have known all that the world has to give—all!) Nothing but shadows, leaving a wound on the heart hard to heal—a dark discontent.

"Now I can more calmly look back on the stormy passages of my life—an eventful life indeed—and see onward and upward a haven of rest to the soul. I used once to think that heaven was a place somewhere beyond the clouds, and that those who got there were as if they had not been themselves on the earth. But life has been given to me to know that heaven begins in the human soul, through the grace of God and His holy word. Those who cannot feel somewhat of heaven here will never find it hereafter."

On another page she wrote: "Tomorrow (the Lord's day) is the day of peace and happiness. Once it seemed to me anything but a happy day, but now all is wonderfully changed in my heart... What I loved before now I hate. Oh! That in this coming week, I may, through Thee, overcome all sinful thoughts, and love everyone.

"Thankful I am that I have been permitted to pray this day. Not long ago I cried aloud in agony to be taken; and yet the great, All-Wise Creator has spared me, in His mercy, to repent. All that has passed in my life has not been mere illusion. I feel it is true. The Lord heard my feeble cry to Him, and I felt what no human tongue can describe. The world cast me out, and He, the pure, the loving, took me in.

"To-morrow is Sunday, and I shall go to the poor little humble chapel, and there will I mingle my prayers with the fervent pastor, and with the good and true. There is no pomp or ceremony among these. All is simple. No fine dresses, no worldly display, but the honest Methodist breathes forth a sincere prayer, and I feel much unity of soul. What would I give to have daily fellowship with these good people! To teach in the school, to visit the old, the sick, the poor. But that will be in the Lord's good time, when self is burned out of me completely."

The next entry was headed Saturday, in London:

"Since last week my existence is entirely changed. When last I wrote I was calm and peaceful—away from the world. Now, I must again go forth. It was cruel, indeed, of Mr. E. to have said what he did; but I am afraid I was too hasty also. Ought I to have resented what was said? No, I ought to have said not a word. The world would applaud me; but, oh! My heart tells me that for His sake I ought to bear the vilest reproaches, even unmerited.

"Good-bye, all the calm hours of reflection and repose I enjoyed at Derby! My calm days at the cottage are gone. But I will not look back. Onward! Must be the cry of my heart. "Lord, have mercy on the weary wanderer, and grant me all I beseech of Thee! Oh, give me a meek and lowly heart!"[44]

Lola was sued, her lease revoked, her furniture attached and she ended up on the street. An elderly couple from Derby, who enjoyed her lectures, took her in to their country estate.

---

[44] Abridged, from *Lola Montez*, Edmund B. d"Auvergne p. 223-226

There she recovered her health and determination to follow Jesus. She attended the Methodist church every Sunday.

She wrote in her diary, "I long to serve the Lord by visiting the sick, helping the elderly and feeding the poor. But alas, how many years of my life have been sacrificed to Satan and my own love of sin! What have I not been guilty of either in thought or in deed, during these years of misery and wretchedness...What would I not give to have my terrible and fearful experiences given as an awful warning to such natures as my own!..."[45]

Being alone in the sedate rural setting of Derby had its healing effects on Lola's body and soul, but her mind craved the intellectual excitement had found in New York. On October 4th 1859 Lola took the steamship *Hammonia* and arrived in New York 14 days later. She traveled as Mrs. Heald, but she retained American citizenship through her marriage to Patrick Hull.

She had forgotten how dynamic New York was. Old habits die slowly; Lola became caught up in the excitement. There appeared an article accusing Lola of degrading America in her talks overseas. She was criticized for claiming a civil war was imminent, and John Brown's raid on the Virginia Amory justified, and his call for Blacks to take up arms across the country was proof.

Lola automatically responded. She sent a rebuttal to the newspaper that very day. It drew enough attention that she was offered several opportunities to lecture. She

---

[45] *Lola Montez*, Bruce Seymour, P 385

demanded and received the largest percentage of the ticket sales. Three thousand people packed Mozart Hall on Broadway. One phrase from her speech that followed Lola for some time, was, "The soul of the negro I love, for the soul has no color."

The Burrs returned to manage Lola's career. From New York, to New Jersey, Philadelphia, Baltimore, Maryland and Washington D.C., she spoke to standing-room-only crowds. In Columbus, Ohio, St Louis, Missouri and Chicago, Illinois, despite bad weather people filled the auditoriums. The Burrs directed Lola north to Detroit, Toronto, Buffalo, Rochester and Albany.

It was the middle of April 1860 when Lola returned to New York City. The theater season and lecture circuit were coming to an end with the heat of summer, but Lola had earned enough money to support herself. Her health had suffered, and lapses in memory became more frequent. It frightened her.

Fear was a unique sensation for her; anxiety was not part of Lola's character. The problem was exacerbated when the Burrs, along with other staunch Republicans, relocated to Washington D. C. They intended to start a newspaper under the new Lincoln administration.

Lola decided to contact Mrs. Buchanan, who had been such a help in the restoration of the Church of the Good Shepherds.

Before she could do that, she was drawn into a court case as a witness for the defense. Her friend, Editor James Bennett of the *New York Herald*, was being sued by David Jobson, a self-proclaimed dentist, lawyer, and writer. Lola knew Jobson from her stay in Montrose, Scotland, and from her residence in Half Moon Street,

London. There he had proposed a business deal where he would write Lola's biography.

"At that time," Lola said, "Jobson represented himself as an attorney, which he was not. Of late my memory sometimes fails me, but on the subject of Mr. David Jobson, I can assure you I remember him as a liar who spent time in jail. He certainly was no lawyer. He did appear to make litigation his profession, in hopes that those he unjustly accused would pay to be rid of him as a nuisance."

Lola's court appearance caused a sensation and drew large crowds. The court clerks printed tickets and charged people to enter the courthouse or peer through the large windows. C.B. Schermerhorn acted as counsel for the plaintiff. He attempted to discredit Lola, but to no avail. She interrupted him and the judge so often the magistrate said, "Madam, will you please be quiet, so this court can proceed in a proper manner?"

She replied, "I cannot remain silent when my reputation is put into question by the likes of Shimmerhorn." She purposely mispronounced the lawyer's name. The audience laughed and applauded. Lola was performing once again, and those in the courtroom relished it. She bowed her head in acknowledgement.

Lawyer Schermerhorn asked, "Isn't it true that while in London Mr. Jobson provided you with a guinea to prevent you from being taken to the poorhouse?"

"No!" Lola replied, and pointed at Jobson. "That scoundrel never had two guineas, and he wouldn't part with his last one for me."

Lola was so disruptive, Schermerhorn threw up his hands in disgust. The audience cheered. The judge attempted to maintain order. Jobson exploded, and with riding crop in hand, he beat the lawyer for the defense and James Bennett about the head and shoulders.

He shouted at Lola. She shouted back. Exasperated at his inability to control the court—the police were outside collecting money for tickets—the judge slammed his gavel, dismissed the case, and fled the courtroom.

On the courthouse steps, Lola gave her admirers and reporters her own rendition of a ditty made popular by a prominent balladeer named Ives. She sang:

> "Lawyer Jobson says he studied law and he gave good advice,
>
> Up above the General Store he'd treat his neighbors nice,
>
> He was righteous in appearance and he looked just like a saint,
>
> Lawyer Jobson looked like one, but lawyer Jobson ain't.
>
> Beware! Beware Of lawyer Jobson! He'll take your teeth so you can't eat your dinner.
>
> He's a bad, badsome man!"

The Burrs had written to Mrs. Maria Buchanan asking her to look in on Lola. Mrs. Buchanan, the wife of New York's foremost florist, was preparing to do just that. She had met Lola when she spoke for the benefit of the Church of the Good Shepherds, but it was only during the Jobson trial—when Lola used her real name as

Gilbert and her married name of Heald—that Maria Buchanan remembered the girl with the fascinating blue eyes, striking beautiful features, and long jet black hair. Liza Gilbert was Maria Buchanan's classmate in the Scotland boarding school.

She met with Lola, and they shared memories of bygone days. Lola asked Maria if she remembered her actions on April Fool's Day. Maria blushed. "No one in school will ever forget. What made you do it?"

"I recall being very bored," Lola said. "It was market day, and the first of April, and I was tired of classes. I went to the market and stripped naked. Sure enough, nobody wanted to touch me or come near me. The policeman didn't know what to do. A fishmonger's wife wrapped me in burlap, and they hustled me back to school. What did the other girls think?"

"We thought you were crazy." The moment Maria uttered these words she covered her mouth and lowered her eyes.

Lola stretched out her hand and said, "If I wasn't then, I am close to it now." She looked across the table and said, "The Burrs wrote to me. I know I am ill. The problem is that I don't always know when."

They shared their memories, and then their passion for following the teachings of Christ and helping the poor. In an exchange of letters the Burrs had explained Lola's physical and mental condition to Maria Buchanan. Reluctantly Lola admitted to hallucinations and loss of memory.

The Buchanans convinced Lola to move to their summer home in Astoria, Brooklyn. The florist and his wife were not only religious, but truly good people; they made provision for Lola in their Astoria dwelling, so she had privacy but was under their watchful eye.

They made prudent investment of Lola's limited funds, so that Lola was enabled to follow the path of religious regeneration. Mrs. Buchanan attended Bible study and church service with Lola, where she was a member of the Episcopal Church of America.

She introduced Lola to Reverend Ralph Hoyt, and the two women directed their efforts to charitable works with the Reverend. Lola wrote and printed several pamphlets of her moralistic lectures, and would buttonhole people on the street and offer them a pamphlet. She stressed the necessity for attending church. She sometimes traveled to New York to promote Christianity. On these occasions Lola took the ferry across the East River, and remained overnight at a modest hotel.

One such evening in New York's theater district, Lola was talking to passersby and handing out her pamphlets when actor Charles Warwick, who had appeared with Lola in Grass Valley, California, recognized her. It was the end of March 1860, but Lola remembered him. He was shocked at her condition. Her cheeks were sunken, her speech perfect but sometimes wandered from the subject. Her hair had lost its sheen that highlighted her electric blue eyes. The eyes appeared even larger in her emaciated face, but still flashed their beauty. Her figure was just as attractive, and her dress modestly fashionable, in black from large hat to high-topped leather shoes.

He wrote a friend of the meeting, "She accepted my invitation to dine. Over good food and fine wine, we reminisced about times past in Grass Valley. Lola," he wrote, "Was evidently suffering from severe mental depression. After dinner we conversed about the theater and politics. I was forced to manipulate our talk around Lola's unrelated comments. She appeared not to notice the concern on my face, and continued to speak about subjects irrelevant to anything previously mentioned. A violent rainstorm pelted the New York streets. I volunteered to have a carriage brought round and take Lola to her hotel. She would not listen to my proposition, and insisted on walking to her hotel in the rain. I argued to no avail. She was elegantly dressed, and her large lace hat had only artificial flowers to protect her from the downpour. She had no umbrella. I sloshed through the puddles at her side. We were both soaked to the skin. Upon arrival at her hotel entrance she was a sight to behold. Her hat had degenerated into an unrecognizable pulp, while the colors of the variegated artificial flowers ran down her face in irregular streaks giving her the appearance of a Comanche chief on the warpath. As I left her in the doorway, I had tears in my eyes. There stood one of the most beautiful women in the world. The guests and employees in the lobby were laughing at her."[46]

Lola's troubled soul at last tasted a bit of peace—thanks, perhaps, as much to the consolations of true friendship with Reverend Hoyt and the Buchanans as to those of her new approach to religion. She left the Methodist Church, and embraced the less gloomy tenets of the Episcopal Church of America.

---

[46] Abridged: *Lola Montez.* James Morton P 314

Lola had periods of lucid thought. She devoted these times to copying a Christian creed and publishing it as her own writing.

## *"THE FIVE TENETS OF CHRISTIANITY*

"1. Read the Word

"Or at least hear God's Word. Romans 10:17 (NKJV-New King James Version) says, 'so then, faith comes by hearing, and hearing by the word of God. If no one had ever told me about Jesus, and about God's plan for my life, or if I had never read for myself about Him, I would be oblivious about the need for faith.

"Reading or hearing God's Word is like planting a garden. If you want to grow or 'build' a garden, you must first plant the seeds, or the actual plant or flower. God's Word is the seed that grows the faith. Knowing His promises, what God says about you, about life, and about Jesus" plan for eternal life won't transplant themselves into your brain by osmosis? Become familiar with the Bible and what faith is all about by meditating on its contents. This will give you the basis for growing or increasing your faith.

"2. Heed the Word

"James 1:22-24(NKJV) offers a second way to increase your faith: But be doers of the word, and not hearers only, deceiving yourselves. For if anyone is a hearer of the word and not a doer, he is like a man observing his natural face in a mirror; for he observes himself, goes away, and immediately forgets what kind of man he was. What I see in the mirror when I first wake up is not the most beautiful sight. Obviously I see there is work to do and makeup to apply if I want to add to my appearance.

"If we fail to heed what we're reading and ignore what God is telling us, then our faith grows stagnant. It took faith for us to become children of God in the first place. Therefore, in order to grow and increase our faith, we need to use that "measure" of faith God gives to everyone and build on it.

"3. Test the Word

"There is a difference in 'testing' God by 'contesting' Him (seeing how far God's patience will go with your own self will) and 'testing,' or proving God's Word is true. Malachi 3:9-11 (NIV) offers one practical way God says we can prove Him faithful to His Word. This passage concerns tithing and being good stewards of the things He has given us: 'Test me in this,' says the Lord Almighty, 'and see if I will not throw open the floodgates of heaven and pour out so much blessing that there will not be room enough to store it.' As you 'test' or act on what God says and experience God's blessing, your faith grows.

"The process of testing the measure of faith you have may involve trials and difficulties. How can you increase your faith in those circumstances? Consider it pure joy, my brothers and sisters, whenever you face trials of many kinds, because you know that the testing of your faith produces perseverance (James 1:2-3, NIV).

"A Personal Example

"The first time King Ludwig and Bavaria were financially challenged, we had several choices to make. The most important was, would we trust God and the promises we had read in His Word? When a new difficulty developed, we faced the same choices. If we chose to believe God, our faith grew a little more. Then the really big crises erupted.

"But each time we looked back and saw the tracks of God's faithfulness. He truly had kept His Word, and we came to understand the true meaning of "perseverance." Trusting Him with smaller problems has built our faith to believe Him for the more difficult issues. Yet, there are still times when I feel more like a baby in my faith than a giant. It's always in need of growing.

"My Prayer for You

"Lord Jesus, increase our faith as we learn to depend on You and trust You more and more. Help us to crave Your Word: to read it, to heed it, and to test it, so it can truly become part of our lives. We long to be doers and not just hearers. Lord, we desperately need more of You and less of ourselves. Thank You for Your faithfulness in always keeping Your Word. Lola Montez, Countess of Landsfeld".

# CHAPTER 19

## THE PENITENT

June 30th, 1860, Southern Democrats were clandestinely engineering a Lincoln, Republican win of the presidential election. They planned Lincoln's success to be the catalyst for the southern states withdrawing from the Union. The moment Lincoln was sworn into office eight Confederate states would secede.

Lola no longer read political, economic, or theatrical news. She subscribed to three religious papers and studied, preached the Bible in public, and attended church. It was a bright sunny day in Brooklyn when Lola left the Burr house for Prospect Park, there to preach. She had her pamphlets, and anticipated explaining the beauty of taking Jesus into one's heart.

A young couple crossed the street coming toward her. She recognized Minnie Follin. On Minnie's arm was a handsome young naval officer. Lola and Minnie had made up by mail some time before, and Minnie had described the young man from a prominent Boston family and asked Lola if she should accept his proposal of marriage. Lola approved. The couple married in upstate New York and honeymooned abroad.

"Minnie!" Lola cried and ran to embrace her, but the woman she hugged fell back in horror, saying, "Madam take your hands off me! You are mistaken. I am not the person you think I am."

"Minnie," Lola pleaded, "It's your Lola! We were sisters. I educated you, trained you, and introduced you to the professional theater. How can you deny me?"

"Madam, I deny any knowledge of you before, now, and certainly in the future."

"But Minnie, you wore my clothes, ate my food, lived in my home!" Lola turned to the naval officer. He shrugged, took the young woman's arm, and they walked away.

Lola stared after the couple and began to doubt herself. Could she be hallucinating? Certainly not: she had seen the look of recognition in Minnie's eyes the moment they saw each other. Lola gagged, and retched into the street.

She returned home, and told Maria Buchanan of the incident. Maria believed Lola was confused. "No," Isaac said, "She spoke to Minnie Montez, whose stage name is now Carolyn Follin. She is married to a naval officer."

"How can you be certain it was them?"

"I made up several congratulatory bouquets ordered by her admirers. They are staying at the nearby Regency Hotel. She and her husband just returned from their honeymoon."

Maria Buchanan held her head in her hands. "I don't know when Lola is telling the truth or not."

"Because Lola doesn't know either. Her lapses in memory are more frequent."

"I'd better look in on her."

Maria knocked on Lola's bedroom door, with no answer. She knocked again, and a third time. There was no sound from within. "Lola?" she called. "Lola! I am coming in."

She opened the door—and saw a pale white hand on the carpeted floor. She rushed in and lifted Lola's head.

The left side of Lola's face was distorted, and she drooled uncontrollably.

"Isaac! Isaac!" Mrs. Buchanan cried.


It was noon when the doctor completed his examination. He shared a cup of tea with the Buchanans, and advised them, "If there is family to be notified, now is the time. Mrs. Montez will not last the night."

"Her mother, Lady Craigie, is the only living relative," Maria said. "Lola despises her."

The doctor shrugged. "There must be friends and admirers."

Isaac Buchanan said, "I will use my office staff to inform the public."

He put out a statement to the newspapers that Lola was ill and not expected to live. English reporters sent word to London, but believing she would be dead by the time the ship reached England, they wrote of her passing. American reporters heard of the English newspaper obituary, and re-printed it in American papers.

Lola did not die that night. She had suffered a full left side stroke; her face, arm, and leg were paralyzed. She couldn't speak, and before the doctor finished his tea Lola slipped into a coma.

Maria Buchanan hired Margret Hamilton, a retired nurse, to care for Lola. The woman sat and slept at Lola's bedside, changed and bathed her.

The doctor was amazed to find Lola alive the next morning. The morning after that she came out of the coma. On July 4, eighty-four years since the signing of the Declaration of Independence, Lola uttered her first intelligible words: "Jesus loves me." They were spoken from disfigured, salivating lips, and difficult to understand, but when Maria Buchanan repeated the words Lola nodded agreement.

Lola's progress was slow but unswerving. The doctor received notoriety for saving his famous patient. Reporters questioned and quoted him every day. He gave his concentrated attention to Lola. With Nurse Margret's help, Lola began to mend and speak again. Her lifelong style of self-discipline, physically and spiritually, became assets to her recovery.

She and Nurse Margret allotted specific times for bodily and linguistic exercise. Together with Maria Buchanan they studied the Bible. Lola had the two women copy biblical passages to be hung around the room for inspiration.

One disruption to her recovery came when Mrs. Buchanan received a letter from Lady Craigie, Lola's mother, saying that she was making the trip from England to see her daughter. Lola became furious and tried to shout. Her words were garbled. She became more frustrated, until Maria Buchanan and Nurse Margret realized Lola was saying her mother was coming to bury her and take whatever inheritance there might be. Both women dismissed this—until two lawyers representing Lady Craigie appeared. They asked Lola to sign a five page document. She refused. After a cursory examination of the document, Mrs. Buchanan agreed with Lola. She ushered the men from her house.

"They wanted me to sign over all my properties to

my mother," Lola said. "That will not happen! Maria, Will your husband recommend a lawyer? I wish to leave three hundred dollars to the Church of the Good Shepherds, and the remainder to you and your family."

Because of the personal care and her indomitable will, Lola's progress exceeded the doctor's prognosis. Her memory did not improve, but her thoughts were lucid. At times the words she spoke came out in garbled patterns. By extreme concentration, persistent exercise, and slowing her speech, she overcame this.

There was nothing wrong with her right hand. She wrote to the newspapers: "To those wishful thinkers who had buried me and wept pools of tears over my passing, I apologize for disappointing you. The Lord in His mercy decided to punish you by allowing me to remain among the living a while longer. Some in this world wish to cast me out, but Jesus Christ took me in."

Impressed by Lola's religious fervor, Maria Buchanan and Nurse Margret invited Reverend Francis Hawks, New York's most popular preacher, to visit Lola. He was pleased to meet the renowned celebrity. She impressed him by insistence on discussing religion and the Bible rather than small talk. He became a regular visitor and consultant to Lola, and he and the three women formed a Bible study group.

He wrote to his Bishop, "The Countess of Landsfeld reads the blessed volume for herself, also, when I am not present. It is always within reach of her hand, and on my first visit when I took up her Bible from the table, the fact struck me that it opened of its own accord to the touching story of Christ's forgiveness of the Magdalene in the house of Simon. I spoke to her of Christ's gentle pity and pardon for this poor woman. 'Ah,' she replied, 'but he loved much. Can I love enough?'

"I am convinced that her repentance and return to Christ is genuine. In the course of long experience as a Christian minister I do not think I ever met a deeper penitence and humility, more real contrition of soul and more of bitter self-reproach than in this poor woman."[47]

As Lola's rehabilitation progressed, so did her thoughts. Her ideas outpaced her physical limitations. Nurse Margaret recognized this as a serious frustration, even as Lola repeated her Nanny's proverb, "Every problem provides an opportunity".

Lola now walked with the aid of a cane. The day she decided to stroll unescorted, Nurse Margret suggested Lola volunteer at the Magdalene Asylum for Women on Fifth Avenue and Eighty-Eighth Street in New York. To each objection Lola raised, Maria Buchanan and Nurse Margaret gave an answer. Reverend Hawks thought the idea brilliant.

"You will move into the Buchanan home in New York, with your own room and toilet, and be within walking distance of the Asylum. What more could you ask but to serve Christ in this manner?"

Lola stood before a full-length mirror and cried, "Look at me! My hair is a mess, my face deformed, I limp, and my left arm is useless."

"You are getting better," Maria Buchanan said. "You need to exercise your mind as well as your body. You

---

[47] *Lola Montez*, James Morton, P 316-317

survived what most of those poor girls are suffering. You can help them find a path to our Lord."

"Isn't the Asylum for the insane?" Lola asked.

"And wayward women?" Nurse Margaret said.

"One look at me and the Staff will think I'm an inmate."

"That is why we wish you to go," Reverend Hawks said. "Without the help of Jesus, you might be one of the internees. Think of it. You experienced what many of these women are now suffering, and you found your way out. Share your revelation with them."

"No," Lola said, "Jesus came into my heart. He guided me out of that world."

"Then open the hearts of these wretched women, so they too may find Christ. Consider the glory that awaits them, if you can lead them to the Lord. It is your opportunity to serve."

Lola took a last glance in the mirror and turned to the two women. "Will you help me dress properly, fix my hair, and if the administrators of Magdalene Asylum try to keep me there as a patient, will you get me out?"

The three woman hugged and the Reverend recited a prayer of thanksgiving.

Lola wrote in her spiritual diary: "Oh Lord thy mercies are great to me. Oh! How little they are deserved, filthy worm that I am."

Lola's mother arrived. Lady Craigie's first words to Mrs. Buchanan were, "Does Lola have children?" Maria Buchanan realized the older woman was worried about heirs to whatever fortune she thought Lola had.

Lady Craigie insisted on seeing Lola. Lola attempted

to avoid the meeting. She made her way upstairs, and climbed a ladder by herself, to hide in the attic. After a day of arguing with Nurse Margaret and Maria Buchanan, they called in Reverend Hawks, who convinced Lola she must obey the Commandment to honor her parents.

It required all of Lola's self-discipline to restrain herself from beating her mother with the cane, but Lola promised she would do as the Bible says and respect her parent. She would not charge her mother with abandoning her as a child, but proclaimed, "I will be damned in eternal hell if I'll leave her a half-penny in my will. My own mother forced me into prostitution."

Maria Buchanan knew this to be untrue—Lady Craigie had paid for her support until Lola ran off and married Lieutenant Thomas James—but Mrs. Buchanan said nothing.

Mother and daughter met alone in Lola's room. Lola never mentioned the conversation, and no one asked. Lady Craigie left for England the next day. She had spent only two days in America.

Lola became a welcome guest at the Magdalene Asylum, where she used the name Fannie Gibbons. She wished to be known for what she was, not what she had been. The staff and patients received her with respect for an older woman.

In fact Lola was only forty years old; the stroke and her disease had aged her. Her smoking cigars amused the women, and when she shared some of her stories, they knew she had been one of them. They listened when she taught Bible.

The group she spoke to expanded to three times the

size after a *New York Times* reporter recognized her entering the Magdalene Asylum and printed the story. The women, young and old, wanted to hear stories of King Ludwig, the Czar of Russia, and the Prime Minister of England—and especially about Jung Bahadur, Maharaja and ruler of Nepal. The discussions, and the exercise of walking to and from the Asylum, brought Lola back to health.

It was Christmas Day, 1860. Lola insisted Nurse Margaret be with her family. The Buchanan's celebrated with their son and family in New York. Lola was alone in the Astoria house.

It was a cold December day, but the sun was shining brightly and warmed the house through the large double hung windows. Lola thought it warm outside. When she realized how cold it was, rather than return for a sweater and scarf, she decided to walk more quickly to keep warm. It was a mistake.

A block from the house, she felt faint. Using the picket fences in front of the homes for support, she made her way back to the house. A passerby helped her up the porch steps and into the house.

The Buchanans, when they returned, found her unconscious on the sitting-room couch and called the doctor. He and Isaac Buchanan carried her up to her room. The doctor examined her, came out and shook his head. "She has double pneumonia," he reported. "Call Reverend Hawks."


Lola clung to life for three weeks. Among her visitors were statesman, ambassadors, politicians, businessmen and stars of the American and international theater. Her constant companions were Nurse Margret and Maria Buchanan who read the Bible to her.

Reverend Francis Hawks, her spiritual mentor, told his Bishop, Reverend Horatio Potter, that he felt Lola was the teacher and he the student. Her humility and penitent soul were greater than any he ever encountered in all his years in the Ministry.

Bishop Potter, the same man who denied Lola the right to donate money to the Church of the Good Shepherd, and whom Lola condemned in the press, requested to meet with her. He did, and was impressed by her knowledge of the Bible and espousal of penitence, remorse, and her total dedication to God and Jesus Christ. He gave her his sincere blessing. "Are you afraid of death?" he asked.

"The Lord is forgiving and all-merciful. Of that I am certain. How he could forgive me is beyond my comprehension, yet I have hope. I have faith that I will be judged fairly in the heavenly court. I have sinned more than most. I am prepared to answer for that."

Bishop Potter laid his hands on Lola's head and pronounced the Biblical blessing:

"May the Lord bless you and keep you.

May the Lord shine his countenance upon you.

May you forever walk in the path of righteousness for His name's sake, Amen?"

He departed wiping tears from his eyes.


On January 17th 1861, with Reverend Hawks at her bedside, Lola whispered, "How many years of my life have been sacrificed to Satan and my love of sin? What have I not been guilty of, in thought or in deed, during these years of misery and wretchedness...? I only lived for my own passions..."[48]

She reached out her hand to the Bible, and her last words were, "Tell me more of my dear Savior."

No longer able to speak, Reverend Hawks asked her to let him know by a sign if she believed she had found true forgiveness and salvation through Christ for her past life. Lola's beautiful blue eyes locked onto Reverend Hawks eyes, and she nodded in the affirmative. The Reverend heard the last breath of Lola Montez whisper through her pale lips – and cease.

Maria Buchanan arranged for the burial in Greenwood Cemetery, Brooklyn, in a plot on a small grassy knoll. It was a cold winter's day, and the snow and ice impeded the large cortege that entered the cemetery grounds. Reverend Hawks presided over an Episcopalian service in the home of Mrs. Buchanan because of the terrible weather. The graveside ceremony was brief.

Lola had explained to Maria Buchanan how she wished her gravestone to read:

***Eliza Gilbert***

***January 17, 1861***

## POSTSCRIPT:

"The spiritual gift of faith is not to be confused with saving faith. All Christians have been given saving faith (Ephesians 2:8-9), but not all receive this special gift of

---

[48] *Lola Montez*, James Varley, P 250

faith Those with this gift have a trust and confidence in God that. allows them to live boldly for Him and manifest that faith in mighty ways."[49]

—The Countess of Landsfeld


Lola is buried in Plot 12739, Section 8, to the south of the cross paths of Summit Avenue and Andean, at Greenwood Cemetery in Brooklyn. Over the years the inscription on her grave weathered away and by 1935 the headstone itself had almost disappeared. It was not until Bruce Seymour (whom I quote often) used the royalties from his biography of her, that a new headstone was inaugurated on 25 April 1998. One side maintains the inscription "Mrs. Eliza Gilbert". The other reads "Lola Montez, Countess of Landsfeld". As is the custom of the cemetery, the original headstone is now buried in the grave. [50]

In my imagination I conceive Lola's life moving past her mind's eye while awaiting death. Her childhood memories would have included caravans of camels in the streets of India, elephants in holiday parades decked out with silks, brocade and semi-precious stones, beggars and street urchins, fakirs and holy men, the starving and the wealthy. She would have turned to tell her mother of these wonders, but her mother (only fourteen years older) saw Lola as a contestant for the attention of men. Little Lola shared her dreams with the slave nanny, Manuela.

---

[49] Faith and Religion, Wikipedia, Lola and her Lovers:

[50] *Lola Montez*, Bruce Seymour, P 325

Lola had difficulty acclimatizing to the boarding schools in Scotland and France. Manuela was always there to help. School work was easy for her. She finished class work before the others, and got into trouble from being bored, and saying so.

She had a plethora of memories to call upon: her elopement with Lieutenant James, subsequent dalliances, and love affairs with some of the most powerful men in the world. and with others who just happened to cross her path.

Through the Bavarian throne she experienced the passion and poetry, intrigues and liaisons, of the rich and powerful. Her rise to authority was meteoric. For a period of two years, Lola Montez became the second most powerful woman in the world (Queen Victoria being the first).

# *EPILOGUE*

The following is a letter written by Maria Buchanan to former King Ludwig:

April, 28th 1861

Sire,

In early childhood having been school companion in Scotland with a young girl who I little thought would have requested me on her death bed to write to your Majesty...She often spoke to me of your Majesty, and of your kindness and your benevolence, which she deeply felt...and wished me to tell you she had changed her life and companions.

And now I redeem the promise I made to the late Mme. Lola Montez, known as Eliza Gilbert, and add that she wished me to let you know she retained a sincere regard for your kindness to the end of her life.

She died a true penitent, relying on her savior for pardon and acceptance, triumphing only in His merit...

I have the honor to be your Majesty's Obedt. & Humble Sert.

Maria E. Buchanan

King Ludwig replied.

Mistress Maria Buchanan,

With great satisfaction I was hearing the repentance of L. M. of her former behavior,
and I am very fond of it that she has given the
commission to inform me. It is a great consolation to hear her dying as a Christian. L. M.
was a much distinguished lady. My sincere
thanks for your kind letter....

Yours much affect.,

*Lewis*

*Lola Montez is the vehicle that carried you through the 19th century. I hope you enjoyed the trip. —Dov Silverman*

# THE HISTORY OF THOSE IN LOLA'S LIFE

Lola's life was a compilation of excesses and excellences. The generosity she displayed was from her heart. Alas, her faults also rested there.

Of Lola, Aldous Huxley said, "When you met Lola Montez, her reputation automatically made you think of bedrooms. Her beauty enhanced the thoughts."

Lola's father, Lieutenant Edward Gilbert, died in India of cholera. Her mother, Marie, re-married to Captain Patrick Craigie who became Adjutant General of the English Army in India.

Lola at age sixteen seduced her mother's lover, First Lieutenant Thomas James. They eloped and married. Lola soon realized he was a shallow fraud and obtained a legal separation (not a divorce). He finished his career in the Army under a cloud. Accused of stealing mess funds, he was never convicted, but never promoted either. He fathered three children out of wedlock, and died of a stroke on May 18th, 1871.

Captain George Lennox was advisor to Lord Elphinstone in India in 1841. Lola seduced him aboard the *Larkin* on the voyage from India to England. He set her up in a London apartment for two months and visited her every day. They parted on good terms.

Henry John Temple, 3rd Viscount Palmerston, KG, GCB, PC, was a British statesman who served twice as Prime Minister of England. He died on October 18, 1865.

Sir Robert Peel, 2nd Baronet, died 2 July 1895, was twice Prime Minister of England and Lola's lover. The first police force he established in Ireland; the policemen were called Peelers from his last name, and are to this day. When he established the police force in England, they were called Bobbies, an idiomatic derivation from Robert.

Lord Brougham was among the few men who disliked Lola. He reached the office of Lord Chancellor of England, later left England for France, where he entered politics but never succeeded, being considered by the French to be an odd person. He invented the renowned Brougham carriage and designed the checkered Brougham trousers.

George Sand was the pen name of Amandine-Lucile-Aurore Dudeant Dupin, died in France June 8, 1876. She was the most famous woman writer of her time. She flouted social norms, and entertained in her Salon the most powerful and influential men of her day. For better or worse she was an important influence on Lola's life. She introduced Lola to four famous lovers: Alexandre Dumas, (*The Three Musketeers, Count of Monte Christo*) Victor Hugo, (*Les Miserables, The Hunchback of Notre Dame*), Franz Liszt (composer, virtuoso pianist) and her first true love, Alexandre-Honoré Dujarier (1815-1845) journalist and newspaper editor. He was killed by Jean-Baptiste Rosemond de

Beauvallon in a duel—of which Jean-Baptiste was later convicted of fixing the outcome. This case helped put an end to dueling in France.

Pier Angelo Florentine was an Italian author, a theater critic for *Le Corsaire* newspaper in Paris. He published novels, poems, and dramas. I did not include him in the story as there was not enough room in Lola's story, though he did find room in her bed. He died May 31, 1864.

Ivan Fyodorovich Paskevich, Prince of Warsaw and ruler of Poland under Czar Nicholas of Russia, offered to build a castle for Lola and promised the riches of Poland to her if she would become his concubine. As a vassal of the Russian Czar, Paskevich went on to successfully fight the Turks and Persians, and pacified the Caucases. He became commander of the Russian Army in the Crimean War, where he was wounded and died.

Russian Czar Nicholas I Lost the Crimean War to the Turks when Britain and France came in on the Turkish side. He is said to have died of shame. He was buried in the St. Peter and St. Paul Cathedral in St. Petersburg, March 1855.

King Louis Ludwig I may have been one of two men Lola really loved, Alexander Dujarier being the other. Ludwig continued to support Lola as he promised. Many of his counselors and subjects considered him a fool. Others called him a hopeless romantic; he gave up his throne for Lola. He continued writing poetry, had other female consorts, and lived long enough to see his son, who inherited the Bavarian throne, lead his country into bankruptcy and become involved in a blatant homosexual affair with the famous German composer, theatre director, and conductor, Richard Wagner.

Prince Klemens Wenzel von Metternich was one of the few men who detested Lola. She was the motivating force that upset von Metternich's political, economic, and military plans for Europe. He held her responsible for the revolutions of 1848: the Italian states, France, the German states, Denmark, Schleswig, the Habsburg Empire, the Kingdom of Hungary, Galicia, Sweden, Switzerland, Greater Poland, the Danubian Principalities, Belgium and Ireland. That year, the Prince and his family fled Austria for sanctuary in England. He had commanded the armies of Austro-Hungaria and through secret agents, military force, and negotiating skills, and was able to dictate terms to the individual German states, keeping them separate and weak. After the defeat of Napoleon, von Metternich convened the Congress of Vienna in November 1814. He negotiated terms that maintained peace in Europe, and divided up the eastern hemisphere. His policy was mostly successful until WWI, because of his strategy of maintaining a "Balance of Power"—which in modern times was adopted by American Secretary of State, Henry Kissinger. Von Metternich eventually returned to Austria, and died in 1859.

Heinrich Maltzahn, one of Europe's renowned playboys, was briefly a lover when Lola first arrived in Munich. He died in 1851 of cancer. He is also not mentioned, as Lola's bed was more importantly ocuppied.

Lieutenant Fredric Nusbammer was a favorite of Lola's, who suffered greatly from his association with her when Ludwig found out. The King had him exiled, then discharged from the army with restrictions of how he could earn a living. He died in an insane asylum in March 1859, not yet forty years old.

In contrast to Nusbammer, student leader Fritz Piesner—a long time playmate of Lola's—came penniless and in debt to King Ludwig. He confessed his affairs with Lola and recounted Lola's escapades. Ludwig rewarded the young man, who used the money to immigrate to America. Piesner became a Professor of languages at Union College, Schenectady, N.Y. He raised a Battalion of German immigrants during the Civil War, trained them, and attained the rank of Colonel. He died leading a charge at the battle of Chancellorsville. He was respected and loved by his students and troops.

August Papon was a complicated character. He didn't fit into the telling of the story, but did have substantial influence on Lola. He at one time managed Lola's affairs, then attempted to blackmail her. When that failed, he tried to blackmail King Ludwig with very intimate love letters sent to Lola by Ludwig. Failing that, he returned the letters to Ludwig and entered a monastery. Monastic life proved too Spartan, so Papon started an insurance company. He insured churches for their religious relics, which was their main source of income derived from pilgrims. He proved the need for his insurance policy by stealing the churches' relics, ransoming them, and selling the insurance policy to cover future thefts. He was eventually caught, convicted of theft and fraud, and sentenced to ten years in prison. He disappeared before he could be incarcerated.

As for Jung Bahadur, Maharaja of Nepal: when Lola seduced the Nepalese King, it is not certain if she was then working for Lord Palmerston and British intelligence. She had her own agenda, which was to do what a courtesan does, and do it for a lot of money. She received a soup bowl full of jewels from Jung. In the description of her meeting in the Munich shooting gallery with Jung, she gave him one of two pistols presented to her by the Colt Firearms Company. She later had the Colt Company send him a matched pair. He never returned the first weapon, but he did give her a large emerald ring. When she tried it on, it was too large for her finger. She said, "I'll have it resized."

"It is not for wearing," he said. "If, in the future, you ever need a favor and it is in my power to fulfill, send this ring to me with your request. Your wish will be granted." It is believed that when the Indian (Hindu) Revolution of 1857 threatened the East India Company and England's rule in that area of the world, Lord Palmerston was attempting to influence Nepal to stop Indian renegades form seeking refuge in the mountainous regions of Nepal. Lola is believed to have delivered the ring given her by the Maharaja to the British consulate in New York. It is a known fact that Bahadur helped the British quell the mutiny, and became a dependable friend of Britain in administering that area of the world. The Maharaja died a natural death in 1877.

Noel Follin was married with two children when he became Lola's manager on the trip to Australia. Lola was impressed by a picture he showed her of his sister, Miriam (Minnie) Follin. Without ever meeting the girl, Lola paid for her dancing and acting lessons. On the return voyage to the states, Lola threw Noel out of her bed. He went missing at sea, and was believed to be a suicide. Lola felt guilty, supported the mother, adopted his sister Miriam, trained and educated her using the stage name of Minnie Montez. Minnie dallied with many men, and was discharged by a disappointed Lola, who was becoming more religious. Yet Minnie asked Lola's advice before marrying a U.S. naval officer. Miriam reverted to her real name on stage. She publicly denied knowing Lola and is believed to have contributed to the fatal stroke Lola suffered. Minnie had moderate success on stage and lived to the age of seventy-four.

George Trafford Heald, the richest and most eligible bachelor in Great Britain at the time, was eight years younger than Lola. His infatuation is believed to be the cause of his demise. He had a guaranteed income of eight thousand Sterling a year, at a time when professionals, doctors, lawyers, and architects received fifty Sterling a year. He was the sole inheritor of his father's fortune. Not being of age (21), he was assigned a legal guardian—his aunt Susanna. Within days of meeting Lola, he proposed marriage. She knew his financial status, and agreed. Aunt Susana attempted to block the marriage which took place July 19th 1849. She failed, and then brought bigamy charges against Lola; She found proof that Lieutenant James, Lola's first husband, was alive in India and they were not legally divorced. It is said by many that Lola drove George Heald to drink, but he was already well on his way to alcoholism as an officer in the elite Life Guard Regiment. Although I wrote about Lola's plan to kill her husband, there is no proof that it occurred. The Coroner's report, and that of the chief Constable, were examined by Aunt Susanna's lawyers and found to be meticulously accurate. Conclusion: death by drowning.

Sayville Morton is likewise not mentioned, as Lola's bed was crowded. He was the lover of many women, fought two duels over other men's wives, but lost the third in October, 1852.

"Frank O'Brien" was really Patrick O'Brien, an internationally renowned musician and short-term lover of Lola's. The real Frank is a friend of mine, a pianist living and working on Long Island, New York.

Dr. Kirke Adler, said to be of German aristocracy, met Lola on one of her hunting forays. They lived together for several weeks in a tent during the spring of 1853, while Lola's new husband Patrick Hull remained in camp with his whiskey. The circumstances of Adler's death were initially called a hunting accident. His weapon discharged while he was on horseback. The incident was questioned, as Adler was an experienced hunter and had handled weapons since childhood. However, he was also known as a drinker. Lola was with him at the time, and never commented. The case was eventually closed as a hunting mishap.

Patrick Hull, Lola's third husband, died of a stroke on May 21st 1858. It was said of him that he was a hail-fellow-well-met who always had a smile, a joke, and an abundant supply of Jameson's Irish Whisky.

There were many claimants to be the children of Lola Montez. Most serious researchers agree that these were all false. Whatever Nanny Manuela taught Lola about contraception, it appeared to work.

Reverend Hawks was later appointed Archbishop.

Mrs. Marie Buchanan and her husband, although later maligned by improper researchers, were good people who attended Lola with all the care and concern attributed to those who believe, "Thou shalt love thy neighbor as thyself."

Nanny Manuela died in her bed, surrounded by her daughter, grandchildren, and great-grandchildren. Her son-in-law became one of India's richest merchants, a shipbuilder, and a benefactor of the poor.

Guru Rama Singh greatly influenced the vast population of India. He challenged British rule by advocating civil disobedience. Decades later Mahatma Gandhi copied Rama Singh's non-violent approach to oust the British from India. Guru Rama Singh died at age 70, in 1876.

*Secrets of Beauty*, edited and condensed from Lola's lecture, is on pages 300-301 of *Lola Montez* by James Morton. She recommended a pomade of rosemary and nutmeg massaged into the scalp, and she warned against commercial cosmetics that could be dangerous to the health.

Lola considered baldness for men and women most detrimental to the perception of beauty. Lola preached the use of natural products to attain results; the fat of a stag used to anoint the body kept the skin elastic. The binding of raw beef around the face delayed wrinkles. To promote a larger bosom (rather than plastic surgery) the recipe was: half an ounce of tincture of myrrh, four ounces of pimpernel water, four ounces of elderflower water, one gram of musk and six ounces of rectified wine. The mixture was to be gently rubbed into the breast for ten minutes, three times a day. Lola was adamant on the use of natural cosmetic products, believing they were more economical, better, and safer than commercial merchandise.

Whatever conclusions you have come to about Lola Montez, you must admit she greatly influenced the past, and gave the present the legend: "WHATEVER LOLA WANTS... LOLA GETS!"

# THREE SONGS INSPIRED BY LOLA.

## She's More To Be Pitied Than Censured
## (circa1900)

### William B. Gray

At the old concert hall on the Bowery,

`Round a table were seated one night,

A crowd of young fellows carousing.

With them life seemed cheerful and bright.

At the very next table was seated

A girl who had fallen to shame,

All the young fellows jeered at her weakness,

Till they heard an old woman explain:


She is more to be pitied than censured,

She is more to be helped than despised.

She is only a lassie who ventured

On life`s stormy path, ill-advised;

Do not scorn her with words fierce and bitter

Do not laugh at her shame and downfall.

For a moment, just stop and consider

That a man was the cause of it all.


There`s an old-fashioned church `round the corner

Where the neighbors all gathered one day,

While the parson was preaching a sermon

O`ere a soul that had just passed away;

`Twas this same wayward girl from the Bowery

Who a life of adventure had led.

Did the clergyman jeer at her downfall?

No! He asked for God`s mercy, and said:

She is more to be pitied than censured,

She is more to be helped than despised.

She is only a lassie who ventured

On life's stormy path ill-advised.

Do not scorn her with words fierce and bitter,

Do not laugh at her shame and downfall,

For a moment just stop to consider

That a man was the cause of it all!

The lyrics below were inspired by Lola Montez. Written by Songwriters RICHARD ADLER, JERRY ROSS for the hit musical Damn Yankees, in 1955.

### *Whatever Lola Wants, Lola Gets*

Whatever Lola Wants, Lola Gets.

And little man, little Lola wants you.

Make up your mind to have (make up your mind to have)

No regrets (no regrets)

Recline yourself, resign yourself;

You're through


I always get what I aim for.

And your heart and soul is what I came for.

Whatever Lola wants (Lola wants), Lola gets (Lola gets)

Take off your coat, don't you know you can't win

(Can't win, You'll never, never win)

You're no exception to the rule.

I'm irresistible, you fool.

Give in (Give in, You'll never win)


Whatever Lola wants, Lola gets

I always get what I aim for

And your heart and soul is what I came for

Whatever Lola wants (Lola wants), Lola gets
(Lola gets)

Take off your coat, don't you know you can't
win

(Can't win, You'll never, never win)

You're no exception to the rule.

I'm irresistible, you fool.

Give in (give in, You'll never win)

Give in (give in, You'll never win)

Give in.

Joanna Newsom's song and title track "Have One on
Me" inspired by Lola Montez. 2016

## Have One On Me

From the courtyard, I floated in

And watched it go down.

Heard the cup drop;

Thought, "Well

That's why they keep them around."

The blackguard sat hard, down

With no head on him now

And I felt so bad

Cause I didn't know how

To feel bad enough

To make him proud


By the time you read this

I will be so far away

Daddy longlegs, how in the world

Am I to be expected to stay?

In the night—

In the night, you may hear me call

Pa, stay your hand

And steel your resolve

Stay where you are

So long and tall


Here's Lola—ta da!—to do

Her famous Spider Dance for you!

Lighten up your pockets!

Shake her skirts and scatter, there

A shrieking, six-legged millionaire

With a blight in his sockets

Miss Montez

The Countess of Lansfeld

Appealed to the King of Bavaria

Saying, "Pretty papa

If you are my friend—

Mister daddy longlegs, they are at it again!—

Can I see you?"


Poor Lola! A tarantula's mounting

Countess Lansfeld's

Handsome brassiere

While they all cheer


And the old king fell from grace

While Lola fled

To save face and her career


You caught a fly, floating by

Wait for him to drown in the dust;

Drown in the dust of other flies

Whereby the machine is run

And the deed is done

Heaven has no word

For the way you and your friends

Have treated poor Louis

May god save your poor soul, Lola

(But there is nothing I adore

Apart from that whore's black heart.)


Well, doesn't that just beat all!

Miss Gilbert

Called to Castlemaine

By the silver dollar and the gold glitter!

Well, I've seen lots

But never, in a million years

Would think to see you, here


Though the long road

Begins and ends with you

I cannot seem to make amends

With you, Louis

When we go out

They're bound to see you with me


At night, I walk in the park

With a whip

Between the lines

Of the whispering Jesuits

Who are poisoning you against me

There's a big black spider

Hanging over my door

Can't go anywhere, anymore

Tell me, are you with me?


I called to you, several times

While the change took place

And then arrived, all night

And I died

But all these songs

When you and I are long gone

Will carry on

Mud in your eye


You asked my hand

Hired a band

"In your heart is all that you need;

Ask and you will receive," it is said

I threw my bouquet

And I knocked 'em dead


Bottle of white, bottle of red

Helpless as a child

When you held me in your arms

And I knew that no other

Could ever love me as you loved

But help me! I'm leaving!


I remember everything

Down to the sound of you shaving—

The scrape of your razor

The dully-abrading black hair

That remained

When you clutched at me

That night I came upstairs, half-dead

And, in your kindness

You put me straightaway

In the cupboard

With a bottle of champagne

And then, later, on a train

It was dark out, I was half-dead

I saw a star fall into the sky

Like a chunk of thrown coal

As if god himself spat

Like a cornered rat


I really want you to do this for me

Will you have one on me?


It was dark; I was drunk and half-dead

And we slept, knocking heads

Sitting up in the star-smoking air

Knocking heads like buoys


Don't you worry for me!

Have one on me!


Meanwhile, I will raise my own glass

To how you made me fast

And expendable

And I will drink to your excellent health

And your cruelty

Will you have one on me?


—helpless as a child

When you held me in your arms

And I knew that no other

Could ever love me—


From the courtyard, I floated in

And watched it go down

Heard the cup drop;

Thought, "Well, that's why

They keep them around."

The blackguard sat hard, down

With no head on him now

And I felt so bad

Cause I didn't know how

To feel bad enough

To make him proud


Well daddy longlegs, are you?

Daddy longlegs, are you?

Daddy longlegs, are you proud?

# ACKNOLWEDGEMENTS

The basis for my historical research comes from my education as a history major at Stony Brook University N.Y. under the chairmanship of Professor David Trask, who became Chief Historian of the U.S. Army. My wife Janet catalogued much of the information I collected over forty years. Wikipedia I accessed so often it would be impossible for me to estimate its use for leads to verification. The touchstones for confirmation were Bruce Seymour's book, *Lola Montez*, Yale University Press 1996 and *Lola Montez*, by Eduard B. di Auvergne, 1909—Fox, Jones and Co. Oxford England. Lola Montez's Autobiography is far more fictitious than this novel.

*Lola Montez*, James Morton, 2007—Portrait Publishing Co. 5 Windmill St. London.

*The Uncrowned Queen*, Ishbel Ross, 1972- Harper and Row, New York, U.S.A.

*Lola Montez*, Helen Holdrege, 1957—Alvin Reidman, London.

*Lola Montez*, 1996—James Varley, 1996— The Arthur H. Clark Co. Spokane, Washington

*The Divine Eccentric*, 1969—Doris Foley, Western lore Press, Los Angeles, Calif.

With thanks to Maestro Taguir Abazov for historical information about 19th century

Russia and Poland, to David Rivlin for background on Ireland, to Steve Bolsom and David Barrett for the lifestyle of period England.

To editors K.J Joyner and Leslie Fish.

To my readers: Barbara Sher, Anav Youlevitch, Loriel Sher and Hilary Waldman of Israel, Elaine and Louis Lehe of Stony Brook, N.Y. Bathsheba Manes, who I am proud to say is a former student, living in China for the past 18 years.

Thank You for encouragement, to Eddie Shapiro and his family (Mom, Miriam), and to Deborah Davidson of New York. Norm and Char Plotsky of Florida

*In Memory of my wife Janet.*